Thursday's
Children

Thursday's Children

RUMER GODDEN

THE VIKING PRESS   NEW YORK

Grateful acknowledgment is made to Chappell & Co., Inc., for permission
to reprint lines from "Some Enchanted Evening," by Oscar Hammerstein.
Copyright 1949 by Richard Rodgers and Oscar Hammerstein II, © renewed.
Williamson Music Co., owner of publication and allied rights throughout
the Western hemisphere and Japan, administered by Chappell & Co., Inc.
International copyright secured. All rights reserved. Used by permission.

LIBRARY OF CONGRESS CATALOGING IN PUBLICATION DATA
Godden, Rumer, 1907–
    Thursday's children.
    I. Title.
PR6013.O2T5   1984   823'.912   83-40252
ISBN 0-670-71196-9

Printed in the United States of America
Set in Sabon

Monday's child is fair of face,
Tuesday's child is full of grace,
Wednesday's child is full of woe,
Thursday's child has far to go. . . .

Old rhyme

My most grateful thanks to The Royal Ballet Schools, The Royal Academy of Dancing, the Merle Park School of Dancing and their staffs for allowing me to watch classes and generously sparing me their valuable time, particularly James Monahan and Barbara Fewster: Joan Lawson – who gave me the idea of the book and has supported me throughout. Especial thanks to Helen Kastrati: to John Ard: to Stuart Beckett, who answered endless questions and allowed me to use his diaries, and to Rachel Hester for permission to adapt an essay she wrote while at school. I must also thank Peggy Taylor of Lockerbie for advice on Ma's emeralds and John and Nicholes Jane Cameron, florists and greengrocers, of Lockerbie too, who taught me how Pa Penny should run his shop.

All the characters in the book are imaginary – except one.

R.G.

for Ninette de Valois

List of Characters

William Penny (Pa), *greengrocer of Pilgrim's Green, London*
Maud Penny (Ma)

Will
Jim
Tim
Hughie
Crystal
Doone
} *the Penny children*

Beppo
Mrs Denning
} *assistants in Mr Penny's shop*

Madame Tamara, *teacher of dancing in Pilgrim's Green*
Mr Felix, *her pianist*
Mrs Sherrin, *her cleaning woman*
Ruth, *Mrs Sherrin's daughter*

Angela
Mary Ann
Joanna
Zoë
} *pupils of Madame Tamara's school*

Mrs Carstairs, *headmistress of Pilgrim's Green Primary School*
Philip Brown, *president of the Association of Dancers and of the London Dance Academy*
Ennis Glyn, *a principal of Her Majesty's Ballet Company and owner of the Ennis Glyn School of Dancing*
Stella, *her assistant*
Miss La Motte, *her pianiste*

Charles
Sydney
Sebastian
Mark
Valerie
} *pupils of the Ennis Glyn School*

The Lady (Madam)
Baroness Lötte von Heusen, *concert pianiste*
Giles Hereward, *television film director*
Michael Yeats, CBE, *director of the Senior and Junior Schools
of Her Majesty's Ballet*
Miss Elizabeth Baxter, FISTD, *ballet principal of both schools*
Mrs Clio Challoner, MA (Oxon), *headmistress of the Junior
School*

HOUSE STAFF
Mrs Gillespie, *housemistress (girls)*
Christopher Ormond, *housemaster (boys)*
Miss Polly Walsh, *boys' house matron*
Miss Thompson, *boys' assistant matron*

BALLET STAFF
Jean McKenzie, FISTD, *ballet mistress*
Leopold Max, FISTD, *ballet master*
Stephen Vince
Olive Hurley, FISTD, ARAD
Gilberte Giroux
and others

BALLET PIANISTS
Jonah
Jacques
Mrs Isobel Smyth
and others

Humphrey Tyrone, *régisseur for Her Majesty's Ballet*
Peter Morland ⎫
Anthea Dean ⎬ *principals of the Company*
Yuri Koszorz, *guest artist of the Company*

Melissa ⎫
Amy
Galina Posniakoff
Kui
Norman
Peter ⎬ *pupils of the Junior Ballet School*
Gregory
James
Claude
José
and others ⎭

Prelude

IT WAS a gala night at the Royal Theatre, London.

The World Première of Yuri Koszorz's
LEDA AND THE SWAN
In the gracious presence of
HER MAJESTY QUEEN ELIZABETH

Music	Creatures of Prometheus by Beethoven
Edited by	John Courtald
Choreography	Yuri Koszorz
Staged by	Stefan Jacobi
Design	Liane Makropopolis
Lighting	David Knight
Leda	Anthea Dean
Zeus/Swan	Yuri Koszorz
Hera, Chief Wife to Zeus	Ennis Glyn
Eight goddess wives of Zeus	Artists of Her Majesty's Ballet
Cock	Peter Morland
First Hen	Bette Cooper
Second Hen	Annette Severin
Bantam	Robinson Gee
Cockerels, pullets, pigeons	Artists of Her Majesty's Ballet
Cygnet	Doone Penny

Doone Penny is a pupil of Her Majesty's Junior Ballet School.

He stood in the wings waiting for his moment, Mr Max, the school senior ballet master, behind him. Though not as small now for his age – he used to be an elf – Doone still barely came

xi

up to Mr Max's breast pocket; naturally – he was only thirteen. No boy of that age, in Mr Max's remembrance, had been entrusted with dancing a solo role in a ballet at the Royal Theatre. 'Tamara Trepova danced the Nightingale in *Le Rossignol* when she was twelve,' said Olive Hurley, doyenne of the ballet mistresses at the Junior School, whose memory was that of an archivist.

'That was in Monte Carlo,' said Mr Max, 'not here.' The directors had tried to persuade Yuri Koszorz to accept a boy from the Senior School, but Yuri had been adamant: 'I need Doone's slightness and smallness; above all, his elevation, *and* his musicality and feeling for my Cygnet.'

The other boys had teased Doone: 'Swans are for girls.' In ballet, with rare exceptions, they were. Anthea Dean herself had just danced the Swan Princess in *Swan Lake*; Doone's own Ennis Glyn of the enigmatic face and long graceful body *The Swan of Tuonela*, and 'Flutter, flutter, flap, flap,' mocked the boys, and 'You'll wear a white tutu and a little crown of feathers.'

'All swans can't be girls,' Doone had retaliated. 'Yuri's dancing the grown Swan *and* he's Zeus.' That silenced them. Who could be more male than Yuri Koszorz or a greater dancer?

The hierarchy of Her Majesty's Ballet and the Royal Theatre made their plans well in advance: *Leda* had been planned a year before and kept secret, and it was not until an afternoon late in last summer's term that Doone had caught a glimpse of his cygnet dance. Coming through the garden of Queen's Chase, Her Majesty's Ballet's Junior School, on the way to an English lesson, he had heard music pouring through the windows of what had once been the salon of the big white house and, as always with music, drawn as by a magnet, he had run up one of the flights of double steps that led to the balcony outside.

The panelled walls of the salon, its ceiling of delicate plasterwork, its marbled fireplace suggested minuets or chamber music. This music was anything but that delicate intimacy – a torrent of sound, eloquent, forceful – and Doone had pressed his face against the window to see what on earth was being danced.

xii

It was not quite of earth; it seemed, too, of air. Though Doone had as yet no inkling it was anything to do with him, Yuri Koszorz was in fact showing Mr Max how he wanted Mr Max, presently, to coach him, Doone. 'Wings are power, speed.' Doone could hear Yuri through the window. 'You must make him lift himself up. Up!' The swift circling did seem like flight. Then why, when the music changed, was Yuri driven into a corner, afraid? He made quick darting movements of his head as if hurt came from every side, fast small attacks like pecks.

The music changed again, and now Yuri seemed to be alone, away from his persecutors; he stood, slowly looking himself over in wonder – a wonder that grew greater. 'He must have his chest *out*,' Yuri was telling Mr Max, 'be proud and as tall as he can.'

Now Yuri's arms were held wide, first one, then the other, the free hand caressing, stroking downwards. 'I see. He's feathering,' said Mr Max. Then, with music, came a brief flight, a tumble, despair; and Doone felt his heart wrung as Yuri's hands stretched out again and again, pleading, as if asking the whole world for help. He was a wonderful actor, and the music sounded as if Jonah, the pianist, was tearing the old upright piano apart. Then, suddenly, courage, a new flight, more sure now, even and beautiful, and 'Ah!' breathed Doone. 'Ah!'

'You're supposed to be at our English class.' Amanda, Doone's special friend and contemporary, had come up beside him. 'Come on. We'll be late.'

'Hush,' said Doone.

'You had fourteen spelling mistakes in your last essay. Better come.'

'Hush! Listen,' said Doone.

'Never mind if he's clumsy,' Yuri was telling Mr Max. 'He's meant to be clumsy. It's his first try at flying.'

To tell a dancer he could be clumsy was perplexing, and Doone and Amanda looked at one another puzzled. 'What *is* it?' asked Doone.

'Perhaps it's a bit of Yuri Koszorz's new ballet they're beginning to talk about,' said Amanda. 'Though why he's doing it here I don't know.'

'But what's it about?'

'Something to do with the story of the Ugly Duckling,' said Amanda but, along with the hundred thousand things Doone Penny had never heard of, was the story of the Ugly Duckling, and 'A duck! That's not a duck,' he said. 'It's something else.'

It was indeed something else. Yuri's ballet differed from the legend. It began with Leda, the young virgin, innocently looking for shells on the lake shore. Now, beyond the standing green stage reeds, Doone could see the suggestion of the lake into which presently he himself would have to look, as in a mirror, to see his own reflection. There were, too, palisades and bales of straw to suggest a poultry-yard. Above, in the flies, were blue curtains like clouds that would suggest Olympus. Leda/Anthea Dean wore a little looped maroon gown that opened to show a line of scarlet as she skimmed and turned. Besides being endearing, Anthea was the prettiest and neatest of dancers. It was only a prelude; the music changed, the clouds came down, and Doone could feel an almost magnetic stir in the audience beyond the orchestra pit. 'This is new, quite new.'

He knew the auditorium of the Royal Theatre, one of the greatest opera and ballet houses in the world. Paris, Milan, New York, Copenhagen, Sydney – he would come to know them all, but the Royal Theatre, for an English-born dancer, was not only the Mecca, the peak of ambition, but also home.

He had seen it in rehearsal – rows and rows of empty velvet-covered seats; tiers of balconies in white and gilt, their rose-shaded lights unlit; the cavernous stage with its great depth and heights, its mysterious walkovers and steel ladders given over to the stagehands or to shirt-sleeved men working on the lights – just as he had seen it packed with those all-important people, the audience. 'You dance for them,' said Yuri. 'Always remember that.' If he looked through a narrow crack at the side of the curtain, Doone could see the people – though hardly see them, the lights in the orchestra pit were too bright. Far back, across semi-darkness, he could see exits, light-marked, but the audience was there between, waiting, breathing, alive. 'If you dance for yourself,' said Yuri, 'the dance stays hidden. You must feel it, of course, but you must tell them. *Tell* them.'

The first time Doone had been in that audience was when he was five. That had been by a lucky accident; but, then, everything that had happened to him had been by accident – or was it luck? As one of the children of Her Majesty's Ballet School, he had sat up in the amphitheatre – twelve seats were always kept for them and given strictly in turn – sat watching the tiny oblong of stage whose floor, which in a moment he would have to try to cover, now looked so wide and bare. He had danced on it at the School's annual performance as one of perhaps twenty boys and girls; had been a page and one of the children in *Konservatoriet*, but then surrounded by the Company. Now he would be alone.

Perhaps for a dancer there is no greater exhilaration than the moment when, after weeks, months of rehearsing in class-rooms, rehearsal rooms, even the theatre, to a piano, suddenly he has to dance that same role with a full orchestra. It brings an euphoria. 'You can do anything – anything,' said Doone. 'I think even if you broke your leg you'd go on.' It takes a trained experienced dancer to sustain that impact and, even after all the rehearsals, it had broken afresh in Doone; his heart seemed not to be thumping but whirring in his chest and stomach; again and again he flexed his legs. He was raring to go, but Mr Max laid a restraining hand on his shoulder. 'Steady.'

Zeus, in his splendour, had looked down and seen Leda, but now his nine wives, headed by Hera, stopped him in his headlong rush to earth. They had had enough, they told Zeus – it was an extremely funny mime – had had enough of Zeus descending on Danaë as a shower of gold, a bull for Europa. If he wanted to be a swan he could, but he would have to take on swanhood completely: first as an egg, then as an ugly dark cygnet – echoes of the Ugly Duckling Amanda had talked of. The great Zeus, too, was to be henpecked in a humble farmyard and know what it is to be penned, yearning for the world outside. At first he was too clumsy to fly, then, lifted by the innate wildness and strength of his kind, flew. Yuri's ballet had almost Christ-like overtones; Zeus, God, had to suffer in his earthly form.

As Doone danced, he would have to cast off shreds and pieces from his dark-feathered tunic to show the white down beneath; his final flight circled the great spaces of the stage –

'Use all of it,' Yuri had commanded. Will I ever be able to? thought Doone. It ended in a leap off so high that Mr Max had to catch him and, as the music of the dance slowly ended, a single feather would fall from the flies on to the stage. A swan's wing-feather, pure white.

The Cygnet grown, Doone's part would be over, but the ballet went on. Leda, in her wandering dance, came back and the Zeus Swan appeared, immense, white-winged – at rehearsal Doone had heard Yuri give a most down-to-earth curse as his foot caught a stanchion. He and Leda danced a wooing *pas de deux*, its tenderness overcoming Leda's terror. Yuri had the Swan's preening virtuoso's courtship solo; then for Leda an adage of yielding until, as the music rose to a crescendo, in a final giant swoop, the Swan swept her off her feet and, half-hidden by the great wings, they fell together, locked.

On stage the lights were hot; Doone was sweating even before he had danced. Behind, and all around him, in the dim spaces off-stage, were other dancers in their costumes, tense in a last-moment warming-up, turning and stretching, bending legs and bodies, arms and heads; others were testing their shoe ribbons once again or were at the resin-tray. Peter Morland, who in minutes would be dancing the Cock, was throwing one leg, then the other, high in *grands battements* as he held on to an iron wall-ladder – it was perilous to go near those powerful legs. Doone heard the Company's ballet mistress's agonised 'Where *are* Joyce and Natasha? They should be here by now,' and a fierce 'You're *late*!'

The Goddesses had finished their scene and the music changed back to the theme of the poultry-yard; he could hear the Cock crowing and, though he could not see the audience, Doone knew from the laughter, the oohs and aahs of tenderness, that the egg had now been pushed on and the minute Claude, smallest boy in the Ballet School, in his costume of brown fledgling down, had opened the egg and come out. 'He'll steal all the applause,' Yuri had smiled. Yuri had been as gentle with little Claude as he had been stern with Doone over every step, every move. Claude had only to pick himself up, walk and waddle, moving his tiny bent-elbow wings as he was coaxed away by a Mother Hen, while he, Doone. . . .

The Hens gathered, dancing with the Cock, who was showing off. Then the conductor held his baton still: Mr Max felt Doone shivering under his hand, shivering not with nerves but with impatience. The opening of the Cygnet music began; a stagehand whispered 'Good luck'. Doone could not thank him because 'Now,' said Mr Max, lifting his hand. 'Now.'

PART ONE

Chapter One

'CRYSTAL, you must take Doone with you today,' said Ma. It was Saturday morning when Crystal went to her dancing class. 'Do I have to take him?' Crystal almost wailed. 'Why do I always have to have him tagging along?'

'Well, I can't have him under my feet all morning; besides, he ought to go out and get some fresh air.'

'And he's your little brother, Chris.' Ma winced; she did not like Pa calling Crystal 'Chris', but 'Madame Tamara says he sits still as a mouse' was all Ma said.

'Which is more than you would have done at his age,' Pa told Crystal. 'Sitting for an hour or more, just watching.'

'Oh, well!' said Crystal. 'I suppose he can carry my shoes.'

Carrying Crystal's shoes was the beginning.

Ma was Mrs Penny, the big brassy wife of William Penny, greengrocer and florist of Porlock Road, Pilgrim's Green, a northern suburb of London.

Pilgrim's Green, though officially part of the great city, was almost as much a village as the village in Devon from which Pa, Mr Penny, came. 'Near Porlock it was; I was born on the farm there'—so it had seemed a happy omen when he found the shop in Porlock Road. Pa's elder brother, John, had inherited the farm, he and his wife Mary. 'So I had to do something, didn't I?' and Pa had become a greengrocer and prospered. He now had a second shop in the larger suburb of Stonham — 'Right in the High Street,' he boasted — but Porlock Road was home and he liked the quiet of Pilgrim's Green; there were people living there who had never been — never wanted to go — to, for instance, London's West End.

Pilgrim's Green had its town hall, its schools, its cinema that doubled as a bingo club, its churches — on Sundays the air was

1

filled with the sound of bells. It had a common with cherry-trees, stretches of grass, and ducks on a shallow pond. 'Everything one could want,' said Pa.

'Depends who the "one" is,' said Ma.

From the day she was married, Ma had 'longed and prayed for a little girl' – that was the family saga – 'And then,' she always said it reverently, 'God sent me Crystal.'

'He took a long time about it,' said Hughie.

First there was Will – William, after his father. It had looked as if Will would be an only child, but five years later there had come 'the Blitz', as Ma called it: the twins, James and Timothy – Jim and Tim; a year afterwards, Hughie.

'You certainly made up for lost time, old girl,' said Pa. 'Three in two years – all boys!'

'Don't you think four's enough?' asked the doctor, but 'One more try' – Ma was not finished yet – 'and I was right!' Two years after Hughie, there was another baby and it was a girl.

'A little girl,' the nurse told her.

'Are you sure?' Ma had not dared believe it.

The nurse had laughed and held the baby up for her to see. 'Look! It's clear as crystal'; and 'That's how your sister got her name,' Ma told the boys. Privately she thought it ought to have been Diamond.

Pa had always known that Ma had 'notions'. She had read that in the royal family the children called their parents Papa and Mamma and thought it would be pretty if her children did the same. 'But we're not royal,' Will had pointed out and all of them refused, so that Mr and Mrs Penny ended up as Pa and Ma. 'Worse than Mum and Dad,' Ma had said. 'Well, Papa, Mamma, does sound sissy to me,' said Pa.

She would, too, have liked to have lived in one of the houses on the Green. 'But they wouldn't have allowed a shop there,' said Pa. The Pennys lived over theirs at number 19 Porlock Road, a roomy Victorian villa with its staircase coming down into a hall that had a front door to the street and two doors at the back, one leading to the shop, the other opening on to a courtyard that could have been a garden but was needed for the van, for the delivery lorries and a shed. 'I should have liked a garden with roses.' Ma had visions of a pergola with rambler

2

roses, flower-beds and a rockery, bright purple in the spring with aubretia set off by daffodils; but 'We have to earn our living, Maudie,' said Pa.

It was difficult to believe Pa had once been a romantic young man who, when he was not learning to be a greengrocer, willingly went without tea or supper to go to a musical or a revue. He had picked Ma out 'at once', he often said, and had waited at the stage door with a bunch of roses. Ma had never had roses before, 'and that was that,' she said but, 'Still,' she said wistfully, 'I used to be a dancer.'

'In the third row of the chorus,' said Pa.

'Yes. I never made the West End.' Ma had to admit that. 'Pa saw me in Golders Green, but it runs in my family'; and she added what the Pennys knew by heart: 'My Great-Aunt Adelaide Turner used to be a Gaiety Girl.' Ma had a suspicion now that what the Gaiety Girls did in their musicals was 'vulgar', a word she winced from, just as a split or a high kick filled her with distaste. 'Vulgar!'

'Nonsense, Maudie. It was fun and pretty.'

'I meant from the point of view of dancing.'

'What dancing?'

'Ballet. That's what I should have done – could have done.' She could not say that to Pa, but 'ballerina' was a beautiful title. There was another more beautiful: 'ballerina assoluta'. It was a shock to Ma when she was told: 'We don't use those names now. They are just called "principals",' which was sad because 'ballerina' matched Ma's dream exactly.

It was more than a dream, it was a vision, because she knew it was real, though where she had seen it or heard of it she did not know – perhaps from a glimpse on television. She was in a huge theatre, the most famous in London, all red and gold, with tiers and tiers of balconies rising up to a great dome, and each tier lit with rows of candelabra. The seats were filled with 'elegant people!' The stage curtain was velvet, embossed with the initials of the Queen, and below the stage the pit held a whole orchestra, whose gentlemen were tapping their bows on violins and cellos to join in the applause as the curtains opened to show a young girl in a full-skirted white net dress with a little satin bodice and flowers in her hair; beside her was a handsome young dancer, a prince, but Ma's dream was on the

3

girl as, gracefully and modestly, she curtsied. Single flowers were thrown down from the balconies on to the stage, but footmen in livery and white wigs brought on bouquets and baskets of flowers. The girl broke a rose off from one, kissed it and gave it to the Prince, who kissed it, too, then kissed her hand, and the clapping and cheering went on and on. Ma heard it in her sleep. 'Maudie, you're kicking me. Is anything the matter? Got a pain?'

Not a pain – an ache. She could not tell him that, but Pa was astute.

'Maudie,' he cautioned her. 'You know a dancing mother is a kind of joke.'

'But what if you are one?' asked Ma, and 'I think I am justified,' she said with dignity.

Crystal certainly showed signs of being able to dance. 'From the time she could toddle,' Pa said proudly.

'She *never* toddled,' said Ma. 'From the beginning she walked on the tips of her toes.'

They had all heard that story, too. 'It must be in her stars or as if she was born with a mark on her forehead,' said Ma.

'But how did I come?' Doone asked Will.

'You? You came out of an acorn,' teased Will.

Two years after Crystal, Ma had had at last to accept the unwelcome fact that another baby was on the way. 'How dared it come! How dared it!' she almost shrieked at Pa when she told him.

Pa was upset because she made him feel guilty. 'It's not its fault,' he said.

'No, it's mine.' Ma was furious. 'I couldn't believe it. After five children my times are all upset; now it's too late.'

'Too late? Maud, you don't mean you would have . . .?'

'Indeed I would.'

'But our child. Yours and mine.'

'We've five already. Isn't that enough? All those great lumps of boys. . . .'

'Look, love.' Pa tried to comfort her. 'Now we have broken the' – he was going to say 'spell', but instead he said 'pattern' – 'most likely it'll be a girl.'

'I have a girl. I don't want another.'

'Think of a pair – you could have a duo.' Pa still thought of dance in terms of revue and of the music-hall. 'They could do an act together. You hadn't thought of that, had you?'

'Don't be silly' was all Ma said, and Pa tried another tactic. 'Crystal's yours. Well, this one's going to be for me. I tell you, Maudie, often I'm quite jealous of you and your Crystal. This one'll be mine and I'll call her after that Exmoor book: *Lorna Doone*.'

'Lorna's a pretty name,' Ma conceded, but the baby was a boy and quite unlike the others, who had all been fine babies. This one was small, dark-haired, with a little pointed face. 'Sweet,' said the nurses.

'Take him away,' Ma almost screamed at them, and, 'You and your Lorna!' she said to Pa.

Pa looked at the small dark head of the bundle sleeping happily unaware in the hospital cot, and, 'I guess you'll have to be just Doone,' he said. Poor Pa. He had no inkling of what that would mean.

There was no room for a baby at Porlock Road. The shop and storerooms took up all the ground floor of the house. On the first floor there was the big sitting-room; next it, the kitchen where the family also ate; then Pa and Ma's bedroom, next to them Crystal's, then a smaller one, Will's, and the bathroom. Above, in the attics, another bathroom had been made and a big bedroom with a steep sloping ceiling, shared by the twins and Hughie. 'If we put Doone in there . . .,' Pa began, but 'Not on your life,' said Hughie. 'We don't want a squalling baby,' said Jim, and, 'He'll keep us awake,' said Tim.

The natural thing – it had not occurred to Pa that it would not happen – was to turn Crystal's room into a nursery. 'What does a two-year-old want with all that?' asked Pa, but 'It's a little girl's room,' Ma said firmly; in pale blue and white, it was the best room in the house, 'And Crystal will need it later on,' said Ma. 'Our only girl.'

The only place for Doone was the boxroom. 'But there's no window there,' said Pa. 'That's not good for a baby.'

'We'll put in a ventilator,' said Ma. Pa put in the ventilator, papered the walls with a nursery-rhyme paper, bought a rug and repainted the family cot. 'There – it's as nice as can be,'

5

said Ma, but Pa was still worried. 'Maybe, till he's older, Maud, we should take him into our room.'

'No, thank you,' said Ma.

It seemed strange that Doone belonged to the Penny family. Their hair varied from Will's neat mouse-brown to Hughie, who had gleams of gold in his like Ma's, while Crystal had golden curls. Doone's hair was dark and, cut into what Ma called 'a pudding-basin' shape, gave him the look of an elf. Their eyes were grey or blue, Crystal's so dark a blue they were almost violet – she was a beautiful little girl. Doone's were green hazel without a hint of blue and looked large in his pointed face. Will said his ears were pointed, too. 'Nonsense,' said Ma, who hated anything peculiar, but it gave her an added resentment against Doone.

In any case, he was an unsatisfactory child. The others 'paid for dressing', said Ma, but Doone was persistently ragamuffin, his socks falling down, his shoes scuffed; his feet were never still. He usually had a gap showing between his jersey and his shorts or jeans, or else the jersey hung in folds. Ma had forgotten his clothes were seldom bought for him but handed down from the others, who were far plumper, and he had to wear them until they were too tight. His hair seemed unbrushed from his habit of ruffling it up when he was puzzled; he was often puzzled and, often, when spoken to seemed curiously absent, too dreamy to be trusted with the simplest message. He was to be a failure at school – every term a worse report – did not learn to read properly till he was ten and was so silent that he seemed to Ma secretive. 'Well, you don't exactly encourage him,' said Pa.

The first word Doone learnt to say was not 'Ma' or 'Pa', but 'Beppo'. Beppo was a mixture of a porter and a shop boy, though he was no boy, a squat little man, so short he was almost a midget; his stubble of stiff brown hair was like coconut fibre and his eyes were so black they looked in his white face like currants in a bun. Beppo was strong enough to carry a sack of potatoes as easily as if it were Doone. 'Well, he used to be an acrobat,' said Pa.

'An acrobat?' The boys were interested. 'In a circus?'

'Till he got his face burnt when the Big Top caught fire.' Beppo had been badly burnt which was why the skin on his

6

face was thick, white and stiff as paper. 'Poor soul,' said Pa, 'but he was lucky to keep his eyesight.'

'Ugh!' said Ma.

From the first she had objected to Beppo. 'Circuses! We don't want anything from them!'

'What's wrong with circuses?' demanded Pa. 'All that lovely razzmatazz!'

'Exactly.' Ma pursed her lips. 'It's vulgar.'

'Vulgar!' Pa spluttered into his soup, which made Ma angrier still. 'Not as vulgar as some of your turns, my girl. What about that time when you had to be an ostrich with feathers and wriggled your bottom?'

'Never,' said Ma. 'I was a powder-puff.' But the boys were guffawing.

Crystal had been a powder-puff, too, the first time she danced in a competition, when she was five years old. Doone, at three, was too young to remember, but now and again, as he grew older, he was allowed to look in the cupboard where Ma kept Crystal's costumes. Sometimes he was allowed to touch the powder-puff dress with its pleated blue silk folds and border of swansdown; there was a swansdown hat to match, and Ma had kept the little white kid shoes. 'Sure you don't want a glass case,' Pa had teased, but he had been as proud as Ma when Crystal won the competition. 'Of course she won,' said Ma.

It was partly because of Crystal's competitions and dancing classes that Doone had spent most of his baby life among the fruit and vegetables at the back of the shop where Beppo watched over him. Beppo taught Doone to crawl by rolling an orange in front of him and made him a playpen with crates of cauliflower. When Doone could walk, Beppo would take him out into the yard at the back of the shop where the lorries and vans came in and give him a seesaw on the scales that weighed the sacks. As he grew older, when the yard was empty, they would play ball with a cabbage, and when Doone was tired Beppo would play him to sleep on his mouth-organ.

Sometimes Doone cried in the night. Pa would hear, but Ma said: 'Leave him. You need your sleep.' She herself would not get up – she had had enough of getting up for babies. 'He'll go off on his own,' she said, settling herself down, but Doone did not go off. He cried and cried; often he was wet and uncomfortable, but soon he learnt to climb out of his cot and make his way downstairs. The door leading to the shop was locked on the inside but, if he tapped softly, Beppo would hear and come at once, unbolt the door and gather him up, make him dry and comfortable with a towel and take him into his bed where they slept peacefully together. Ma never knew; Beppo had to be up at dawn to make Pa a pot of tea before he drove to the market, and Beppo would carry Doone, fast asleep, upstairs and put him back in his cot. 'You see,' said Ma. 'He settled.' Pa guessed but kept quiet because 'I don't know how Doone would have grown up without Beppo,' said Pa.

'He gives me the creeps,' said Ma. 'Looks like a horrid clown.'

Beppo slept in the small storeroom behind the shop. There was just room for a narrow iron bed he had picked up in a junkshop; the mattress was thin as was the pillow; it had some old army blankets, and Pa had added a quilt. An old china sink served as a washbasin, and there was a strip of carpet on the floor and a small electric fire; some hooks over the bed held Beppo's few clothes, and in a basket under it he kept what underclothes he had and his pair of acrobatic shoes; in a shed in the courtyard he had a trapeze on which he still practised. 'When you big I teach you,' he told Doone.

Besides the trapeze, Beppo had three other private possessions, which were kept on an upturned orange-box beside the bed; on it were Beppo's comb, the mouth-organ he played so beautifully – 'I teach you that as well,' he told Doone – and there was, too, a little plaster figure in blue and white whom Beppo called 'Our Lady'. 'Can I play with her when I'm big?' asked Doone, but Beppo was shocked. 'Never!' said Beppo. 'Never. She not for play' – by which Doone knew she must be somebody important; perhaps, though she looked too young, a statue of Madame Tamara, Crystal's dancing teacher, to Doone the most important person he knew.

At first Ma had taught Crystal herself from what she could remember; it was not until she saw Ennis Glyn's classes for four- and five-year-olds with free running and skipping, foot exercises done on the floor to strengthen insteps and ankles, the careful placing of the small feet for *pliés* – knee-bends – the clapping of rhythm and simple mimes that made the children listen to the music that she knew how over-ambitious she had been. 'Get the basics right, then you can begin' was the ballet tradition. Crystal had had no basics because Ma had grown more ambitious still when she heard of Madame Tamara.

'Is she good?' asked Pa.

'She must be. She's Russian. Ballet started in Russia' – in which Ma was mistaken. Soon, though, Crystal was going to Madame Tamara's school on Tuesdays and Saturdays for special teaching and, on Wednesday afternoons, attending the open classes held at the Empire Rooms, classes of a kind that in fact belonged to Madame's youth, and used to be called 'fancy dancing', truly 'fancy': a mixture of elementary ballet and Greek, with a simplified character dance thrown in for interest, besides waltzes and polkas.

'At least I teach the children to hold themselves up, to run and stretch, to curtsy properly and not tread on their partners' toes,' said Madame Tamara. 'Those classes do no harm.' They were, too, the largest part of her income, being popular, almost a social event, for the Pilgrim's Green mothers. To Ma they were her pride and joy, especially when Crystal was called out to show off a scarf dance or a tarantella with her tambourine to which Ma lovingly tied a whole rainbow of ribbons.

'An odd kind of tarantella to be danced by a seven-year-old,' Stella, Ennis Glyn's fiery little assistant at the Ennis Glyn School, was to say when Ma told them of it.

'They'll dance anything,' said Ennis Glyn. 'It's how they dance it that's so pathetic.' All the more pathetic because Ma thought it was perfect. 'Of course, Crystal has extra classes,' she boasted to the other mothers, 'but I must say Madame Tamara's a good teacher.'

'She is, when she's allowed to be.' That was Mr Felix, Madame's old pianist. Ma had not realised she was sitting so near the piano, nor that when Crystal danced she did not keep time with Mr Felix but Mr Felix with her – 'For Minnie's sake,' he would have said. Mr Felix called Madame 'Minnie'. Ma could not think why. He was an innate pianist, sympathetic to any child who was in earnest, but, for him, playing for the classes at the Empire Rooms was routine; he simply had to beat the music out, 'so that any little donkey can hear it!' and so, at the same time, he read a book propped up on the music-stand. Ma found the book an insult. 'Couldn't be less interested. At least he could be polite,' but there were certainly no smiles for mothers or little girls, and 'Such a disagreeable old man!' said Ma.

Wednesday was early-closing day for the shop, but Pa sometimes used it for clearing out and rearranging stock. Then he needed Beppo, and Ma had to take Doone, as well as Crystal, to the Empire Rooms. 'You must sit still as a mouse,' Ma said as she always said. Mice are not still unless they are frightened but, as he sat beside Ma, Doone did not know he was still because he was transported: the music, the lights, the little girls – it seemed to him a hundred little girls – all in party dresses and dancing shoes, moving to the music in what seemed to him a miracle of marching, running, leaping; doing intricate little steps, using their arms in a wonderfully pretty way and, in the midst of them, Madame Tamara, in a black dress glittering with what Doone thought were black diamonds, giving commands in a clear high voice. When, at the end of the class, the little girls came from the corner two by two and curtsied to Madame Tamara, Doone almost swooned with delight. 'Ma, can't I go to dancing class?'

'Of course not; you're a boy.' Ma seemed to have forgotten that, without boy dancers, there would have been no prince for her visionary girl. There were certainly no boys at the Empire Rooms, and it was only now and then that Doone went there. Usually he had to stay with Beppo. 'Never mind,' said Beppo. 'I teach you other things.'

For Doone's fifth Christmas, Beppo made him a Christmas tree; it was the tip of a tree that had been left unsold, and Pa had said Beppo could have it. He planted it in a pot covered with red paper made pretty with the paper grass that came with the boxes of tangerines. Beppo threaded strings of holly berries and nuts, wound them like necklaces in the branches and hung them with walnuts. 'I no use silver,' he told Doone, 'because, after, we give it to the birds.' He hung tangerines, too, and for a star at the top he used a scarlet poinsettia flower

10

that had broken off its plant. Doone thought the tree beautiful and it was his own.

There was a big tinsel tree in the living-room, but this was private and he left it where it was, in Beppo's storeroom. Only one thing he took off it – the best of all. On the tree was a present, hanging by a ribbon; it was a mouth-organ, smaller than Beppo's, primrose colour with silver chasings. Beppo could have given Doone no greater treasure. 'I play big one. You play little one and quite soon you learn,' said Beppo. Doone's eyes shone as none of the family had seen them shine, and that night, when ostensibly he had been sent to bed out of the way, he took a cracker he had saved down to Beppo. They shared a crystallised pear that had fallen out of a broken box. Beppo cleaned Doone's sticky hands and mouth with a shop paper bag and he fell asleep while Beppo played 'Silent Night' softly on his big mouth-organ.

It was not long before Doone was playing that on his mouth-organ and other music as well; not the sort the boys listened to. 'What they call "pop",' said Beppo. 'I can do that, too.' He could, and extremely well, but he liked to play songs, 'O sole mio', 'Lucia', or arias from opera, 'La donna è mobile', 'Vesti la giubba' and others, some soft-sounding, some exciting when he stamped and danced. Doone liked the melodies best of all and soon he, too, could play them. Now and then he was allowed to play Beppo's big mouth-organ, and, 'That boy has an ear,' said Pa. 'He's quite a little musician.'

'Gets it from me,' said Ma. 'I had a sweet voice, remember?' and she sighed.

To play the mouth-organ was not the only thing Doone learnt from Beppo. As a tiny boy, Beppo had made him do exercises and now he hung a small trapeze beside his big one in the shed. Below he laid a mattress he had bought in the secondhand market so that, if Doone fell, there was something soft to fall on. Beppo taught him to swing on the trapeze, legs taut, feet held together like a true acrobat and, presently, to swing his body up, up, and, still holding, turn a somersault and swing down. Sometimes Doone fell, but on to the mattress, and 'Had enough?' Beppo would ask; but as soon as the little

11

boy had recovered his breath he shook his head. 'Try again.'

Besides the trapeze, Beppo bought a strip of coconut matting and, on it, taught Doone to somersault. He played leap frog with him – not ordinary leap frog but with the acrobats' way of leaping and landing – and Doone began to be able to jump into a somersault. He tried, too, to copy Beppo's flip-flaps, when he threw himself over on his hands and landed standing upright, but it was too difficult. 'Soon, soon you will,' encouraged Beppo. 'Flip-flap *and* back somersault.' He was amazed at Doone's agility and was all the more careful, making him bend and touch his toes after everything he did. Doone could catch hold of his heels and raise his legs above his head, sit on the ground, hold his ankles and knock his forehead on the ground – and do cartwheels. 'I couldn't, not at five,' said Beppo. 'But you must balance right.' To teach Doone to stand on his hands Beppo would hold his legs. 'Head! Head up,' and 'Soon,' said Beppo, 'soon,' but Doone had to finish learning handstands by himself because he and Beppo ran into trouble. Bad trouble.

It happened in the February after that Christmas, one of those fine February days that can be as warm as spring. Beppo had fetched Doone from school. As Doone was now five, he had begun school and usually came home with Crystal, but on Wednesdays she and Ma were at the Empire Rooms, so Beppo fetched Doone, which both of them liked. Beppo always bought Doone an ice cream.

As it was so warm and sunny he brought the mattress and matting into the courtyard. No one was about. The boys had a football match. Pa was checking accounts in the other shop. With two shops now he was more than busy, and 'Maud, couldn't you take over this one for me?' he had asked Ma.

'Me! Work in the shop?'

'You did when we first married.'

'It was different then – just you and me. We hadn't the boys, nor Crystal.'

'Nor Crystal.' Pa said it a little bitterly. With Crystal, he often thought, had come even more 'notions'. 'You could get a woman to help you in the house,' he suggested – one came in already for the mountain of washing and ironing – but 'I like to do the rest myself,' said Ma and, to give her her due, in spite of

12

the 'notions', she looked after them well; no boy was ever sent to school in a dirty shirt or muddy shoes; Pa's greengrocer apron was ironed impeccably; the house was shiningly clean and smelled of polish and good cooking and was full of the pot plants that Pa got at cost price. But the shop! Ma wrinkled up her nose, and Pa had to engage Mrs Denning, a plump good-natured woman with a frizz of dark hair and cheeks red as apples – 'Beauty of Baths. Delicious!' said Pa.

She was, of course, not there on Wednesday afternoons and, on that particular one, Beppo and Doone did not notice how quickly time passed and, suddenly, when Beppo had just done a double somersault and was encouraging Doone to try, a voice sounded from the downstairs house door which opened on the courtyard: 'Beppo!' The voice was ecstatic. 'Beppo! *You* can do that!'

It was Crystal in her spring coat and matching beret, white socks and shoes with buckles. 'Beppo!' she cried like any ordinary little girl. 'I'd love to do it.' She threw off her coat and beret, dropped her shoebag, and: 'Teach me, Beppo. Beppo, please.'

Beppo was flattered. This was Miss Crystal, who never spoke to him; he had always looked on her as someone apart, but still he hung back. 'Mamma?' he questioned. 'I think she no like.'

'She's upstairs.'

'But – what she say?'

'She can't say anything if she doesn't know. Anyway, it's part of dancing. Beppo, please.'

'Not in that dress. Not in those shoes – you can't.'

In a moment Crystal, who usually argued about everything, had stripped off the party dress, so carefully ironed by Ma – she would not trust it to Mrs Simms – tossed it behind her in the doorway and took off her shoes. 'Will socks do?' she pleaded. Beppo had never heard Crystal ask like that before. 'Teach me, Beppo. Please.'

It was not as easy as with Doone, which amazed all three of them – Doone had thought Crystal could do anything – but Madame Tamara seemed to have made Crystal slightly stiff and her feet were not flexible. 'You must hold on with your foot,' Beppo had said when he tried her on the trapeze; and on

13

the mattress: 'You must land steady. Foot must be like your hands.' But Crystal's were not. She could somersault but not use the trapeze, nor cartwheel. 'Never mind,' said Beppo. 'It will come if you work'; but Crystal did not like work, and 'Beppo,' she called, 'could I do the splits?'

'Anyone can do splits,' said Beppo – he called them 'e-split' – but Crystal had to try and try. 'I'm nearly there. I'm *there*'; and 'Bravo! Bravo!' Beppo started to clap when from the courtyard door came a screech: '*Crystal! God Almighty! Crystal!*' It was Ma standing in the doorway. She had no idea that splits and handstands were part of a true dancer's training; to her they were a dangerous vulgarisation. 'Do you want to *ruin* your dancing?' She advanced into the courtyard; she had picked up Crystal's dress and shoes. 'Go upstairs at *once*. You, too, you naughty little boy,' she said to Doone, who had done nothing. 'As for you,' she said to Beppo, 'how dare you!' Beppo, who had always been afraid of Ma, quailed. 'How dare you come anywhere near Miss Crystal! Teaching dangerous things to children! Well, I'll teach you,' stormed Ma. 'A clown like you! Out! Take your things and go.' She went into the shop, driving Beppo before her, opened the till, took out some five-pound notes and threw them on the floor. 'There's your money. Pack your things and go, and never, never show your face here again. Out! Out!' screamed Ma.

'You should have asked me first,' said Pa. When Pa was angry, unlike Ma, he became quiet, so quiet now that Ma was frightened. 'But handstands,' Ma defended herself. 'He might have broken Crystal's back – and splits!'

'You used to do the splits.' Ma ignored that.

'Circus tricks!' she said, and, looking at Pa's face: 'I'm sorry, William, but I couldn't risk spoiling Crystal's career.'

'How do you know she's going to have a career?'

'I know,' said Ma, but she did not feel comfortable.

'And what about Doone?' asked Pa.

Doone had not gone upstairs when Ma had ordered him but had followed her and Beppo into the shop.

'Doone, I told you. . . .' Doone had paid not the slightest attention. He was frightened; he could not understand what had happened or why Ma had screamed 'Out! Out!' He only knew something was happening to Beppo and he clasped Beppo round the legs and pressed his face against him. It was Beppo who gently removed his hands and stood him back. 'Be a good boy,' said Beppo, 'and, Doone, remember. . . .' Beppo could not go on.

Doone's mouth quivered. 'What, Beppo?'

'You practise every day. You promise.'

Doone nodded.

Most people can show by their faces if they are glad or sad, shocked or frightened, but Beppo's had been so badly burnt that it could not. Only his mouth twisted like one of the clowns Ma had called him. Then 'Go like Mamma says,' he told Doone. 'Go upstairs.'

Beppo left his blankets neatly folded on his bed, the quilt on top of them. He left the clothes Pa had given him, the five-pound notes on the floor where Ma had thrown them. He had taken the basket with the underclothes and shirts that belonged to him and his acrobatic shoes, his comb and the precious little statue, but propped against his pillow was his mouth-organ and a two-word message printed in large letters: 'For Dune.' Pa and Ma looked at it, and 'How are you going to explain this?' asked Pa.

'Doone's just a baby,' said Ma. 'He'll forget,' but it was now that Ma had a taste of what she was to call 'Doone's obstinacy'.

'Where's Beppo?'

'Where's Beppo?'

'Where's Beppo?' It went on, day in, day out. 'Where's Beppo?' Until Ma, exasperated, said flatly, 'Beppo's gone.'

Then it changed to real anxiety. 'Mamma' – Doone was the only one who had realised Ma's wish and, brought up by Italian Beppo, said 'Mamma' – 'Mamma, Beppo'll come back? Come back?'

'Of course he will.' 'Anything for peace,' she told Pa, and perhaps she really did think Beppo would come back. 'He knows which side his bread is buttered,' but Beppo did not come back, and 'I'm not surprised,' said Pa. 'When you lose your temper, Maud, it's not nice, not nice at all.'

15

Soon there were no more questions. There came a night when Doone woke and, as in all the other nights since Beppo had left, struggled out of bed and went down to the door which he tapped. That night he did not tap. He stood by the door, put his cheek against it, then climbed wearily back to bed. Presently he reached out his hand in the dark, found the big mouth-organ and softly, under the bedclothes, played himself to sleep.

Perhaps Ma was sorry. She was less impatient with Doone. Sometimes she even put her arm round him, drew him close and kissed him; but Doone, who once would have been filled with happiness and kissed her back, freed himself as soon as he could. It was not that he held anything against Ma; he knew she had sent Beppo away but, then, Beppo, in some way he could not understand, had hurt or threatened to hurt Crystal. Crystal, Doone knew, was all-important, but suddenly he was no longer what Ma said he was, a baby; he was an independent little boy who had somehow grown proud, and not only with Ma; it was no use Pa patting him on the head and giving him money to buy an ice cream; no use Will being kind and offering to jump him up on the trapeze – he could reach it himself if he stood on a stool. It was just that Doone knew quite well and quite clearly that now there was nobody who wanted him.

He would have loved to go and play football with Hughie, Jim and Tim and their Gang on a piece of waste ground they had taken for their own, but when he ran after them Hughie commanded him to go back.

'You're too small,' said Hughie.

'And a thudding nuisance,' said Jim.

'Go home,' ordered Tim.

'Home! Push off,' the Gang told him.

Crystal had her own important life with her dancing and her friends; Doone had no friends. Even Mrs Denning in the shop could not put up with him. 'I really can't be responsible for Doone,' she told Pa. 'Now Beppo's gone I seem to have so much to do.'

There is an emptiness in being unwanted, an aloneness when there seems nothing to which you belong and, 'Maud,' said Pa, 'that child's not right. He's grieving.'

16

'Grieving? He's just growing,' said Ma and, though she was tired and did not want just then to be bothered with Doone, she said what was the wisest thing anybody could have said at that moment: 'Let him grow,' and presently Doone discovered he did have something to which, mysteriously, he seemed to belong.

'Doone!' Ma's voice was so shrill that he heard it in the shed and came out. 'Where *have* you been? It's long past tea-time.'

Doone did not know it was past tea-time; he hardly knew that time had passed. He had been working on the trapeze – not his small one, but Beppo's big one – standing on the stool to reach it, then kicking the stool away. True, he had fallen, but he had been careful to do as Beppo had told him, 'Always put the mattress underneath.' He had been trying to do handstands, too, and was nearly there. When he was tired he had sat on the stool and played the big mouth-organ – Ma could not hear him in the shed – and he played 'Lucia' and other things Beppo had played. Time had meant nothing, nor food; he was rosy and tousled – and happy, thought Ma, surprised and, 'What have you been doing?' she asked.

'I. . . .' Suddenly Doone decided he was not going to tell Ma, or anyone and, 'Nothing,' he said, but it was from that afternoon that Doone discovered he had two things that, quite apart from the family, were his companions – had had them all the time; acrobatics and music were his as well as Beppo's, so much his that he wanted to keep them secret.

Other things began to blot Beppo out but when, as a bigger boy, Doone saw the ballet *Petrushka*, with its strange other-world music, and the poor Clown puppet with his stiff face beating on the wall of his booth for love of the Ballerina with her rouged cheeks, Petrushka was so like Beppo that Doone could not bear to watch.

Chapter Two

IT WAS strange that the one in the family who least wanted Doone now had the most of him. Crystal had to take him to and back from school, which neither of them liked; she made him walk behind so she could talk to her friends and, if he dawdled in the slightest to look at something interesting or was slow at a crossing, she would pull his arm fiercely or punch him. If his socks came down, or his anorak was not done up, she would put them right with fingers that pinched, and she often slapped him; it was, too, not only going to school.

'What are you going to do with Doone now on Wednesday afternoons?' asked Pa. 'He can't stay here alone.'

'He'll have to come along with Crystal and me.'

'And Tuesdays and Saturday mornings?'

'Crystal will have to take him to Madame Tamara's.'

The dancing school was just round the corner; Crystal always walked there on her own – Pa was sure Pilgrim's Green was utterly safe – and, 'I have spoken to Madame,' said Ma.

Madame Tamara was kind. 'What would you like to do, little boy? Look at your comics or watch?'

'Watch,' said Doone.

As he watched, his eyes seemed to grow bigger and bigger, and something else was happening in Doone; it was a certainty that this dancing, too, was where he belonged, another thing that was his own, or was going to be his own.

The classes at the school were quite different from those at the Empire Rooms. There was no coming or going or chatter, no lit chandeliers or glistening floors – Doone was to learn how dangerous a polished floor is for dancers. Here, in the corner of the classroom, was a tin tray of resin in which the girls rubbed their shoes to stop them slipping, even on the bare wooden boards. There were no mothers sitting round the

18

walls; if they came, they mostly had to sit in the waiting-room, though some, like Ma, marched into the classroom. There were no party dresses, chiffon scarves or tambourines, few solos or stamping peasant dances, no waltzing or polkas. There were only ten girls in plain tunics, leotards, or vests and tights, but their shoes were pale-pink satin. Madame held a long thin stick like a wand with which she touched their feet or arms; Doone would not have been surprised if magic had come out of it. Except for Madame's voice and the piano, the room was quiet, the girls earnest.

The class began with work on what he had not seen before, wooden bars that ran along the walls, so that the dancers could rest one hand on them for balance while they did their exercises; sometimes their feet were up on them, too, as they stretched their legs. Every class began with work at the barre, twenty minutes, even half an hour – 'So boring,' said Crystal, but to Doone it seemed sensible, even comfortable. He tried some of the exercises holding on to the rail of his bed. The barre, for Doone, was to become like the trapeze, a helpful dependable wooden friend.

When the girls came to the centre it was prettier. Doone loved the armwork: '*port de bras*', Madame called it. He said it over and over again, '*Port de bras . . . port de bras . . .*,' like a charm. He saw an *arabesque* – the leg pointed behind, one arm stretched forward, both knees straight, the weight shifted to the front leg, while the back leg was slowly raised as high as possible when the girls tilted slightly forward, which lifted it even higher; some of them made a beautiful line, even if they wobbled. What they did with their feet in some of the exercises fascinated Doone so much that he got down from the chair that had been allotted him near the piano and knelt on the floor to see their quick changes in the air while Madame chanted, 'And one – and two – and one and two – and three.' The feet beat in time with the music – or not with the music. 'Ah, no!' cried Madame and, once, exasperated, 'Have you no ears!'

Doone did not see that the classroom was shabby with dingy walls, a cracked ceiling and windows that were seldom cleaned; the stuffing was coming out of the seats of the padded benches under them, and the corner of the piano seat was worn through. The piano itself was old and tinkly. He only knew that he loved the dancing and, for the first time, sniffed the smell of a dance classroom, a smell of dust with a tinge of resin, the smell of dance shoes, especially when they were new, and of hot young bodies as the class warmed up. In Madame Tamara's there was also a slight smell of gas from the old-fashioned gas-fire; dancers, when they stop, stand still, rest, must not get cold.

Soon, though, as the first dazzlement wore off, Doone began to notice things – and differences. All the girls' hair was tied back, Crystal's in a pony tail from which her curls cascaded and tossed; only one had her hair neatly plaited into a band round her head so that Madame could really see her neck and shoulders. Always in the back row, this girl was slender, not pretty, but with brown hair and eyes and a dignified small face. Madame hardly ever spoke to her, and she was so quiet and pale that, behind Crystal with her vivid colouring and charm, few people would have noticed her. Doone noticed her at once. 'What are you looking at?' Mr Felix, the old pianist, asked.

'That one.' Doone stabbed a finger at the pale girl.

'At Ruth?' Mr Felix played on, then said, 'You have good taste, young man.'

Obviously Mr Felix was surprised. He was a thin old man with a head of proud white hair; except that it was silky and set off a fine brow, why it looked so proud was difficult to explain because the rest of Mr Felix was shabby, even dirty.

'I wonder Madame keeps him,' said Ma. Madame kept him because his music came faultlessly, exciting or gentle, slow, fast, coaxing. It is not easy to be a dance pianist; they never know what they may be asked to play and have to watch the teacher, the dancers, and find music that fits the steps and has the right beat and feeling, but Mr Felix seemed always able to conjure it. Now he looked down at Doone and asked, 'What makes you watch Ruth?'

Usually, if anyone asked Doone a question, he was tongue-tied. To be the youngest in a family is supposed to be enviable, but that is in fairy-tales; with four older brothers and an important older sister, Doone rarely had a chance to speak. Once he had burst out to Pa, 'Papa, I don't get *any* moments!' There had been a hush of surprise. Then, 'That's true,' said Pa.

'What is it you want to say, son?' Pa often called his boys 'son', as if he could not remember which was which. 'What is it you wanted to say?'

'We're listening,' said Hughie.

'Come on, tell us,' jeered Tim.

'Open up,' said Jim.

'It isn't fair,' Crystal had unexpectedly intervened, and she commanded, 'Give him a chance', but the sudden attention had made Doone lose what he had been burning to tell them and he could not utter a word. 'Silly baby,' Crystal had said; but now, with Mr Felix, it was as if he, Doone, were back with Beppo and, 'She . . . makes it look easy.' That was what Beppo had said acrobats had to do, and Doone explained to Mr Felix, 'You mustn't make people look at your hands or your feet but at the all of you.' He was only repeating what Beppo had told him, but Mr Felix stopped playing to look down at Doone.

It was only for a moment. He started playing again, then, 'What did you say your name was, boy?' asked Mr Felix.

'Doone. Doone Penny.'

'Penny? Then . . .?'

Doone nodded. 'I'm Crystal's brother.'

'*Crystal!* That one?'

'Yes.'

'Not possible,' said Mr Felix. 'Not possible.'

Doone felt crushed. He knew he was a queer kind of small brother for someone like Crystal to have but evidently Mr Felix could not have thought too badly of him; he took to asking him questions.

'Who's not pointing her feet?'

'Zoë or Angela . . . .' Often 'Crystal.' Small as he was, Doone could not help noticing that Crystal seemed to wave her arms, use her eyes and neck as if she were showing off her pretty hair, but often did not pay attention to her feet.

'Who's not using her head? Who's not holding her arms properly?' And once Doone had to give the surprising answer: 'Madame.'

Seen closer, away from the glamour and lights of the Empire Rooms, Madame Tamara, in her everyday black dress, looked worn and old; her feet were knobbled; though she could still point them, they obviously hurt, and when she walked she

21

limped. Her arms, for all their grace, were thin, and sometimes she seemed too stiff to use them. She had dark stains under her eyes, and sometimes there was stale powder in her wrinkles. Doone discovered another thing about Madame: she was afraid of Ma.

'Crystal says she can't do all that work at the barre,' Ma told Madame.

'But, without work at the barre, how...?' Madame sounded bewildered.

'We don't want the child to lose her enthusiasm, do we? I'm not one of those mothers who want to push their children.' Ma sincerely believed that. 'But she's had a great many lessons from you, Madame. If you would give her a few more little solos. ...'

Soon Madame was teaching her class a great many little solos; there was also a day when, 'What funny shoes!' said Doone as he saw Ma sewing ribbons on a new pair of pink satin ones with strange hard tips. 'What funny shoes.'

'Block shoes,' said Ma, beginning to darn the tips. 'Madame's putting Crystal up on points,' she said importantly and, presently, in the waiting-room Doone heard her say to Ruth's mother, Mrs Sherrin: 'I see your Ruthie's not on her points yet.' Ma did not attempt to say *'en pointe'*.

'Certainly not!' Mrs Sherrin said it severely. 'Madame knows Ruth's not nearly ready yet.'

'Crystal is.' But Doone heard Mr Felix say to Madame, 'You shouldn't have done that, Minnie. You know you shouldn't have done it. She's hardly eight years old.' He was stern, but Madame only made a helpless little gesture. 'I know.'

'At eight years old! That's wrong. The others will want the same,' he warned.

'I know,' Madame said again, and her dark eyes had a look of panic as if she were being hunted.

Crystal was not only the avowed star of Madame Tamara's dancing school; she was also 'her bread and butter', said Pa.

'I don't think there's much butter,' said Ma. 'Dancing doesn't pay much, and Madame has a bedridden sister. Think what that must cost.'

'Yes, but every time Crystal dances at a matinée or charity show she brings perhaps another dozen little girls to the

22

school. Madame ought to take her for nothing.'

Pa was joking, but Crystal flashed, 'She takes Ruth for nothing.'

That was not quite true, as Ma felt bound to say. 'She takes Ruth in exchange for Mrs Sherrin helping with the housework and Madame's sister, poor soul.'

'Well done, Mrs Sherrin,' said Pa.

From the first, Crystal had tried to patronise Ruth. 'You don't come to the Empire Rooms?'

'No.' Ruth said it quietly. 'I don't want to.'

'Why not?'

'It isn't dancing.'

'Of course it is.'

'That hotchpotch! It's only a very old-fashioned teacher who has those kind of fancy dancing classes these days. I think they were started by Madame's mother.'

Crystal was indignant and told Ma, but Ma pondered and said, 'Ruth's probably jealous; I can guess she hasn't a proper dress to wear, poor little thing.'

Ma could often be thoughtful and kind, and next Saturday morning she made a point of coming to Madame Tamara's and, after class, sought out Mrs Sherrin and Ruth. 'I have brought a dress for you, dear,' she said to Ruth, and to Mrs Sherrin, 'I hope you don't mind. Crystal has so many and she has only worn this once or twice – she grows so quickly. She's taller than Ruth. I got it at the girls' boutique and it's so very pretty. Pink would suit your. . . .' She was going to say 'paleness', but changed it to 'complexion'. 'Wouldn't it, dear? Look,' and she shook out the pink skirt. 'Pure silk.'

Mrs Sherrin flushed and drew back. 'It's kind of you, Mrs Penny, very kind, but I'm afraid Ruth would have no use for a dress like that.'

'Wear one of Crystal's dresses,' Doone heard Ruth flare when Ma had gone – under her quietness, Ruth was passionate – 'I'd rather be dead,' and what had begun as a rivalry became a war.

'You don't slap me in the face twice!' said Ma.

'Mrs Sherrin's probably very proud. People who are poor often are,' said Pa. 'How would you like it, Maud, if someone gave you a secondhand dress for Crystal?'

'But she's just a cleaning woman,' said Ma.

Doone could have told her that Mrs Sherrin was not a usual cleaning woman. As the Tuesday afternoons and Saturday mornings went by, he had found he not only wanted to watch the class but also to join in, and had discovered that, if he went into the corridor outside the classroom, he could still hear the music and Madame Tamara's voice. There was a radiator there he could hold on to for a barre, and soon, instead of going straight into the classroom, he stationed himself by it and, as the music began, gravely making a preparation and holding out his arm as the girls did, he would sink into the *pliés* with which every class began.

He had been aware of a lady – a young slim brown-haired lady – in an overall who dusted and vacuumed and polished. Now, coming down the corridor, she stopped as if she were astonished. For a moment she watched; then, putting down her dustpan, she said, 'No, Doone' – she knew his name – 'not quite like that. You're letting your feet move as you go down. Make them grip the floor.' She put an experienced hand on his ribcase to set it straight. 'Back straight, too, head up, and don't clutch the radiator. Just keep a hand on it to steady you.' She gently adjusted his arm. 'Let it fall in a curve. That's better. Now try in the second position.' And Doone set his feet apart – he knew all the positions. 'Get your knees out, over your toes.' It made him ache, but he did it. After that she often helped him. He had not known she was Ruth's mother until he heard her say to Madame, 'I'll stay and cook supper if you'll give Ruth twenty minutes at the barre.'

The class did less and less at the barre, and Madame seemed to have given up criticising. Not so Crystal.

'You don't get your leg very high,' she told Ruth. 'Look at mine,' said Crystal.

'Yes, but yours isn't turned out,' said Ruth, 'and it wobbles.'

'It doesn't.'

'Look at it,' Ruth was withering, 'and you don't hold your body still. Can't you keep your bottom in?'

It was in front of the whole class and Doone, too, burned with shame. He liked Ruth but Crystal was his sister.

'Is Ruth a better dancer than Crystal?' he asked Mr Felix.

Mr Felix did not answer at once; he seldom did. At last,

'Your sister,' he said as he played, 'would dance very well if she paid attention and would take a little discipline.'

Doone did not know what 'discipline' meant; it sounded like a medicine, and that evening, 'Does discipline taste nasty?' he asked Pa.

'Well, most people don't like the taste of it,' said Pa. 'Why do you ask, son?'

'Mr Felix said Crystal ought to take some. It would do her dancing good.'

'Mr Felix!' Ma was annoyed. 'What does Mr Felix know about it?'

'Just about everything, I should think,' said Pa. 'He must have been playing for dancing classes for something like fifty years.'

'Do you know, Ma,' said Crystal, 'Doone can play almost all the music Mr Felix plays in our classes.'

'Doone? Nonsense,' said Ma.

'He can – on his mouth-organ.' For once Crystal was praising Doone. 'Listen,' and she commanded, 'Doone, play what Mr Felix plays when we start class with our *pliés*. See! she said to Ma as Doone played. 'Now for *port de bras*.'

'But Mr Felix plays different things for that,' objected Doone.

'Well, play one of them,' Crystal said impatiently. 'See,' and she showed Ma. 'It fits.'

'Of course it fits,' Doone could have said, because he knew the positions, too, but he said nothing – only played, which led to a dispute.

'Doone ought to have music lessons,' said Will.

'Just because he tootles on the mouth-organ?'

'Pa, he doesn't tootle. He plays,' said Will. 'That's the point.'

'Do you think I'm made of money?'

'No, I don't,' said Will, 'but why should so much of it be spent on Crystal?'

'That's different,' and Ma said seriously, 'when, in a family, one child has real talent, the rest have to make some sacrifice.'

Crystal's crowning battle with Ruth was about shoes. As Mr

Felix had predicted, when Madame Tamara gave in to Ma and put Crystal *en pointe*, the other mothers wanted that, too, and soon all the class was on points – except Ruth. 'Pity you're so far behind,' said Crystal. 'I suppose your feet are not strong enough.' For answer Ruth, in her bare feet, walked across the room on the tips of her toes. Doone would dearly have liked to show them he could do that, too, but he sat still. The class was tittering at Crystal, which made her go red; Doone hunched his shoulders and made himself small. He hated fighting.

'If you're so strong,' said Crystal to Ruth, 'why aren't you on points?'

'Madame says I'm not ready.'

'If *we* are. . . .'

'You're not.' Ruth said it firmly. 'It's your mothers,' and she shrugged, an insolent little shrug.

'Our mothers!' Crystal was indignant. 'I expect it's because *your* mother can't afford to buy you block shoes'; and Crystal called to the girls, 'Just look at Ruth's shoes. All dirty and frayed.'

Ruth's shoes were far more worn than the other girls', but that was because she practised and worked in her own free time; evening after evening found her in the empty classroom, working at the barre, watching herself in the mirror. It had to be by candlelight – Madame would not let her use the electricity – but, even if she could not see well, Ruth tried to feel, as Madame said, 'from your feet to your head, to your very fingertips.'

'You need new soft shoes, let alone block ones,' said Crystal and jeered, 'Ask your mother to do some more scrubbing.'

Wham!

Crystal was bending down to tie her ribbons as Ruth's foot came up in a fierce *grand battement* that almost threw her off her balance. Her toe caught Crystal in the eye. 'Who said my leg couldn't go high?' asked Ruth, breathless. Crystal had given a yelp of pain; now she began to cry noisily, holding her eye, and the other girls gathered round her as Madame burst into the room. 'What has happened? *Crystal!*' Everyone answered her at once and, in the hubbub, Mrs Sherrin, too, came in. She was as calm as she was dismayed. 'Let me take her

26

and bathe that eye,' said Mrs Sherrin. 'Ruth, get your things and go home at once.'

'You naughty, naughty girl.' Madame was beside herself. 'What am I to tell Mrs Penny? What? You're bad through and through. Ungrateful!'

'I don't care,' said Ruth. 'I'm glad I did it – and I hope it hurts.'

Ma had seldom been as angry. Crystal was due to dance that Saturday, the 5th November, at a gala evening for the Royal Benevolent Society. 'We were so looking forward to it. She was to have been a rainbow with scarves in all its colours, and how can she be a rainbow with a black eye?'

She obviously could not; the bruise had spread down her cheek and, 'I must say,' said Pa, 'when that little girl hits—'

'Kicks,' said Ma.

'Kicks, then – she means business.'

'Ruth, if you must lose your temper and kick someone,' Doone heard Mr Felix tell Ruth, 'don't do it in the eye or face. You might damage them for life.'

'Exactly what I wanted to do,' said Ruth.

Mr Felix had chuckled but, 'I'll sue that woman,' said Ma, 'and Madame Tamara.'

'Maud, it's just a little girls' tiff. . . .'

'Tiff!' shrilled Ma. 'Crystal might have lost an eye! But what can you expect? A girl of that class. No idea how to behave.'

Ruth came up to Crystal with an envelope. 'Mother says I'm to give you this.'

Crystal was wary. 'What is it?'

'Tickets.' Ruth almost gave a sob. 'Two tickets for the Royal Theatre.'

'For the ballet?'

'Yes. On November the fifth. Madame gave them to us. She was sent them by a girl she used to teach who is dancing her first solo part, but Madame can't leave her sister. Now. . . .' This time there was a real sob. 'Here – take them.' She thrust the precious envelope into Crystal's hand, 'and Mother said I was to say I was sorry.'

'You're not really sorry, are you?' asked Crystal.

'I'm sorry about the tickets,' said Ruth and went quickly out of the room.

'I don't want to go,' said Crystal.

'Don't want to go!' Ma could not believe her ears. 'To Her Majesty's Ballet!'

For a moment Ma had been tempted to play tit for tat and hand the tickets back – 'We have no use for them, thank you' – but Her Majesty's Ballet! And, 'I must say it's decent of Mrs Sherrin,' said Ma. 'Only right, of course, but those seats cost goodness knows what. Pounds and pounds. I never dreamed. . . .' And she was dumbfounded when, 'I won't go,' said Crystal.

'But, Crystal, Her Majesty's Ballet.'

'It's Bonfire Night,' said Crystal.

The boys had built a bonfire in the courtyard. For weeks and weeks they had been dragging a dressed-up Guy Fawkes round the streets in the family's old pushchair. Doone, hoping to be allowed to join in, had donated his pyjamas – they had been Tim's and Hughie's and were tattered, but Ma made as much fuss as if they had been new and he was suitably punished. 'No sweets, and you don't go out for a week.' But 'Twopence for the guy', 'Fivepence for the guy', the boys chanted – Doone could hear them and knew he had contributed. Now they had plenty of fireworks and had asked their Gang and were going to have sausages and chips and apples roasted in the bonfire.

'You had to miss it anyhow,' Pa told Crystal.

'Because I was going to dance. I would miss it for my own dancing,' Crystal was quite candid. 'Not for other people's.'

'But, Crystal, these are some of the best dancers in the world.'

'It's Bonfire Night. I want to ask my friends.'

'I can't go alone.' Ma was almost in tears. 'William?'

'Maudie, you know I have to be here. All those kids and a fire.'

'I know.' Ma sounded helpless. 'Will? You?'

'I can't, Ma. I'm taking Kate to the theatre.' Kate was what Ma called 'Will's young lady'. 'Girl,' Will corrected her and now, 'I'm sorry, Ma'.

'Go to see ballet?' Jim, Tim and Hughie pronounced it 'bally'.

'Not on your life,' said Jim and Tim.

'Catch us,' said Hughie.

It was then that Ma felt what had been going on for a long time – a tugging at her sleeve. 'Doone, what do you want?'

'To come,' said Doone. 'To go with you. Please.'

'It goes on late,' said Pa. 'You'd go to sleep.'

'I wouldn't,' said Doone. '*Please*, Mamma.' He had not called her that since Beppo went.

'You'll miss the fireworks,' said Will, but Doone did not seem to hear. 'Mamma, please, please.'

'It seems a waste of a seat,' said Ma. 'But if there's no one else.'

'Ma, will you wear your emeralds and diamonds?'

They really were emeralds and diamonds. A fine Edwardian pendant necklace, the pendant a large cabachon emerald drop held by twin chains set with small brilliant cut diamonds that themselves hung from a bar, like a brooch, with another cabachon emerald flanked by delicate diamond foliates that matched the holder of the pendant. 'A most desirable piece, sir,' the insurance man had told Pa.

To Ma they were her greatest asset, not only because of their worth but also because, in a way, they proved her pedigree. 'They were left to me by my Great-Aunt Adelaide, the Gaiety Girl, and given to her by an . . . an admirer.'

'You mean her lover,' said Crystal, though it was difficult to think of a great-aunt with a lover.

Now and again Pa would take the necklace out of the safe and let the children look at it – Crystal had even tried it on – but tonight Ma wore it with her best flowered dress, regretfully her old coat, but she had been to the hairdresser's and had her hair retinted. 'Looks like the finest brass,' said Pa. He liked Ma as she was, but was gratified to see how pretty – *handsome* was a better word – she still was.

Doone was wearing one of Crystal's outgrown tailored coats with a velvet collar. 'It buttons the wrong way for a boy,' objected Will. Doone did not mind. He had new brown corduroy velvet shorts, a new white shirt and a brown bow-tie.

His hair had been brushed till it shone, and Pa had polished his shoes – they, too, had been Crystal's and had silver buckles. 'Sissy! Sissy!' Jim and Tim had teased. 'Nonsense,' said Ma. 'He looks a proper little gentleman,' and to Doone she said: 'I'm proud of you.'

Doone glowed.

For that evening, Ma and Doone were completely at one; they both grew more and more excited as they came out of the Underground – it had been quite a journey from Pilgrim's Green – and found their way through the labyrinth of little streets until they came to the Royal Theatre where Doone was dazzled by the lights, the long lines of cars and taxis and, particularly, by a gentleman in a magenta-coloured coat and top hat who was opening car doors and seemed to be welcoming people. 'Is it his house?' asked Doone.

'Sh! He's the commissionaire.'

Doone did not know what that was, but it sounded even grander and,'Commissionaire, commissionaire,' he whispered to himself. Inside, in the big rose-walled foyer, jostling with people, he seemed as small as a mouse in a wood, but he did not feel lost, only more and more excited.

They climbed a staircase, wider than the sitting-room at home, with a brass rail down the middle and, on the landing, 'Look, Doone,' breathed Ma. 'Look at the flowers! What would Pa and his pot plants say to those?' She and Doone stood transfixed; the flowers in their vases were taller than Ma.

They went to their seats and Doone had never imagined anything as big or gorgeous as the auditorium; deemed too young to go to the Stonham pantomime, he had only been to the cinema at Pilgrim's Green.

The orchestra was below; Mr Felix had told Doone a little about orchestras, and Doone recognised instruments – a piano, three harps in a box at the side – and the music-stands waiting for the players. Best of all he liked the huge drums. 'I'd like to play those,' he said to Ma. He and Ma were sitting in the third tier; the rest went up and up; high above he could see people, small as ants, craning their heads to look over a rail and, if he put his head right back, he could see the pale-blue dome of the ceiling.

It was exactly as Ma had dreamt it. 'How did I get it so

30

right?' she was asking herself. 'It must be an omen.' She was too awed to do anything but whisper, but Doone felt oddly comfortable. He had a glossy programme, but when Ma tried to read it to him it seemed an interruption. He waited, his knees pressed against the seat; he had to sit on his coat and Ma's to see, and his legs could not reach the floor.

Slowly the house lights dimmed; the stage curtain lit up. 'Those are the Queen's initials on them,' whispered Ma. There was a crackle of applause. 'That's for the conductor.' The only conductor Doone had seen was a conductor on a bus, but now, far below, he saw a little man – little because he was so far away – lift his hand in which he could see a little stick. 'That's his baton,' whispered Ma. She should not have whispered because a hush had fallen on the house. The baton moved and music stole out, music sweeter than any Doone had heard; he seemed to be carried away on it, away, far out of himself, and then the curtain rose.

'Well, was it wonderful?' Pa had waited up for them. All signs of the bonfire party had been cleared away and hot cocoa and sandwiches were waiting for them. 'Was it?'

'Not at all what I expected.' The last ballet, *Elite Syncopations*, had upset Ma. 'Elite!' she sniffed. 'Lowest kind of music-hall.' Then she melted. 'But the first two! Especially the second.'

It was *Le Spectre de la Rose*. 'A young girl falls asleep after her first ball, holding a rose her partner had given her,' said the programme, 'and in through the window comes the Spirit of the Rose.' 'You never saw such a leap.' That was the first time Ma saw Yuri Koszorz dance. 'I never thought to see a man dance a rose!'

'A bit precious, I should think.'

'Oh, no, William. He was strong and so beautiful.'

Pa did not want to spoil it for her or he would have said more.

'The first was about a shop, *La Boutique fantastique*'; and suddenly Ma and Doone bubbled into laughter.

'It was a toyshop on the Riviera. French.'

'The toys were people.' That was Doone.

'Two old maids, English, came in and an American. A Russian family. . . .'

31

'Lots of children. The shopman had a shop boy with a runny nose.' Doone doubled up with laughter.

'The dolls danced. Dolls from Italy, Poland, Russia. A pair of lovers.'

'They danced something called the CanCan.'

'The English old maids were shocked.' Ma was laughing, too.

'And there were poodles,' said Doone.

'Dancers dressed as poodles,' corrected Ma.

'One of them lifted its leg!' Doone was overcome with delighted giggles.

'Not a very nice thing to ask a dancer to do on the stage,' said Pa.

'It *was* nice. I'd love to be that poodle. . . .'

'The lover dolls were sold separately, but at midnight the other dolls let them out of their parcels.'

'And they *all* danced the CanCan.'

Doone was hilarious, and Ma had been so titillated, refreshingly elated, that she looked almost like the young Maud Pa had courted nineteen years ago. 'So you did enjoy it?' Ma sobered. 'I've learnt more tonight than in all these years. You should have seen the dancing, William.' Something in Ma sensed she had been near its living nerve. 'Doone was thrilled to the bone,' she told Pa, 'like me', and, when in the interval, they came out into the crush bar and he asked, 'Could I have a sandwich?' Ma had answered, 'You can have anything you like tonight, lemonade as well. As for me, I'm going to have a glass of champagne.' She even let him have a sip. 'And then they went and spoilt it with those "syncopations",' she told Pa. 'I suppose it was meant to be very funny, very smart. A tiny little man dancing with a tall ballerina. She jumped into his arms and he fell flat down. Slapstick,' said Ma with derision, 'and all that jigging about and pulling funny faces. Horrid, I thought. I suppose it was clever – the audience liked it. Not at all what I mean when I say "ballet",' said Ma. Then she melted. 'But that *Rose* . . .'; and as Pa picked up Doone to carry him to bed – he was staggering with tiredness – 'Just think,' said Ma, 'one day Crystal might be the girl with the rose, mightn't she, Doone?'

'Crystal?' Doone raised his sleepy head from Pa's shoulder.

What had Crystal to do with it? He, Doone, was the rose.

That September, Pilgrim's Green was to have a Festival of Arts; it was announced in the local newspaper and, as part of the festival, there was to be a dancing competition held under the auspices of the LDA. 'That's the London Dance Academy,' Ma said solemnly. The competition was open to any school in Pilgrim's Green, Stonham and in the north-west suburbs for children between seven and ten years old. 'Just right for Crystal.' Heats would be run off the week before and the twenty finalists would dance on the stage of Stonham's best cinema, open to the public, when the children would be given marks. The Council was awarding a gold, a silver and a bronze medal for the three highest marks, and six children, including these, would win scholarships to some of London's famous schools, three for the Academy itself. They had set the programme.

'Of course I know about the Academy,' said Ma, who had never heard its name until she read it in the newspaper, 'but these other schools – are any of them good?' asked Ma.

'Indeed they are,' said Mrs Sherrin. 'I only wish I had the money to send Ruth to one of them. I believe, with a scholarship, they even pay the fares.' Her eyes were bright with longing. Ma, though, was not interested in scholarships. 'If Crystal won the gold medal. . . .' but she and Mrs Sherrin and the other mothers had a surprise. When Ma took the leaflets to Madame Tamara, Madame said quickly, 'I have had those.'

'Who will you be entering?'

'No one,' said Madame. 'I don't approve of competitions.'

'But why?'

'It's not good for the children. These tests are all the same – hidebound,' said Madame. 'Makes them like a pattern. I . . . I prefer them to be free. It's the same with examinations – all these grades. I never let my pupils go in for them.'

'We wouldn't pass, that's why,' Ruth said under her breath, but Crystal caught it.

'Why wouldn't we?'

'Because we're not taught enough.'

'Well, I wouldn't want to take them anyway.'

'I would,' said Ruth. 'I would,' but she and Crystal were at

33

one in wanting the competition. 'Madame, why not?'

'Mine is the oldest school in Pilgrim's Green.' Madame drew herself up. 'Perhaps the oldest in all north London. I do not need to compete.' Nobody saw that she was shaking.

'Madame, please.'

'I prefer not.'

'It's a pity – those scholarships are such a chance – but perhaps she's wise.' Mrs Sherrin accepted it, but not Ma. 'Madame Tamara, we' – 'we' were herself and the mothers of the other little girls, Angela's mother, Zoë's Mary Ann's, Joanna's – 'we *want* our children to go in for this, so you will please arrange it. . . .' They did not say 'or else', but Madame understood and, once again, gave in.

'You'll regret it, Minnie,' said Mr Felix.

There were three sections in the competition: a set variation, one for boys, one for girls, arranged by one of the judges; then, for the girls, a solo, simplified from the classic *Nutcracker* ballet.

'That, at least, I know by heart,' Madame sighed, relieved.

'It's Clara's dance. She's the child in the ballet,' said Ruth. 'A sort of polka.'

And on the day of the competition each school could present a character dance which could be for two or three dancers, even a group. That cheered Madame – she had been noted for folk dancing. 'A Russian peasant dance,' she said.

'Everyone will be doing that,' Ma objected.

'Neapolitan?'

'Can't we be original?' said Ma and then, 'I remember a *Harlequinade*,' she said.

'Harlequin?' Madame's eyes lit up. 'You mean as in the *Commedia dell'Arte*?'

'*Comm*-what?'

'The old Italian travelling players who first had those classic characters, Harlequin, Punchinello, Pierrot. . . .'

'Nothing like that,' said Ma. 'We did it as a threesome when I was a girl. Harlequin, Columbine and a Clown. I was Columbine. You wouldn't believe it, but I was as light as a piece of thistledown,' said Ma. 'I still have the music at home. It's ever so pretty. I'm sure no one else will think of it, and not too much hard work for you, Madame – just a few rehearsals.' And she coaxed, 'Of course, *you'll* choose the parts,' but all of them, including Madame, knew Crystal would be Columbine. 'In a white flounced dress, painted with cherries.' Madame was thinking of Columbine in the ballet *Carnival*.

'Pale pink with rosebuds,' corrected Ma. 'Rosebuds,' Ma said it firmly. 'I'll make the costumes for you, and who will you have for Harlequin?'

'Ruth,' said Madame.

'Ruth! Oh, no!' That was Crystal, in dismay. 'I can't dance with her, Madame,'

'You'll need her. She's strong.' Madame seemed to know Ma would insist on points for Columbine. 'If there are turns, she can steady you.'

'Otherwise you'll fall over.' Doone had been listening. 'You often do, you know.'

Crystal gave him a warning look.

'But. . . .' Madame was dismayed again. 'Someone will have to be the Clown.'

'Angela Burrell,' said Crystal. 'She's always doing acrobatics. She can walk on her hands.'

'But. . . .'

'Angela would love it,' declared Ma. 'That's decided, then. I have the music at home. I'll send one of the boys over with it. It's so pretty and catchy.'

Mr Felix raised his head in alarm.

'But what,' Madame almost wailed, 'what am I going to say to Mrs Burrell?'

'Say it's a character part with a great deal of acting; that's true, and Angela acts very well. Don't mention clowns.'

'But when she knows?'

'It will be too late. She won't come to rehearsals, will she?'

'N-no. But then. . . .' Madame recoiled.

'It's all settled.' Ma was triumphant but, when they had all gone, Madame sank down on the piano stool and hid her face in her hands.

Doone was worried. 'Madame, are you all right?'

Madame took her hands down and shook her head. 'I'm tired, Doone. Tired to my bones.'

'So was I, often,' Doone said earnestly. 'I ached, but Beppo said that was good because it showed I was trying really hard and it was making me strong.'

'But I am not strong,' said Madame. 'Not strong enough.'

Doone did not know how to comfort her, so he patted her knee; then inspiration came and, 'Do you know, Madame,' he said, 'when I grow up to be a dancer, a *very* great dancer, I shall tell everyone that it was you who taught me.'

Madame looked at him in astonishment. 'But, Doone, I have not taught you anything. I haven't given you one lesson, so it's not true.'

'It *is* true,' said Doone and did what he had not done with anyone but Beppo – put his arms round Madame and hugged her.

The Academy had agreed to appoint the judges and now their names were announced, two women and the senior judge, a man, Mr Philip Brown.

'Brown! What an ordinary name. I shan't expect much of him,' Ma decided.

'Except that he is president of the Association of Dancers,' said Mrs Sherrin.

Ma blinked; blinked still more when she showed the paper to Madame Tamara.

'Philip!' cried Madame. 'Oh, no, not Philip! I had heard but I hoped it wasn't true.'

'Why? Isn't he nice to the children?'

'Of course, but. . . .'

'But?'

'He's severe. He doesn't overlook little faults.'

'Faults?' Ma's voice was high.

'There are always faults. Crystal has her faults. We all know that.'

'Do we?' Ma sounded on the warpath.

'Yes.' Madame was unaccustomedly fierce. Then, 'Well. . . .' She gave a wan smile. 'At least Philip knows a dancer when he sees one.'

'Ah!' Ma was satisfied.

'The children will be marked in accordance with their age and experience' was in the competition rules, though not for the character dance; that award would go to the teachers but,

for each child, there was a marking for 'overall performance' –
'Which means on everything we do,' said Ruth. She read the
rules over and over again, and worried about them – 'Mother
will be so disappointed if I come very low' – but Crystal
seemed to take them for granted; having, she thought, plenty
of experience, she worried far more about the clothes.

'Ruth, what are you wearing for your Variation?'

'My tunic.' Ruth seemed surprised. 'Aren't you?'

'No, I'm not. My mother's making me a tutu.'

'A *tutu*! For the Variation? Crystal, you can't.'

'Why not?'

'You'll look such a silly.' Ruth was blunt. 'Sometimes they
make you wear swimsuits, or vests and briefs.'

'*Swimsuits?*' It was Crystal's turn to be horrified.

'So they can see you properly.'

'I'll wear what I like.' Crystal, though, did not sound quite
as certain. 'But Clara's dance? That has to be in costume.'

'I don't think so. Ask Mother.'

'No, thank you,' said Crystal. She knew Ma would not like
that. 'Anyway, I don't care – a stupid little polka thing.'

'I think it's *delightful*.' Then the delight faded. 'If only it
wasn't so difficult.'

'Difficult! What's difficult about it?'

'The style,' said Ruth. 'It could so easily be made too saucy
and it's the style that counts,' but Crystal had never heard of
style.

Not all the class was entering the competition – 'Mary and
Joanna haven't been here long enough, Zoë's too young' – but
all the girls worked on the Variation. Some tried the Polka, but
the real interest was in the Character Dance, all the more
because it was secret. Crystal, Ruth and Angela were the
chosen ones and, in a way, the dance seemed 'chosen', too;
though it was short, not more than three minutes, Madame
found steps for it and created 'a lovely little thing', Mr Felix
had to admit, 'if it were not for the music'.

'Minnie, you're not going to let your pupils dance to *that*!'
he had said as soon as he saw the sheet.

'Mrs Penny brought it.' Ma seemed to have taken over.

'Ta tata rum-tum. Ta ta ta ta.

'Rum-tata rum-tum, ta ta ta ta! Grrrh!'

37

I know, Felix.' Madame made the same helpless gesture. Mr Felix said no more.

The *Harlequinade* was spirited and deliciously funny. 'If only Crystal doesn't overdo it!' That was Madame's great anxiety, but Crystal was dancing as she could dance when she was really interested. Ruth was a graceful Harlequin – and steady enough to keep Crystal from wavering when she was on points – while Angela put all her zest into the Clown. Even Madame was beginning to be less fearful; she even had a sparkle in her eyes until, two days before the Competition and at the final dress rehearsal, Mrs Burrell came bursting in.

Ruth and Crystal had already found Angela, still in her outdoor things, sobbing in the cloakroom.

'Angela, you told.'

'I had to. Mum found me painting my nose and I've only come to get my things. She's here now.'

'And she won't let you . . .?'

'*Let* me!'

'Angela! My Angela – to be a clown . . .,' stormed Mrs Burrell. 'You said Pierrot.'

'Well, Pierrot is a sort of clown.'

'Not with a red nose and white face and frills like a Toby dog. You knew I wouldn't have consented, you deceitful double-dealing old trickster.'

'In my School, you will not call me names.'

'That's what you are. Angela, my Angela, to be a clown, while Crystal Penny. . . .'

'This is a character dance – *character*, Mrs Burrell.' For once Madame was proud and certain. 'I have many little girls who could dance Columbine – not as well as Crystal, of course.' Madame had to remember Ma was in the room; she and the girls had followed Mrs Burrell into the classroom. 'Many little girls,' said Madame, 'but only Angela could dance the Clown because it needs acting – and Angela can act. She is the only one, too, who is good enough at acrobatics to somersault and walk on her hands.'

'Crystal can somersault.' Doone spoke from under the piano where he had retreated. 'Crystal . . . ouch!' Crystal's hard little heel had come down hard on Doone's hand, but they had all heard and, 'That's an idea,' said Mrs Sherrin, who

38

had come in. 'If Crystal and Angela changed places. . . .'

Ma went red. 'Crystal is cast as Columbine. . . .' and 'Wouldn't *you* mind,' she said aside to Mrs Sherrin, 'if Ruth had to be the Clown?'

'Not if she were suitable.' Mrs Sherrin said it loudly as if she meant Mrs Burrell to hear. 'Not if she were suitable and it taught her something. If you want to be a dancer,' and Mrs Sherrin sounded oddly wistful, 'you have to dance all sorts of parts – a clown. . . .'

'Or a naughty poodle,' put in Doone, nursing his hand.

'Or a naughty poodle.' Mrs Sherrin smiled at him and, encouraged, he said again: 'Crystal can somersau—'

'Doone, go outside! Go outside at once,' commanded Crystal. Doone went, mystified. He had only been trying to help; besides, he did not like Madame saying Crystal could not do what he knew she could. He hunched himself in a chair in the corridor but he could still hear what was being said.

'I *chose* Angela,' Madame was saying; she made it sound as if it were a privilege. 'Clowns are an important part of dancing and you want Angela to be a dancer. Think of *Petrushka*,' but Mrs Burrell refused to think of *Petrushka*.

'Angela, get your shoes.'

'But you can't do this.' Ma was almost weeping. 'The costumes are made. The names have gone in. By now they're *printed*. The final's on Saturday. Today is Thursday. . . .'

'Mrs Penny, please.' Madame was still dignified as she turned to Mrs Burrell. 'Mrs Burrell, Angela will be so disappointed; she has worked hard, come through the heats. Think of her.'

'Exactly what I am doing.' Mrs Burrell said it bitingly. 'You won't make a fool of her. You can keep your Competition and you can keep your school. Angela will not be coming here again.'

They swept past Doone in the corridor, leaving the door open. Then, 'Minnie, I think you had better sit down,' he heard Mr Felix say.

'I suppose,' Ma spoke uncertainly, 'I suppose Harlequin and Columbine could dance without the Clown?'

'It would be meaningless,' said Madame. 'Without the

Clown it's ruined. Ruined.'

'She's quite right,' said Mrs Sherrin.

'But it would still look quite pretty.'

'*Pretty!*'

'It was the Clown who redeemed it from prettiness,' but Mrs Sherrin saw Ma did not understand and began again. 'It's the contrast. . . . Just as in a recipe, you don't want too much sugar.'

There seemed nothing more to be said and Madame got up. 'Fool!' she said. 'Fool that I am! I knew this would happen. I knew when I listened to you – you *mothers!* We can only withdraw from the Competition.'

'Withdraw!' Ma and Mrs Sherrin spoke together.

Madame nodded.

'But there's the rest,' they said. 'The Variation; *The Nutcracker.* . . . Crystal and Ruth have come through the heats, too.'

'Only just. . . . The *Harlequinade* was my hope to save me from shame,' said Madame Tamara.

That silenced them until into the silence came a little sound:

'Ta tata rum-tum. Ta ta ta ta.
Rum-tata rum-tum, ta ta ta ta'

Madame held up her hand for silence. 'Listen.' They listened.

Then, 'It's our *Harlequin* music,' said Ruth.

'But?' Mr Felix was sitting silent on his piano stool; besides, the sound did not come from a piano. 'But who . . .?'

'It's Doone,' said Crystal. 'I sent him outside. It's Doone on his mouth-organ.'

It might be only a mouth-organ, but the music was sweet and true, the rhythm exact, and, 'He can really play it!' said Madame.

'Not only play it,' and Mr Felix spoke. 'Minnie, that boy could dance your Clown.'

The stage at the cinema was big. 'I hope you don't lose your way,' Madame said to Doone. 'I wish I could chalk off a circle on it for you.'

40

'He knows it's there,' said Mr Felix, and Doone did, as clearly as if Madame had drawn it.

'How can he learn it in the time?' Madame had asked.

'He knows it already,' and Mrs Sherrin said, 'He has been doing it for weeks out in the corridor. I could have laughed and laughed except he was so serious.'

'He'll be better than Angela,' said Ruth. 'You'll see.'

But Madame was anxious. 'You *must* keep to your corner so that people can see Harlequin and Columbine, but first you run right round them and offer Columbine a rose.'

'I know,' said Doone.

'Again at the end.'

'I know.'

There was nothing to help anyone on the stage. 'They might have had some flowers or potted palms,' said Ma. There was only a shabby grey backcloth and an upright piano down on the right for the pianist of each school, but the audience was full of parents and their friends, people from the Council, old pupils of the schools and some too young to compete. There were 'reporters', whispered Ma, excited and, at a table facing the stage and covered with papers and with a loudspeaker, were the Judges, two ladies and a man, the most important of them, Mr Philip Brown. 'That must be him,' whispered Ma, 'with the bald head and spectacles.' Somehow she had never thought of a dancer going bald. She had to concede that there was something kindly about him, fatherly and yet quietly important. 'He doesn't look severe,' Ma whispered to Pa. She was longing to hear what they thought of Crystal. 'Looks a picture in that dress,' said Ma.

Doone had vomited his dinner. 'Don't *you* go getting nerves,' Ma had told him, but Doone did not really care how sick he was, or frightened. In a way it was not fright; he was excited, but there was a sharp edge of, Will I be able to do it? Will I? – and 'Are *you* frightened?' he asked Ruth as they waited in a big room behind the stage. Neither Ruth nor Crystal had danced their Variation or Clara's Solo yet, and Ruth had her foot up on a chair as she retied her shoe ribbons for, perhaps, the tenth time. 'Are you frightened, Ruth?'

'My mum says if you're not nervous you're not going to do your best.'

'Then I must be very best,' shivered Doone.

To his surprise Ruth gently patted his Clown wig, then gave him a kiss. 'You are very best,' said Ruth. 'Mum and I both think so.'

The room was filled with a hubbub of voices and excitement. Different teachers with their pupils had their own groups; Madame Tamara's was the smallest with only Ruth, Crystal and Doone. Costumes for the character dances hung on the backs of chairs; the time to change into them was not yet. The caller, a woman in a white blouse and black skirt, with a list and pencil in her hands, was still calling – only two minutes were allowed for each dancer unless the Judges asked a question. Most mothers were out in front watching and, 'I'll put you into your costume now,' Ma had told Doone at two o'clock, the opening of the afternoon session, 'then I'll have plenty of time to watch and be able to change Crystal.'

All the girls were in tunics, Ruth in her usual pale grey one carefully washed and ironed but Crystal – she had hastily warned Ma off the tutu – was in a new one in white satin edged with blue with forget-me-nots at the waist; she had a bunch of forget-me-nots in her hair, too. 'They can't object to that,' said Ma. 'Looks are half the battle,' and, as they waited, 'How do I look?' Crystal asked Ruth.

'I'm warming up,' said Ruth, holding the edge of a table; then she did look and, 'If I were you, Crystal,' said Ruth, 'I'd take those flowers out of your hair.'

'Just because you're shabby. . . .' But there was no time for argument. 'Ruth Sherrin,' said the caller and, to Crystal, 'Crystal Penny, you're next, so get ready. Ruth Sherrin', and, 'I hope you fall flat on your face,' said Crystal.

'Crystal ill-wished me,' said Ruth.

'That's silly talk,' said Mrs Sherrin but it was strange that, when Ruth had made her preparation, standing in the fifth position, left foot in front, arms held low, while Mr Felix played the opening chords and then began the Variation waltz, and she started – *chassé* back on her right foot, *tendu dégagé devant* with her left, balance *en avant*, arms in *arabesque*, balance *en arrière* – there was a loud bang, a cry of pain and the music stopped abruptly. The piano lid had fallen on Mr

Felix's hands.

One of the women judges got up and went quickly to him as he sat, bowed over with pain. For a moment Ruth went on – *posé, temps levé* – then stopped, too, and was left standing bewildered in the middle of the stage.

'That's torn it,' Crystal, who was waiting ready for her turn in the wings, whispered to Doone, who had crept up behind her to watch. She did not say 'Poor Mr Felix,' or 'Poor Ruth,' but aghast, 'It's my turn next,' she said. 'Who's going to play for *me*?'

Ruth was slowly walking off, her face ashen, when Mr Felix lifted his head. 'I'm all right now,' he said, though his face was as white as Ruth's. 'I can play.'

'Are you sure?' asked Mr Brown.

'I can play.'

'Then, Ruth,' Mr Brown called from the Judges' table, 'will you come back, please?' and, as she appeared, 'It is Ruth, isn't it?'

Ruth nodded, unable to speak.

'That was a shock, I'm afraid.' Mr Brown was sympathetic as well as kind. 'We don't usually let a dancer start again once she has stopped, for *any* reason, but this wasn't your fault, or the pianist's. Now, get your breath, then go back and start again.'

Ruth went to the corner and waited, Mr Felix managed the first four bars as she made her preparation again, then . . .

All that the audience saw was a fraction of hesitation, skilfully covered by Mr Felix, but Ruth knew, and the Judges knew, that for a second or two it had hung in the balance; her eyes had widened in panic. I can't remember. I can't remember a single step. Mercifully she did not say it aloud, because there came a small voice from the wings, whispering in the kind of chant that Doone had picked up from Madame Tamara: '*Chassé* back, *tendu dégagé, devant* with your left foot, balance *en avant* . . . arms in *arabesque, balance en arrière*' – and Ruth was able to begin and danced the Variation and Clara's Solo that followed it with certainty, neatness, yet making them flow. When she had finished, Mr Felix was smiling and there was a torrent of applause.

'Well done.' Pa clapped loudly, but Ma was vexed. She felt it

43

was taking away from Crystal but then Mr Brown announced, 'Next, Crystal Penny, eight years old,' and Crystal came on to make the identical preparation – 'Only it wasn't identical,' said Will.

As this had seemed to be such an important occasion for the Penny family, Pa had felt he should take the afternoon off, leaving Mrs Denning in charge, and Will had announced he was coming, too – 'I'm not coming for Crystal but someone ought to support young Doone.'

Will's heart had gone out to Ruth. 'Brave kid,' he said to Pa and clapped her loudly. Instinctively he liked and trusted Mr Brown but now, as Crystal danced, Will began to be uneasy. The two dances were the same, but Crystal was making them different – fussy, thought Will – and ought she to be thinking so much about her hands and her hair? Will knew his sister, and, She's not paying attention, he thought, and she shouldn't smile at the Judges like that.

He looked across to their table and saw they had their heads together and were talking, not watching closely as they had watched Ruth.

Crystal drew an applause equal to Ruth's but Will noticed there was little clapping in the two centre front rows around the Judges' table and, 'They're talking Crystal over,' he said uneasily.

'Of course.' Ma was rising to go backstage. 'I'm sure they were impressed. She looked so pretty and confident after poor Ruth. I must go and help her change.'

The character section began: there was a Chinese dance from the Winston School, eight little girls with fans, charming in their black wigs; a Russian quartet, two girls and two boys. 'You see, boys *do* dance,' said Doone. 'Dance! Just stamping about in boots,' Crystal dismissed them. There were more boys in a *Pastoral*, shepherds with milkmaids. 'Wishy-washy,' said Crystal. In fact she saw nothing that seemed to threaten their own *Harlequinade*, though as they waited in the wings for their turn there was a *'Victorian Bouquet'* of six girls, immaculately danced. 'They're from the Winston School, too,' Ruth whispered to Crystal. 'They're very good, particularly

44

that tall girl, Janet Abercrombie.' Even Crystal had no answer. Then Mr Brown's voice came over the loudspeaker: 'Madame Tamara – Harlequinade.'

At Mr Felix's instigation, Madame had altered the end and the beginning especially for Doone and now the lights went out on the stage and auditorium and, into the darkness, on a mouth-organ playing alone, came a tune, one only too familiar to all the Penny family, but to the people in the big cinema auditorium it sounded lost, forlorn, and as the lights came up they showed, in the middle of the bare empty stage, a figure, small and lonely, a tiny Clown, sitting cross-legged in his frills and ruff and wig, playing his tune. His tinyness roused the audience to clap but he did not stop; his tune grew more cheerful, less forlorn; as the piano took over and the bright melodious tune began, the little Clown did a back somersault; then three, one after the other, so quickly the audience gasped as he scurried to the corner of the stage, waiting for the entrance of Harlequin and Columbine.

Doone only knew that he did what the music told him, except that he remembered what Madame had said and kept out of the other two's way, or thought he did. He tried to do the steps Angela had done, but the pompoms on his shoes kept catching his feet, putting him off balance; yet every time he stumbled the audience laughed. He walked on his hands, pretended to copy Harlequin and did what Angela had done, but to the audience, making a sad face, then a glad one when he had to offer the rose to Columbine. Crystal had to take it, but her eyes were furious. 'Stop it,' she hissed. 'Everyone's looking at you, not us,' but Ruth said quietly as they were dancing, 'Go on, Doone.' He had to try to kiss Columbine's hand; she was supposed to give him a light slap, but the slap was so hard that it made his eyes sting with tears. He could not find the red-spotted handkerchief the Clown had been provided with, so he wiped his eyes on the back of his hand, wiped the wet hand on his waist frill and then wiped his nose on the frill because he still could not find the handkerchief. The audience laughed again and, to hide his embarrassment, Doone did three somersaults so quickly he nearly tumbled off the edge of the stage, just saved himself and sat in his corner rocking himself in unhappiness.

45

Will heard the Judges laughing, too. He could have laughed himself but he was too embarrassed by what Crystal was doing – 'over-doing', Madame Tamara, watching in the wings with Mrs Sherrin, said in despair – making eyes at the audience, tossing her head, arching her wrist in affectation, ogling the Judges. 'Oh, no!' Madame covered her eyes.

The two minutes seemed to last a long time but, at last, Doone heard Mr Felix, in the music, reminding him what he had to do at the end. Harlequin and Columbine had gone and Doone had to go back to where he had begun, sit down and play his mouth-organ – only he couldn't find it. Frantically he felt among his clothes, ran round the stage where he had danced, searched among his clothes again and found it in his pocket underneath the spotted handkerchief he had not been able to find, either. The handkerchief was a relief; he had to blow his nose again because he was beginning to cry, but at last he was back, sitting cross-legged in the middle of the stage, ready to play the mouth-organ.

He tried to play; the first few notes were clear; then he could not help it, a sob came – after all, he was only a small boy. Another four or five notes and then Mr Felix was wise enough to lift his hands from the keys and let Doone go on alone, which he did for three mouth-organ bars; a sob, then two notes . . . one . . . and Doone threw the mouth-organ away, bent double and began really to cry.

Someone – 'inspired', as Madame Tamara said afterwards – put the lights out. The clapping was deafening as Mr Felix picked Doone up and carried him away.

The dancers, most of them still in costume, joined their families in the audience while the teachers waited on the side of the stage. There was a buzz of expectation and all eyes were on the Judges, who were still conferring and comparing notes. Then one of the women called, 'Madame Tamara?'

Madame, in her black and jet, came forward on the stage.

'Madame, we are puzzled. Your little Clown in the *Harlequinade* surely was not Angela Burrell, aged nine.'

'N-no.' It was plain that Madame Tamara was terrified. 'I – I sent you a note saying Angela could not dance.'

'The Variation and Solo, yes. You didn't mention the

46

character dance.'

'N-no, but when, at the last moment . . . I thought to cancel would have spoiled the chances of the others, so . . . so I had to substitute another child.' Madame was going to say 'pupil', but in honesty could not say that.

'Who is this child?'

'His name is Doone Penny, six years old.'

There was a stir among the audience and among the judges. 'Only six.'

'Yes. He is too young to enter. That's why I thought it would not matter. I'm sorry if I was wrong,' said Madame.

'So are we, because unfortunately this disqualifies your *Harlequinade.*' There was a sigh of disappointment but, 'Rules are rules'. Mr Brown had taken the loudspeaker. 'No child is eligible unless he, or she, had been through the heats and taken all sections of the competition but I must say,' said Mr Brown to the audience, 'if Madame Tamara has in reserve pupils of the calibre of that small boy, she is a fortunate teacher. Where is he, Madame?'

'He – Doone is a little overcome,' said Madame. He was still sobbing and shaking with Mr Felix.

'No wonder,' said Mr Brown, and then, 'Let's go on to what I know you are all waiting to hear – the results of the Competition.'

They were read out by one of the women.

'First and winner of the gold medal, Janet Abercrombie of the Winston School with the astonishing total of eighty-six marks,' and, 'Really good style and ability and beautifully danced,' added Mr Brown. Janet was the girl Crystal and Ruth had picked out. Crystal made a wry face. The Winston School took the silver medal and second place as well. Another school was third with the bronze; fourth, a boy; each time Mr Brown added a comment: 'You will have to watch that left foot, Sylvia'; 'James, your beats could be better and I'm sure if you work hard you can jump higher than that'; 'Monica, if you look at the floor, dear, you lose all feeling of poise and lightness. You've nothing to be ashamed of – far from it. You danced very well, so look at the audience or your partner, and you could, sometimes, smile.'

'Fifth, Ruth Sherrin, Madame Tamara,' and Mr Brown said,

'Ruth would have come higher if she had not had that small crisis of nerves. One of the first things a dancer has to do is to overcome shyness and nerves, but I'm sure Ruth will soon learn to control them. Well done, Ruth!'

Ruth had crimsoned and had to be impelled to do as the others had done, stand up and bow.

Ma could not believe it. Ruth before Crystal? Ruth better than Crystal? Crystal, though of course she had to clap, sat upright and bit her lip. She would not look at Ruth. 'You can't win all the time,' Pa tried to comfort her but she pushed his hand furiously away. The place numbers went on: sixth . . . seventh. . . . The marks getting lower until nineteenth – fourteen marks, and there was still no mention of her. Fury gave place to puzzlement. 'What *has* happened?' asked Ma, and then whispered, 'They must be keeping something in reserve, perhaps a special medal.' She was sure Crystal was better than 'that Janet Abercrombie', certainly better than Ruth, but the judges had gone on to the character dancing. First, *A Victorian Bouquet* – the Winston School again; second, the *Pastoral* that Crystal had said was 'wishy-washy'; third, the *Chinese Dance* – Winston School again. Then Mr Brown announced, 'The panel has decided to award an extra prize for Madame Tamara's *Harlequinade*, which would have won, in spite of poor music, had it not been for the breach of rules; a prize for originality, for design, for humour as well as romance, for the supportive dancing of Ruth Sherrin as Harlequin and the really remarkable performance of the little Clown.' There was a roar of approval, but no mention of Columbine. No mention of Crystal? Ma was bewildered, Pa sat on the edge of his seat, while Will had paled; he had a dreadful feeling that he knew what was coming.

Mr Brown held up his hand. 'To return to the placings: there is one name we haven't mentioned and I expect you are wondering why, because she figured very prominently among today's young dancers – too prominently,' said Mr Brown.

The audience stirred in expectant curiosity.

'It's a great great pity,' Mr Brown went on, 'that Crystal should have come so low because obviously she has talent, and I should like to talk to her parents afterwards. Meanwhile I'm sorry to have to say: twentieth, Crystal Penny. No marks.'

48

There was a stunned silence. Ma was stunned, too, and Crystal, sitting beside Pa, gave a gasp of astonishment. She heard Ruth cry, 'Oh, no! No!' and wanted to put her hands over her ears but, conspicuous in her pink dress and rosebuds, knew that everyone was looking at her. Then Pa did one of the things he sometimes did suddenly and no one dared stop him. He scooped Crystal up in his arms and made his way out, past all the people in the row who respectfully stood up for him. 'Fetch her coat,' he snapped at Will who had followed him. 'I'm taking Crystal home.'

'Not a penny more,' said Pa. 'Not one penny.'

'Mr Penny won't spend a penny.' Hughie was trying to be witty but, 'You shut up,' said Will. Even the twins knew that something serious had happened and now, 'Out! All of you!' roared Pa. 'This is between your Ma and me.'

When he and Will had taken Crystal away, Ma had stayed in her seat quite still as the people, going out, flowed round her. Then she had risen, gone down the aisle and across to a door through which she had seen the Judges go out. She did not walk, she marched; on each cheek was a burning spot of red, and she held her bag as if it had been a hatchet, but if anyone had looked at her eyes, they would have seen she was not only hurt but utterly bewildered and holding back tears.

In a small private foyer, the two women Judges were talking to the children who had won – five girls, one boy. Ma saw Janet Abercrombie's fair head and Ruth, who looked as if she had been part of a miracle – to her she had. 'Fifth, and a scholarship when I had been so stupid!' When she saw Ma, she pressed herself back against the wall.

'Where is Mr Brown?'

'In there.' One of the women pointed to an inner office. 'He has someone with him. If you would like to wait. . . .'

'I can't wait,' said Ma. 'I'll see Mr Brown *now*.' She would have flung the door open, but it was a padded swing door that opened silently. Ma opened it, blinked and stopped. Mr Brown indeed had someone with him. Madame Tamara was sobbing and he was holding her in his arms. 'Now, Minnie, now,' he was saying. 'It's not the end of the world.'

49

'It is for me. I should have gone out cooking, cleaning, anything rather than desecrate – yes, desecrate – my art.'

'Minnie, you're being theatrical.'

'But it's true.'

'Come. You did very well for that little Ruth.'

'She's Judith's daughter. Not as gifted as her mother but still. . . . A good pupil brings out the best in a teacher. You know that. But the others. . . .' Madame gave a shudder and reverted to tears. 'If I have damaged that little girl. . . .'

This time Mr Brown had no answer.

'Just because Madame Tamara was Russian . . . ,' Pa was saying to Ma.

'She isn't Russian,' and Ma felt almost as shamed as she had felt when she tried to defend herself to Mr Brown. 'I thought, being Russian, Madame Tamara must be good' – and he had smiled. 'She's no more Russian than I am. Her real name is Minnie Price,' and he added what Mr Felix had once said, 'She's a good teacher – when she's allowed to be,' and he had looked sternly at Ma.

'Not Russian – another fraud.' Pa said it bitterly.

'Not – not exactly,' said Ma. 'She's nearly eighty, William, so she belongs to the time when people thought all dancers should have foreign names. Ignorant people.'

'Like us.'

Ma winced but had to say, 'Yes, like us.'

'Madame Tamara!' mocked Pa.

'William, don't. She was crying, heartbroken over Crystal.'

'So she ought to be.' Pa was still wrathful. 'I'm going to talk to that lady.'

'You can't. She's giving up – at least, the school's being taken over by Mrs Sherrin.'

'Mrs *Sherrin?*'

'Yes.' There seemed no end to the surprises of this day. 'Mrs Sherrin was Judith Clement, quite a well-known dancer.'

'I know,' Crystal was to say when she would talk about dancing again. 'I didn't tell you, Ma, because I thought it might upset you and then you would have come and upset us, but it was Mrs Sherrin who coached us for the Variation and for Clara's dance, and was she strict! I've never been spoken to

50

like that.' Oddly enough, Crystal had not complained; she was quite astute enough to see they needed more drilling, more meticulousness than Madame would have exacted from them. 'That's how we got through the heats.' It had given Crystal a new respect for Mrs Sherrin and Ruth or she would never have consulted Ruth about her clothes.

'I always wondered why she seemed to know so much,' said Ma. 'It seems she broke her ankle so badly she couldn't dance again – but she has danced in Paris and in all the big towns in America and Australia, too.'

'Well, that explains a lot,' said Pa.

'Yes, but why couldn't she explain to *me*?'

Those very clothes: 'Pretty dresses, presentation, though of course they help, do not compensate for carelessness in dancing,' Mr Brown had said, 'and I'm afraid we cannot give marks to a dancer, however young, who is full of self-consequence and airs and graces. Hard words, I know, Mrs Penny, but I have to say them,' and now anguish overflowed. 'Why didn't she warn me?'

'Would you have let her?' asked Pa. 'You know you wouldn't, Maudie. You always knew best.'

'Yes.' Ma almost whispered it. 'He . . . Mr Brown said . . . I bullied Madame into putting Crystal on points when she shouldn't have been.'

'And did you?'

'Yes,' whispered Ma. Mr Brown's words still burnt in her mind. He had not minced them. 'Have you ever seen a sickle foot, Mrs Penny? That's what you can do to a child's tender feet, distort them, turning them inwards. You can damage the joints so that, very young, she might get arthritis, be crippled for the rest of her life. Mrs Penny, it's a *wicked* thing to do,' and, 'Where is Crystal now?' Ma asked Pa in panic.

'In her room. She had hysterics. I slapped her. I had to.'

'After *that*!' Ma was appalled.

'I *had* to.' Pa was so distressed that he spoke curtly, almost brutally. 'I think she might have bitten me, she was so shamed and angry.'

'Poor baby. Poor baby.' Ma rocked herself back and forwards in her misery.

'So I gave her a spanking and sent her to bed. Will says she's

51

asleep. I couldn't bear to look,' and Pa said, 'We'll have no more dancing, Maud. This is the end.'

'No, William.' Ma stood her ground.

Although Mr Brown had shattered many dreams that afternoon, in the end he had been more than kind and, too, Ma had heard Madame say, 'The worst of it, Phil, is that Crystal *has* talent,' and, 'I know,' Mr Brown had answered. 'That's why we Judges decided we must do as we did.' And to Ma he had said, 'It was meant as a lesson, not only to your little girl, but to all the others.'

'But Crystal?' Ma did not care twopence for other little girls. 'Is her dancing spoiled – for ever?' She could hardly bring herself to say it.

'Not if Crystal doesn't want it to be,' Mr Brown had sternly emphasised. 'Crystal – not you, Mrs Penny. Remember that.'

'And what,' asked Pa, 'has His Royal Highness Mr Philip Brown commanded us to do now?'

Mr Brown had said, 'Tell me, Mrs Penny, can you afford to pay for lessons?' and, 'He said Crystal should go to a school he knows well in London. If you let her, William, and she wants this herself – Mr Brown said it's she who must want it – to help you pay for it, I'll . . . I'll work in the shop.'

'Maudie!'

Later in the evening Ma took the little Clown's wig and costume and hung them up in the wardrobe with Crystal's dresses. Ma had found Columbine's dress stuffed in the dirty-clothes basket and left it there. She did not know quite why she labelled Doone's, as she had all Crystal's, with the date and 'Doone's first costume. Clown in *Harlequinade*.'

Doone had no inkling of what had happened except that Ma had told him there would be no dancing for a week – 'Madame Tamara's tired' – and, on Monday, that Crystal would not be going to school. 'She's tired, too.' 'I can't.' Crystal had been hysterical again at the thought. 'It'll have been in all the papers. The girls!' 'and so I kept her back, just for a while till it's blown over,' Ma told Pa. 'Was that wrong?'

'Quite wrong,' said Pa. 'She has to face it, poor little love,' and, on Wednesday morning, 'School,' he said firmly to

Crystal – the boys had already gone. 'You as well as Doone.'

They had reached the Green when Crystal stopped. 'You go on,' she ordered Doone. 'I'm not going to school.'

'Not going?'

'No. I'll be here at half-past three to bring you home.'

'But . . . what'll you do all day?'

'Amuse myself,' said Crystal loftily. 'I might go for a bus ride or to a film. Walk about, buy some fish and chips.'

It was an alluring picture and Doone lingered. 'Go on, can't you?' cried Crystal, 'and, Doone, you're not to tell anyone, see?'

On Thursday it was the same but a neighbour saw Crystal lurking in the summer-house on the Green and called in at the shop to tell Pa, who put on his overcoat at once. 'So! You've chickened out. We don't do that, Chris. Come, I'm taking you to school.'

That afternoon, for the first time, Crystal walked home without a following of friends. She kept her head high but, instead of making Doone walk behind her, she held him tightly with one hand and walked so fast he had to trot to keep up with her.

Doone still did not understand that his whole small world was turned as upside down as it had been with Beppo. Ma had said Madame Tamara's was closed for a week – one week, thought Doone – and the next Tuesday he left his class at three o'clock as usual and got himself ready, trying not to be ragamuffin, washing his face and hands, combing his hair with the private pocket-comb Will had given him. Then he went to the girls' cloakroom to find Crystal.

She was not there; instead she came out with the others at half-past three.

'We'll be late.' Doone jumped up from the shoe-lockers where he had been sitting. 'Madame Tamara. . . .'

'Sh! Stop it!' hissed Crystal. 'We're not going to Madame Tamara's.'

'Not going!' When Crystal was ready Doone would not move. 'Not going!'

'I've told you.' The other girls had clattered and banged their way out; Doone and Crystal were alone, and Crystal spoke aloud, 'I've told you.'

'But I want to see Madame and Ruth and Mrs Sherrin and Mr Felix' – Mr Felix was most urgent of all.

'Well, you can't. We're finished with that lot.'

'That . . . lot?' Doone could hardly believe what he had heard but, 'Yes,' said Crystal. 'Yes,' and, 'S'matter of fact I've finished with everybody. Funny, isn't it?' she mocked.

Doone knew it was not funny but, just as with Madame Tamara, he did not know what to do. He went to Crystal, put his cheek against her coat, and Crystal did not shake him off. Instead she said wearily, 'I suppose we must go home.'

On the next Tuesday, when she came out of school, Doone was not there, nor in the boys' cloakroom or playground. When she reached home he was not there, either. 'Where is he?' asked Ma. 'He shouldn't be out alone,' but 'I know where he is,' said Crystal, 'I'll fetch him,' and, sure enough, when she got to Madame Tamara's, he was sitting on the doorstep.

'The door wasn't open,' he said. 'I rang the bell. Nobody came.'

'They couldn't,' said Crystal. 'It's closed. Look,' and out on the pavement, by craning his neck, Doone could see that the first-floor windows were all shut and blank, except one – the waiting-room, where he glimpsed a ladder on which was a pot of paint. 'I told you,' said Crystal. 'Madame's gone and they're painting and tidying the school up. Then it will be Mrs Sherrin's.'

'Mrs Sherrin's.' Doone brightened at once. 'Then we can come back.'

'Never,' said Crystal vehemently. 'Never! Doone, you're only little so you can't understand, but they're all stupid, stupid!'

'Mr Felix isn't stupid.' Doone fixed his eyes unflinchingly on Crystal. 'Mrs Sherrin isn't stupid. Ruth isn't stupid – and I want to see them.'

'Well, you won't see them by sitting on the doorstep.' Crystal said it crossly, but she took out her handkerchief – Ma always saw she had a clean one – and wiped his face gently, not with her usual angry jerks. Then she said, 'Doone, would you stick with me like you do with them, even if I'm horrid?'

'Of course I would,' said Doone, surprised and, 'I believe

you would,' said Crystal. 'I believe you would.'

'This has gone on long enough,' Pa told Ma. 'Put an end to it.
Tell her.'

'You mean ask her. . . .'

'Surely you don't have to ask, Maudie. Why, you and
Crystal. . . .'

'Not any more. Every time I try to talk to her she breaks
out.' 'Lashes out,' Ma could have said.

'Dearie, I'm only trying to help you.'

'You don't. You never have,' and Crystal had turned on her.
'Go away,' she had shouted. 'Go *away*.'

She's just upset, Ma had tried to tell herself but that Crystal
could look at her, 'as if she hated me,' with eyes like blue
stones, lock the door against her – shut her out! Ma winced
every time she thought of it.

The culmination was Mrs Carstairs, the Headmistress,
ringing up from school. There had been a scene in which
Crystal had thrown her – 'quite heavy,' said Mrs Carstairs –
wooden pencil-box across the classroom at another girl.
'Fortunately it missed but if it had caught Mary's head. . . .'

'I thought it was boys who were violent. It seems it's little
girls,' said Pa.

Crystal had been sent to sit outside in the corridor. 'Well,
she wouldn't put up with that,' said Ma. 'It's like being put in
the corner.' She had run away. 'I hope home,' said Mrs
Carstairs but it was not until after five that Pa had found her.
'Alone in the cinema!' Pa exploded. 'How can she behave like
this?'

'She's Crystal,' said Will.

'Yes, and I've a good mind. . . .'

'No, William', and Ma gathered herself together and
knocked at Crystal's door – she had never knocked before.

'What do you want?'

'To talk to you.'

'Go away.'

But some of Ma's spirit had come back. 'Open the door at
once. I have something important to tell you,' and the door
opened.

Ma knew Crystal had been sitting on her bed as she had

55

taken to doing lately. 'Just sitting,' Ma told Pa. Her room was pretty with its blue walls and white furniture. Crystal used to bring her friends to it, enjoying their envy, but now she sat alone, playing her transistor. She had turned it up as Ma came in and Ma was suddenly annoyed. 'Switch that off,' she said in her old way. 'Off – and pay attention.'

Crystal turned it off but did not move from the bed. 'Well?'

It was cold and hostile, but Ma made herself ask, 'Pa and I must know if you want to go on with your dancing?'

'Oh?' Crystal's eyebrows went up.

'You needn't – if you don't want to.'

'Why shouldn't I want to?'

'After the Competition. . . .'

'Oh, that! Can't you make a mistake?' but Crystal was as tense as Ma. 'Do you think I want to be just an ordinary girl?' It was biting. 'Of course I want to go on. But how do you think you' – Crystal said 'you' in scorn – 'can possibly arrange that now?'

'I have arranged it,' said Ma.

Crystal stared, then flushed with consternation. 'You're not sending me to Mrs Sherrin.'

'As if I would.'

'To that Winston School where everybody knows.'

'We have *some* sense,' said Ma. 'As a matter of fact we're sending you to Ennis Glyn.'

For a moment Crystal sat so still that Ma thought she had not taken it in; then 'Ennis Glyn,' whispered Crystal. 'Ennis Glyn – but . . . she's *famous*! She's a *ballerina*.'

'In Her Majesty's Ballet. Right at the top of the tree.' Ma was complacent.

'She can't be a teacher.'

'She has her own exclusive school,' said Ma.

'In *London*?'

'Yes.'

There was all the astonishment Ma had hoped for. 'But how?' asked Crystal. 'How *could* you know about her?'

This time Crystal did not mean to be rude; it was sheer curiosity, and Ma was happy as she said, 'Mr Philip Brown advised us that you should go there and wrote a letter for you. I'm taking you to see her on Tuesday.'

The blue eyes were not hard now; they shone. 'Wait till they hear this!' 'They' were the girls at school. Crystal turned and looked at Ma as if she were seeing her for the first time. 'You and Pa would send me there', and Crystal burst into tears and flung herself into Ma's arms. Ma was in tears, too.

'There's been enough tears over this silly business to wash away Waterloo Bridge,' said Pa, but even he had to blow his nose hard.

Only one thing worried Crystal. 'Will Ruth be there?'

'No. She's going to the Academy', and, to reassure Crystal, Ma said, 'I don't think you need meet Ruth again.'

But something worried Ma, too; when she had sent Mr Brown's letter to Miss Glyn, Miss Glyn's reply had ended, 'Please bring your little boy.'

Crystal had only to set eyes on Ennis Glyn to know that here was one grown-up she could not twist around her little finger. Anyone more different from Madame Tamara would be hard to imagine. 'She's quite young!' Crystal whispered to Ma while they were waiting – Miss Glyn was on the telephone. She was not only young but also good-looking, her chestnut-brown hair smooth and twisted into a knot at the back of her head – Crystal was to learn that all dancers have neat hair. Her grey eyes were friendly but, Crystal sensed, could be stern. They were assessing her, Crystal, now. Miss Glyn was not small, nor too tall, with a slim quick body, dressed in a blouse and black skirt that divided – 'So she can kneel and do steps,' Crystal explained to Doone. '*She* doesn't stand in the centre and give orders and poke you with a stick. She shows you. . . .'

Miss Glyn wasted no time. 'The cloakroom's in there. Go and change quickly, both of you, and we'll go to the classroom and you can show me what you can do', and to Ma, 'I should like to see a few simple exercises.'

'Crystal could dance one of her solos. I've brought her music.'

'I think the exercises will be enough.' Miss Glyn did not say they would tell her all she needed to know; as though she sensed Ma's hurt and bewilderment, she was gentle with her. 'Your little girl is exceptionally pretty,' she said and Ma's hopes rose, but Miss Glyn added, 'And your boy has an uncommon little face.' A great teacher had once said of a boy, 'I could do something with that face,' which was what Ennis Glyn was thinking now, but when Doone emerged behind Crystal – obediently he had trotted in behind her – he was still in his corduroy shorts and jersey.

'I said both of you.'

Crystal and Ma looked at one another, then Crystal spoke. 'Doone doesn't have dancing things or shoes.'

'Oh, well, he can dance in his socks. Take off his jersey and shirt.'

'Then I'll be in my vest,' said Doone, shocked, but Miss Glyn gave him a quick warm smile. 'Perfect,' she said. 'Most of the boys dance in vests.'

'Boys?' Doone was astounded but, 'Come along,' Miss Glyn was saying. Ma rose but, 'Would you mind staying here?' said Miss Glyn.

The classroom was not at all like Madame Tamara's, either; three times as big, it was airy, glitteringly clean and warmed by radiators, but all round the walls were the familiar barres, and in the corner was the same sort of upright piano – 'only better,' said Doone – and the familiar tray of resin on the floor. Doone went over and gravely dipped the toes of his socks in it and waited for what this strange lady would want of him. 'Go behind Crystal on the barre and try to do what I ask her to do.'

'What did she ask you?' Ma was longing to know.

'Ordinary things – exercises at the barre, then in the centre, arms – port de bras – skip to the music. Jumps.' But Crystal did not dismiss them as she had before. 'She tried my legs to see if I could turn out . . . and my hips. Then I had to do a mime.'

'What's a mime?'

'Pretending you're something or that something is happening to you. I had to be the Sleeping Beauty waking up after a hundred years.'

'Could you?'

'I'm not the Sleeping Beauty.' Crystal sounded dismayed. 'Doone was better than I was but his was easier. She told him to be a frog.'

'Well!' said Ma.

'I liked it,' said Doone. 'I did big leaps and puffs with my face. The piano person helped. She made music that jumped, so I jumped, too.'

'That isn't dancing,' said Crystal.

'It is,' said Doone.

'Certainly it is,' Miss Glyn had come out. 'A most important part. Now, if you are really serious, Crystal. . . .'

'I am. Oh, I am.'

'Shall we try for, say, six months – if you can manage it, Mrs Penny? Saturday morning and two afternoons a week.'

'Two?' Ma had hoped it would be one, on Wednesday, early-closing day. 'It's quite easy,' Ma told Pa. 'Crystal has only to get on the Underground from here to Swiss Cottage and it's direct. Two minutes' walk. . . .' but, 'No child of mine is going to be in London on their own,' Pa had laid down. 'You'll have to take her and fetch her, Maud, and how, with the house and the shop, will you manage that?' but, 'It's what Crystal needs,' Miss Glyn said now. 'It will be a long rough road, Mrs Penny. It's so difficult to undo what has been done.'

'Will she have to have . . .?' Ma could not say that terrible word, 'remedial', but Miss Glyn said it for her. 'I think we can deal with the foot problem. It hasn't gone too far, and fortunately Crystal's feet are strong and well shaped, but she must do foot exercises every day at home, not once but twice a day,' and Miss Glyn said, with a smile, 'I shall give you a hard time, Crystal. For a year, perhaps more, just work at the barre and in the centre. Some mime and country dancing. Though we have an annual "Open Day" for parents and friends, I don't allow outside engagements, so it will be slog, slog, slog. Can you stand that, Crystal?'

To Ma's amazement, 'Yes, please,' said Crystal and, on the way home, 'I think she's fabulous,' she said reverently and, 'Ma, aren't you happy, too?' Ma was happy, but also unhappy; Miss Glyn had gone on, 'Now, about Doone.'

'Doone? But . . . he just came along,' Ma tried to explain 'We never thought about dancing for Doone.'

'I think you should. He has real aptitude.'

Ma took refuge in, 'Other things apart, I'm afraid we couldn't rise to the expense, Miss Glyn. Not for more than one.'

'I see . . .' Miss Glyn was visibly disappointed, and Doone said suddenly, 'I don't want to learn dancing from you. I want to learn it from Mrs Sherrin.'

'*Doone!*'

'You rude little boy.'

Ma and Crystal spoke together, but Miss Glyn looked down at Doone with amused eyes. 'You don't?'

'No,' said Doone. 'You see, Mrs Sherrin used to teach me.'

'She never did,' said Crystal.

'She did. Outside in the corridor,' and to Miss Glyn he said, 'I like you – I like you very much.' He was anxious not to hurt her feelings. 'But I like Mrs Sherrin better.'

'That's enough of Mrs Sherrin,' began Ma, but Miss Glyn was speaking to Doone with as much respect as if he were grown up. 'Loyalty to your teachers is a wonderful thing, Doone; you must never forget them. . . .'

'Like Beppo.' Doone suddenly remembered Beppo.

Miss Glyn did not ask who Beppo was, but said, 'Like Beppo and Mrs Sherrin – but there comes a time when you have to move on. Suppose you ask Mrs Sherrin what she thinks because' – and now Miss Glyn spoke to Ma – 'I'm going to make you an offer, you pay for Crystal's lessons and I'll take Doone without a fee – if,' she added with a twinkle, 'if he and Mrs Sherrin agree.'

'Mrs Sherrin! He's not going near Mrs Sherrin.'

'I should let him if I were you,' and Miss Glyn asked, 'Well?'

'It's very kind of you, Miss. . . .'

'Not kind at all. I believe he could do me credit.'

'But his Pa. . . .' Ma forgot to say 'Papa'. 'I don't think he would ever allow a boy of his to dance.'

'Not even if he has a gift? You can see it for yourself, Mrs Penny.'

'Can I?' Ma blinked. She did not say she had not seen it because she had not looked. 'Think it over,' said Miss Glyn. 'But I hope – I'm sure – you want to do the best for him as well as for Crystal.'

'Of course,' said Ma, but she did not sound convinced and, 'What are we going to do?' she asked on the way home.

'I think she's fabulous!' Crystal said again. She was still in this surprising rapture.

'Yes, but what are we going to do about Doone?'

Crystal became her usual calculating self; though she would not have admitted it, she had a feeling that Miss Glyn would not have taken her if she could not have had Doone but, 'I'll show her!' Crystal said that through clenched teeth. Meanwhile Doone had to come. He must, thought Crystal.

The train swayed; she, Ma with her tired perplexed face, and Doone swayed with it. Doone was still being that frog. Jump, jump – on a frog's long legs. Pull your cheeks in – blow – puff them out, jump. . . . Then 'Ma,' said Crystal – she had to speak loudly because of the noise of the train – 'Ma, she said she would take Doone free?'

'Yes. Two for the price of one. It's a bargain, I know, but . . . your Pa.'

'If Pa doesn't have to pay, why should he have to know?' asked Crystal.

At the end of Miss Glyn's, or her partner, golden-haired Stella's, classes Crystal often found she was sweating, something she had never done at Madame Tamara's; sometimes her legs or arms ached, but if Miss Glyn had smiled at her, even once, she came out radiant.

Miss Glyn had taken away her *pointe* shoes. 'I'll get them back when I'm ready,' said this new Crystal. She never scamped the foot exercises she had to do at home, morning and evening. 'She's really working,' said Ma. 'New broom,' said Pa, but it went on, week after week, month after month.

'I'm not surprised,' said Ma. 'There's one thing, William, I haven't told you. Just before Madame Tamara left Mr Brown on that – that day' – Ma could hardly bring herself to speak of the Competition – 'Madame said, "Perhaps my excuse, Phil" – Phil is Mr Brown – "my *only* excuse for holding on, was because ever since I started teaching I had hoped, believed, that one day I would discover one. . . ." '

'One what?' asked Pa.

'One really gifted child; and I'm sure,' said Ma, lifting her chin, 'William, I'm sure that she meant Crystal.'

At the end of six months there was no question of Crystal leaving Miss Glyn but it was strenuous for all of them. Ma kept her word and helped in the shop but there were the

61

Saturday-morning and two afternoon trips to London every week. Luckily, Mrs Carstairs had agreed to let Crystal and Doone off on those afternoons, 'on condition they don't fall behind'. As soon as they had come home and had tea they, even small Doone, had to settle down with their books. Strenuous, but even Ma knew they were getting closer to the real world of dancing.

Ennis Glyn's school had a quiet elegance that extended down to the smallest pupil; Crystal now had a glimmer of what Ruth had meant when she talked of style. For one thing, there was compulsory dress. 'I never knew dancing schools had uniforms,' said Ma. Miss Glyn's girls wore short white tunics and socks, pale-pink satin shoes, their hair tied on top of their heads with a pale pink ribbon; Ma had to knit Crystal a white cross-over, a little short-sleeved woollen jersey that kept shoulders and chest warm. The boys wore black briefs, white vests with a monogrammed EG.

'Suppose Doone talks,' Ma had said.

'He doesn't talk – or, if he does, nobody listens,' said Crystal.

Doone's classes were in a different room from hers. There were four other boys. 'Four!' Doone thought that a marvel but, 'Still twenty girls to one boy,' lamented Miss Glyn.

The four were all older than Doone. Mark, Sydney, Sebastian and Charles. 'Mark, Sydney, Sebastian and Charles.' Doone said them over and over like a chant. 'Mark, Sydney, Sebastian and Charles.' None of them took much notice of Doone. 'They live in London,' he explained, which separated them from the home world of Pilgrim's Green. They called him 'the Penny'. 'Not big enough to be a twopence,' said Charles. At first, led by Sebastian, he, Mark and Sydney had objected to Doone's being in the class. 'We're not a kindergarten.' 'Wait,' said Stella, who taught them and, when they saw Doone jump they were quiet and began to help him, moving him into line, nudging him when he was not quick enough to take his turn and explaining the French of the steps. 'Why is it French?' Doone asked, and Charles said, 'Ballet has to have a universal language because it's all over the world.'

'All over the world! Then why French? Why not English?'

'Because it started in France.'

'Ma says Russia.'

'No, France, but in old-time Russia the language of the Court was French.'

'Oh,' said Doone. 'Thank you, Charles.' Soon the chant 'Mark, Sydney and Sebastian' was dropped and became simply 'Charles, Charles, Charles'.

Charles – Charles Ingram – was the same age as Crystal and, like her, far superior to him, Doone. Charles had bright-red hair, kindly brown eyes, a good well-knit body and, 'He's the best dancer I've ever seen, better than Ruth and Crystal,' Doone told Will. Charles was now Doone's hero and, 'I'm glad I go to Miss Glyn,' he said.

He had gone to see Mrs Sherrin; Miss Glyn had said he should, so he did not ask Ma. This time the door was open.

It was the same but not the same. The old classroom walls were clean and painted white; the gas-fire was gone, the windows shining, but the barres were there, the upright piano. Mrs Sherrin was not wearing an overall but was dressed like Miss Glyn. Best of all, Mr Felix was at the piano. A class was going on and Doone did not interrupt it; he went quietly in and sat in his old place on a footstool by the piano. Mr Felix may have been startled, though he gave no sign; he went on playing but, as he played with his left hand, he put his right hand down for a moment and touched Doone's hair.

'Does your mother know you're here?'

'No,' said Doone. 'But she knew I would come.' Class was over and, alone with Mrs Sherrin and Mr Felix, it all came tumbling out: Miss Glyn and the interview; what he and Crystal had done – Doone showed them his frog – and what Miss Glyn had offered Ma.

'Ennis Glyn said she would take you and teach you without fees?' said Mrs Sherrin. 'You lucky, lucky little boy.'

'I don't want to be lucky,' said Doone. 'I want to go on learning dancing with you.'

Mrs Sherrin became serious. 'Doone, listen to me. I can't teach you. To begin with, your mother wouldn't let me – not even without fees – but it isn't only that.' Mrs Sherrin sat down on the piano stool and drew Doone to her. 'You want to be a dancer like the ones you saw at the Royal Theatre.'

'The Rose?' asked Doone. 'Or a poodle? Yes. *Yes!*'

'Then, if you want that, you must go where your dancing takes you – take every chance that means you could get better and better and better. I am only an ordinary teacher. Why do you think Ruth has gone away?'

'She got a scholarship.'

'Yes, a scholarship to learn from someone far far better than I. That's what has happened to you. It's like ... like climbing a ladder. You have to leave people behind.'

'That's what Miss Glyn said.'

'I'm sure she did, and it's true.'

'No,' said Doone.

'Yes,' said Mrs Sherrin, but Doone was still only a little boy and his face began to pucker. Mrs Sherrin turned hastily away.

Then, 'May I speak?' asked Mr Felix. 'Listen to me,' he told Doone. 'You do as Mrs Sherrin and your mother say. You learn to dance from Miss Glyn. Right?'

'Right,' quavered Doone.

'But that is no reason,' said Mr Felix, 'why you must leave us.'

Mrs Sherrin turned round, puzzled, but Doone's face had lost the pucker. He looked at Mr Felix in absolute faith. 'There is something else you need to learn,' said Mr Felix, 'if you are to be this true dancer. You must learn music.'

'M-music?'

'You play the mouth-organ. Yes, very nice but, I think, what you need now is an instrument.' That was a word Doone had not met before. 'Shall we say the piano?'

'The piano?' Doone was so dazzled it took every other thought away. 'You mean you would learn me the piano?'

'Teach you,' Mr Felix corrected severely, 'and not on this old tin kettle.' He gave the upright a thump. 'On my piano. That is, if your mama will allow me. I will call and ask her.'

'Will you teach Crystal as well?' asked Ma.

'No,' said Mr Felix.

'*Something* must teach you to listen,' Miss Glyn had told Crystal. She was as exasperated as Madame Tamara had been with her anguished, 'Have you no ears?' 'You *must* have music lessons,' said Miss Glyn.

'I haven't time,' Crystal tried to dodge but, 'You must make time.' Miss Glyn was the oracle and, 'Suddenly I thought of Mr Felix,' Ma told Pa. She did not tell him that, to her, Mr Felix's visit had seemed providential and she did not mention Doone.

'We would pay you for Crystal,' Ma had told Mr Felix and, 'Surely he must need the money,' she said to Pa. 'His overcoat's a disgrace, that horrible old muffler, and he's so thin. He can't have enough to eat, but when I asked his fee. . . .'

'I have no fees.' For all his shabbiness, Mr Felix, with his height, his proud face and head of silvery hair, looked majestic in the Penny sitting-room. 'When I teach, I teach for love,' and Mr Felix said, 'I will teach Doone.'

Ma was vexed for Crystal. 'I don't understand,' she said. 'These days it seems to be Doone, Doone, Doone.'

'Well, it's a change from Crystal, Crystal, Crystal,' said Will.

Mr Felix lived in two rooms on the third floor of an old Victorian house, and Doone could not imagine how his piano got up to them; he would not have been surprised if it had flown there, but Mr Felix said they took the legs off, wrapped it and put it on its side.

The piano was a Steinway Grand; immense and gleaming, it took up almost all the sitting-room. Both rooms were even more untidy than Madame Tamara's, strewn with books and sheets of music, unwashed cups and saucers – Mr Felix did not like mugs – plates with food he had forgotten to eat, clothes he had flung down on chairs or on the floor. There were cobwebs in the corners, ash on the hearthrug which had holes burnt in it from the ancient stove, but the piano was immaculate and when, on that first day, Mr Felix wound up the stool and put four telephone directories on it so that Doone could reach the keys and, for the first time spread his fingers on them, Doone felt as most small boys would have done if they were being given a chance to drive a Rolls-Royce.

'Can I make it sound?' he had whispered.

Mr Felix had to suppress a smile. The piano looked so big, Doone so small but, 'That's what you're here for, isn't it?' he asked. 'Now. . . .'

*   *   *

65

Doone wished Mr Felix could be as cherished and cared for as the piano. Once he went into the bathroom and found the bathtub full of socks; it seemed Mr Felix wore all that he had, then put them in the bath with soapflakes and stirred them round, but he had forgotten to take them out, rinse them and hang them up. Doone tried but felt he had better not interfere – in any case, the socks were worn thin and full of holes. Did Mr Felix sometimes go barefoot? Doone worried, especially as there seemed nothing to eat in the flat except bread, and he took to bringing a small punnet of fruit – an orange, banana and pear – and leaving it on the keyboard. 'Always,' Pa had told his children, 'take any fruit you like. Fruit is good for you.' 'Frut is gud for you. Eat it,' Doone wrote on a card on the punnet. Neither he nor Mr Felix mentioned it but, when Doone came again, the fruit had always disappeared.

As the weeks went on, it still seemed to Doone an increasing wonder that he, Doone Penny, should have power over this great instrument and that, slowly, he was gaining more and more power; he who had such difficulty over reading English seemed to be able to read music.

Mr Felix taught in the old-fashioned way: first, five-finger exercises; then scales; then chords and arpeggios. When Doone heard his first arpeggio, the notes, as they ran up, sounding out in the room, it was like feeling his first *arabesque* at Miss Glyn's. Mr Felix gave him his lessons on Saturday afternoon; and, every other afternoon, except Tuesday and Thursday, dancing days, he came to practise. At those times Mr Felix had to play for Mrs Sherrin, but he trusted Doone with a key. Alone with the piano, Doone found, as he had found with the mouth-organ, that he could pick out music he had heard. At first it was only single notes with his right hand but, as Mr Felix taught him thirds, then fifths and sevenths, he began to use his left hand, too.

Would Mr Felix be angry at his, Doone's, playing like this? Doone did not know, but it was irresistible. Sometimes at the end of his Saturday lesson Mr Felix played to him and, 'Can I learn that?' Doone asked often. 'One day, perhaps,' said Mr Felix. What he did not know was that Doone could play parts of it, or something near it, already. I wonder, Doone thought, if Mark, Sydney, Sebastian and Charles have piano lessons. I wonder if Charles . . . but he was still too shy to ask them or to touch the pianos at Miss Glyn's – in any case, they were not at all like the Steinway. When, reluctantly, he got down from the stool – 'Half an hour, no more,' Mr Felix had commanded, but later 'Very well, an hour' – Doone always stroked the polished wood after he had gently put the lid down; it was like saying goodnight to his dearest friend.

More and more the Penny family seemed divided into parts – or apartness; Will, as the eldest, had always stood alone. Jim, Tim and Hughie lived their own lives and had little interest in the others, though they all, of course, knew about Crystal. Doone, at the tail, was even more alone than Will had been – no one knew or cared what he did or where he went, though Will had begun to guess the secret. As the months went by, he saw Doone, in his box of a room, exercising by the bedrail, noticed that on Tuesdays and Thursdays his small brother seemed unusually tired, saw the small-size black shorts and white singlets drying beside Crystal's tunics on the washing-line, saw, too, how happy and absorbed Doone was nowadays but, 'It's a secret, Will,' said Doone. 'Ma says we mustn't tell Pa.'

'I don't see why,' said Will. 'Why shouldn't you have lessons as much as that thumping nuisance Crystal?'

'She doesn't thump half as much since she went to Miss Glyn,' Doone said earnestly. 'Really she doesn't, Will,' but under the hard work, the obedience and new control, Crystal was still Crystal.

One Tuesday of their second summer term, Ma told them they had to be at the Ennis Glyn School half an hour earlier, 'so that you can have a short class. Miss Glyn says you mustn't miss that, but it seems there's an important exhibition of ballet costume she feels you ought to see.'

Ma no longer came to the school with them. Crystal was almost ten now. 'Think! You have been at Ennis Glyn's for nearly two years!' Ma said.

It had been a hard two years for them all, and it often seemed to her that all the fun and excitement had gone out of dancing; 'Nothing but exercises, exercises, exercises,' she had once said, exasperated.

'You don't understand.' Crystal had been lofty. 'You don't understand anything at all.' Again Ma had been too hurt to speak and, perhaps because the exhibition was of ballet costumes, when she had seen Crystal and Doone off she went upstairs, opened the wardrobe and looked at the dresses hanging there, all dresses she had so carefully made. She had rescued Columbine's but still could hardly bear to look at it. The rainbow dress was there, the tarantella's wide skirt and ribboned tambourine, and the tiny powder-puff, though she could scarcely see it for a mist of tears. Gone, she felt, were all the pretty things: the lights and flowers and the clapping; music she could understand. There was no one to tell Ma that it would all come again, more wonderfully than even she could dream; she put out her finger to stroke the blue silk folds, but a hanger swung in the way and she found that what she was caressing was Doone's Clown ruff.

The exhibition was at the Victoria and Albert Museum. 'Here's a pass that will get you in,' Miss Glyn told them. 'The bus goes straight there. Valerie will take you.'

'Valerie!' Crystal was pleased.

'Yes. She knows her way about London and at twelve she *ought* to be responsible.' There was a certain anxiety in Miss Glyn's voice as she said 'ought'. 'She'll bring you back here. The Museum closes at five, and I have promised your mother we'll put you on the train for home.'

Crystal had long admired dark-eyed, dark curly-haired, red-cheeked Valerie and envied her. The red was rouge – 'She uses eye-shadow, too, and has had her ears pierced. Pa says I have to wait till I'm sixteen!' On the way to the bus, Crystal did her best to impress and charm Valerie. When Crystal wanted, she could be fun and entertaining, and Valerie soon lost her sullenness. 'Having to lug two infants about,' she had said, but soon she and Crystal were chattering and laughing. Valerie did not speak to Doone.

At the Museum, which was bigger than any building Doone could have imagined, bigger than the Royal Theatre, he would have liked to have stayed and gazed at the huge arched entrance, the even bigger entrance-hall with its marble pillars and uniformed attendants, the corridors leading away, but Valerie hustled them along. 'Let's get it over,' she said. 'This'll be the third time I've seen this flipping exhibition.'

Crystal stopped. 'Tell you what,' she said. 'There's a film on at the Odeon. You can't see it without an adult.' Valerie's bright eyes grew brighter. 'But if you got the tickets – you look eighteen – we could slip in behind somebody. If we took the next bus to Marble Arch, we could just catch it.' Crystal always had plenty of pocket money and, 'I'll treat you,' said Crystal.

'But what about Miss Glyn? She'll ask you about the costumes. . . .'

'You've seen them twice already so you can tell me, and so can Doone. He's good at things like that. We'll leave him here . . .' but Doone protested. 'I want to see the film we mustn't see.'

'No, you don't,' said Crystal. 'You want to see the exhibition. Here's your pass. We'll tear ours up. We'll buy you a catalogue. Miss Glyn said we should have one', and she told Doone, 'Look at everything and mark it carefully, mind. You have heaps of time. We'll come back for you at five, so be here at the entrance, see?'

'I won't stay here, I won't', but Crystal gave him a push and Doone was inside.

He found himself in a passage with glass cases full of strange things, though some of them now were not as strange to Doone; there were ballet shoes, block-toed and soft, all reverently laid out, yet they were worn, and some of them had writing inside the instep. What a funny place to write, he thought. There was a golden wig with queer little horns: 'Wig worn by Nijinsky' – he made out 'Nijinsky' – in a ballet with the word 'faun'. Who was Nijinsky? And what was a faun? There were fans, a muff, flowers, combs, wide ribbons and strange pear-shaped wooden things, each pair held together by tassels – 'Castanets,' read Doone – but what were castanets? He had to move along, there were so many other people, many other children. 'This way,' said an attendant. Doone went through what seemed a tunnel and then was suddenly in darkness; after the lights outside, its black was completely black.

For a moment he was afraid, as when he was little and used

to find his way to Beppo, but music began, music like the music he had heard at the Royal Theatre, an orchestra, and he went in on tiptoe and stood still as, slowly, lights like footlights came up on the edge of the platform, more lights shone overhead and, against black curtains, black platform, he was looking at a model in a tutu of pink, with a deeper pink hem-frill embroidered with silver and gold. Down went the lights – he gave a gasp of dismay – but they came up, this time on a group of young men models with plumed helmets, tunics with gold embroidery and falling lace cravats. Darkness again and, as the lights shone, there was a crouched and glorious toad with a pillbox hat. The toad had dappled cream tights and a metal skin of rough fabric covered in stones like dull jewels.

Doone began to see how the exhibition worked: the figures were numbered; they, too, were black but they all had, he thought, lovely serene faces. They were lit up in turn and there were small stands which also lit up, in front of each group, showing the names of the ballets and, sometimes, of a famous dancer who had worn that very costume. He moved round, stopping to look at a costume until it blacked out while the music sounded like dancing, though the figures were still. 'Lady into Fox.' How? he wondered, and what a strange dress, woolly red-brown, tight all over, with a falling white neck-frill; the tights came over block shoes that had black tips and there were little black gloves. He saw, too, as the lights came round again, perhaps for the third time, that with the Sleeping Beauty – he had made out her name – was a glorious Prince in orange tights and a tunic of orange and gold brocade. Doone looked at him and only him until the lights dimmed. He had quite forgotten Crystal and Valerie.

He did not stay all the time. Two and a half hours is a long while and, as if he needed to rest, he wandered outside into the Museum's hall and the place where they sold postcards and books, and looked at them, but always he came back – the attendants let him come and go – and soon he stayed on. Sometimes, because his legs ached, he sat on the edge of the platform, close to the costumes – he could have touched them if he had dared; sometimes he shut his eyes because they were dazzled and then the music seemed to play inside him.

The tape lasted for perhaps twenty-five minutes and, after a pause, started again, but it always ended in the same way with a strange, half-eerie wistful melody, played as the lights came to rest on a big showcase in the centre of the room and on one dress made all of white feathers except where, on the breast, a deep-red jewel shone. The second time round, as Doone stood there, a voice behind him whispered, 'That's where the arrow struck – it's a drop of blood. It's Pavlova's dress for *The Dying Swan*.' The voice went on, 'When Pavlova was dying, she asked for her swan dress, then the dancer, like the swan, died,' Doone felt as if he had a lump in his throat as slowly, quietly, in a quiet last breathing, the music finished, too.

Each time it came round to that end, Doone went back to that showcase and stood there.

At the fourth time the crowd was beginning to thin and he was almost alone as, looking at the deep-red jewel among the feathers, he waited for those last sad lonely notes. Suddenly, 'I must say Oswald's done it marvellously well.' A man's loud booming voice shattered the moment. 'Really imaginatively.'

'Quiet!' said a furious small voice. 'Don't talk now. Be quiet!'

Doone hardly knew he had spoken, he was so angry, but the music had gone and, as he turned outraged, his eyes blazing with temper, he saw a group of grown-ups. The gentleman who had spoken was as big as his voice, wearing a dark-blue overcoat with a velvet collar. There were two younger gentlemen, one in grey flannels and a jersey who looked as if he belonged to the Exhibition, and with them a Lady – instinctively Doone gave her the capital letter. As she had grey hair he supposed she was old, but she was upright and slim, her eyes as blue as Crystal's.

'Well! Well! *That* put me in my place,' said the big gentleman. The other two were laughing, and Doone wished he could have sunk into the floor, but the Lady did not laugh. Instead she said: 'He's quite right. I think we could do with more of that respect.' She came over to Doone and looked down at him. 'What is your name, little boy?'

'Where *have* you been?' Miss Glyn, for once, was not calm.

71

Valerie and Crystal joined in, 'What have you been doing?' and, 'Who was that?'

As was to be expected, the film they should not have seen ran late. 'It's after five,' Valerie had said uneasily but, 'Never mind,' said Crystal, 'Doone will wait. He always does what I tell him.'

'But what are we going to tell Miss Glyn?'

'That we liked the costumes so much we stayed till the last minute.'

'Oh!' said Crystal as they got off the bus. The Museum was closed and there was no sign of Doone. 'I'll skin him for this,' said Crystal. 'Now we'll have to tell.'

'Yes, and Her Highness Glyn will be furious – a film instead of her precious Exhibition.'

But, 'I don't mind about the film,' said Miss Glyn. 'I might have done that once myself. I mind about the deceit.'

'It was Crystal's idea,' Valerie said quickly.

'And I suppose you weren't in charge – and two years older.' Miss Glyn was withering. 'You're cheats, both of you – but where, oh, where is Doone?'

She rang the Museum. There was no little boy there. Could he have been shut in when the Exhibition closed? 'You know what he is,' said Crystal but, 'Certainly not' was the answer.

'If you would just look,' Miss Glyn begged and, when no Doone was found, 'I shall have to ring your mother.' Miss Glyn tried not to sound distraught and it was then that Valerie, who had gone to the window as if she were trying to dissociate herself from what she called 'the fuss', cried, 'Here he is! In a car – a car with a chauffeur!'

It was the chauffeur who brought him upstairs – 'All right now, Doone?' – touched his cap to Miss Glyn and went downstairs as they pounced on Doone. 'Where have you been? Whose car was that? Who was that with you?'

'It was the big gentleman's car and she was the Lady', and Doone explained, 'Crystal and Valerie weren't there, so they brought me here.'

'What lady?'

'The Lady.' More and more that seemed to Doone the proper name for her.

'You know Ma says we're not allowed to talk to strangers,'

Crystal began.

'She wasn't a stranger. She was. . . .' but Doone could not say what she was.

'Do you love dancing so much?' she had asked.

'Yes.' All Doone's world was in that 'yes' and he found he was telling her about Madame Tamara, Mrs Sherrin and Miss Glyn.

'Ennis Glyn?' she had asked. 'Good. Go on,' and he told her about *Le Spectre de la Rose*, the French toyshop and the poodle. She said, 'Nothing could have been better.' Then the music and lights came on again and she took Doone by the hand and led him, stopping at three or four places to explain a ballet to him – he noticed the music stopped while she was talking. Other children had gathered round. Doone heard their mothers whispering but she took no notice of them.

They came to the shoes and she explained about the writing. 'For a ballerina to give you one of her shoes, inscribed with her name, was a great great compliment,' said the Lady.

'But they're so old.'

'Not old, worn,' which was the same word that had come to Doone. 'One day you will see the ballet of *The Sleeping Beauty*, when the Princess dances with her four suitors in what they call the Rose Adage; in that one dance she wears right through the toe of her right shoe.'

'Why doesn't she wear out the other?'

'Because most of the time she's *en pointe* on the right one, but in the Finale she wears out the other, the left.' When it was all finished, the Lady had paused and said to Doone, 'Now we'll do it properly, no talking, just the music and lighting.'

'Madame, they're closing,' said one of the gentlemen. The other children were being bustled out but, 'Tell them they must give us ten minutes more, ten minutes of the end of the tape,' and she said crisply, 'It won't hurt them,' and, though now the exhibition was empty except for themselves and the gentlemen, once again she and Doone moved with the lights and the music. When they came to the big case and the white-feathered dress there were no interruptions, and she stood in silence with him. As the last note died away, Doone could not bear it; he bent his head and, where she was holding his hand, a tear dropped on the Lady's.

73

For a moment she looked down at it. Doone was thankful she made no comment. 'Boys don't cry,' he could hear Pa's voice but, What if you can't help it? thought Doone. Gently she let his hand go. 'It's time we went,' she said, but drew her finger down Doone's cheek. 'One day I'll come and see you dance.'

That alarmed Doone. 'Miss Glyn doesn't let visitors come.'

'I think she'll let me – and I don't think she'll be cross that I have kept you,' and, holding out her hand to the big gentleman, she had said, 'Lend me your pen, Alex.' She wrote across Doone's catalogue: 'Doone – at the Exhibition of ballet costumes', and signed her name.

When Miss Glyn saw the programme she said what Mrs Sherrin had said, 'You lucky lucky little boy,' and, 'You must keep this always,' but Crystal interposed: 'Please keep it for him, Miss Glyn. If he takes it home, he'll show it to everyone and he mustn't show it to Pa.'

Then, 'Your father *still* doesn't know about Doone?' asked Miss Glyn.

That was becoming a problem for Ma.

Every year the Ennis Glyn School of Dancing held an open day for the pupils' parents and friends; old boys and girls came, too, and it was known that some of Her Majesty's Ballet Company came to look. In their first year Crystal and Doone had not taken part. 'They haven't been with me long enough,' Miss Glyn told Ma, who, all the same, had had an invitation. This second year was different. Crystal was one of ten girls and boys chosen to show a demonstration class; she was also to dance a *czardas*, a Russian dance, for two girls and two boys, Sebastian and Charles. 'One of four.' Ma was disappointed. 'At least I wear red boots,' said Crystal. Then Pa announced he was coming.

'Could you leave Doone out of the display?' Ma asked Miss Glyn.

'Wouldn't that be rather unkind, Mrs Penny?'

'Doone won't mind. He's used to being left out.'

'That's not how I treat children.' Miss Glyn was curt, and Ma flushed. Then Miss Glyn relented. 'I've put him in a

74

children's version of the Chinese Dance from the *Nutcracker* ballet. He'll be in costume and made up.'

'And Mr Penny won't be looking for him – he'll be so taken up with Crystal.' Ma was cheered and, as she had predicted, Pa did not notice Doone; he was too impressed with Crystal. She looked 'so neat and modest', he said with surprise and, 'That child can really dance, Maud.' He was even reconciled to paying for Crystal's music lessons – Miss Glyn had found Ma a teacher, one of her own pianistes, Miss La Motte. 'Always shelling out for our little Madam,' he said, but good-humouredly. 'Only, is it fair on the others?'

'Some children need different things,' said Miss Glyn.

'Yes,' Ma sighed and, 'I keep hoping Doone will grow out of it,' she told Miss Glyn.

'On the contrary, every day he's growing more and more into it. Mrs Penny, you'll have to tell your husband,' but Doone, though he did not say a word, was beginning to tell Pa himself.

'It's Doone's birthday on Wednesday,' said Pa. 'What does he want, Maud?'

Ma hesitated. 'William, he wants a book.'

'A *book*!' No Penny child had wanted a book for their birthday. 'He's barely learnt to read.'

'I know, but he still wants it.'

Will had won books as prizes at school; the boys sometimes took books out from the school library – spy stories or science fiction – but all anybody actually bought were comics or magazines and, 'This book costs eleven pounds,' said Ma.

'Eleven pounds for a book!' Pa was shocked. The odd part was that if it had been a bicycle costing ten times as much, like the one Hughie had asked for, though Pa would have demurred, he would have given it to Doone. 'We must be fair,' but, then, Pa understood bicycles. 'What is this book?' he asked.

'He saw it at Miss Glyn's. It's got lots of pictures and it's called *The Magic of the Dance*.'

' "The Dance"! For a *boy*?'

'It's because he sees so much of it when he goes with Crystal.'

'Then he had better stop going with Crystal,' growled Pa, and, 'Is there anything else you want for your birthday while we're at it?' he said sarcastically to Doone.

'I wouldn't mind a grand piano,' said Doone.

'A grand piano. You say Doone has been having piano lessons.' Pa sounded dazed.

'Not what you could call lessons', and Ma explained, 'Mr Felix is teaching him – he has always had a fancy for Doone. Not proper lessons like Crystal's, and he doesn't expect us to pay.'

But it was not the money Pa was thinking of. 'You mean Doone wants it? *Likes* it?'

'He goes there several afternoons a week to practise. At least it keeps him out of mischief', and Ma pleaded, 'William, it's difficult to know what to do with Doone. The boys don't want him – they are so much older – and Crystal has her own friends.'

'Doesn't he have friends?'

'He doesn't seem to. . . .'

'Of course I have friends,' said Doone. 'Mr Felix, Mrs Sherrin, Ruth. . . .' Perhaps Charles, thought Doone, but did not say it aloud.

'I meant friends at school to play with.'

'I haven't time,' said Doone, which was true. If these two years had been hard on Crystal, they had been far harder on Doone, which nobody realised. He had school and the catching up with schoolwork at home, his dancing – unlike Crystal, he practised – and he had his music, practising for that, too. He would have liked to play football and cricket after school and at weekends like the other boys, but how could he? In any case, he liked his own things better but, 'It seems so odd for one of ours,' said Pa.

'Wait till he gets into the team,' said Ma. 'They say he's good at games.'

That comforted Pa. 'You think he'll grow out of it?' Ma did not tell him what Miss Glyn had said – 'he's growing more and more into it' – and Pa bought Doone a cricket bat for his birthday. Doone stood it proudly in the corner of his room where it stayed.

76

'What I don't understand,' said Miss Glyn, 'is why, Mrs Penny, it all seems so strange, such a new world, to you. You're interested in dancing and there has been, for instance, so much about the ballet on television.'

'We have the one set in the sitting-room,' Ma said slowly. 'Mr Penny and the boys, they like to watch football, sport, Westerns, the serials, *Top of the Pops*, the news.'

'And Crystal?'

'She has her own telly, of course.'

'Don't you watch it together?'

'Well, no – not now. You see' – Ma hardly dared confess it to Miss Glyn – 'she likes what the boys like, and to tell you the truth, Miss Glyn, come evening, what with the shop – Mr Penny leaves in the morning at a quarter to four – and the house and all of them, the arranging and cooking, it used to be taking Crystal backwards and forwards, but still it's seeing her off, come evening, I'm too tired to take in much', and Ma said miserably, 'I suppose it's true and I don't understand,' but to her surprise Miss Glyn leant forward and kissed her. 'I think you do wonders,' she said. 'Wonders! They wouldn't have got anywhere but for you,' said Ennis Glyn.

She would have been surprised if she had known how much that kiss heartened Ma, and also that Miss Glyn allowed Crystal to dance in the Pilgrim's Green Primary School concert – true, not as a rainbow or anything special. The dance was simply called 'Waltz'; Miss Glyn had arranged it for her.

'What about Doone?' Mrs Carstairs, the Headmistress had asked. 'Shouldn't he dance?'

'He's too junior,' Ma said hastily. Pa was coming.

Crystal wore a draped tunic Ma had made for her, her hair drawn back, the curls falling from a silver binding. Ma had asked Mr Felix to play for her.

'What is the music?' he had asked suspiciously. 'It's a Brahms waltz in A major.' Ma had read that on the sheet.

'Ah!' Mr Felix was contented, and, afterwards, 'I wouldn't have known it was the same girl,' he said. 'Congratulations.'

Ma was not sure she liked that; nor did Crystal, and she despised the dance. 'It's so dull,' and, 'I'm sure the girls thought it dull,' she said as she came off, still breathing hard from the quick ending of the waltz. 'Oh, I wish I could have done a "number," ' – that was what Valerie called them – 'tap in a top-hat and tails and a cane.'

Before her talk with Miss Glyn, Ma would have said it would have been more fun, but now, 'Mrs Carstairs lets you off school to learn ballet,' she said severely. 'Classical ballet.'

Crystal gave a deliberate little yawn; Ma knew it was deliberate because it was meant for her and she felt a cold little fear clutch her heart. 'It has to come from the child,' Mr Brown had said. 'Never force a child that doesn't want to dance,' and, 'It's the child that decides,' Miss Glyn's Stella had echoed it. Did these ballet people know something she, Ma, was blind to? Yet, next minute, Crystal was running on to the stage again, curtsying prettily at the applause and, afterwards, getting praise from the teachers, excitement from the other children, but, She's running out of interest at Miss Glyn's, thought Ma. I must think of something else. I must.

She met Mrs Sherrin in the High Street. 'Crystal danced a solo at the school concert.'

'I know,' said Mrs Sherrin. 'I read about it in the *Gazette*. It seems she's shaping beautifully.'

'And how is Ruth?'

'Getting on. As a matter of fact, in October she's auditioning for Her Majesty's Junior Ballet School.'

'Her Majesty's. . . .' Ma's mouth was open in a mixture of surprise and dismay. 'They have a school?'

'Yes, Queen's Chase at Buckingham Park. You see, Ruth's nearly eleven and the time has come, if she's to try to be a professional, for full-time training at a school where she can go on with her academic work as well. At Queen's Chase she can and, if she's lucky, go on to the Senior School.'

'But Buckingham Park is the other side of London.'

'Yes. She would have to be a boarder.'

'Boarding school!' Ma felt dizzy, then longed to ask how Mrs Sherrin would be able to pay for that, and Mrs Sherrin said, as if Ma had asked, 'I should have to apply to the education authorities for help. I don't suppose Ruth will get in; they say over a thousand girls are auditioned and there are

78

only twenty or so places to fill,' but Ma hardly heard the last words; gripping her shopping-bags tightly, she was saying to herself, 'Now, why didn't I think of that?'

'It's not that we don't think you're teaching Crystal beautifully,' Ma began.

Only Doone, sitting in a corner, waiting for Ma and looking through the school copy of the *Dancing Times*, was in the room with them. Crystal had gone with Valerie. She had discarded all her other friends for Valerie and had been immensely flattered and pleased by Valerie's asking her to spend the night. Pa had let her go, though he had demurred. 'At twelve to make friends with a ten-year-old? Doesn't seem natural,' and, 'Who is this Valerie?' 'She's a doctor's daughter,' said Ma as if that settled it but, when Miss Glyn heard she had given a little frown and, now, 'Do you think Valerie's the best friend for Crystal?' she asked.

'She's a doctor's daughter.'

'The doctor is her mother, a busy doctor; she doesn't have much time to spare for Valerie.'

'Only too willing to fob her off to anyone who will have her.' Stella had come in. Ma had noticed that Miss Glyn did not treat Stella as an assistant but as an equal – 'Of course!' Miss Glyn would have said. 'Doesn't she run the school when I have to be away?' – and now Stella went on, 'Valerie's father doesn't seem to know what to do with Valerie, either.'

'Which is partly why we have kept her,' said Miss Glyn. 'She's a capable little dancer, of course.'

'And precocious. *And* an accomplished liar,' said blunt Stella.

'You mean Crystal might catch bad ways.' Ma spoke as if bad ways were measles.

'Crystal can be deceitful, too.'

'Never!' Ma ruffled up. 'I've never had a day's trouble with Crystal.'

'Little girls can be very baffling,' was all Miss Glyn said and then, 'but you wanted to see us, Mrs Penny.'

'Yes,' and Ma took a deep breath. 'It's not that we don't think you're teaching Crystal beautifully, but next year she'll be eleven and changing schools. There'll be homework and all

79

that and they may not be as understanding about her dancing as Mrs Carstairs. Besides, she should have much more – I mean more dancing.' Ma was getting breathless.

'So?' asked Miss Glyn.

At last Ma brought it out. 'Miss Glyn, don't you think she should apply for Her Majesty's Ballet School?'

When Doone heard that name he put down the *Dancing Times*. The words 'Her Majesty' conjured up for him a world of magic. The School, he thought, must be a palace; he saw a façade like Buckingham Palace with soldiers. No, a castle like Windsor Castle – Pa had taken them there one Sunday. A castle with ramparts and towers. . . . It was almost a shock to hear Miss Glyn say in a matter-of-fact voice, 'Her Majesty's Ballet Junior School. You mean Queen's Chase?'

So it was not a palace. Still, Queen's Chase was an intriguing name. Why 'Chase'? wondered Doone.

'Yes, Queen's Chase.' That was what Mrs Sherrin had called it.

Miss Glyn became so quiet that Ma brought herself to say, 'You do encourage children to try to get there?'

'Some of them. In fact, Charles is trying for it this autumn.'

'Charles!' Doone was listening now with both his ears. Then boys did go to that majestic-sounding school. Mark, Sydney, Sebastian, Charles – and Doone? A new excitement woke in Doone.

'It's important for Charles. His father, Colonel Ingram, has just been made military attaché in Paris.' Ma did not know what an attaché was, but it sounded grand. 'He'll be posted soon, and Charles's mother wants him to do his training in England.'

'*She* wants?' That seemed to make a bond between Mrs Ingram and Ma, but Miss Glyn went on, 'If ever there were a worthwhile balletomane, it's Isabel Ingram; in fact, she's one of our Governors.'

'Then Charles is bound to get in.'

'The Governors have nothing to do with auditions.' Miss Glyn withdrew into coldness as she always did when Ma made what Will called 'insinuations'. 'That rests with the Members of the Panel, who judge purely on merit', but, 'Charles is the boy with red hair, isn't he?' Ma was saying. 'He's the same age as Crystal, yet you didn't think of her?'

'No.' It was so firm that Ma felt uneasy.

'Because you thought she wouldn't get in?'

'No, because I thought she might,' said Miss Glyn, which seemed to Ma a strange answer. Before she could speak, 'Mrs Penny,' asked Miss Glyn, 'what gave you this idea of Queen's Chase?'

'A dancing friend' – Ma almost said 'enemy' – 'a little friend of Crystal's is going to audition this October, and I thought, if Ruth, why not Crystal?'

'Perhaps Ruth's a different sort of child,' said Stella.

'What do you mean?' Ma was even more ruffled. 'What's different about Ruth and Charles? Doesn't Crystal dance well enough? If not, why not, I should like to know? Haven't we been paying you good money these two years?' Ma recollected herself. 'I'm sorry, Miss Glyn, but. . . .'

'It's not the dancing. In fact Crystal's dancing can be excellent when she tries. It's not the dancing.'

'Then what is it?'

'Crystal herself, Mrs Penny. Her Majesty's Ballet School sounds glamorous; it is, of course, and yet, in a way, it's not. Every boy or girl there knows that he, or she, is in for years of gruellingly hard work – if they are successful, seven or eight years; struggling to make their dancing better and better, yet loving it so much that they are ready to give up all sorts of things that other children like and do and yet, at the end, be ready to take the smallest, probably unnoticed parts just for the privilege of dancing them. Parents should be very careful before allowing a son or daughter to commit themselves to that.'

'And really,' said Stella again, 'in the end, it's the child who decides.'

'I have decided,' said Doone, but none of them heard him and, 'I only know,' said Ma, 'that from the time she was a tiny mite Crystal has thought of nothing else but dancing.' As she said it, Ma knew it was not quite true.

'Yet she gets bored with it,' said Stella.

'Yes, I'm not fabulous now,' Miss Glyn smiled. 'Just a tiresome nagger. No, Mrs Penny, to be blunt, I think Crystal doesn't dance for love of the dance, the magic of the dance; she doesn't feel the magic, because she dances for the love of Crystal. Don't blame her,' said Miss Glyn. 'Only one child in a thousand, perhaps a hundred thousand, is born with that "extra" quality. I suppose you could call it a "plus". Crystal's gifted, but she needs stimulus, a spur. Let's see if we can get her into a full-time training school that offers more drama, more theatre.'

'She would get parts at once,' said Stella, 'she's so pretty: parts in pantomime, films. . . .'

Ma knew how much Crystal would like that, but she held her big bag even more tightly and sat upright. 'I still think she should go to Her Majesty's Ballet School. You were there, Miss Glyn. You're one of the most important dancers in the Company, so I'm asking you to put in a word for Crystal, and I think you ought.'

Miss Glyn was not a Madame Tamara to be ordered about and, 'I'm afraid I can't do that,' she said. 'For one thing, it isn't necessary. True, I have to sign the application form and I'm proud to say that the examiners take my name as a guarantee that I'm not just sending in "possibles", but "probables".'

'And Crystal's neither?' Ma was red in the face.

'I have told you, Mrs Penny, I don't think the school is right for Crystal or Crystal for it.'

'Ma, if Crystal can't go, can I?' Ma jumped; she had not realised Doone was in the room.

'What are you doing here?' she asked sharply.

Waiting for you – What else? Doone could have said but was too intent. 'Ma, can I?'

'Of course you can't. Go and wait outside, you silly little boy.'

When he had gone Ma gathered herself together. 'Well, if you won't help Crystal, I will. I suppose I can ask for an audition?'

'Anyone can apply. I'll give you a form.'

'Will you sign it?'

'I shall have to.'

'But you don't want to', and Ma's misery burst out. 'Why? Miss Glyn, why?'

'Because – and of course I could be wrong – one can always be wrong – I'm afraid you'll both be disappointed', and, 'Mrs

Penny,' said Stella, 'Doone isn't a silly little boy. If you have set your heart on having a child in Her Majesty's Ballet, wait two years for him.'

In the train going home Ma suddenly turned on Doone. She was so upset, astonished and dismayed that, 'I couldn't help myself,' she told Will afterwards. 'What I don't like about you,' she told Doone – he was rocking with tiredness as well as with the train – 'what I don't like is the way you worm your way into people so they do favours for you.'

'I don't worm. . . .' Doone was so astonished he could hardly speak.

'You do. Mrs Sherrin, Madame Tamara, Mr Felix, Miss Glyn and that Stella.' Doone always saw things in pictures and he saw a pink-brown worm, with his own head and green-brown eyes, wriggling into those people whom he loved, and, 'I don't worm,' he said, horrified.

'You do,' said Ma. 'Teacher's pet.'

'Teacher's pet?' Mr Felix said thoughtfully when Doone told him. Doone knew that was what Crystal called him, the boys following suit but, until now, not Ma, and he was still shamed and hurt.

'Is it so bad to be that?' asked Mr Felix. 'Teachers naturally like the boys and girls who are interested in what they teach. I think it's honourable to be a teacher's pet.'

'They laugh at me,' said Doone. 'Jim, Tim, Hughie.'

'Let them laugh. Silly hyenas.'

'What are hyenas?'

'Creatures that run in packs – and eat what other animals kill for them.' Mr Felix was fierce. 'They make a noise like laughing, but they don't know what they are laughing at. Now, don't waste time. Turn to page seven. The scherzo – but play it slowly first. . . .'

Will helped Ma fill in the form. Will, now openly engaged to Kate, had grown to be slim with soft brown hair and a small moustache, grey eyes behind steel spectacles which made him look older than twenty-one; he was, in any case, mature for his age. 'How could I help it with all that lot coming after me!' he used to ask. Now, 'Height of father? Height of mother?', and

Will asked, 'Why do they want to know that?'

'It helps them tell how much she'll grow. A dancer can't be too tall or too small.'

There had to be photographs. 'In my leotard,' Crystal objected.

'Back and front,' said Ma, 'and your hair out of the way.'

The photographs had to be paid for, and there was the audition fee. 'Will, can you lend me twenty pounds?' asked Ma. 'I'll give it you back bit by bit from the housekeeping.' Ma needed new shoes, 'but I'll manage,' said Ma.

'Occupation of father.' Will was going to write 'green-grocer', when, 'Put "merchant",' said Ma. 'It sounds better,' and, as she saw Will's look, she said, 'It's true. He is a kind of merchant.'

'I thought you hoped they would give us a grant,' said Will. ' "Merchant" sounds as if Pa had bags of gold,' and, 'Ma,' said Will, 'why won't you give up all this pretence? And why won't you tell Pa?'

'Crystal may not be chosen. Until we know, why bother him?'

'It isn't only Crystal. There's Doone. It isn't fair to either of them.'

'You leave your father to me,' said Ma. 'He has to get accustomed. You know he does. I'll tell him in . . . in. . . .' Then proudly she found the right words, 'In due course.'

'Is that you, Miss Glyn? I wanted you to be the first to know. Crystal has had her audition and been chosen.' Ma could not keep the triumph out of her voice. 'Yes, lovely, isn't it? And how did Charles do?' Doone listened anxiously. Charles, with his sunflower burst of hair, his bright brown eyes, the power of his dancing – to Doone, Charles could easily have danced the Rose – and Doone let out a breath of delight as Ma said, 'Oh, he did, did he? Congratulations,' but Ma sounded disappointed. 'Crystal's friend? Oh, you mean Ruth. I haven't enquired.' This time Ma was hostile, though, 'Ma, ring Mrs Sherrin and ask about Ruth,' Crystal had urged. 'I want to know, I must know, if she got through.' 'I wouldn't demean myself,' Ma had said, but now to Miss Glyn, seriously, even humbly, 'They said Crystal might still have trouble with her

84

left foot and would have to work on it meanwhile. Thank you, Miss Glyn,' and, as Ma put down the telephone, she told Crystal, 'Miss Glyn says of course you'll work at it with her, so that you'll be ready in March. You see, there's a second audition,' Ma told Pa.

'Another? They're not half choosy,' said Pa.

'They have to be, to make sure.'

Ma had told Pa 'the truth but not the whole truth', said Will. Not, for instance, about Queen's Chase and Crystal having to be a boarder, but what she told him was told with a flourish. 'Think, William! Just twenty chosen out of hundreds of girls, and from all over, not only Britain; some are from overseas.' Pa, in his innocence, had thought it was a different kind of competition. 'Not in the least like the last,' Ma had assured him – a kind of assessment by which a child could get a grant from the education authorities for dancing lessons from an accredited ballet school. 'After all, these classes are expensive,' said Ma.

'Indeed they are.'

'So we could use a grant. It could be well over a thousand pounds a year, William.' Ma deliberately understated but, even so, he gasped.

'We couldn't need all that.'

We shall soon, but Ma did not say it. Instead, 'You have been a good Papa to Crystal' – Ma still used 'Papa' on state occasions – 'you deserve a little reward.'

'Little! It seems queer – so much money for a child Crystal's age.'

'That's talent,' Ma said convincingly. 'She'll get through again in March, I know she will. William, she's perfect – or near-perfect,' with a modicum of sense Ma added that; but perfect Crystal was soon to give her two surprises which, though small, were unpleasant little stings.

Pa had taken Crystal to buy her a present. 'One of twenty out of over a thousand,' he had said. 'Even if she isn't chosen next time and doesn't get the grant, this calls for something handsome.' He had chosen a brooch, 'a little circlet set with pearls, real pearls, and turquoises, just right for Crystal's colouring and age'. It was more expensive than he had thought, 'but it was so pretty', he said. Crystal had spent the next day with Valerie and, that night at supper, as always after being with Valerie, she was boasting and putting on airs until Pa said, 'That's enough, Chris. You're not a ballerina yet. Don't let this go to your head.'

'It has gone to her head,' Hughie giggled. 'She's had her ears pierced.'

'What if I have?' Crystal tossed her curls, showing the temporary rings. 'But you haven't any proper earrings,' said Ma.

'I have.' Crystal had the grace to blush. 'Pa, I changed your brooch. I knew you wouldn't mind.'

Pa did mind. 'I chose it for her,' and, 'Had her ears pierced – at eleven,' said Pa.

'Lots of little girls do.' Ma defended Crystal, though she, like Pa, was hurt. 'It's Valerie she goes by nowadays, not me,' but, 'She's growing up,' she told Pa, and, 'If she passes this audition. . . .' Ma broke off. At least at Queen's Chase there would be no more Valerie. Miss Glyn had said the discipline was strict. 'It has to be,' said Miss Glyn.

Ma could not console Pa with that because he did not know yet about Queen's Chase but, 'I'm ashamed of you,' she told Crystal.

'You're not.' Crystal put her arms round Ma and rubbed her face against Ma's in the old irresistible way. 'You're proud as proud of me as you can be, you know you are, and you're glad, glad you didn't listen to Miss Prissy Stuck-up Glyn.'

'What do you mean, I didn't listen . . .?'

'Do you think I don't know what she said?'

Ma pushed Crystal away from her. 'You heard? I thought you had gone with Valerie.'

'Not at all,' Crystal said coolly. 'We knew you were discussing us, so we listened.'

'Eavesdropped!' said Ma, but Crystal was mimicking, ' "Not a good friend for Crystal. . . .", "an accomplished liar",' and Crystal mocked, 'Poor Ma, do you think I'll catch bad ways? And I get bored – sometimes I'm bored with everybody.' Then Crystal broke off. She had remembered something else and her face clouded. 'But what did Stella mean, Ma, when she said, "Wait for Doone"? Does she think

86

he's better than I am?'

'Little snoopers often hear what they don't want to hear.' Ma said it severely but, '*Is* he better?' asked Crystal and, under her breath, 'He's not to be. He's not!'

That summer was the end for Doone of the cocoon that had wrapped him round as a little disregarded grub; while it had lasted it had been, in a way, snug, but now it was as if, little by little, the threads were breaking and he was being forced out into the light.

For one thing, he had a friend who was not a grown-up, one he had not dreamt he could aspire to – Charles. Ever since he came to Miss Glyn's, Doone had admired and followed Charles as best he could, and Charles had been kind in a lofty kind of way. 'Not *en dehors*, which means outwards; *en dedans*, inwards,' Charles would explain and, 'Look, you're letting your tummy sag. . . .' 'Not that foot, the *left one*, you clot'; but the 'clot' had been affectionate, and 'You'll find it easier this way,' said Charles. Then, suddenly, they were equals. It had begun in class.

'Where's Miss La Motte?' Miss Glyn had said, coming into the classroom.

The piano was closed, and Charles had answered, 'I don't know. She isn't here.'

'She's ill.' Stella had followed Miss Glyn. 'Flu. She can't come in.'

'How annoying!' For once Miss Glyn was not sympathetic. 'I have Monsieur Fleurie from Paris coming to watch our classes. I can't spare John from the girls.' John was the other pianist. 'Bother!'

'Would you like me to play?' Doone was suddenly moved to say, his heart beating. Would this be what Ma called 'showing off'? 'Would you like me to play?'

'You?' Miss Glyn had been more than startled.

'I can.' Doone said it with quiet confidence. 'If you put up the stool.'

'But . . . Miss La Motte has all the music,' said Stella.

'I don't need music,' said Doone, 'if you tell me what you want, and what steps', and, when Stella had wound up the stool, he went into one of the mazurkas the boys used for

87

jumps, timing it just as Miss La Motte did, so that the dancers went up on the strong beats, down on the softer. It was Charles who, after the first astounded moment, began the jumps.

'Cor!' said Mark when they had finished. The others were dumb with amazement but, 'All right,' said Miss Glyn. 'To the barre, boys, for *pliés*. A slow waltz, Doone, please', but Doone already knew.

'It's unbelievable,' said Stella.

'No, it's true.' Sydney, who took everything as literally as Doone, had answered her. 'It's true.' Doone could not, of course, follow the dancers, playing with them, allowing for what each dancer could compass, as Miss La Motte and Mr Felix did – he was pretending he was Mr Felix – the boys had to adjust to fit with Doone, 'which won't do them any harm,' said Miss Glyn. She handed over the class to Stella and went to meet her Monsieur.

When she came back from the classrooms with him, Ma, who had come up with Crystal and Doone that day, heard him say, 'I see you have a small prodigy, Mademoiselle.'

'I'm hoping he'll be more than that,' said Miss Glyn. Ma had taken it they were talking of Charles and felt a pang for Crystal.

When Doone had changed, Miss Glyn had called him back into the classroom. 'Before you go,' she said to Doone, 'tell me, can you play all of that Chopin nocturne we use for *port de bras*, or just the part that Miss La Motte plays for us?'

'We only need the parts,' said Doone.

'I know, but can you?'

'Mr Felix made me, but the middle bit won't come right. I'm not very good, you see,' said Doone.

'I see,' and Miss Glyn asked, 'Have your father and mother heard you play?'

'No, we haven't a piano.'

'And your mother doesn't come to Mr Felix's.'

'She doesn't like him. He wouldn't give lessons to Crystal, but he's my best friend since Beppo.'

Beppo again. Slowly, bit by bit, Miss Glyn was beginning to piece out Doone's life and, 'I can guess Beppo accounts for your agility,' she murmured almost to herself, then said, 'Your mother's in the waiting-room. Would you like me to call her and you play for her now, here, just as you did for class?'

Doone sat still. He was tempted, but he shook his head. 'She would tell Pa, and he might stop it. You see,' said Doone, 'Pa wants proper boys.'

'But Doone. . . .'

'Anyway,' said Doone, 'Mr Felix says one day he'll have it out with my Ma.'

'I think,' said Miss Glyn, 'one day I'll have it out with your Pa.'

'Was it like a castle?' asked Doone.

'Why should it be like a castle?' Crystal answered crossly. 'It's a school but in a house.' Then some of the glory came back. 'A beautiful house, creamy white with white pillars, big. Princesses were brought up there.' Doone nodded. They would be. 'But, of course, now there are classrooms and dormitories, a canteen.'

'Classrooms . . . dormitories . . . a canteen!' Doone's dream came tumbling down but, 'Was it full of music?' he asked.

'A horrible lot of pianos,' said Crystal. 'Even in the dormitories.'

'A-ah!' said Doone, then, 'Why are you so cross?' he asked.

'Pa,' said Crystal curtly.

Crystal had come through her second audition and Ma had had, at last, to tell Pa 'everything', said Ma – though it was still not quite everything. 'He'll go through the ceiling,' she had said.

Pa did not go through the ceiling; he was oddly quiet, even about the boarding school. 'It might be the best thing for Chris,' he said.

'Crystal.'

But Pa had gone on, 'She's getting beyond us, Maudie.' Since Crystal had changed his brooch for her earrings, Pa seemed to try to avoid her. He had given Ma the money for the auditions and the photographs. 'You should have asked me, not Will.' He had even joked, 'When Chris has gone, perhaps I shall have a wife to myself again.'

*   *   *

That June, Pa, Ma and Crystal were invited down to Queen's

89

Chase – to see it 'in action', the Director had said.

'Can't I come, too?' Doone begged but, 'He's not to come,' Crystal almost shouted. 'I don't want him near.' Ma had understood but Pa looked at his daughter in astonishment. 'There's nothing to get excited about,' he said, and to Doone, 'It wouldn't interest you, son.' Doone was opening his mouth when Ma's hand came down on his shoulder. 'You'll stay here with Will – and don't upset your sister.'

They drove to the Park in the van. 'Does it have to be the van? Couldn't we hire?'

'A van is what we have,' said Pa but when they had driven through the gracious park, up the drive and turned into the wide sweep of ground before the big porticoed house he was shaken. More shaken still when he saw the glass-topped showcases in the museum off the hall, and the hall itself with a wide blue-carpeted staircase going up and a life-sized painting of a girl in a white flounced dress patterned with cherries. 'That's Columbine,' whispered Ma, remembering what Madame Tamara had said. 'She may be,' said Pa, 'but, Maud, this is no place for us.'

'It isn't for us,' hissed Ma. 'It's for Crystal', and indeed the house seemed alive with girls and boys running up and down the stairs, waiting by the classrooms or in the classrooms. Girls and boys – and music – thought Pa. He had to admit he had never seen a better-kept, livelier and healthier-looking lot – 'and all of them completely at home,' he said, marvelling. The boys wore blue tracksuits, the girls scarlet, 'to keep them warm,' Crystal explained – one was among the listed uniform Ma had had to get ready for her which was not quite like the lists of other schools; there was a green skirt and cardigan, white blouses, a green red-lined cloak, but also leotards, white knitted cross-overs, quantities of white socks; later on there would be tights. 'But you can get all these from the wardrobe at reasonable prices,' Mrs Challoner, Headmistress at Queen's Chase, told Ma.

They saw Mrs Challoner in her study, which had once been the library – Ma and Pa had never seen a private library. Mrs Challoner was warm and friendly and, though her dark hair was as beautifully dressed as she herself, she did not make Ma feel like a bundle as she felt with Miss Glyn. They were introduced to the girls' housemistress, Mrs Gillespie – the boys were in a separate wing. They saw the dormitory where Crystal would sleep, 'Not like a dormitory at all,' said Ma.

'Well, the lady who took us over said it used to be a picture gallery,' said Pa. He would have liked to ask more about the history of the house, but Ma and Crystal were only interested in its present, and, 'I must say, it's a rum kind of school, this.'

'For such a posh place,' said Ma. The point was that it was not 'posh'. Both of them were taken aback by the narrow beds and lack of room. The Senior girls had a separate floor in what used to be the servants' attics. True, some had been knocked together to make a common room and they had their own pantry, but, 'Five beds to one small room,' Ma exclaimed.

'Well,' said Mrs Gillespie, 'when dancers go on tour they have to get used to sleeping in all kinds of beds, berths in trains, bunks in cabins, lodgings.'

'But where do they keep their things?' asked Ma.

'They have two drawers each and share a cupboard, and each has a locker.'

'Such tiny lockers.'

'Well, again, when they come to do their make-up in a dressing-room with perhaps forty other girls, they can only use the smallest space and must hang their costumes up carefully or they'll be in trouble with the Wardrobe Mistress. We have to teach them to be tidy and think of one another,' and, 'Bring as little as you can, dear,' Mrs Gillespie said to Crystal. Ma thought of Crystal's innumerable possessions – her collections of china animals, dolls from all over the world, records, cupboards full of clothes and, 'You're going to miss your room all right, Chris,' said Pa. 'But, then, it's good training and I expect the money has to be spent on the dancing and classrooms.'

'As long as the food isn't poor,' Ma was worrying.

'We feed them six times a day,' Mrs Challoner said when Ma asked her. 'To begin with, a big breakfast. If they don't eat at least two courses, they're not allowed to dance – for them the utmost penalty – then elevenses, lunch, orange juice or milk and biscuits for tea, then supper and a hot drink at night.'

'I don't think you need worry, Maudie,' said Pa.

They saw schoolrooms where school lessons were going on

and the big airy mirrored dancing-rooms, one in the old Salon. 'That must have been a beautiful room,' said Pa. He stood amazed and bewildered at the lessons. Countless girls in pale blue, their hair plaited up on their heads or, with the older ones, drawn up in a knob, and many boys in black shorts, white singlets. 'Boys,' said Pa, more amazed. They saw the Senior Ballet Mistress, Miss McKenzie. 'Masters teach us as well,' said Crystal. Her excitement and Ma's was growing. They walked round the gardens. 'What a place for children!' said Ma. The space and air seemed to her marvellous after Pilgrim's Green. 'In summer we're not allowed in the Four Yews Garden or the Lily Pond Garden until we reach the fifth form,' Crystal told them. 'Four Yews Garden', 'Lily Pond' – To Ma that seemed romantic, but 'Humph!' said Pa. How quickly she had slipped into 'we', 'our', Pa thought wryly, 'we girls'. Then, suddenly, she stopped. 'Look, Ma – look. Who's that going in?' She drew a sharp breath. 'It's Ruth.'

It was unmistakably Ruth, grown taller but still with the same slim graceful body and legs. Ruth with Mrs Sherrin, standing where Pa, Ma and Crystal had stood an hour ago before they rang the bell. 'So she did get in', and Crystal breathed, 'She would. The one person in the whole world I didn't want. She would!'

In the van going home, while Crystal chattered and chattered, Pa was silent. When they reached the house, Ma and Crystal went up to the sitting-room; he put the van away and followed them. His step was heavy as he came up the stairs, and Ma and Crystal looked at one another. 'Go and take your things off,' said Ma. 'Leave your pa to me,' and, 'What is it?' she asked Pa as he came into the room.

'I'm not letting her go there,' said Pa.

'*William!*' Ma was aghast. 'I know it's a posh place. . . .'

'That doesn't matter.'

'Then what is it?'

'I never thought . . .,' said Pa. 'It hadn't dawned on me until today that Crystal's dancing could be . . . her job.' Pa did not know what else to call it, but Ma did. 'Not a job – a career.'

'Slavery,' said Pa. 'I feel I'm selling her. It's over four

thousand pounds a year they're giving her; and remember, Maud, what the Director gentleman said.'

'Mr Yeats?' For a moment Ma was silent.

At their interview with him, 'When and how often shall we see Crystal dance?' she had asked. The Director, Mr Yeats, and Miss Baxter, Principal of both Senior and Junior Schools, had looked at one another. Then, 'I'm afraid not for five years, Mrs Penny,' said Mr Yeats.

'Five years!'

'Unless she's chosen for the School annual performances, which are open to the public, but you would have to buy tickets.'

'You must understand,' Miss Baxter had said it as kindly as possible, but plainly, 'from the day Crystal comes to Queen's Chase, you will have to trust her to us. Of course we'll consult you about her health and schoolwork, but not about her dancing, which is what she will be coming for and with which you must not interfere', and, 'You'll stand for that, Maud?' asked Pa now.

'I'll have to. We'll have to,' said Ma. 'What do we know about classical ballet? And, as for the money, she's earned it, William. Think! There must be about a hundred thousand little girls who would give their eyes to be where Crystal is now.'

'I don't care about a hundred thousand little girls. I care about mine, and I don't feel it's right, and I can't let her go.'

'Can't let me go!' Crystal burst into the room. 'What do you mean?'

'You've been listening again. . . .' but Crystal took no notice of Ma. She was facing Pa like a furious kitten.

'You can go to one of those other schools your Ma told me about, and I'll pay for it – schools not as grand or as serious.'

'I don't want other schools. I'm going to Queen's Chase – I am, I am, so there,' spat Crystal, but Pa shook his head.

'I've got in. You can't stop me.'

'I'm still your father. I have to give my consent.'

'If you don't let me go, I'll kill myself. I've got my suitcase and my uniform. I'm all ready,' and, 'I've worked and worked,' Crystal wailed.

'That's true, William. She has worked all these years for this'
— Ma could have said 'we' — 'Now, at the last moment . . .
William, please.'

Pa shook his head again. He could not speak.

'I hate you,' screamed Crystal. 'I'll hate you all my life. You
spoil everything. Anyway, why pick on me? Why me, me, me?
You let the boys do as they want.'

'They don't want this — this highfalutin . . . this . . . this. . . .'
Pa was still groping for words but at last managed to say,
'They want ordinary things.'

'Oh, they do, do they?' And Crystal crowed, 'What about
your precious Doone? If you want to spoil dancing, why don't
you spoil his?'

'Crystal, you promised . . .,' began Ma, but, 'Go on — spoil
Doone's,' spat Crystal.

'Doone's?' Pa stopped, bewildered.

'Yes, Doone's. I know Ma said I mustn't tell, but now I'm
going to', and Crystal flung at Pa: 'Doone's been learning
dancing, just like me, at Miss Glyn's, for the last three years.'

Pa sat down as if his legs had given way under him. 'But
how?' he asked. 'How?'

'Well, he had to go with Crystal.' Ma was trying to defend,
not Doone, but herself. 'It — it kept him out of mischief.'

'Mischief.' To Pa, dancing was the mischief. 'But why didn't
you tell me?'

'I didn't think it mattered; it wasn't as if we were paying
anything. You see, Miss Glyn said if we sent Crystal to her she
would take Doone free.'

'*Miss Glyn took Doone without being paid* — and you let
her? That's charity, Maud. We're not beggars.'

'She didn't do it for nothing — it was to get Crystal,' but
suddenly a doubt rose in Ma. Was it really to get Doone? Ma
hastily put that thought away and, 'Does it matter so much?'
she asked Pa.

'I gave him a cricket bat.' Pa sounded dazed.

'He would much rather have had money for his dancing
shoes,' Crystal put in. She's trying to make things worse,
thought Ma, yet it was true; Doone's shoes had long been a
problem. 'You keep growing,' Ma upbraided him and he could
not wear Crystal's old ones; his feet were a different shape. Ma

94

had tried him in them once and Miss Glyn had been really angry. 'Never let a child wear another child's shoes. It's always wrong, but for a dancer it's criminal.'

'Dancing shoes!' Pa put his hand over his eyes as if he were trying to shut out a bad dream. Then he took it down. 'Doone didn't say anything.'

'He has learnt not to. The boys tease him enough already.'

'Why can't he be like other boys?'

'I don't know, but he isn't.'

'He's got to be.' Pa got up and strode up and down the room. 'Maud, half those boys at least grow up to be queers.'

'Nonsense, William. Look at Charles.'

'I don't know Charles – whoever he may be.'

'Natural as natural,' Ma declared, 'and those beautiful boys we saw today.'

'Beautiful. Ugh! No son of mine. . . .' Pa had to break off. Ma had never seen him as distressed.

'William dear. . . .'

'Don't "dear" me! First there was Mr Felix,' said Pa, 'but at least I paid him.'

'You – you didn't, William.' Better, thought Ma, to confess it all.

'I gave you the money every month.'

'I know, but he wouldn't take it, and as Miss Glyn said Crystal must have music lessons I paid Miss La Motte with it, so it amounts to the same thing, doesn't it?' asked Ma.

'It certainly does not.'

'I've told you, Mr Felix wouldn't take it.'

'Then Doone is not to go there any more.'

'Oh, William, don't be so angry.'

'Angry!' cried Pa. 'When you have fooled me, bamboozled me and gone behind my back? Shut me out from my own children? First it was Crystal – knowing all the time what she would be in for. Now it's Doone.'

'Well, he won't go to Miss Glyn's after the end of this term,' and, 'Oh, William, won't you *see*?' asked Ma. 'I couldn't tell you because I knew you would have stopped it all.'

'Indeed I would, and have you thought why?'

'Because you're prejudiced and ignorant,' flared Ma.

'Ignorant! It's you, Maud, who's ignorant of what your

children are or should be.'

'You say that! If you hadn't been too busy with your two shops to make time for your own children, you might have seen. . . .'

'It'll take more than two shops to support you, Madam, if you go on like this.'

It was the nearest in all their married life that Pa and Ma had come to having a real quarrel. Ma began to weep. 'I can't take any more.'

'Nor can I,' said Pa, 'but I suppose I'll have to.' He could not bear to see Ma cry. 'All right,' he said. 'All right. Do as you like.' He sat down wearily in his chair and let Crystal cover his face with kisses.

Doone had come in and, with consternation, had seen Pa turn his head away from Crystal's kisses. 'Do as you like.' Then he caught sight of Doone. 'Not you, my lad,' said Pa. 'You're finished.'

No dancing, no music, no Crystal.

It was strange how much Doone missed her; though she had often hurt him and bullied him, at least she spoke his language. Doone went into her room and looked at the smooth white bed, the dressing-table bare without its frills – Ma had only taken them away to wash and put on freshly when Crystal came back for weekends or the holidays. There was no daily sound of Crystal's shrill peremptory voice. She was in Queen's Chase, that enchanted place of dancing and music; Charles, too; and he, Doone, was not just left behind but banned.

'Now Crystal's gone,' Ma had told him, 'you won't be going to Miss Glyn's any more.'

Doone had blinked.

'There's no need now,' said Ma.

'There is, there is.' Doone was in a panic. 'How shall I go on dancing?'

'You'll have to put that out of your mind – music, too. Pa says so. Miss Glyn's been told, so has Mr Felix.'

'But . . . what'll I *do*?'

'Just get on with being at school and your games and that, like the other boys.'

'I'm not the other boys.' Doone said it helplessly yet with a certain dignity that made Ma feel guilty; but soon, as well as no Crystal, there was no Ma. In the middle of cooking Sunday dinner, she had felt faint. Pa and Will had just had time to help her to bed, leaving the boys open-mouthed, before she lost consciousness. She lay, her eyes shut, her face drained of all colour, for what seemed to them all an aeon, before she opened her eyes and whispered, 'Don't worry – it's just the strain.' That final battle for Crystal had worn Ma out more than the long years of toil. She had won but now, 'Can't', was all Ma would say. 'Can't any more.'

For years, from the time Will was born, the Pennys, every summer, had closed the shop and house and driven down in the van to Devon and the farm, but for the last three years Pa had not been able to come. 'You've all grown so expensive,' Pa told them but now it was to Porlock, to Uncle John and Aunt Mary, that he sent Ma. 'A long rest,' the doctor had said. 'No stress, no strain. Away from the family.'

'But how?' asked Ma. 'How can I go?'

'Will and I can manage,' Pa assured her, 'and the boys will help.' With one voice they promised Ma they would but, until the last minute, she went on with distracted instructions about washing socks and airing sheets, not leaving food in the refrigerator more than two days, making out shopping-lists.

'And what about our shop?' she had asked.

'Mrs Denning will come back. She's offered. Stop worrying, Maud,' ordered Pa, but even at the station Ma had given him a book of easy-to-cook recipes. 'We'll just have fry-ups,' said Pa when he got home.

'Or buy pizzas,' said Jim.

'Fish and chips,' said Tim.

'Or Chinese take-away,' said Hughie.

For a while it was fun being without Ma, but the fun soon wore off. Pa looked harried and grew more and more irritable; he missed Ma every minute of the day and could not sleep at night without her comfortable mound beside him in their big bed. Will became dictatorial, the boys rebellious. Doone, too, missed Ma. Though she was often so sharp with him, it was to Ma he always went as for granted, when he was cold or hungry, when a cut finger needed a plaster; he had only to come and sit by Ma to feel the reassuring rock of her presence;

while she was there, the world would not fall to pieces. After Beppo had gone, she had always come to tuck him up in bed. Doone did not know this was from that feeling of guilt. True, at first she had peremptorily turned the light off. This was another time Crystal, surprisingly, had intervened. 'He'll go to sleep much better, Ma, if you let him look at books.' Ma, too, always looked in on them before she went to bed herself, making sure they were safely in bed. Safe. That was Ma. In spite of this, Doone seemed strangely happy.

'No dancing, no music.' Doone had stood it as long as he could, but he was not a little boy now; he would soon be nine years old, and he knew he had to look after himself – no Crystal was there to open the way. He knew, too, that his vital self was in those very things Pa had forbidden – dancing and music. 'Very well,' said Doone to Doone, 'you'll have to make your own arrangements.'

Though Pa tried to look after them all equally, Doone, at a different school from the others, could not do what they did and it was difficult to keep track of him. 'What do you do when you come back from school?' Pa asked him.

'Usually play.' Pa was satisfied, but play meant a different thing for Pa than it did for Doone. For Doone it meant playing Mr Felix's piano.

At what would have been his Saturday music-lesson time, he had taken himself to Mr Felix's. He had not rung the bell or used his key, but sat on the doorstep hoping, and sure enough the third time Mr Felix came down and opened the door. 'It's no good, Doone,' said Mr Felix. 'I can't teach you.' He sounded not only sorry but also disgusted. 'I can't go against your father.'

No – but I can. Doone did not say it, but asked, 'Mr Felix, can I keep your key?'

The old man looked down on the boy and they understood one another. 'Yes, you have no alternative,' said Mr Felix. 'You know my times' – the times when he would be out. 'What you do with yours is your affair.'

When, next afternoon, Doone used his key, as soon as he touched the piano he knew what those long days of silence had meant; it was as if he had been a butterfly caught in a tight mesh and now was set free, able to fan his wings and fly.

98

Perhaps in that first hour of coming back, Doone played as he had not played before. Mr Felix had left music for him on the stand, music marked with written instructions and Doone, as he tried to follow them, had to be careful not to get too engrossed and overstay his hour; he had to be home by half-past five for tea. Once it was nearly six and Pa asked awkward questions; every time Doone came, he put his small offering – an apple, grapes, a banana – on the keyboard like a sign; when he came again, it had always disappeared.

He did not go on Tuesdays and Thursdays; on those afternoons he left school after school dinner as he and Crystal had always done – Ma had forgotten to tell Mrs Carstairs that Doone no longer needed to be let off for dancing, and nobody stopped him as he washed his face and hands, brushed his hair and picked up his bag with his dancing clothes and shoes in it. He caught the familiar train and presented himself at Miss Glyn's.

'I've come,' said Doone.

'But, Doone, your mother told me. . . .'

'Yes, I know,' said Doone, 'but I have made arrangements', and, as he saw Miss Glyn and Stella look at one another, 'Don't worry, it's all right,' he insisted, and, 'I'll go and change.'

'I ought to send him home,' said Miss Glyn. Then, 'Or ought I?'

Even more than with his music, it was bliss for Doone to be back in this, his element – that released butterfly again.

'We thought you'd left, like Sydney,' said Mark. 'He said he'd had enough.'

'I'll never have enough,' said Doone. He was not the youngest now; there were new boys: Giles, eight years old, and two smaller, Italian twins, Pietro and Guiseppi. Doone had to show them exercises and steps as Charles had shown him. 'Watch Doone,' Stella told them, and Mark and Sebastian looked at him with increased respect.

'He'll be here again on Saturday, Ennis,' said Stella.

'I'm sure he will.'

'You're not going to tell me to send him away.'

'I'm inclined to leave it to Doone,' Miss Glyn said slowly. In any case she had no choice. She was going with the Company to America next day.

'Is everything all right, Doone?' Will often asked.

'Quite all right,' answered Doone, but it was not quite. He was beginning to have difficulties. 'Stella,' he asked, 'Do you think Miss Glyn would let me play for some of the classes and pay me?' but Stella shook her head.

'What would happen to Miss La Motte and John? Besides, you haven't time.'

'Pa, can I do a newspaper round?'

'No, you can't.' Jim promptly interfered with that. 'I do it.'

'Could I help tidy the shop?'

'Well, Doone, that's Tim's task.'

'Would you pay me if I swept up the leaves in the courtyard?'

'Hughie does that.'

'What *can* I do?' asked Doone.

'Get lost,' said Hughie, and that was what Doone was beginning to feel – lost for ways and means, particularly means.

'Those shoes are far too tight,' said Stella. 'You mustn't wear them. You must have a new pair. You'll have to ask your father.'

Doone shook his head.

Stella noticed his clothes too; he and Crystal had always arrived with clean fresh leotards or briefs, singlets and socks. Now Doone's briefs looked dusty, his singlet and socks grey. 'While your mother's away,' said Stella, 'leave your dancing clothes here. I'll wash them with mine.'

'That would be nice,' Doone had said. 'You see, I'm not a very good washer'. He did not add, And I have to dry them in my bedroom where no one sees. Kind Stella, though, had to say, 'You must ask your father for the shoes. You must, Doone, or you can't dance.'

'Will, how can I earn some money?'

Will was surprised. 'You had a lot for your birthday.'

'Had' was the right word. 'I spent it.'

'On what?' On things Will would not have dreamt of: Underground tickets, white socks, a bun or a roll – dancing made a boy so hungry.

Will gave him a pound. 'That's not enough,' Doone cried in anguish.

'Give it back then,' and Will took it back.

Doone went and sat down on his bed to think. He thought and thought, then reluctantly went downstairs to the shop.

'Mr Penny,' said Mrs Denning. 'There's something I'm afraid I have to tell you.'

'Do you have to tell me *now*?' poor Pa asked. It was nine o'clock on Saturday morning when, as soon as the shop was opened, it would be packed. Pa had already had to think of the weekend and send Jim out shopping, set Tim to clean the house, Hughie the courtyard, and all of them had argued. 'Mrs Denning, does it have to be now?'

'Well, it's the end of the week,' said Mrs Denning. 'We shall have to tote up the takings, Mr Penny, and for some time now money has been missing from the till; not a great deal, but once it was three pounds. I couldn't account for it and thought I had made a mistake and, to save worrying you while things are so difficult with Mrs Penny away, I made it up, but when I came in today. . . .' Mrs Denning broke off, distressed.

'Today?'

'I hate to tell you, Mr Penny, but I caught Doone taking a five-pound note from the till.'

'Doone, did you take this?'

'Yes,' said Doone. 'I had to.'

He had been ready to go to London when Pa had called him down and taken him to Beppo's room behind the shop.

'You *had* to. Why?' bellowed Pa. 'I give you pocket money. Isn't that enough?'

'Not enough for what I need.' Doone did not mean it, but there was a suspicion of haughtiness in the way he said it and that finished Pa.

'I'll tell you what you need,' said Pa. 'Being cheeky and obstinate is one thing – stealing is another.'

'I *didn't* steal,' Doone protested. 'I only *borrowed* it.' But, 'Take down your pants,' was all Pa said. They were purple corduroy trousers that had once been Hughie's pride. Now Doone clutched them to him. 'No, Pa, no.'

'Take them down.' Pa was unbuckling his belt.

Because of his exasperating morning, because Ma's being away gave him too much to do and to worry about, besides the ache of missing her and his sleepless nights, Pa hit harder than he meant to do. Even loyal Mrs Denning pleaded, 'Stop, Mr Penny, please, stop' but, 'Leave me to manage my own children,' Pa shouted at her and, when he had finished, 'That'll teach you.' Then, 'Pull up your trousers,' he panted and strode into the shop. Doone was just able to walk to the corner where Beppo's bed had been and which was now filled with potato-sacks; he fell on the sacks and lay spreadeagled, numb with shock and pain.

Presently Mrs Denning tiptoed in. 'I'll bring you some fresh orange juice and sugar,' but Doone shook his head. When she had gone, he stood painfully up, tidied himself, then put his hand under the bottom sack, which was where he kept his money, and hobbled as fast as he could to the station.

When he arrived at the school, class had begun, but there was Miss Glyn outside the office. 'You're back!' It seemed too good to be true; mysteriously it was Miss Glyn he had to see, not sympathetic Stella.

'I flew in yesterday. Doone, what's the matter?'

Doone had begun to quiver from head to foot; the quivering turned to shudders that shook him, and he felt such a welling-up in his throat that he knew he was going to sob. 'I'm sorry . . . I'm late,' he managed to say, 'but I can't dance,' and, in a crescendo, 'Pa beat me. He beat me – Pa!' The sobs burst.

Miss Glyn drew him into the office, but the desperate cry went on. 'Pa beat me,' and, 'What can I do? What can I . . .?' Miss Glyn held him tightly.

'She's always so remote,' Ma used to complain.

'I think teachers of ballet have to be,' Miss Glyn would have said. 'They can't teach if they get too emotionally involved.' She was always telling Stella this, Stella 'who plunges right in', said Miss Glyn, but now she held Doone close until the sobs subsided; gently she let him go, tidying his hair. 'Tell me about it,' she said. A torrent came out, from the time Pa and Ma had quarrelled over Crystal. It was an incoherent jumble but Miss Glyn seemed able to understand; it ended again with that despairing, 'What can I do?'

'For now,' said Miss Glyn, 'you'll stay and watch the rest of the class. You're too sore to dance.' Sore outside and inside, she might have said but, 'Come, we'll wash your face, then you can go in and watch. You'll like that. Charles is here.'

'Charles?'

'He's home for the weekend and came in to see us.'

'He mustn't see I've been crying.'

'He won't when you've washed your face. Meanwhile, I'll have a good think, and when you come back I'll tell you what we'll do.'

Charles did see the swollen eyes and stains of tears but said nothing about them, was only extra kind and, after class, told Doone about Queen's Chase, quite differently from Crystal; nor did he laugh when Doone asked, '*Is* there a castle?'

'It's far more beautiful than a castle and think, Doone, we dance every day. The only thing,' said Charles, 'is I'm so bad.'

'*You* bad?'

'You should see some of the others, the older ones.' Charles's eyes were looking at visions. 'It makes you want to work and work.'

'I'll come there.' Doone was fired, then he remembered and, 'I don't see how,' he said. 'I don't see how I can go on dancing.' The tears were coming back, even though Charles would see them but, 'Wait,' said Charles. 'Wait. Miss Glyn will arrange something, you'll see.'

'Doone, I want you to be brave,' said Miss Glyn, 'and come here as usual but not on Tuesday – on Wednesday. Wednesday is early-closing day in Pilgrim's Green, isn't it?'

Doone could not see what that had to do with it, but he said, 'Yes, Miss Glyn.'

'Here's the money for your fare so you won't get into trouble and I'll see about your shoes. When you come, I want you to play for the class and perhaps play something for the boys – they have never really heard you. Then you can join the others.'

'Yes, Miss Glyn, but – what should I do about Papa?' Doone was recovered enough to remember that Pa was Papa when they talked to Miss Glyn. 'What'll I do?'

'Nothing,' said Miss Glyn. 'Leave Papa to me.'

*   *   *

103

Usually on Wednesday afternoons, as they were shut, both Pa's shops had a thorough cleaning, but this Wednesday he seemed so worn out that Will said, 'Put your feet up, Pa. I'll see to it.' Truth to tell, Pa had hardly slept since Saturday.

'What's the matter with Doone?' Will had asked. 'I gave him a good hiding,' Pa made himself boast, but Will had said at once, 'Are you sure it was good?' and Pa found he was not at all sure. He could not forget the sight of Doone's white face and of him lying, face downwards, on the sacks and, too, that he ran away – away, not back to him to ask forgiveness. 'He'll get over it,' said Pa.

'He won't, not Doone', and it was true that Doone had become even more silent and secret, not cowed but 'proud' was the only word Pa could think of. 'He won't hold it against you' – of that Will was sure – 'but it's a pity you did it,' which was no comfort to Pa, but now Will brisked up the fire and brought his slippers. 'The boys won't be in till late. There's a Rugby match on. Read the paper and have a snooze and forget about all of us,' said Will and Pa was doing exactly that when the door-bell rang.

'Pa, it's Miss Glyn. Miss Ennis Glyn.'

'Miss . . .!' Pa struggled to his feet, clutching the newspaper with one hand; he knew his shirt buttons were undone, his tie hanging half-down, that he was in his slippers and his hair, what was left of it, on end.

'She's on the stairs,' hissed Will. 'Quick, let me tidy you up.'

Expertly he took away the paper, buttoned Pa's shirt, pulled his tie up and smoothed his hair. Then, 'Come in, Miss Glyn,' he called. 'This is my father.'

'Good afternoon, Mr Penny, I'm afraid I have disturbed you.' Pa had seen Miss Glyn at the annual displays but never as close as she was now; he had not realised how melodiously she spoke, nor how elegant she was. It was not that she was beautiful or expensively dressed; it was her poise, the way she moved her hands and turned her head with its brown chestnut hair – bronze, thought Pa – coiled into a chignon. 'May I sit down?' asked Miss Glyn.

Will pushed a chair forward. 'Please,' and, as she sat down, 'You'll want to be quiet. I'll go and get on with the shop.'

Will, Will, don't leave me, Pa wanted to cry; he was

104

sweating, but Miss Glyn began by talking of everyday things. How was Mrs Penny? Had they heard from Crystal? Was she happy? Was it true she had four older brothers? Was Will his son? Then she admired Ma's chrysanthemums, 'I've seldom seen such lovely ones,' and Pa found himself saying, 'Of course, being in the trade, I have a pull. If you're ever wanting pot plants, Miss Glyn, I'd be happy. . . .'

'Thank you,' and, 'She meant it,' Pa told Will afterwards, but then a little silence had fallen until she said, 'I expect you know why I have come.'

'No.' Pa was genuinely puzzled.

'Then you should know why. Mr Penny, have you and your wife ever thought seriously about Doone?'

'Doone? Of course we have.'

'Compared to Crystal?'

'Crystal's different.'

'Yes, quite different,' and, 'I'm going to ask you to do something, Mr Penny – to come with me.'

'If it's for Doone and dancing – no, Miss Glyn. In any case, I'm not coming anywhere for a boy who steals from his own father!' but, before Miss Glyn could answer, Will came running up the stairs.

'Pa, look what I've found.' It was a sheaf of little pieces of paper torn from an exercise-book, each with a date and a sum of money.

Pa. IOU £3. I'll pay you back when I'm famous. Signed, *Doone Penny.*

Pa. IOU . . . pay you back, Doone Penny.

IOU . . . Doone Penny.

There were at least a dozen, all for the same amount of pence. 'Why pence,' asked Will, 'and all the same?'

'A child's fare from your station to mine,' said Miss Glyn.

'So. . . .' Pa sat staring at the pieces of paper. 'So. . . .'

'So he wasn't stealing,' said Miss Glyn. 'At least, not to his way of thinking.'

'I see. He left all these for me to find underneath the till, and I beat him. I beat him!'

'I know you did. I saw the welts.'

'*Welts?*' Pa was horrified.

'Welts,' Miss Glyn said plainly. 'A child's skin is tender,

Mr Penny.'
'Don't!' said Pa.
'Over the money,' said Miss Glyn, 'I'm sure Doone will pay you back a hundred times over. Now, please, Mr Penny, will you come with me – and please come, too,' she said to Will.

In one of the classrooms of the Ennis Glyn School a glassed slit had been made in the wall so that anyone wanting to watch a class or a dancer could sit and watch unseen. 'If they know they're being watched, they can get self-conscious,' Miss Glyn explained to Pa. 'If Doone knew you were here, he probably wouldn't dance at all. See if you can find him,' said Miss Glyn.

The class was in full swing. Four boys, all in black briefs, white singlets, white socks and shoes, were working at the barre. Pa and Will looked along them but none of them was Doone. The teacher, a young fair-haired woman, dressed in black, too, was calling out what to Pa were incomprehensible words. 'We use French for the names of ballet steps and exercises,' explained Miss Glyn. 'These that they're doing now are *grands battements*.'

'And the children understand?' Pa marvelled.

'They learn to.'

Erect at the barre, feet tightly closed together, the boys began, in time with the music, to throw the outer leg, fully stretched, upwards as high as it would go, then closed it tightly against the other foot; up it went, front, side, back.

'But Doone's not here.'

'He is,' and Will whispered, 'Pa, he's playing. Do you realise? That's Doone at the piano.'

'It can't be.' But it was Doone, sitting on the piano stool made higher by two telephone directories – he no longer needed four. He was following the teacher. As the music came clearly – and beautifully, thought his astounded father and brother – from Doone's small hands, she counted, 'And one and two, three, four, five and six and seven, eight, nine, ten.' The exercises changed and there was a quick beat, 'and one and one and one and one'. Then, the boys left the barre and came into the centre, 'for what we call *adage*,' and a slow rippling melody began.

'Doone can play like *that*. I never dreamed. . . .'

106

'He is extremely musical, but we only let him play to show you. Now just watch him dance.'

Doone had got down from the stool; a woman took his place as he joined the class, and Miss Glyn said: 'They are going to practise their jumps.'

First small ones – simple changes – then higher, the feet beating. Then higher still, Doone seemed to spring as naturally as he breathed, out-jumping the other boys. 'And remember,' said Miss Glyn, 'he's a year younger than Mark, almost two years younger than Sebastian. Now watch this.'

They were coming from the corner one by one. Not the little boys but Mark, Sebastian and Doone. With heads turned over their right shoulder, and focusing on the opposite corner, the boys turned swiftly from one foot to the other, eight times before stopping, feet apart, and spinning round twice on one leg in a pirouette.

They repeated it from the opposite corner, each boy running into position without being told, ready to follow, each finishing with a double pirouette on the last and taking his stance. The boy called Mark wobbled precariously on this, then, '*Grands jetés en avant*,' ordered Stella.

'A *jeté* is a leap,' explained Miss Glyn.

'Careful how you land,' called Stella.

In two leaps Doone had covered the distance. 'Do you think one of your "proper" boys could do that?' Miss Glyn could not resist the little taunt. Pa shook his head and passed his hand in front of his eyes as if he could not believe it. 'I never saw Crystal, or any of the others, dance like that.'

'Well, Doones don't grow on blackberry-bushes, Mr Penny,' said Miss Glyn.

'Maudie, that boy's worth twenty Crystals.'

'*William!*'

Ma had come back, rested and well, but now was having shock after shock.

The greatest shock was the reversal in Pa. 'Talk of a right about-face!' Ma said to Will.

Pa was so strangely humble. 'You were quite right when you said I was prejudiced and ignorant.'

Stella had rubbed that in. 'So you've come to see your boy

dance at last, Mr Penny,' she said when Miss Glyn brought Pa into the classroom; he had been feeling remorseful enough when he saw Doone's eyes widen with surprise, then fear as he quailed and took refuge behind Stella. 'I never dreamed. . . .'

'Because you never looked,' said indignant Stella.

At that Pa had raised his head. 'You must remember, Miss Stella,' he had said, 'this is all very difficult for me. I have four other boys. They were babies, grew older, went to school; gave us bad times with things like measles, throwing a ball through a neighbour's window – Jim was bit by a dog – they got into mischief, made a lot of din, but that was normal,' said Pa. 'If I took them to a football match on a Saturday as a treat, or to the seaside or a pantomime at Christmas, that was enough and I could understand – but these two! Dancing lessons, music lessons, shoes, clothes, fares. With Crystal, it grew up with her, so I kind of didn't notice – besides, she's a girl – but Doone! I knew he wanted books . . .' Pa spoke as if books were dangerous territories and, 'I don't know where people like us got him from,' said Pa.

Stella said no more but made the boys bow to Pa and Will, the bow with which boys – for girls it is a curtsy – thank their teachers at the end of the class and with which one day, for some of them, they would thank their audiences for applause, coming on stage in front of the curtain. They pointed their feet to the left, brought them both together and bowed from the waist; again to the right. Pa had never been bowed to before and he felt a strange spring of joy, partly of relief because Doone was not a little thief, partly from this new pride in him, yet there was something more; it was as if he, Pa, had shed a heavy armour of – of obstinacy, Pa told himself – and, 'That boy's going to have every chance, Maud, every chance. Which reminds me. . . .'

'Doone tells me he hasn't had a piano lesson for two months,' Miss Glyn had said.

'Because of me.' Pa had reddened and, 'I tried to put that right,' he told Ma now. 'I wrote to Mr Felix and sent him a cheque.'

'He sent it back?' guessed Ma.

'No. He hasn't answered,' said Pa. 'Odd.'

*   *   *

It was the Sunday before Christmas. Crystal, who was home, had taken Doone's new status with calmness. 'It's time Pa understood,' she told Ma and, 'Of course he thinks it's wonderful but, remember, Miss Glyn and her Stella have always had a thing about Doone. Well, they haven't many boys. . . . *We* only have the cream,' and, 'When you go back, give my love to Ennis Glyn,' she condescended to say to Doone. 'I hope she doesn't let Stella push you *too* far. These smaller schools so often do,' said all-knowledgeable Crystal.

Doone kept out of her way and, that afternoon, she was alone with Ma and Pa; dinner had been cleared away and they were sitting comfortably by the fire – 'for a few minutes' peace', as Ma said – when Will came up from the shop. 'It's Mrs Sherrin. She wants to see you, Ma and Pa.'

'Mrs Sherrin?' Ma reared herself up in her chair. 'She's not coming up here,' but Pa had got to his feet. 'Wait, Maud. For Mrs Sherrin to come it must be something grave,' and he said, 'I think it's to do with Mr Felix.'

It was. 'The people in the flat below found him at the foot of the stairs last week,' said Mrs Sherrin. 'They took him to hospital. He died this morning.'

'Died!' Ma said it in a whisper.

'Yes. I wouldn't have come,' said Mrs Sherrin, 'but I thought I should tell you at once so you can break it to Doone before he discovers it himself. It seems he has a key and has been letting himself in to practise.'

'We didn't know.'

'I think it was a pact between Doone and Mr Felix.'

'Crystal, fetch Doone.'

'You said "no lessons", Pa, but you didn't say no practice,' Doone defended himself but he, himself, had been uneasy. He had rung the bell to tell Mr Felix his wonderful news about the dancing but there had been no answer; when he had gone in to practise on Friday, the fruit he had taken to Mr Felix was still on the keyboard and the apples had gone brown. The room had looked dustier than ever and the fire was cold. On Saturday afternoon the fruit had disappeared as had the dirty cups and saucers; the books were piled tidily, the grate emptied; the whole room was clean and the piano lid was shut. There was a smell of dankness as if the flat had been shut, too, and it was so cold that Doone had kept his anorak on and had had to blow on his fingers.

Now, 'You have to give Mrs Sherrin that key,' Pa told him. 'But. . . .'

'You can't go there any more,' said Ma. 'Mr Felix has gone away.'

'Gone away?' Doone lifted his head and looked at Ma. 'Mr Felix wouldn't have gone without saying goodbye.'

'He had to.' Mrs Sherrin came forward, put her hands on Doone's shoulders and told him the exact truth. 'Mr Felix was taken ill last Monday. I was with him when he died just an hour ago.'

'While we were having dinner?' That seemed suddenly terrible to Doone, that they were eating while Mr Felix. . . . Doone swallowed, sick at heart, but Pa was saying, 'Mrs Sherrin, *you* haven't had anything.' She was pale and shivering. 'Maudie. . . .'

'Of course, I'll make some tea. The kettle's hot.' Ma got up, but, 'I'll do it,' said Crystal.

'Just a cup,' said Mrs Sherrin and when it came she drank it gratefully. 'I've been at the hospital all day.'

'Wasn't there anyone of his own?'

'No one. There were very few people Mr Felix allowed to know him,' and Mrs Sherrin spoke plainly. 'So it was a terrible loss for him when you stopped Doone's lessons.'

'You can't blame Mr Penny . . .,' Ma began but, 'I'm not blaming anyone,' said Mrs Sherrin. 'You did what you thought was for the best.' A little colour had come into her cheeks from the tea, and she stood up. 'Doone,' she said, 'your father's right. I must ask you for that key.'

Doone took the key out of his trouser pocket, but his fingers tightened on it. 'Couldn't I . . . couldn't I have a last play?' he asked.

Mrs Sherrin, Ma and Pa looked at one another; Pa nodded, and, 'Very well,' said Mrs Sherrin.

'Just for half an hour,' Ma put in.

'Then perhaps you would let him bring the key to me,' said Mrs Sherrin.

Again Pa nodded. 'All right, boy,' he said.

It was not all right. Quite why, Crystal did not know, but

she followed him downstairs and found Doone standing in the hall. A look at his stricken face, the small shivers that were shaking him was enough and, 'You're scared,' said Crystal. She found her coat, cap and gloves. 'I'll come with you.' She could tell by his eyes how grateful he was but he was still cautious. 'You won't say it's shabby and dirty?'

'I won't even come into the room,' said Crystal. 'I'll wait on the landing or stairs.'

'And you won't tell Ma.'

'Who do you think I am?'

Doone could have said, 'Crystal – Crystal who breaks promises as easily as she makes them,' but not now, thought Doone. This was the Crystal who, once or twice before, had been suddenly, unexpectedly, kind. She did not even say he was silly when she saw the little punnet that, from habit, he had filled with fruit to take with him.

Outside, Pilgrim's Green was like a Christmas card; the sky was still blue, the sun flooding the town with winter sunshine. The green was powdered with snow and, though the pond had frozen into thin ice-patches, the ducks were quacking lustily. A robin sang; the streets were bustling with people carrying parcels, carrier-bags and bunches of holly and, in almost every window, there was a lit Christmas tree. 'I don't believe anyone could be dead on an afternoon like this,' said Crystal and Doone looked up at her with a gleam of hope, but when they came into the house it was hushed and cold, and Doone did not protest when Crystal took his punnet from him as they went silently upstairs.

The familiar room was as Doone had seen it on Saturday; if Crystal had come in, she would have thought it shabby, but it was clean, tidy and had been emptied of papers, tins, coals, kindling – as if Mr Felix were being cleared away, thought Doone with a catch of the heart – but not all of Mr Felix; the piano was as big and shining as ever and, as soon as Doone opened the lid and touched a key, the deep note answered and he seemed to hear Mr Felix's voice, too: 'Begin with the scherzo. One, two . . . three, four and. . . .'

Crystal had perched herself on a chest on the landing and had begun to eat the fruit when the music began.

Pa had said how good Doone was, 'over and over again',

111

until they had all grown impatient, and Crystal had expected something of the kind she had heard at Queen's Chase where some of the boys and girls played the piano well, but this run of quick sure notes, their speed and firmness, came as such a surprise that she stood up, a half-eaten orange in her hand. It couldn't be Doone. Someone else must be playing. Perhaps Mr Felix was not dead, perhaps he had come back and, for a moment she felt her scalp prickle under her hair, her skin goose-fleshing but, as she peeped round the door, she could see Doone, and only Doone, in his old anorak that had belonged to Hughie; Doone, sitting at the piano, his face rapt, his hands that Crystal knew as small and grubby, drawing that power of music and beauty from a piano of such magnificence that she was awed.

Crystal did not know, or care, about music except as it affected dancing – Doone, on a different scale, was at one with her on this – she could not tell when Doone made mistakes, as he did when the music ran away with him. Mr Felix would have stopped him abruptly. She only knew that Doone played as she had never heard a child play before, as she had not dreamed a child could play – and she stood spellbound, amazed, by the door, as Doone played on and on.

The Town Hall clock struck four. The half-hour was over and Crystal went in. With a new respect she put her hand on Doone's shoulder. 'Doone, it's time.' He took his hands down and sat still on the stool, his head bowed. Crystal gently closed the piano lid.

Stella was worried about Doone. 'He's getting so thin.'

'He always sparks up when he comes to class,' said Ennis Glyn.

'He would, but he's unhappy through and through.'

'At least it isn't my fault this time,' said Ma. She was still haunted by that persistent child voice that had said, 'Where's Beppo? Where's Beppo?' – 'until I was nearly driven mad,' said Ma – but Doone's silence was more haunting still. 'It's like living with a little ghost,' and, 'Mr Felix was an old man,' she told Doone, trying to be kind. 'I think he was very very tired.'

'Why should he be?' asked Doone. 'He didn't do anything different.'

'Old men are tired,' Ma went on as if Doone had not spoken. 'You must try to put Mr Felix out of your mind.'

'Out of my mind!' Doone looked at Ma as if she had committed blasphemy.

All the same, he pondered over what she had said. 'Will,' Doone asked when he was alone with Will, 'did Beppo die?'

'Beppo? I thought you had forgotten him long ago.'

But Doone shook his head.

'I nearly had, but now every time I do a flip-flap or a handstand or a jump. . . .' and Doone asked again, 'Is he dead?'

'I don't know,' said Will, 'but why?'

'Beppo's gone and . . . and Mr Felix . . .' It was still difficult to speak of Mr Felix. 'He's gone, too, but they haven't gone. There's bits of Beppo in me, lots – lots – of Mr Felix,' and, as if Doone suddenly realised what Mr Felix's going really meant, he burst out in desolation with the old cry, 'What am I going to do?' and, 'Pa chose this time, this very time,' Will told Kate, 'to let out to the boys about Doone.'

It was a pity. The boys knew Mr Felix had died. 'Doone's terribly upset,' Ma had told them. 'Don't tease him,' and over Christmas, in their way, they had tried to be kind – even Hughie – and, on the first Saturday of term, Jim had said at breakfast, 'You can come with us today if you like, Doone.'

'No, he can't,' said Pa. 'He has a dancing lesson,' and, looking round at their surprised faces, 'Crystal's not the only one in this family who dances, I can tell you.'

'But – Doone's a boy!'

'And don't boys dance?' All that Pa had said on that very point should have echoed in his ear, but he chose not to hear. 'How do you think,' he asked, 'that a ballerina could dance, or ballet exist, without men dancers?'

They had, of course, never thought, but Pa went heedlessly on, 'You don't know a thing about your brother,' he declared and the damage was done.

> 'See me dance the polka
> See me skim the ground. . . .
> I'm a marionette,
> See me pirouette.'

113

Every time Doone went out or came in, he met that barrage. 'Sissy. Sissy. Pouffda!'

'Teacher's pet.' Hughie caught him on the courtyard doorstep.

'Teacher's pet yourself,' said Doone, which, if he had known it, was completely on the mark; Hughie had a good deal of Crystal's charm, curly gold hair, blue eyes and the same innocently appealing look. 'That he's the worst little rascal in Pilgrim's Green has nothing to do with it,' said Will and had to laugh.

'Teacher's pet yourself.'

'Cheeky, aren't you?' Jim, Tim and the Gang closed in. Tim gave Doone a hard punch. Doone punched back. 'Want to fight?' asked Jim.

'I can't fight you all,' said Doone. 'I'll fight one of you.'

'You'll fight who we choose,' said Jim. 'At him, boys,' but just then Will drove into the yard and at once saw what was happening. He jumped from the van and, 'No, you don't,' said Will. 'That's not fair, you scum. Doone, you'll fight Hughie. You lot make a ring.'

'Yoicks!' said Hughie. Neither he nor any of the other boys was prepared for what happened next.

Hughie was thirteen to Doone's ten, but he was a plump boy, the one who was fondest of Ma's cakes and pies; he had no idea that Doone's slimness and smallness were built of muscle, firm and trained; that he could twist and turn with the quickness of a cat and that his fists were like small hammers. In no time at all Hughie was on the ground groaning, while Doone, panting a little, stood over him. 'Strewth! Blimey!' said the boys, astonished and, 'Anyone else you'd like to fight?' Will asked Doone as a buzz of approval went up. 'And everything might have stopped,' Will told Kate, 'if it hadn't been for that old idiot, Pa.'

He had heard the noise and came quickly out of the shop. 'What the hell do you think you're doing?' he roared at the boys.

'It's all right,' said Will but Pa had taken in Doone's dishevelled jersey and hair; a mark was beginning to show on his cheek and, 'Your hands! Show me your hands. Your

114

knuckles,' cried Pa. Doone reluctantly showed them; they looked worse than they were – they were covered in blood. It was Hughie's blood, not Doone's, where Doone's fist had caught his mouth, but one knuckle was split where it had hit a tooth and, 'This evening I'm taking you, or was supposed to be taking you, to arrange about piano lessons,' scolded Pa. 'How can you play like *that*?'

Doone looked at his knuckle perplexed; it was beginning to be sore, but not as sore and dismayed as he was himself when Pa went blundering on. 'Don't you know by this time,' he said to the boys, 'that your brother has a gift?'

'Pa, I don't want piano lessons,' but, 'Gifts,' Pa had corrected himself. 'He's not the same as you are. You've got to treat him differently.'

'I am treating you differently, Doonie darling,' and at tea, under the table, Jim ground his heel into Doone's toes.

It went on all week. 'Come and play football, Doone. We'll buy you a fluffy ball.'

'Mustn't bruise his precious little hands,' and again,

> 'I'm a marionette,
> See me pirouette.'

'Run and tell Pa, grease rat.'

It culminated at another Sunday dinner. 'Don't use your fork, Doone, it might prick you.' The double joke, which Pa and Ma had no idea of, made the boys fall about in their chairs laughing. Then, as Doone tried to eat, every time he lifted his fork, Jim, who was sitting next to him, jerked his elbow so that he missed his mouth and the food spattered.

'Jim, let the poor child eat,' commanded Ma.

'He doesn't like his food, Ma. Steak and kidney pudding's *far* too coarse for him,' and Jim put on a falsetto voice, 'Can I tempt you, Doone, to a little roast pheasant?'

'Or a teeny sip of pink champagne?'

'Shut *up*!' said Doone.

'Temper! Temper! Tut tut!'

'Pa,' Doone appealed desperately.

'Mustn't be teased – mustn't.'

115

'Miss Glyn's little petty mustn't be teased.'

'Run and tell her, darling,' and Hughie chanted: 'Sneak, sneak, your pants leak.'

'Hughie! At the table! Be quiet, all of you!' but before Ma could say any more, Tim had jeered, 'Pity you can't run and tell old scarecrow Felix.'

'You'll not speak of the dead like that,' Pa had begun but, at Mr Felix's name, Doone stood up, his eyes blazing. 'You're hyenas!' He had remembered Mr Felix's words. 'That's what he called you and that's what you are. Hyenas – running about in packs and laughing at what you don't know. Hyenas!' And he took his plate of steak and kidney pudding, potatoes, cabbage, gravy and flung it straight into Tim's face.

'Taking notice is the worst thing you can do.' Will went to see Doone in his room where he had taken refuge.

'It's worst already,' said Doone, and Will had to admit it was.

'He won't speak and he won't play.' It was Pa who came to Miss Glyn, not she to him. 'I took him to a piano teacher Mrs Sherrin recommended.'

'Judith?'

'Yes. He wouldn't even sit on the piano stool. What would you do, Miss Glyn?'

'For the present, leave him alone.'

'That's what Mrs Penny says.'

'She's wise.'

'But – he'll lose all he's got.'

'I don't think he will. If you agree, I'll suggest to him he comes here an extra afternoon a week and plays for the babies' class – our youngest children. I'll pay him – yes, that's quite fair – and nothing could teach him rhythm – and patience – better than that, *and* it will keep him in practice.'

'And then?'

'Then we'll see,' and Ennis Glyn quoted softly: ' "A star danced when I was born." '

'I beg your pardon,' said Pa. 'What did you say?'

'Nothing,' or everything, thought Ennis Glyn.

Just four days later the telephone rang for Ma; she answered it

116

in the shop, came upstairs to the sitting-room and sat down heavily. 'Believe it or not,' she told the family, 'Doone's been offered a part on television.'

'All of ten minutes,' Miss Glyn had said – the call was from her. The theatre school where she had sent Valerie needed a boy, nine to ten years old, who could play the piano to a high standard, 'a boy not too tall, preferably dark-haired. In fact, Doone.'

The film was a documentary: 'The life of a composer called Debussy,' said Ma. 'It seems he was a strange dark man – which was why they want a dark-haired boy – and wrote strange music.'

'It's strange, but I like it,' said Doone. 'Mr Felix played me some.' As Miss Glyn had said, Doone was to make only a brief appearance. 'All the same he has to have a licence,' said Ma, which sounded important. Pa had to sign it.

The boy Debussy had to walk down an alleyway – 'It's supposed to be in Paris' – walk as if he were dreaming. 'He does that all the time,' said Ma. Boys threw stones at him – 'Well, they do,' Doone could have said – and he had to escape by dodging behind a street barrow. 'That will be shot in some town with cobbled streets. 'We needn't go to Paris,' the director, Giles Hereward, had told Miss Glyn. 'Then there'll be a studio scene for the piano; he'll have to play for perhaps a minute. Can he take direction?'

'Yes.' Miss Glyn said it positively. It was she who had taken Doone for the screen test. 'At most, two days' shooting,' she told Pa and Ma, 'and perhaps a day's recording, so Doone can spare the time.'

Spare the time to go on television! Ma was astonished, but that matter-of-fact way was how Miss Glyn treated it, as did Doone. He was the least excited of the family; it was simply part of his life.

'But what was it *like*, Doone? What did you do?'

'I did it,' said Doone.

'Ar – come on!'

'Well, there was this nice man, Giles,' Doone made an effort, 'and cameras and lights and things, but the set was nice, a sort of study with pretence books, but the piano was real, an upright. I had to play the beginning of *Clair de Lune*. It's

117

lovely, really like moonlight.'

'Never mind what you had to play. What was it *like*? What did you wear?'

He was a nineteenth-century boy in breeches, a tunic, buckled shoes. Ma could describe it minutely; it was she who had gone with Doone, but with the now familiar pang, 'I would have thought if anyone should have been on television it would have been Crystal.'

'She wouldn't be allowed to,' said Will. 'You know her ballet people won't let them do anything outside.'

That consoled Ma and she had to confess it had been glorious to be fetched by a studio car and an uniformed chauffeur and be driven to the village where they were shooting and where Doone had to do his first day; to have a special seat; to be allowed to look through a camera, watch the lights, the sound boom, the continuity girl and the make-up man who kept on dabbing Doone's face. 'He did very well,' she told the boys. Then, 'What was it you said to Mr Giles about the stones?' she asked Doone.

'You needn't be scared,' Giles had told him. 'We'll see the stones won't hurt you,' and, 'Don't worry,' Doone had said. 'I'm used to it. Sand and gravel are worse. Sand stings.'

'Was that true about the stones?' Ma had asked on the way home. 'Is it the boys who throw them at you? Jim . . . Tim . . . Hughie?'

'And the Gang, Chuck, Thomas. . . .' Doone said it as a matter of course.

'This never happened with Crystal. Doone, you cause nothing but trouble', and Ma sighed.

That hurt even more than the stones and Ma, too, made a mistake. 'Boys, you're not to touch Doone.'

There were plenty of things they were able to do without touching Doone; they took his dancing socks and briefs out of his case and sewed them up; took his schoolbooks out of his satchel and put in a dead rabbit that Tim had filched from the butcher. They still threw stones, gravel, sand and mud. The worst day of all was when they put dog dirt in his dancing shoes. 'You'll have to tell your father,' Stella had said.

'I can't.'

'Then I will.'

118

'Please, Stella, don't. It'll only make it worser.'

'Ennis, won't you go and see Mr Penny?'

'I think not,' Miss Glyn had said. 'If Doone can weather this, we'll really know what he is made of.'

The Debussy was shown and there came an immediate lull.

'Our brother's on telly,' Jim, Tim, Hughie were boasting.

'Go on!'

'He is.'

'That's likely.'

'It's true.'

'Crap!'

''S true, and he plays the piano in it.'

'Like at the Albert Hall?'

'Yes,' which was not true.

Pa had worried about that. 'Doone hasn't played for weeks, and this about the moon sounds a difficult piece.'

'Miss La Motte is taking him through it, and. . . .' Miss Glyn paused. 'You don't know how lucky Doone is. They've gone to the very top and the great pianist, Lötte von Heusen will be playing the Debussy music in the film. The actor, of course, will simply mime.'

'So it's only Doone who'll act and play.' Pa was proud until 'Will he be able to?' he asked anxiously.

'Miss von Heusen has kindly agreed to coach him.'

'Not like that, Um Göttes Willen!' Lötte von Heusen had cried when Doone first played her his part of Clair de Lune. 'Not like that!' Then, remembering he was only ten years old, 'My little man, we don't want to make poor Debussy turn in his grave.'

It was an unfortunate beginning. Doone was immediately stiff and pale. 'Mr Felix wouldn't turn in his grave. That's how he played it.'

'Ah!' Lötte von Heusen remembered what Ennis Glyn had told her and, 'Mr Felix — your teacher. I beg your pardon, Doone.'

No grown-up had begged Doone's pardon before and he began to warm to this great piano lady — it seemed she was not just Miss von Heusen, but a baroness of whom his loved Ennis Glyn was fond, and who had come to the dancing school on

119

purpose to meet him where he could feel at home. 'A great privilege,' Miss Glyn had said – three words Doone would come to know well.

'Perhaps Mr Felix did not play much of Debussy,' said the Baroness – Doone had been told to call her 'Baroness'. 'No pianist can play every composer. Suppose we try another way. Listen.' Doone had to admit Mr Felix had never played like that. When she had finished, the Baroness lifted her hands from the keys and looked into his face. 'Beautiful, hein?'

Doone nodded; he could not speak. The Baroness began to chuckle. Chuckle! Doone was astounded. 'You are such a little solemn!' said the Baroness and Doone found he was laughing, too.

The Baroness was jolly – a strange quality in a musician; she was also impressive; large, high-complexioned, her white upswept hair held by a diamond comb, her clothes rich and sweeping; she wore a great many rings and would discard them in a glittering heap at the end of the piano, which she had only to touch to show her difference from other pianists, 'and this is on our old piano,' said Stella, and told Doone, 'Lötte von Heusen has a Blüthner concert grand. It goes everywhere with her.'

'Even to Australia and America.' Doone was learning about Lötte von Heusen.

'Even to Australia and America, and she takes her own tuner.'

'Baroness,' Doone asked, 'is a Blüthner better than a Steinway?' The big face looked down into the small one and perhaps divined the loss that lay behind the question, because, 'Nothing could be better than a Steinway,' said the Baroness. 'I think you used to play one. Yes?'

'Yes.' She had spoken so gently that Doone was able to confide what he had not confided to anybody. 'When I'm grown up and famous, Baroness, I shall find my Steinway and buy it, and bring it back to Mr Felix's rooms and go and live there. Of course,' he added, 'I'll have to get the money first.'

'Of course,' said the Baroness, 'and the first step is to get our Debussy right. Take the opening eight bars. . . .'

When it came to music the Baroness was anything but jolly. Doone was corrected, 'and corrected and corrected – and

120

corrected,' he told Pa. There was to be no more playing for dancing classes while the film was on. 'It keeps you alert, I know, but gets you into bad ways. You will think only of the music, Doone.'

'Would Baroness von Heusen teach Doone?' Ma asked Miss Glyn.

'Mrs Penny! Lötte von Heusen teaches pianists, not small boys.'

The first time Ma heard Doone play was in the film studio, with the same effect as with Crystal. 'Who's that playing? It can't be Doone.' In the visitors' gallery she could see the set on television, Doone at a piano in a book-lined room but, 'It can't be Doone' and, 'Who is playing?' She asked one of the lighting crew. 'It must be someone else – Miss von Heusen?'

'Miss von Heusen?' The man laughed. 'It's your son – go and look.'

Ma tiptoed round the gallery, looked down and there was Doone on the set alone; she could see the Baroness and Mr Giles standing on the floor, listening, watching, while Doone played as Ma, like Crystal, had not heard a child play, had not dreamed a child could play and, 'Mr Felix might have told us. Should have told us,' she said to Pa when she got home. 'Surely Doone is exceptional,' she said to Miss Glyn.

'Not in the von Heusen world, but he has had her coaching which I'm sure he'll never forget.'

Doone had tried with all his might, not only because of the film but also because, in those few days, at the Ennis Glyn School and in the film studio, a rare comradeship had grown up between the Baroness and him. 'Miss von Heusen, I'm afraid we shall have to take Doone through that again,' Giles Hereward had had to say two or three times. 'I hope you don't mind.'

'Mind? We are old troupers, Doone and I. Come, Lausbub.' The Baroness often called him names: 'Lausbub', which meant ragamuffin; 'Dümmerchen', 'little stupid', but with the Baroness it was affectionate. Besides being large, there was a largesse about Lötte von Heusen that made Doone love and trust her.

'It's kind of the Baroness to take so much trouble,' Pa

121

had said.

'It isn't just kind,' said Miss Glyn. 'I assure you Lötte does nothing that doesn't amuse her.'

Doone did amuse her. When the filming was over, Pa asked Miss Glyn — 'or Miss Stella if you're busy' — to take Doone to thank the Baroness and present her with a basket of fruit. The basket was gilded, with wide gold ribbon on the handle, and was filled with pineapples, avocados, satsumas, crowned with grapes, and was so heavy that Doone staggered under its weight — he would not let Ennis Glynn help. 'But how *beautiful!*' exclaimed the Baroness. 'How munificent! And *how* extravagant!'

'It's all right,' Doone assured her. 'We get them at cost price.'

It was, though, more than just amusement. When Lötte von Heusen had first changed Doone's position on the piano keys, she had not touched hands as small. She had not known, either, that a child could have the courage and the sternness to rebuke a grown-up, and a famous one. 'Mr Felix wouldn't turn in his grave.'

'Ach!' she would often exclaim as if she had bitten on an excruciatingly tender tooth. 'No, Doone, *no!*' but she coached him with all her heart — 'and her peculiar magic,' said Ennis Glyn — and, 'Bravo!' she said when the recording was over. 'Bravo, Doone. We shall make a musician of you yet.'

Doone knew he had done well. 'There's a picture of him in the *Radio Times*,' the boys marvelled and, coming back with Ma in the studio car, she had said, 'You are the luckiest boy! Three things are open to you!'

'Three?' Doone was mystified.

'You can act.'

'A bit.'

'You can play.'

'A little bit.' After being with Lötte von Heusen, Doone knew how little that was.

'And dance.'

'I can dance. Mama,' said Doone, giving her the full title and fixing his eyes on her — she had not noticed before how those green-brown eyes could speak. 'Mama, I'm learning dancing with Miss Glyn and Stella. *Dancing*,' said Doone and, 'He's weathered it,' Ennis Glyn told Stella. 'Getting stronger every day. Be patient – the audition is not far off.'

'Boys, numbers thirteen to twenty-four, please come in now.'

The twenty-four boys had been divided into two sets of twelve. Since October, these auditions had been held in north, west, east and south England, and Scotland, Wales and Ireland, while some of the children had come from even farther away, from overseas. Two hundred and thirty-four boys had entered – and twice as many girls. Now, on this March morning, from the twenty-four who had survived those auditions, ten boys would be chosen for places at Queen's Chase, the Junior School of Her Majesty's Ballet.

The boys, all eyeing one another, were gathered at a quarter past nine in an enormous and austerely bare classroom which had been set aside as a waiting-room at the Senior School in Hammersmith, headquarters for both schools. Stella was with Pa and Doone, number 19. Ma had refused to come.

'An audition? What audition?' Crystal had asked.

When she had come home at Easter she had not been at all upset about the television, nor when it was shown and Doone had indeed been in the *Radio Times*. 'It's all right for him. We don't think a great deal of television. You see, we get so much,' but a gifted brother at home was one thing; to have him in the same ballet school was another; and there was the question that had rankled in Crystal since the *Harlequinade* and particularly after Stella had said, 'If you want a child in Her Majesty's Ballet School, wait for Doone.' 'No. Ma, please,' begged Crystal and, 'Not there, William,' Ma said when she saw the entry forms. 'Not there. It'll only lead to trouble.'

'I see – because of Crystal.'

'Yes, because of Crystal. She has never wanted Doone anywhere near Queen's Chase. She just doesn't want him.'

'May I point out that Miss Crystal Penny doesn't own Her Majesty's Ballet School?'

Doone had come through the October audition and now, on this March morning, he faced the final.

'I had a Good Luck card from Charles,' said Doone, 'and

from Miss Glyn, and one from the Baroness, and Ruth and Mrs Sherrin!' His eyes were as glowing as Pa's were anxious.

To Doone, that summer, autumn and winter had been perhaps the smoothest his short but troubled life had known. True, the boys still teased him, 'But it isn't horrid now, and I can tease back – sometimes.'

In his dancing he had passed the grades Stella seemed to think important and, at the School's open day, he had danced the Bluebird solo from *The Sleeping Beauty*, 'Made easier, of course. The beats were taken out and the flying steps, though I did manage the *grands jetés en tournant*.' He had worn the true bluebird costume, blue tights, a short, sparkling, brilliant-blue tunic, small wings of feathers in his hair. 'The music's great,' he told Pa. 'It whistles like a bird.'

He was, too, in a skating dance for six boys and girls, 'when we wobbled and fell about and sat down on our tails,' he chuckled. He had also made his peace over music.

That was the Baroness's doing. On the day he had taken her the basket of fruit, she had said, 'I understand from your father, Doone, you want someone to teach you the piano.'

'No, I don't. I don't.' He was passionate. 'Mr Felix taught me all I need to know,' said Doone.

'Come here, you silly boy,' the Baroness had commanded. Doone had come unwillingly. 'Mein kleiner Dümmkopf,' said the Baroness, 'my little simpleton. No one, not you or I or the finest musician in the world, knows all of music that he needs to know,' and over his head she had asked, 'Ennis, could you bring Doone to my concert on Saturday?'

'I can't – I'm in a matinée. Perhaps Stella . . .' and, 'He was so transported,' Stella told the Baroness afterwards, 'I had to hold on to him tightly, or he would have let himself be run over.'

'Ah! Would you like to come to another, Doone, on Saturday week? A student of mine is playing.'

The concerts had won Doone over. Sometimes Will came with him, sometimes Stella; sometimes he went alone. 'Do you like them so much?'

'They're . . . they're. . . .' Doone could not say what they were, but the Baroness understood and, 'So! You will have a teacher of piano and you will practise, practise, practise.' The

124

'r's came rolling out. 'Hein?'

'When I get to my proper school,' Doone promised.

It was now or never.

Everyone knew the morning would be long and taxing. 'Both sets of boys will dance for an hour and a quarter,' the Secretary had told them as they waited. 'There will be a pause after each. The panel has to discuss you and, I'm afraid, some boys won't be chosen; we can't take you all. Those boys can go home. The others, one by one, will be examined by our doctor. We have to be sure, you see, that you are strong enough for classical ballet training.

'After both sets have danced, and been discussed and "sieved",' she said with a smile, 'the boys who are left will dance again. Then the Panel will watch while you have tests for physique, which means the right sort of body for training. No legs on back to front or heads put on the wrong way.' Boys and parents tried to give an answering smile but failed as the Secretary became serious. 'After that, the Panel will choose the final ten.'

The final ten. Most of the boys were shivering now, even though they still wore their anoraks or coats.

In the room next door, the feeling was almost as tense; expectant, too, though an expectancy tempered with reserve – there had been so many disappointments. The panel sat behind a long table, a row of men and women, each with their papers, each with the knowledge of a lifetime's experience and dedication to the dance and, in spite of the reserve, each was hopeful. One day one of these children might turn out to be . . .?

Only 'might'.

Looking down the line, there was first, and in the chair, the upright figure of Elizabeth Baxter, Principal of both Senior and Junior Schools. She was taller than the other women and quietly commanding. 'Rightly so – her perception is extraordinary,' the Director, Michael Yeats, often said. 'Elizabeth can see what the rest of us often miss.' With her was the top rank of this particularly eminent ballet world, Michael himself, Director of the Schools: the director of ballet at the small but renowned Princess Theatre where Her Majesty's Company had begun. There were, too, from Queen's Chase, the Senior Ballet Master, Mr Max, the Senior Ballet Mistress, Miss McKenzie, and an even more Senior Teacher from the Upper School; to the left sat Mrs Challoner, watchful for perhaps different traits.

What was marked in all the Panel, though perhaps especially in the men, was a tenderness towards these unknown and embryo dancers, yet that would not influence the strictness of their judgement. They had to be strict, the standard of Her Majesty's Ballet had to be maintained, 'and the cost will not be only in money'. They all knew that and, 'One of these little "urchins" ', as the Director called them, 'might hold the future of our ballet in his small fist.'

Now the pianist was ready, as was Margaret Duval, head teacher from the Associate Junior School who would lead the audition, explaining each exercise to the boys, demonstrating it, sometimes dancing with them and, expertly, easing tension, even fright.

'Come in now, boys.'

'You didn't give him any hints, tell him anything,' Pa had reproached Stella. She had only helped Doone take off his coat, straightened his singlet, combed his hair and let him go with a pat on his shoulder. 'Mrs Penny said Miss Glyn told Crystal to enjoy herself – though how could the poor child!' Pa was walking up and down. 'No one should let children in for this,' he said.

'Not ordinary children,' said Stella. 'Some are not ordinary and there was no need, Mr Penny, to tell Doone to enjoy himself. He will.'

'Those heartless judges!'

'They're far from heartless. This audition is something they have to judge quite unemotionally, Mr Penny, and to Doone they won't be judges, they'll be friends. He knows at once when people understand him; it's only when they don't that he gets frightened,' and 'Come and sit down,' said Stella. As Pa obeyed, she slid her hand into his. Pa had not felt a woman's soft hand for a long long time; poor Ma's was hard with work, Stella's was not only soft but also firm, confident and, 'Leave it to Doone,' she said.

126

There was a hush as the boys filed in. Much the same age, ten or eleven years old, they were still all heights; some had shot up, some were small, 'But fortunately,' the Secretary had explained to the parents, 'if there's any doubt, we can tell how tall they will eventually be – there's a band of cartilage around the wrist that will be X-rayed and our doctor can assess from that.' Some boys were plump, with even a prominent small stomach; some slim or thin; some were tow-headed, some brown or dark; there was a mop of ginger curls. Skins were rosy, pale, sun-browned or freckled; eyes eloquent or withdrawn. All the boys had been told to try to smile.

They were dressed identically in black briefs, white singlets bearing a number, white socks, black or white soft-soled kid-leather dancing shoes and all of them had their heads up, determined to give as good an account of themselves as they could.

They circled the room, walking round and round, then, at Margaret Duval's command, broke into skips until they were warmed and relaxed. Then to the barre and, to a slow waltz, showed full *pliés*, a deep bending of the knee, heads up, small bottoms held in, all deeply serious.

There were simple foot exercises, still at the barre; all twelve pairs of feet moving in unison, each boy scrutinised from pointed foot to the top of his head.

In the second set, there was number 15, Norman, a proud, poised boy with a straight nose, disdainful nostrils, brown eyes from which now and again he shot a scornful look at the other boys, and well-cut, well-brushed fair hair. In contrast Peter, number 21, was a minnow of a boy with anxious blue eyes and a fuzz of brown hair. He had skipped joyously, tried with the whole of his being, though it became obvious he had never heard of most of the steps.

The Panel watched some boys for a short while but did not look at them again – they did not need to; others they watched thoughtfully, looking again and again, pencils to lips, then wrote a note. Their papers had a division for each boy with headings: height, body, hips, legs, extension, feet, Achilles tendon – if that were too tight, the boy would be discarded – and room for remarks. The dancing school from which they

127

came was noted, and if they had passed any Royal Academy grades – 'My Rupert has passed them all,' Rupert's mother had boasted in the waiting-room.

'Oh dear! I'm afraid Peter hasn't done anything like that.' Peter's young mother, a single parent, was agitated. 'He's just bewitched with dancing. He did get through the preliminaries, but perhaps I shouldn't have brought him here.'

'It's for them to say, isn't it, dear?' Rupert's mother was condescending. 'For Rupert really it's only a formality.' Yet Rupert was not one of the ten chosen, while Peter was. 'It *is* puzzling for parents,' Elizabeth Baxter said. 'They can't understand when a child, obviously well trained, is passed over, while another, a complete beginner, comes through.'

What were the Panel looking for? Not just a child who could dance, if not at present, when trained; not even for the right physique, though that was necessary for the demands that would be put, little by little, on the growing body. Not just for enthusiasm; most of the boys clearly had that 'or they wouldn't be here,' said Miss Baxter. They were looking for a child born with a talent so strong that already it was dedicated, as if it did not belong to the child but he to it; for what could be called an echo of the Gospel's, 'Ye have not chosen me, but I have chosen you.' A child 'marked' – as Ma had once said – and how hard it was to find that mark. 'Even Elizabeth can be deceived,' said Michael Yeats. The boy with the mop of red curls had an excellent body and real power, yet there was an odd jerkiness in what he did. 'It might be nerves, or a habit, but I think we should wait for his orthopaedic report' was the verdict. Another, lit with enthusiasm, had such an alabaster skin that a candle seemed to be burning through its transparency; they noted he sweated a great deal. 'He doesn't seem strong enough.' Many were clearly gifted – to this experienced audience, 'normally gifted'. They would have shone in their own schools, but the Panel had seen many hundreds of equal level. In the second set the small dark boy, number 19, caught their attention; Doone was manifestly enjoying every moment and, when he smiled, the gravest of the Panel could not help smiling back. 'He's one of Ennis's,' Miss McKenzie whispered to the Director. 'Ah!' The name was on his paper, 'Ennis Glyn School of Dancing'. That spoke for itself.

All the exercises and steps were easy, 'Child's play,' Norman's face seemed to say, but each was carefully set for a purpose; to show footwork, arm movements, potential strength, elevation.

The programme for each set of boys was the same. After the barre work, Margaret Duval called them to the centre of the room.

'Step forward, right arm in second position, look right.' She showed them.

'Step forward to left, left arm in position, look left, back-foot *tendu* pointed. Repeat four times. Be proud like a young prince.' Twelve young princes went through it. Norman was especially proud.

'Thank you,' said Miss Baxter. Her thank-yous were completely noncommittal.

It was noticed if the other boys grew muddled or could not keep up they stood aside, but the small Peter kept on.

Next were *arabesques*. 'Never mind if you wobble,' said Miss Baxter. 'Just see how high your legs will go.' Norman's was held in perfect balance, Peter not only wobbled but almost tumbled onto his face.

Jumps. *Changements* – changing feet in the air. 'The ceiling's not too high – try to hit it,' Miss Baxter encouraged them.

Peter did his utmost, but even with the simplest changes his feet fell over one another. 'We mustn't laugh!' Mrs Challoner whispered to Jean McKenzie, who said in an equally quiet whisper, 'I could do something with that child.' Peter entangled himself again; Norman, whose feet were correctly pointed like arrows as he soared, glanced contemptuously at him.

'We had to do the hornpipe faster and faster,' Doone reported with glee. 'She, the lady, said we could end any way we liked. I looked through a telescope. It was fun.'

'A *hornpipe*!' Norman, who was one of Doone's batch, told his mother with scorn.

'I fell down,' said the small boy, Peter.

'You can go now, boys,' said Miss Baxter. 'Thank you.'

'Make your bows,' Margaret Duval ordered – two bows on

129

two chords. Norman bowed formally, Peter with relief. 'Say thank you to the Panel,' said Margaret Duval. Murmured thank-yous. To a march they went out.

In the outer classroom it was the Secretary's task to read out the chosen, and unchosen, names, trying to read them in an even unemotional voice as if this were everyday, not a triumphant or a devastating moment. 'I'm afraid the Panel doesn't feel Simon – or Richard – or Anthony – is quite up to it. Rupert, you can go home, and Garry, Ian and Jan.'

For the final half-hour, fourteen boys were left; of those fourteen, four would have to go.

Only two exercises were given them, but each several times over.

'Again, please, Margaret.'

'Again, boys.'

'Thank you . . . thank you . . . thank you,' with no indication of feeling. Then, 'Shoes and socks off,' ordered Miss Baxter.

'The worst part was the end,' said Doone. 'The ladies and gentlemen all watched, all the time, never took their eyes off us. We had to go into the middle, just two of us, and bend over, keeping our legs straight, and touch the floor three or four times; after that we had to lie on the floor on our backs, put our feet together and draw them up, so we looked like frogs and the young lady pushed our knees to see how far down they would go; it hurt. Then we had to stand, with our feet together, straight, not moving, while they looked at us for ages and ages, all those eyes, until the head lady said, "Thank you." '

'Sounds like a cattle-market to me,' growled Pa.

It was, but not quite. These were small humans, children, and children are not helpless. Some boys had looked downcast or embarrassed under that scrutiny and stared at the floor; some looked anxious, scanning the Judges' faces. Several could not manage to stand still and had fidgeted, but a few retaliated; Norman looked proudly face to face; Peter beseeched; and one or two smiled at the Judges, who smiled back. One of these was number 19, Doone.

As soon as they were gone the Panel's discussions began; at first a hum of voices as notes were compared until, authoritatively, Miss Baxter called, 'Number 1,' and, quietly in order, judgements and opinions were given.

'Number 1?'

'Just possible.'

'Could – perhaps.'

'Number 7?'

A unanimous decided 'No,'

'Number 9?'

'Extremely good elevation.'

'I liked the way he held himself.'

'Neat footwork.'

'I think we should say "yes". '

Now and again there was a touch of acrimony. 'You're too hopeful, Mr Max.'

'I happen to believe in hope.'

'Well, I think we would be wasting our time.'

When it came to Norman, number 15, there was a pause. 'There's no doubt about the training,' said Miss Baxter, and they all had to agree. But 'There will be problems of character,' someone predicted and, 'I could guess it's not the boy's fault.'

'I should say,' Miss Baxter summed up, 'that at the moment the training exceeds the talent. Still. . . .'

'Wait till I get him in my class,' murmured Miss McKenzie.

With one boy, number 17, there was a good deal of demur, but Mr Max had taken a liking to him and was hopeful again. 'Let him try for a year,' he urged. 'Then we can think again.' Mrs Challoner intervened. It was the first time she had spoken. 'A year with an almost certain doubt? The boy's eleven, time for his senior school. If you put him back a year, he'll be at a grave disadvantage. Is that fair?' It was clearly sensible and, 'I don't think it would be fair,' said Miss Baxter.

'I wonder what they said about me,' Crystal was to say, 'when I auditioned.' She would, too, have liked to know what they said about Doone.

'Number 19?' But there was no need to ask. 'I think we all liked number 19,' said Miss Baxter.

131

'Doone's in!' It was Hughie who gave the news to the other boys and the boys of the Gang. 'Only ten passed out of four thousand' – four hundred had quickly become four thousand – 'and our brother's one,' they boasted and Doone even found himself being congratulated on his way home from school; if his hair was pulled now, it was almost affectionately.

This time it was a proud Pa who telephoned Miss Glyn.

Doone, though, did not get the 'something handsome' like Crystal's brooch. Pa was too upset; he had had a quarrel with Ma that was even more serious than the quarrel over Crystal. 'There seems something about the Ballet School that tears this family to bits,' said Pa.

Ma had been so silent since she had heard the news that at last Pa asked, 'Well, Maud?'

'I don't think it's well,' said Ma.

'He can act,' Crystal had said. 'Why can't he do that?' Ma put it to Pa now. 'Even after that small part, Miss Glyn says they're always asking for him.'

'He doesn't want to act.'

'Music,' Crystal had said. 'He's brilliant,' and Ma said now, 'I'm sure he could get a scholarship.'

'Maud! He wants to dance.'

'So you're going to let a child of eleven choose for himself?'

'That's what your Mr Brown said we should do, but I don't think you did with Crystal. You suggested and suggested.'

'I'm not suggesting now. She doesn't like it.'

'If she doesn't like it, she can leave.'

'*She* leave!'

'Yes,' said Pa. 'Doone did this on his own, his very own, and *no one* is going to interfere.'

'Thank you,' said Ma. 'Then I need have nothing to do with it – and that's what I'm going to do,' said Ma. 'Nothing.'

PART TWO

PART TWO

Chapter Three

IT WAS better than any castle. Doone knew now that a castle, or a palace, was the imagination of a little boy but, from the moment he and Pa and Crystal had driven in from the Park with its beautiful deer in herds under the trees and among the bracken – in autumn they were the same colour – and then up the drive and on to the broad sweep of the gravelled courtyard in front of the big cream-stuccoed porticoed house, Doone felt he had come where he belonged. It might almost have been a kingdom in which he was to be one of its young princes by inherited right. 'Well, it is a sort of inheritance,' said Charles. 'We're following a long long line of dancers: Ennis Glyn was here and Peter Morland and Anthea Dean.'

There had been princes, too, or at least princesses. Outside the garden walls stretched the spaces and woodlands of the park made by King Charles I for his deer – and in the time of King George I the house had been a royal hunting-lodge – but now the herds grazed in peace.

The big house was built on a slope. The front, with its wide sweep of gravel, its magnolias and great portico, the hall and salon were on ground level but, on the garden side, a double flight of steps led up to the balcony that gave on to them, and the balcony, itself one storey higher, looked down over the lawn with its great cedar – Queen Mary, 'our Queen's grandmother', the children were told, had climbed it when she was a little girl – overlooked the Four Yews Garden with its lily pond Ma had admired so much and away to wide swathes of grass open between the trees, the Chase that had given the house its name.

The Salon had necessarily been defaced, fitted with full-length mirrors and triple wooden barres round the walls. A new sprung floor had had to be laid over the original parquet

135

of solid oak which had been cruel on a dancer's feet.

The main house had two wings, the King's Pavilion and the Queen's; to both new buildings had been added, on one side to separate the boys' dormitories and their House Master's flat and, on the other side, a range of modern schoolrooms; even the old coach house with its cobbled yard was a schoolroom now. The two pavilions were linked on the garden side by two long semi-circular corridors that had been converted into the junior girls' dormitories with small white beds and lockers.

Below them, the basement corridor opened on to a maze of kitchens, storerooms, dining-rooms. No child was allowed to run along that corridor – its stone flags were too uneven, 'and if they fall,' said Mrs Gillespie, the House Mistress, 'sure enough they damage their legs or knees'. Those carefully guarded legs and knees.

Nothing could have shown the dedication of the Queen's Chase staff more than the way they accepted the inconvenience and limitations of the house; except for the Salon, all the dancing classrooms and most of the schoolwork classrooms had been purpose-built or converted, as in the Queen's Pavilion, but the staff dining-room had to serve as a common room as well. Mrs Challoner's study, once the Library, had to act as a reception room. The ballet teachers used the Yellow Drawing-Room, once hung with yellow silk; the ballet secretaries worked in its ante-room.

In the Orangery, built as part of the front of the house, there were now no carefully prized tubs of trees, covered in spring with their small waxen over-fragrant blossom. One part of the Orangery had become the school library, the other its museum – a strange museum for a school, with showcases of old theatre programmes, letters, posters, manuscripts; worn satin shoes with ribbons; a fan; a wig. Photographs covered the walls, and there was a bronze statue of a girl wearing a tutu whose gauze was metallic.

There were no tutus in the school; the girls wore pale-blue leotards with, for those in the first year, rose-coloured belts to distinguish them; belts for the older girls were blue or dark blue.

For two hundred years the ladies who had lived in Queen's Chase had been entitled to wear coronets, if not crowns. Now the 'ladies' were the girls who, when they came for their daily ballet classes in the Pavlova or Frederick Ashton dancing classrooms or in the Salon, wore, especially the younger ones, coronals made of their own plaited hair, put tidily out of the way so that the ballet mistress could see the shape of their heads and necks, but, 'Maybe one day', as most of them hoped, one day one or two of them would wear another sort of crown.

Charles came out to meet Doone. All new children at Queen's Chase had an older boy or girl as 'guide' to steer them through their first puzzling weeks, and Charles had volunteered for Doone. He took him and Pa to meet Mr Ormond, the boys' House Master. Pa could not get over his being so young 'and with a beard', but Doone thought he looked like a king. Charles showed Doone his dormitory that held eight bunk beds and had a glazed-in balcony overlooking the garden where the duchesses and royal ladies used to sit. He showed him the basement corridor and its labyrinth of rooms where Doone thought he would never find his way. He was introduced to other boys wearing, as he himself was wearing, grey shorts, a dark-green jersey, a green tie.

It was the boys he could not get over; boys and boys and boys, forty or more of them, all cheerfully and naturally doing what, alone, he had struggled so long to do – living for their dancing. Amongst them he was not odd or peculiar and, though he had gone back again to being a nobody, merely a first-year child dazzled by some of the older boys' dancing and, though his body often ached and he despaired of trying to please the teachers – especially Miss McKenzie – Queen's Chase to him was like coming home at last, his true home; he was confident, comfortable, and it seemed as if he would never need to be lonely again.

'Jean, that's a good batch you have in your "first years",' Miss Hurley said to Miss McKenzie in the staff dining-room, where teachers drifted in and out in the times that they were free, and helped themselves to lunch or tea, mostly a hasty cup of coffee and a sandwich. 'A good batch.'

It may have seemed odd that the Senior Ballet Mistress

should teach the first-year boys, but Jean McKenzie trusted no one but herself or, now and again, Mr Max to do it. 'Let them get their basics right,' that was the perpetual axiom, 'then they can begin.' She was not given to eulogies but now her face lit up. 'Some are a delight to teach but,' she sighed, 'every year I forget what hard work the first-year children are, from trying to remember their names to having to show them everything. Of course it is bewildering for them.'

It was. Doone had never been the concern of so many grown people, some of whom, it seemed, had little to do with the dancing, yet were tightly bound up with it: Mr Ormond, the Matrons – he loved Miss Walsh – even the 'ladies' who served in the canteen and who smiled at him. There was Sister in the infirmary; the housekeeper lady – 'Were the chips nice and crisp, Doone?'

'Not as crisp as my Ma's.' Doone was too honest to be tactful. There were secretaries, two for ballet, and kind Daphne, Mrs Challoner's private secretary who seemed always to know where everyone was and what they were doing – for quite a long while Doone had thought Queen's Chase belonged to Mrs Challoner. Under her were what seemed to him a small army of schoolteachers. 'Well, we have to be a double school,' she would have explained and, 'They teach you everything,' Doone lamented to Will at the weekend. 'English, *French*!' he said in horror. 'Maths, science, history, art. I thought this was a school where they taught ballet.'

Will did not sympathise. 'You don't want to grow up an ignoramus.'

'I wouldn't mind,' said Doone.

Crystal took this – her first – opportunity. 'I'm afraid Doone, my little brother, isn't good enough at lessons for Queen's Chase.' She had come to Mrs Challoner with a suitably grave face, regret in the blue eyes she lifted to look at the Headmistress. 'He's finding it too hard, Mrs Challoner. He can't keep up and so he's worrying.'

'I don't think he worries at all,' said Mrs Challoner and laughed.

Crystal bristled. 'Is it funny that he still can't read properly?'

Mrs Challoner became serious. 'A boy who can read music will read English – when he's ready,' and, 'Suppose you leave

138

Doone to us,' said Mrs Challoner. 'We're used to funnies.' That was true; the academic staff at Queen's Chase had to be unusually adaptable and patient. Children were always being fetched from their classes for reasons of dancing. 'But somehow we manage to get them through their examinations,' said Mrs Challoner. 'Fortunately there's affection on both sides,' which was true. The ballet staff had to be more aloof.

Doone did not know all of them. He knew Stephen Vince who taught the second and third year boys, a young dancer with curly gold hair who had injured his back so badly on stage that he could not dance again. 'Not properly,' Charles told Doone. 'He can't lift a girl or jump high,' but Vince refused to be unhappy and trained as a teacher. To Charles, Stephen Vince was a hero.

For the girls, besides Miss McKenzie, there was Miss Hurley and a lissom young French woman, Gilberte Giroux – Mamzelly – as well as two other teachers; as in all ballet schools, girls far outnumbered boys. Other teachers came for folk dancing, Morris dancing and, as Doone was to find out later, there was a master who came from the Senior School to teach *pas de deux* to the older girls and boys and called them 'ladies and gentlemen' because he did not know their names, 'and each teacher has to have an accompanist,' said Pa. At Queen's Chase there were four full-time pianists, headed by Jonah, whom everybody loved.

Miss Hurley was the oldest of them all; she had been at Queen's Chase since it opened and was one of the old school – 'a strict traditionalist, and none the worse for being that,' said Miss McKenzie. 'She keeps us in line.' Miss Hurley had, too, the knowledge of an old servant which could be deadly and, 'How is little Prince Norman getting on?' she asked.

'Wrong from the waist down,' sighed Miss McKenzie, 'but he could learn, if he will.'

'And little Peter?'

The worry-line on Miss McKenzie's face came back. 'I know I said I could do something with that child. I could physically. He loves it, and he tries almost too hard, but he's so slow. He'll never keep up. . . .' Miss McKenzie was haunted, especially at night, by Peter's beseeching eyes but, 'You can't. You mustn't,' she told herself. 'If you care too much about one child, it

139

unbalances your care for the dance, which is what you are here for,' and, 'He'll have to go,' she told Miss Hurley.

'Then the sooner the better. Tell me about Doone Penny. How is he?'

'Coming on. Coming on.' Miss McKenzie said it cautiously.

From his first year at Queen's Chase, Doone kept a journal, writing it in a Gentleman's Pocket Diary in bed at night.

The diary had one page for a day and every page began the same way: 'Today. . . .'

Today we had to do 'dog walks'. You walk on all fors, your hands flat on the floor, your legs strait. They ache and ache. We all said 'No – *pleese*, no.' Miss McKenzie said, 'Yes,' Norman wudn't do it but Peter trid hard. Miss McKenzie says you can have 'sad knees', when you let them sagg and 'smiling knees', when you pull them up strait. It's troo, your knees can look like faces.

Today was good, thogh I'm very stiff and had to go and see Miss Walsh because my knees are sorr; she said she would talk to Miss McKenzie and has excoosed me from gym. If annyone had told me how much dancing could hurt, I wudn't have beleeved them, but it dus. Gregory says he's goin to runn away.

Doone had to use a pencil after the assistant matron, Miss Thompson, had found ballpen marks on his sheet and scolded him sharply. The boys called Miss Thompson 'Tom Cat'. 'She can scratch and spit,' they warned Doone. He did not like Miss Thompson and, as boys will, quickly divined that Miss Walsh – Polly – their official House Matron, did not like her, either. 'I don't need an assistant,' she had told Mr Ormond.

'Look, Polly. We used to have twenty to twenty-five boys, now there are over forty. You can't cope with that.'

'I can.'

'No, Polly.'

'Very well, then. Give me a comfortable old body who can patch and darn and sew and *not* invent rules,' Miss Walsh had said indignantly.

140

'No writing anything once you're in bed,' ordered Miss Thompson, but Doone still wrote.

Today was OK. In ballet we did beats. Mine are getting beter but they are stil not good. Miss McKenzie said I have two left feet. Charles says not to wurry, but I do. Norman said, 'You're almost the only one who can't do them.'

Today was roten. I got my English reterned. I'll never never lern to spell. My back aked too. Miss McKenzie said it didn't mattar but it did to me. Greg says we're crazey to keep going and sumetimes I think he's rite'.

But what was impressing Doone all the time was the seriousness of the ballet teachers – Stella, by contrast, seemed light-hearted. At Queen's Chase the ballet mistresses and masters seemed to work as hard as their pupils, with endless, patient demonstration and talking; sometimes, at the end of class, Miss McKenzie's voice was hoarse.

'You'd think we'd never learned dancing before,' said Norman.

'We haven't, not like this.'

'Of course not,' Stella would have said. 'You can't do in three lessons a week what can be done when you are steeped in it day in, day out, and so you have to go back to the beginning to reach a different standard', and, 'One day,' said Miss McKenzie, 'one hopes, in the second term at least, they begin to know our language – it is a whole new language – and to understand a little so I don't always have to show, I can tell them,' and soon, as she spoke, giving out an *enchaînement*, small feet began to twitch and point, arms to stir, eyes look the way she wanted. A boy might do a turn, another a prospective leap. Heads nodded in agreement, 'and then they try,' said Miss McKenzie. 'They may not be able to do all the steps, but they know what I am asking and that *is* a moment,' said Miss McKenzie.

Today was a nise day but we had French verbbs. I got Good for maths. We had a ballet lesson with Mr Max.

141

Haven't been taut by a man teecher before. He made us stretch and stretch. He uses a rolled up newspaper to smack our bottums and legs but he let us try *tours en l'air* . . .

Today was bad. Miss McKenzie said I wasn't wurking. I hate Miss McKenzie.'

'Don't stick your thumb out, Doone.'
'Doone, keep your shoulders *still*.'
'Doone! I said *down* in the *third* position.'
'*Doone!*'
'Why does she always pick on me?' Doone burst out to Charles about Miss McKenzie. 'Why always me?'
'Because she's interested in you.'
'Interested in *me*?'
'Do you think she'd bother if she wasn't? She's *the* one,' Charles said earnestly, 'and when you please her . . .'
'I never will . . .' but,

Today she said my beats have got beter. I don't think so but, if they have, it is becose of Charles, who has really been grate. We spent an hour after prep in the salon, practtersin. Charles can do beats really well. It's funny, Charles helps me and Miss McKenzie said to me, 'Doone, will you help Peter? Practtise with him.' *Me!!*

Today we did some more beats. Miss McKenzie said, 'Well done, Doone.'

Doone underlined that in red. How strange that one word of praise from Miss McKenzie seemed to be more important than all the kindness of Mr Max.

That Easter term a whisper ran through the school and, 'Crystal,' she was asked, 'is it true that your brother is going to be the Indian boy in *The Dream*?'
'Of course he's not,' said Crystal, but soon it was confirmed.

142

Doone Penny, that small dark boy, had been chosen to be the changeling boy in *The Dream*.

'Humphrey Tyrone asked for him,' said Doone's friend, Gregory. 'It seems he once saw Doone.'

'Once seen, never forgotten,' teased the boys.

The boy was only on stage for a few minutes but, all the same, to appear at the Royal Theatre and be named in the programme was something to envy, though not openly. Queen's Chase children knew that any Company decision must be accepted. Kui, the half-English, half-Chinese second-year boy, small for his age, was made understudy. 'He's a second-year. Doone's only first.'

'He has the right face,' Charles pointed out, 'and it's not a dancing part. Anyone could do it.' But Doone was suddenly an object of curiosity.

He had his first rehearsal; unfortunately it was the Tom Cat who took him and Kui to the Senior School where, 'ages and ages ago', they had both had their auditions. The rehearsal was taken by the régisseur, Humphrey Tyrone. With him was his assistant, a woman, keeping track of the notation. 'I didn't know dancing could be written down,' Doone told Charles.

'It is nowadays. It used to be just "handed on", which I think,' said Charles with a certainty strange in a thirteen-year-old, 'is the best way. Suppose you could have a great dancer to coach you in a part they used to dance and which you are dancing now. I would choose Nijinsky.'

Doone remembered that name – everything his Lady had said was engraved in his memory. 'He was the one who wore the golden wig with the little horns.'

'Yes. *Yes!*' said Charles.

'My part doesn't have any dancing.'

At the rehearsal, besides Mr Tyrone, of whom he stood in deep awe, and the notation lady, there was a pianist, Jacques, and, of course, the dancers. Oberon was danced by Peter Morland, Titania by Anthea Dean, and there were fairies – sixteen besides the four important ones, Cobweb, Mustard Seed, Moth and Peaseblossom. Once again Doone was struck by the seriousness of these grown-ups; though they laughed and even teased, under everything was an intensity of work. He watched Peter and Anthea dancing together and saw how,

143

with these exalted beings, Humphrey stopped them again and again. 'No, no, no, Anthea! Go right to him, don't pull away.' 'Peter, move in closer.' 'Anthea, don't look down. The moment you look down, you destroy the lightness. You're Titania – ethereal.' 'You're flying . . . keep up. Up!' And with Doone, even though his part was such a small one, Humphrey went through it again and again and explained it carefully: 'You're in the scene where Oberon – he's King of the Fairies, as I hope you know – quarrels with his Fairy Queen, Titania, because he wants you, the boy, for his page. You're half-Indian, half-fairy – a changeling. Titania has adopted you and won't give you up, not for all the Fairy Kingdom.'

'Look up at her,' commanded Humphrey. 'Now come round behind Titania . . . stand between her and Oberon. You see, Doone, it's you they're quarrelling over. Look up at her as if you were wondering. . . . Remember, she won't let Oberon have you . . . keep close to her. Head back . . . closer. That's good. Now they're going to have a tug-of-war over you. Quick, turn your head from one to another. Now Oberon jerks you away and throws you across the stage. It won't hurt. Good boy! Why, Doone, that was splendid. You might have been tumbling all your life.'

Doone was too awed to speak or he would have said, 'I have. Beppo taught me.'

'Now hop, skip, back to the fairies.'

Later in the ballet, Titania gives the boy to Oberon, who picks him up and kisses him. Doone did not like that and brushed away the kiss, which made Peter and Humphrey laugh. 'Do just that,' said Humphrey. 'It makes the boy alive,' and Doone came back to Queen's Chase in bliss, repeating, over and over again, every word Humphrey Tyrone had said, and practising 'wondering' in front of the looking-glass. He was in a daze of happiness until, in the afternoon tea-break, Crystal waylaid him in the garden where he was sitting on a bench, having run three times round the house chasing Gregory, who had escaped.

'You're going to be in *The Dream*,' said Crystal.

'I am in *The Dream*.'

'We've been doing *A Midsummer Night's Dream* in our English class, so I know all about the boy, and you're going to

144

be him. That's perfect,' said Crystal.

'Why is it perfect?' Already something shrank back in Doone.

'I don't know if I ought to tell you,' said Crystal.

'Tell me.' Doone felt as if he were holding his breath.

'Well, he's a changeling, isn't he? So are you.'

'*Me?*' Then, 'I don't believe you,' said Doone.

'Don't you? Why do you think when Pa and Ma were expecting a girl they got a boy? Why, when all of us in the family are quite tall and fair or, at least, mousy, are you so little and dark? Your ears are pointed, you know, and you have this elevation they're always talking about and you're light and strong like a fairy.'

'There aren't any fairies.'

'No? You should read about Puck', and Doone began to remember what Will had said – 'You? You came out of an acorn' – and Pa's, 'I don't know how we got you.' It was insidious.

'Why do you think Ma doesn't like you?'

'She does', but Doone could still hear what Ma had said in the train, still hear the contempt in her voice when she had called him, 'Teacher's pet'.

'She does like me – she does.' He was getting frantic but Crystal shook her head. 'She knows you were not her baby. That's why she handed you over to Beppo.'

That Doone could not deny but, 'I'm not a changeling. I'm not.' He said it as stoutly as he could.

'I'm afraid you are. At least, we don't know where we got you – and, Doone, it's a family secret, so don't tell Ruth or Charles.'

Crystal sauntered off, highly pleased with herself.

'Doone hasn't come to supper,' said Miss Thompson. 'Where is he?'

Nobody knew.

'He might be in the library,' said Charles. 'He can get lost in a book, or perhaps piano practising. He gets lost then, too.'

'Go and look for him, Charles,' but Doone was not in the library nor at any of the pianos, nor in his dormitory. Charles went out into the garden but someone else had gone there too.

145

Ruth, looking down from a top window, had seen a small figure sitting forlornly alone in the gathering dusk; hidden behind the yews, no one could have seen him if they had not looked from above.

For more than two years Ruth and Crystal had been at Queen's Chase together, often in the same class for dancing or lessons, sleeping in the same dormitory, though not next to one another – 'Thank goodness,' both had said. In all that time they had not spoken. In silence they passed one another, brushed their teeth at basins side by side, followed each other with their trays at the canteen serving-counter, but when Doone came there was an open confrontation.

'Hello!' Ruth had said to him on his first evening. 'How lovely to see you. Get your tray and come and have supper with Charles and me.'

'Doone is having supper with me,' said Crystal.

'Would you like to be my partner?' Ruth had asked Doone when the second and third year girls and boys came to join the 'first years' in *grande promenade* that always ended the Saturday-morning classes in folk dancing.

'Doone's my partner,' Crystal had said.

As each boy had to partner two girls, it ended with Doone taking Ruth and Crystal, who looked daggers at one another over his head. Now no Crystal was about and Ruth ran down; she met Charles in the garden.

'Doone! I've been looking everywhere for you. . . .'

'Doone! What is the matter?'

Doone lifted a face of such misery that Charles and Ruth both broke off and Ruth sat down beside Doone, putting her arms round him while Charles stood by distressed.

Doone had no idea how long he had been there, nor did he know that he was cold, only that he seemed numb. Pa was not his Pa. Ma not his Ma. 'Why do you think Ma doesn't like you?' Crystal's matter-of-fact words still sang in his head. Will was not his brother, nor any of the boys. Crystal was not his sister – he had been so proud of Crystal. He was not really Doone Penny, just a boy come from nowhere. Nowhere, no one, no name, and 'I can't dance the boy in *The Dream*,' he told Ruth and Charles.

'You've been chosen.' Ruth was scandalised and, 'What *is*

146

all this?' asked Charles, but Doone had broken into such shivers that Ruth said: 'Quick! We must take him in to Miss Walsh. He's frozen.'

'Someone's done something,' said Charles.

'Or said something – something to do with *The Dream*,' said Ruth. 'We should tell Miss McKenzie.'

'She's gone home. All the teachers have gone.'

'Tomorrow, then,' but, before Ruth and Charles had a chance, Doone had gone with the Tom Cat and Kui to a rehearsal at the Senior School.

'You remember what I told you last time?' said Humphrey Tyrone.

'Yes, sir,' but it was barely audible.

'Come round from behind Titania. Stand between her and Oberon. . . .'

Doone knew every movement but, when the exciting music began, as if he were made of lead, he could not move. The only thing he felt was a queer thudding in his head.

'Doone, wake up,' and, 'Jacques, please start again,' said Humphrey. Doone still did not move. Jacques started for the third time. Anthea tried to help Doone, to pull him round, but he resisted. '*Doone!*' This time Humphrey shouted and got up from his chair. 'What in the name of thunder has got into you, child?'

'Sir, I can't, I can't,' and Doone pleaded, 'Kui looks quite like an Indian boy – get Kui.'

'Thank you for telling me what to do.' Humphrey was obviously disappointed as well as angry and he said, 'I've done with him. Take him away.'

Doone was taken straight to Miss McKenzie by the Tom Cat who was delighted to tell the shocking story – in Company tradition it was shocking – but, 'Thank you, Miss Thompson,' Miss McKenzie said in an even voice. They were in the Yellow Drawing-room – the ballet secretary had tactfully gone out – but the Tom Cat lingered until, 'Thank you,' Miss McKenzie said again. 'I will deal with Doone.'

Misbehaviour, at Queen's Chase, was Mrs Challoner's

problem, but this was a ballet matter and, 'In a ballet school,' said Miss McKenzie, 'children do as they're told, not as they choose.'

'I know.'

'You've had one rehearsal.' At the misery in the figure standing in front of her desk, Miss McKenzie's voice softened. 'Didn't you like it?'

The whole face changed, was radiant. 'I loved it.' Then the light went out and, in his anguish, Doone asked, 'Miss McKenzie, have I got pointed ears?'

'Pointed *ears?*'

'Please look.' Beginning to have a glimpse of what was wrong, Jean McKenzie dutifully looked. Then, 'Of course not,' and deliberately, carefully, 'You do have an elfin look. That's magical in a dancer. One day you might dance Puck.'

'I don't want to.'

It was a cry and, 'Doone,' said Miss McKenzie, 'tell me why.'

'No.' Miss McKenzie was astonished. As Doone saw when he raised his eyes to look at her, she was not used to having children say 'No' to her. 'It's a family secret,' Doone said miserably.

'I see.' There was a pause in which Miss McKenzie seemed to see deep into Doone. Then, 'A family secret?' she asked. 'Is it one that your father and mother asked you not to tell?'

'They don't know that I know.'

'Don't know that you know a secret that stops you taking a part you like so much?' and, with a kindness that brought Doone, though he was eleven and three-quarters now, close to crying, Miss McKenzie said, 'I think you had better sit down and tell me all about it. I'm sure your father and mother won't mind,' and, trying to keep his voice steady, Doone told.

'Well, you were a clot!' Charles was to say. 'You were born in hospital, weren't you? In hospital, soon as you're born, the nurses put a tag round your wrist with your name on it, just so as you couldn't be mixed up. I saw it on my baby sister. Your Pa and Ma would have seen it. You ask them.'

Ruth said something different, more visionary. 'Suppose you had to be adopted – wouldn't it be gorgeous to be adopted by Titania, the Fairy Queen?'

148

'You mean Anthea,' said literal Doone. 'Oh, yes! It would.'
'Then what was all the fuss about? Doone, you don't think,'
said Ruth.

He was thinking now, and bitterly. 'We can't allow such
behaviour,' Miss McKenzie had said, 'and you have to forfeit
the part. Kui must take your place, so you've missed a
wonderful chance.' She had listened, balancing a pencil
between her fingers as if she had been trying to weigh what he
said, then, 'Even if this happened to be true,' said Miss
McKenzie, 'if you are a real dancer – I believe you may be one
– and you have a part, it doesn't matter what you feel about it
or what happens to you privately, you go on stage and do it. I
have known dancers, Doone, whose husband or mother has
died and yet they danced that evening – and smiled. It doesn't
matter, either, if they don't like their part, or feel there's
something wrong with it – they can go and discuss it privately
with their teacher or the director, but they do not, and I repeat
not, do what no one else in this School or, I think, even in the
Company, has done – defy a Director taking his rehearsal. And
there's something else,' said Miss McKenzie. 'Doone, do you
remember the lady at the exhibition – who took you round it?'

'My Lady?' Doone shone. 'Of course I do.'

'Well, Mr Tyrone was with her at the exhibition that day.'
Doone remembered the young man in the jersey and jeans. Of
course, it was Mr Tyrone. 'They remembered you, and it was
she who suggested you to him for *The Dream*. She will be
disappointed.'

Doone's head was hanging so low it was almost below the
desk.

'Crystal, Mrs Challoner wants you in the study.'

'Who told you this tarradiddle?' Miss McKenzie had asked
Doone when he had finished his telling.

'Tarradiddle?'

'A story without a word of truth in it.'

Doone had looked this way and that as if he were trying to
escape but, 'I think it was your sister,' said Miss McKenzie,
and, 'I never thought Doone would be silly enough to believe
it,' Crystal defended herself.

'If you thought he wouldn't believe you, what was the point

of telling him?' asked Miss McKenzie, who was with Mrs Challoner. 'I think, Crystal, you deliberately set out to try to stop your brother having a part at the Royal Theatre. That's the truth, isn't it?'

Crystal's lips parted but she did not say anything. There was nothing she could say and Mrs Challoner spoke. 'One of the things we will not have at Queen's Chase, Crystal, is bullying.'

'*Bullying?* I never touched Doone.'

'Words can hurt as much as kicks or pinches. Charles and Ruth have told me what a state Doone was in when they found him.'

'Little stupid!' said Crystal scornfully.

'Was he? I hear you have a very convincing way of telling your – shall we call them "concoctions"? – and I'm warning you, Crystal. Children can be dismissed from this school on other counts besides dancing, and that would be a pity, wouldn't it, when otherwise you are doing so well.'

Doone was made Kui's understudy and had to endure the penance of standing in the wings with Miss McKenzie, seeing Peter transformed into nobility by his green Oberon robes, his crown, and Anthea in diaphanous gauze with wings and a crown of flowers as Titania. He could hear the music but not see the orchestra, was cut off from the lights but could feel the stir and bustle, hear Peter curse and, worst of all, see Kui, in my part, thought Doone. Mine! He knew now that what Miss McKenzie had told him was true: nothing that anyone said, nothing that anyone did, even if they died, thought Doone, would stop him again from dancing. If only I could have another chance – but the Company did not do *The Dream* again that season, and, 'Next year I shall be too big,' he told Ruth. It was bitter, but Doone had to accept that never again would there be that particular chance.

Chapter Four

ASSESSMENT time came round as it came every term, when each class was watched eagle-eyed, and every boy or girl knew that he or she would be thoroughly discussed – 'and perhaps sent away,' said Doone in dread. It was his third assessment.

Norman, to Doone's relief, had long been gone. 'We're taught such elementary things,' he had said.

'Yet you can't do them properly,' Gregory had pointed out.

Norman ignored him. 'I should have known how childish it is here when they played "Boys and Girls Come Out to Play" for our skips at the audition. A nursery rhyme!'

'Splendid to skip to,' said Doone.

They had all been sorry, though, about Peter, whom everyone had liked, but for the rest, the more they worked together, the more there grew to be a bond – soon the boys were closer to Doone than his own brothers. 'I do so hope none of us will have to go.'

Some inevitably would and all the children were tense, even those who pretended to be calm or cocksure.

Crystal had come through – 'just', as Miss McKenzie had to tell her after the holidays. 'You're going into your fourth year, which is crucial. It's a question of every day – not just when people are watching you. You danced well enough at the Assessment, even better at the School's Annual Performance.'

The School's Annual Performance had been held at the Princess Theatre.

Doone was in the Morris stick dance, 'which was fabulous', except that Gregory, in his excitement, hit him on the head with his stick, and poor clumsy John had dropped his.

Crystal had been in the Irish dance – 'with seventeen other girls,' she had said discontented, but even the smell of a theatre or public notice quickened her into fresh effort and she knew,

151

too, that their progress was judged partly on how they performed. 'Yes, you always rise to a challenge,' said Miss McKenzie, 'but what you don't realise is that there's a challenge every day, in every class. Both Miss Hurley and Mademoiselle Giroux tell me that you are letting yourself get lax. That won't do.'

Crystal gave a deliberate little shrug.

'Oh, but she is insolent.' Mamzelly had been standing near. 'It is not often that I cannot find sympathy, *rapprochement*, with my girls, but Crystal! She is abominable. Think of poor Doone. She should have been *thrown out*.' Mamzelly was fierce.

'No,' said Miss Hurley. 'She can dance.'

'*Can!*'

'Yes, and abominable she may be but she's also an independent little madam who solves things for herself.'

'Tries to solve them,' said Mrs Challoner.

'Yes, and they're the ones that get there in the end. Once she has got over this hurdle – I think we all know what it is – you'll see. Meanwhile, I hope little brother has some of her stuffing. He'll need it.'

Crystal waylaid Mr Max. 'How did Doone do in the Assessment?'

'That's not for you to know, young lady,' but Crystal wanted to know exactly where she stood. 'Please, Mr Max,' she said. 'My mother's so anxious and I'm Doone's sister.' Mr Max was not versed in the adroitness of young girls; he also found it hard to resist true prettiness, the pleading blue eyes, the diffident little hand on his coat sleeve. 'Did he – please – did he do well?'

'He did extraordinarily well.'

Next time Crystal met Doone she cuffed his ear hard.

'But why does he upset you so?' asked Ma next time they were home. 'He's so much younger; he can't get in your way.'

'To them he's the only Penny that matters.'

'Nonsense.'

'It's true. He's only second-year, but Mr Max has him working twice a week with the third-year boys.'

152

Doone was no longer taught by Miss McKenzie but had moved into a male world, and a harder one.

'Today Mr Vince made us do *ronds de jambe à terre* and *en l'air* till I thought my instep would brake. He's always so sarky. 'John, what *is* so intrishing outside the window?' 'Gregory, use your own brane, not mine.' 'Shut your eyes and *lissen*.' 'Mrs Smyth's not playing for her own amusemant.' 'Count, boy, *count*.' 'Isn't that easy enugh for you?' He talks twice as much as Mr Max and he can make you feel uncomforteble.

There were compensations.

Today is Satuerday. We have cuntry dancing and Morris dancing. We end with a *peromonade* round the room. Each boy takes two gurls. The gurls wanted to dance with me. I chose Amanda and Zara.

Doone had many friends now. Gregory, to his sadness, had gone, but there was Kui, Julian, Tommy, John; among the girls particularly Amanda, who was so delicious, small and compact that she made Doone's heart turn over and, even more particularly, Zara, a curious stormy girl with a dark fuzz of hair, creamy skin and enormous grey-green eyes; she was supposed to be the best dancer of her year and, 'Can you believe it?' said Charles. 'They say you're the best boy. They must be joking, of course, but that's what they say. The best boy!'

'Me?' Doone did not believe it, but Charles was serious as he said, 'Yes, and you should remember that when your precious sister tries one of her games again.'

For Crystal it was not only the dancing; it was the Ingrams – let alone the Baroness.

'This Mrs Ingram – what is she like?' asked Ma.

'Only the most elegant person I've seen in my life,' said

Crystal bitterly. 'She's like Ennis Glyn, only more so – tall, slim.' Ma thought of her own bulk and sighed. 'Red hair, not bronze,' said Crystal, 'and the most beautiful clothes, and he's to match.'

'The Colonel?'

'Yes. Tall – he wears tweeds.'

'Not uniform?'

'He's on holiday, Ma. He has his suits and his shoes made for him. I asked Charles.'

'Did you tell his father you had two brothers in the Army?'

Jim and Tim had enlisted in the Junior Leaders Corps to train as NCOs. Ma was proud of them but, 'The Army!' Crystal had wrinkled up her nose. 'Those horrible clothes! Clumping boots,' and now, 'Colonel Ingram would hardly be interested in corporals and sergeants,' she crushed Ma. 'Besides, *I* never get a chance to speak to him. Doone has all the luck!'

Amy, Crystal's best friend at Queen's Chase, was the daughter of a chemist – 'Might as well be a greengrocer.' When Colonel and Mrs Ingram came over from Paris, as they often did, to take Charles out for the weekend, they sometimes asked Doone as well. 'They take him to hotels.' Crystal had never been to a hotel. 'He's been racing and to theatres. It's not *fair*,' cried Crystal.

What Ma could not get over was that she had to give permission – no child at Queen's Chase was allowed out with another without that – 'And written,' Ma lamented – she found it so hard to write letters. A telephone call was not enough – except from the Baroness.

Now and again the Baroness would sweep down from her Olympian heights and bear Doone off from home or school – without questioning – though, 'Do you really know Lötte von Heusen?' Mrs Challoner had asked Doone in his early days.

'Of course. We were in a film together.' Doone said it as if, again, it were everyday. 'At least, I was in the film and she helped.'

'She *helped*?'

'Yes, she's my friend.'

'I think she's more than that,' Mrs Challoner had said. 'She rang up – about *you*, Doone. She wants you to have piano

154

lessons from our Mr Delaney.'

A pause. Then, 'Couldn't I learn the piano with Mr Jonah?' 'I don't think that's quite what she meant.'

'No,' said Doone and sighed. All the same, it was wonderful to be with the Baroness again and go to more concerts. 'What about the tickets?' Pa had asked his mentor, Ennis Glyn. 'We can't let her go on paying for those.'

'Lötte never pays for tickets,' Miss Glyn told him. 'If she goes to a concert, that concert is made.'

Sometimes she took Doone home to her house where he had to play for her. She might say, 'Um Göttes Willen!' or she might nod in approval but, best of all, she would usually play for him. On these occasions Doone would sit curled on the window-seat or, in winter, lie on the hearthrug in front of the fire, rapt, seeing pictures and completely at ease. 'It's like being at Mr Felix's again,' he told Will.

It could not, though, have been more different.

The Baroness's drawing-room was like her, large and pink, its chintzes bright with roses, furniture polished to lustre, and it was full of silver-framed photographs, all signed for 'Dear Lötte', 'Dearest Lötte', 'Lötte von Heusen with admiration and respect'. The piano in this pink room was a small, sweet-toned upright on which 'I had my first lessons,' said the Baroness, but off it was a big room, empty of everything but instruments.

There, besides the Baroness's concert grand, the Blüthner – 'Almost as beautiful as my Steinway,' said Doone – was a spinet, a small fine one, inlaid inside the lid and above the keyboard with roses and, in gilt letters, its maker's name, Ebenezer Mince. Doone thought that sounded lovely, as did the spinet when the Baroness played it, lovely but curiously sweet and thin. 'It sounds thin,' she told him, 'because each note only has one string.

'Haven't you any drums?' asked Doone. In all concerts, the player he liked best to watch was the orchestra's drummer twisting round on his stool from drum to drum, bringing out the splendid deep loud beat, or making a roll which reverberated through the hall, then smoothing it away with his padded drumsticks. He would have loved to do that and, 'Any drums?' he asked.

155

'I am not an African', but the Baroness played the harp for him. It was taller than she and, when she sat down and drew it back against her shoulder he revelled in its beauty; he had seen harps in the orchestra at the Royal Theatre but never as close. Now he could touch the gilding and polish of its frame, its golden strings and pedals; its sound seemed to echo through the house and, 'A-ah,' said Doone in a long breath. 'How I should love to play that.'

'You will never play anything,' the Baroness said severely, 'if you don't practise. Practise. Practise. Practise – at school and in the holidays, particularly the holidays.'

'I can't practise in the holidays; we haven't a piano.'

'Not a piano?' To the Baroness, that was like saying a family had no bread. 'Not a piano?'

'Pa's not made of money.' Sometimes in what Doone said the Baroness could hear Pa speaking, sometimes Ma. 'It's nothing but ask, ask, ask,' said Doone. 'He's always putting his hand in his pocket.'

'Ma, what's the matter with Pa?' he had asked on one of his weekends that autumn term.

'Nothing that concerns you.'

'That's what grown-ups always say.' It concerned every inch of him.

'William, I've never known you be like this,' he had heard Ma say.

'Because it's never been like this.'

'Like what?' Doone asked desperately.

Crystal enlightened him, took pleasure in enlightening him – it was a part of a new plan. 'A supermarket has opened right here in our street. As they're a big chain they can undercut our prices. Pa's losing half his business.'

Pa tried to be philosophic. 'Our quality's so much better, Maud. Haven't I always gone to market and bought my specialities myself, and all the flowers? The customers'll come back. It's just now. . . .' but Crystal did not repeat those comforting words to Doone. Instead, she took this which seemed a golden opportunity. 'Have you ever asked yourself, Doone, now Pa has all these money troubles, how he can go on keeping both of us at Queen's Chase?'

Doone had certainly never asked himself that, or thought

about it. 'Is Queen's Chase expensive?'

'It costs thousands of pounds a year for each of us and he's only a greengrocer. No wonder he looks so worried and old. I think one of us ought to leave.'

'If you think so, why don't you?' Doone always went straight to the point.

'I?' Crystal's eyes opened wide. 'Of course I've thought of that but, Doone . . . think,' commanded Crystal. 'You are just beginning. I'm in my fourth year, deep in. Besides, there's nothing else I can do, but I'm sure your Baroness would help you to get a scholarship to the Academy of Music, and Pa wouldn't have to pay anything, anything at all.'

'If you asked anyone outside which one of us should go,' went on Crystal, 'I'm sure they would say it should be you – and how much nicer for Pa and me and everyone if, before you're asked to leave, you offered.'

'Offered!' That really took Doone by surprise.

'Yes. If you went to Pa now and said you wanted to leave, not for my sake, or for his, but for your music.'

'It would be a lie.'

'Maybe, but it . . . it would be. . . .' Crystal cast around in her mind for a word that would really impress Doone and, 'It would be noble,' she said. 'Like a prince. . . .'

'I don't want to be noble,' said Doone. 'I want to dance.'

Chapter Five

'Do children ever stay at Queen's Chase for the holidays?' Doone asked Mrs Challoner.

'You want to go home for Christmas, surely.'

'Not this Christmas,' said Doone.

It was a strangely empty Christmas. Will was spending it with Kate and her people. 'Only natural' – Ma tried to be fair, but she found it difficult to accept this extra daughter. 'You'd better get used to it,' Pa laughed at her. 'You'll probably have three more with Jim, Tim and Hughie.' As usual he left out Doone, but it was impossible to imagine marriage for 'that scrap of a boy', as Doone still seemed to Pa. Pa liked Kate, 'a thoroughly nice girl'. Kate was more than a girl, a young woman blossoming, not into the pretty spring flowering of plum or pear, but something as sturdy as apple or the strong clusters of cherry. She was a little stocky – 'I envy you that lovely figure,' she told Crystal. Kate wore her bright brown hair brushed and plaited round her head, 'like the Junior girls at Queen's Chase'. Crystal had been scornful, but it suited Kate, giving her a peasant look that matched her blossom skin, clear brown eyes, 'and sense,' said Pa. 'She might have come from Devon.' He could give no higher praise but, 'No style,' said Ma.

The wedding was to be in the New Year. 'No bridesmaids. No champagne.' Crystal was disappointed. 'My people are not well off,' said Kate, 'and Will and I like things simple; we'd rather put the money towards furnishing our flat.' They were to be married in the little church near her home in the early morning, with a breakfast afterwards for the two families, no one else. They would go away for a few days afterwards. 'To Devon,' Crystal predicted. 'Yes, to Devon,' said Will. 'It doesn't always have to be the bright lights, Crystal. Kate and I are happy just to be alone together.'

They would live over the Stonham shop and, 'I'll have to make it over to Will,' said Pa. 'He's our eldest son and has given up so much and worked so hard. I could do without this just now,' sighed Pa. 'Still, I'm sure she'll be a comfort to him.'

'Why should Will need comfort?' Ma was sharp.

'Every man does.' Pa sounded more than wistful.

'Do you know what?' Hughie had rushed to meet Crystal and Doone as soon as they arrived home. 'They ran away, Jim and Tim.'

'No!' breathed Crystal, excited.

'Yes. In the Army that counts as desertion. The police came here looking for them. Military Police!' Hughie's eyes glistened. 'They wouldn't believe Pa and Ma, and searched the house. Ma says she'll never hold up her head again.'

'I don't want to hear,' cried Doone but, 'Go on,' said Crystal.

'Of course they've been caught,' said Hughie. 'Six weeks' detention, so they can't have leave for Christmas, and Pa's got to go down and see their Colonel. All the way to Wales,' and Hughie mimicked Pa, 'Just when the shop's at its busiest, Maud!'

Hughie had grown into a strapping great boy, golden-haired, blue-eyed, handsome; next to Crystal, he was Ma's pride, but Hughie had one great resentment. He was training to be a mechanic and for a year now he had longed for, hoped for, even prayed for, a motor-bike. 'I'm over sixteen and I should have had one if things was fair,' he grouched. 'I don't go to a fancy school.'

'You couldn't. You haven't the talent,' Crystal said crushingly.

What Hughie did not know was that Pa had bought him a Yamaha for Christmas. It was hidden in Beppo's room behind the potato-sacks but, 'William! That's more than fifty pounds every month.'

'Don't I know it, but we have to try to keep the dish even.'

'It's such a lot of money!'

'Money, money, money.' Doone never remembered hearing

159

as much about it as in those holidays. He tried to retreat into his own world.

'Ma, can I go and see Mrs Sherrin?'

'Certainly not. Do you think I want the whole town to hear about Jim and Tim?'

'It isn't anything to do with Jim and Tim. Ruth is choreographing a ballet for our special dancing week next term. Lots of us are – little short ballets.'

'Isn't it time you had a try?' Mr Max had asked Doone.

'I can't make things up. I can only do them,' which was true and for which he was greatly in demand, for music as well as dancing.

He had planned to get the Baroness to help over the music. 'She has hundreds of records,' he had told Ruth but, to add to the emptiness, the Baroness had gone to her own Germany for Christmas.

He tried to tell Ma and Pa about the ballets. 'I shall be in one called *War of the Worlds* – I'm the planet Mars and fight with everyone and wear red tights – and I'm in one called *Trouble*. There are five girls and only four boys, so there's bound to be trouble!' He thought that a funny ballet but, 'Wait, I must see if the potatoes are done,' said Ma. 'There's a wonderful one called *Nightmare* – that's Roger's ballet. It begins with six of the big boys, all in black, bending right over a girl who's lying on the floor – you know how when you have a nightmare it seems to be pressing you down.' Doone shuddered. 'I have to find music for that, too.'

'Yes, dear,' said Ma. 'Crystal, have you seen my scissors?'

It was impossible to talk to Ma and Pa and, 'I *must* see Mrs Sherrin.'

'Well, you can't.'

'But Ruth's ballet. . . .'

Children's play, Ma would have said. She still had not understood that Her Majesty's Ballet took even a junior boy or girl's effort seriously; all Companies, everywhere, were looking for, hoping for that rare being, a good choreographer, even an embryo one.

'I'd better order a smaller turkey,' Ma said dismally. 'It's not going to seem like Christmas without Jim and Tim – and Will.'

160

'And me,' said Crystal.

'You?'

'Yes.' Crystal went on rather too fast. 'Valerie's down at Southport dancing in a show called *Christmas Crackers* at the theatre on the pier. They're closed on Christmas Day. She's in lodgings with just her grandma, and it'll be miserable. She can't come home, it's too far, so I said I'd go and spend Christmas week with them. Her grandma says she'll pay and be ever so grateful. Poor Valerie.'

'You mean you would rather spend Christmas in lodgings than here?'

'Yes, I would,' said Crystal. 'I could go to the theatre every night.'

'You are going to the theatre. We're booked for the pantomime.'

'The pantomime!'

'We could change it for a musical. . . .'

But Crystal cut Ma short. 'You don't know anything about musicals. You don't know anything about anything. At least Valerie's a professional.'

'Let her go.' Pa had come back from Jim and Tim's camp exhausted and seemed too tired to care any more. 'Let her go.'

On Christmas Day there was nothing on the tree for Doone from Ma and Pa. In this 'money' time he had asked, as he had asked last Christmas and on two birthdays, for money for his china pig. He had saved twenty-seven pounds towards the Steinway and hoped for – 'No, counted on,' he could have said – at least five pounds in an envelope, but all the presents were handed out and, though he had little parcels from Will, Kate, Crystal, Hughie, there was nothing from Ma and Pa.

'Do you think there isn't a present for you, Doone?' Ma had a secret that warmed her and, 'Hughie's not the only one to have a surprise,' she said.

'A surprise?' It was the last thing Doone expected.

'What would you say to a piano?'

Doone's mouth opened but he could only give a gasp.

'A piano that you know,' Ma went on.

'That I know?' A wild idea filled Doone; Ma could, he knew, work miracles but – it couldn't be, he thought, yet she was nodding and smiling.

'Mr Felix?' he said uncertainly.

'Yes, Mr Felix used to play it.'

'*Ma!*' It was a shout of such astonishment and joy that Ma was taken aback. Doone rushed at her and hugged her – something he had never done before – and, 'Where is it? Where?' he cried.

'In Will's room. He says you can keep it there as he's going away so soon.' The last words were lost. Doone had run to Will's room, flung open the door – and recognised the piano at once.

'Doone must have a piano, Ma. He must.' Crystal had been curiously insistent, and it would be nice if I did something for Doone for once, Ma had told herself. She always kept a little store of money, saved from housekeeping and the odd sums that Pa gave her. 'Money I can use to buy little private things,' said Ma. Almost always they were for Crystal but, this time it'll be for Doone, thought Ma virtuously and she went to Mrs Sherrin. 'What happened to that piano of Madame Tamara's?'

'She wanted me to buy it with the other fittings,' said Mrs Sherrin, 'but I really couldn't. Finally I sent it to Richardson's the auctioneers, poor old wreck.'

'Mr Felix used to play it?'

'Mr Felix could play it, but I doubt if anyone else. . . .'

'He taught Doone . . .,' argued Ma.

'Not on that old tin kettle.'

Richardson's still had the piano. When it was polished and cleaned it looked, to Ma, quite good and, 'I got it for eighty pounds,' she told Pa in glee.

When a child is disappointed it is not a sadness; it is tragedy. Doone did not know where to look, what to say, but stood – Ma thought transfixed – he felt too sick to move.

'Well?' asked Ma and, 'Are you happy?'

For answer Doone turned, put his arms round her and hid his face against her – anything but let her look at him – and Ma, flattered and pleased, patted his head and said, 'There, there, boy. There, there. . . .' Then she put him away and, 'Well,' she said again. 'Let's hear from you.'

Doone tried valiantly but the tin-kettle piano had stood two years or more in the auction rooms; the keys stuck together or were dumb where they had lost their strings or the felting had perished; the pedals squeaked.

He tried a mazurka, a waltz, then stopped. 'It won't play, Ma. It can't play. It's Madame Tamara's old tin kettle', and Doone put his head down on the keys in misery.

'Will, make it play,' Doone said desperately. 'Make it.'

'I wish I could,' said Will. 'Poor Ma.'

'Well, really, Maud!' Pa scolded. 'Eighty pounds! Eight hundred would have been nearer the mark.'

'I know.' Ma's voice was so small Doone could not bear to hear it. Pa had given him the five-pound note, but it was with a heavy heart that he put it in his pig; if an upright piano cost eight hundred, a Steinway grand. . . . It seemed, too, though he could not see why, that he was in disgrace. 'I can't do anything right,' said Ma as if it were his fault and, 'If only the holidays were over and I was back at school,' he told Will.

'I've heard of people being homesick,' said Will, 'never schoolsick,' but Doone could not smile.

'I often think,' Mrs Challoner said once to Mr Ormond, 'these children come to belong to us more than to their parents. After all, we have them for more than eight months of the year. Yes, they do belong.'

'Doone Penny for instance,' said Mr Ormond. 'But I wonder about that sister of his. Will she stay the course?'

All the important letters came at breakfast-time. 'Naturally,' said Ma. 'The post's delivered then.' Pa liked a good breakfast when he came back from the market and was usually in a good humour, so in holiday-time the Pennys lingered over breakfast. The letter was for Pa.

'Victor de Vaz?' said Pa. 'For heaven's sake! Who do we know with a name like that? Manager? *Christmas Crackers?*'

'That's Valerie's show they're producing at Southport.'

'What the hell's happened now?' said Pa.

He read it aloud. ' "Dear Mr Penny. . . ." '

'But he doesn't know you,' said Ma.

'Hush, Maudie. "Dear Mr Penny, As you well may have

heard" – I've heard nothing,' said Pa – ' "when our young leading dancer, Valerie Kydd Mortimer, fell ill and could not appear on Boxing Day, either for the matinée or evening show – we perform twice daily – we had no other dancer of her calibre and your daughter, Crystal, gallantly stepped in." '

'But she's not allowed to, William. She mustn't appear anywhere in public while she's at the Ballet School.'

'Seems to me,' said Pa, 'she mayn't be there much longer. Listen,' and he read. ' "She picked up the part immediately, improved it and gave a performance that far excelled young Valerie's." '

'I should hope so,' said Ma.

' "In fact, she brought the house down. She's a wonderful little dancer and has a most engaging personality. Our box office has doubled and no wonder. So we have arranged. . . ." '

'Arranged!' Pa almost spluttered. ' "Arranged for her to take over the part for the rest of our short season. With the Christmas posts there was no time to consult you." '

'I suppose he hasn't heard of a telephone.'

' "There is, of course, the matter of a licence. As this was an emergency, she has been dancing under another girl's name." '

'The twister! He could be had up for this.'

' "Crystal said you would be agreeable. . . ." '

'Oh, she did, did she?'

' "But now I must regularise matters and write to ask your official permission." *My* permission for a piece of dirty work like that.' Pa about choked with fury. 'Crystal to pretend she's helping a friend and then to steal her part. The little cheat!'

'He offers Crystal twice the money.' Hughie had picked up the letter. 'He says he'll give Valerie compensation.'

'What could compensate a girl for that?' And Pa stormed, 'Our daughter, *our* daughter, to behave like this.'

'William, where are you going?'

'To Southport to fetch her. This time Mr Victor de Vaz won't be the victor – but how I'm going to apologise to Valerie and her grandmother, I don't know,' said Pa.

'You can save your breath,' Crystal's voice came from the doorway. 'I've come back.'

The courtyard door had been unlocked because Hughie was cleaning his Yamaha in the yard, and Crystal had come

164

upstairs without any of them hearing. Now she put down her case and flung off her coat. 'Is there any breakfast left?' she asked, and Ma got up at once.

'You must have caught a very early train,' said Pa.

'I did.'

'You've been sacked,' said Hughie.

'Anything but,' said Crystal. 'I simply changed my mind', and, 'All I can say is "Thank God",' said Pa.

'Ma, coffee and scrambled eggs,' Crystal said over her shoulder.

'You're not in a café,' growled Pa.

At that, Crystal's control broke and, 'Shut up!' she screamed at Pa. 'Shut up! Shut up!'

'It was because of Valerie, wasn't it?' Ma had come into Crystal's room to help her unpack and take her clothes for washing. She did not mention Crystal's outburst and, 'It was Valerie, wasn't it?'

'Of course it wasn't.' Crystal was still furious – but with whom? wondered Ma. 'She'd do that to me, so why shouldn't I do it to her?'

'You don't have to behave like other people, especially when they do dirty tricks.'

'It's show business.'

'I was in show business and didn't do things like that.'

'Which perhaps explains why you never went very far.' Then the cold voice softened. 'It was so beautifully easy, Ma. None of that nag, nag, nag, when already you're trying so hard you think you'll break in half. They said I was wonderful – the de Vaz people. They gave me flowers, and Mr de Vaz went up to London to get me shoes. The shops were closed, of course, but he found them; he bought half a dozen pairs. Nothing was too good for me. I had a red tutu with spangles.'

'It must have been pretty.' There was yearning in Ma's voice, too, but, 'There you go!' said Crystal. 'A little ballerina!' She was mocking now. 'What do they know about ballerinas when all the time I knew I'm not ready even to dance the Diamond Fairy. I kept seeing Miss McKenzie and Mamzelly – Amy, Melissa, Galina – all the other girls – and I couldn't. I just couldn't. . . . Then why did I do it at all?' and suddenly

165

Crystal had to be cruel. 'What was it you said when Pa told us about when you wore the ostrich feathers?'

The whole of Ma winced. 'I never had your chances.'

'You said it was vulgar.' For a moment Crystal brooded. 'Yes, I know now what that means, and I get it from you. Oh, I wish I was pure.'

'Pure!' The word startled Ma. 'Crystal, of course you are.'

'I mean, not mixed up – all of one piece and why did I have to be your child?' cried Crystal. 'Why couldn't I be Mrs Sherrin's?'

'Mrs Sherrin's?' Ma could not believe what she heard.

'Yes. Ruth's all in one piece. Little saint Ruth!'

'So is Doone.' To her surprise Ma had found a shield.

'Yes,' said Crystal bitterly. 'Because you left him alone,' and, 'I'm the only one who's wrong. All wrong. It was the Competition all over again.'

Ma lifted her chin. 'Nonsense,' she said. 'That's years ago. You were quite right to walk out of a silly little pier-show when one day you're going to dance at the Royal Theatre.'

'When?' asked Crystal. 'Not for years. Perhaps never. Only two of the Senior School were accepted for the Company last year. Two out of more than a hundred. It's just work, work, work. . . .'

For once Ma had had enough. She rose. 'All that you say, Crystal, may be true. I know I'm not much. . . .' For a moment her voice quavered. 'I make terrible mistakes, even now.' The thought of Doone and the tin-kettle piano rose up and almost choked her. 'But at least there's been one thing; from the day you were born I believed in you. If you don't believe in yourself, that's not my fault,' and she walked out of Crystal's room.

166

Chapter Six

'WHO is that at the Judges' table?' asked Crystal. 'That young man talking to Anthea Dean.'

'Don't you know?' asked Melissa.

'He looks like. . . . He can't be. . . .'

'He is,' said Melissa. 'He's Yuri Koszorz.'

It was the last afternoon of the Special Dancing Week, the afternoon devoted to choreography.

In most schools the Easter term is one of comparative peace – Christmas excitements are over, examinations not yet begun; usually little happens, but at Queen's Chase the Easter term ended, 'and was beset', Mrs Challoner could have said, by this Week when the would-be dancers showed their paces. Parents were not invited – Queen's Chase had no 'open day' – only what Mrs Challoner called the 'hierarchy' of their particular dancing world was gathered: Mr Yeats and Miss Baxter, familiar figures now: senior teachers who taught the advanced boys and girls in the Upper School in Hammersmith. The Director of Ballet at the Royal Theatre was himself to judge the choreography. Well-known dancers might appear, Principals whose names and photographs were in the papers, who were on television, and yet they came to this Special Dancing Week to see the children who might one day succeed them.

As with the official Assessment, most of the children were tense and yet, to some, like Doone, it was a chance to see the very people who had been at their final audition, who had smiled at them like friends. Madam might be there on one or two of the afternoons; Doone had learnt to call his 'Lady' Madam. Last time he had talked to her. 'She often talks to the boys,' said jealous Zara. 'She talks to girls, too,' put in Amanda.

167

They, the first and second year children, only had to show a demonstration class; they were, though, allowed to watch the rest. Being in their fourth year Ruth and Crystal would both dance – 'but in dull peasant dances from *Giselle*,' Crystal had said. 'I'm sick of dirndls.'

'Don't you understand? They have to see how we would do in the *corps de ballet*,' said wiser Amy.

Crystal had also been chosen to dance the famous *Quartet of the Cygnets* from *Swan Lake*. There were two sets of cygnets; Ruth was in the other.

'Poor judges,' said Melissa. 'They have to see that *Quartet* every year, always the same.'

'Always different,' said Miss McKenzie, 'and it's a good testing-ground. If you can dance that *pas de quatre* properly, it goes a long way to help you.'

Also, to her surprise, Crystal had been given a solo. Usually it was only fifth-year girls and boys who danced those, but this time three fourth-year girls, Crystal, Ruth and Galina, had been put forward by Miss McKenzie. The dances were set by the judges, but she allotted them and, to Crystal's delight, she had been given the Diamond Fairy – 'in a simplified form, of course,' said Miss McKenzie – and that was not all.

'Crystal, will you be in my ballet?' Ruth had asked at the beginning of term. 'Will you?'

'No, thank you.'

'Look,' Ruth had said. 'We're in the same school, the same class. One day we may be in the same Company. We can't go on hating each other.'

'If we do, we do.'

'Oh, don't be so *silly*,' said Ruth, exasperated. 'I don't hate you. How could I when, as I thought of my ballet, the chief part was for you. You and two boys.'

'No other girls?'

'How could there be? It's Adam and Eve and the Serpent. Charles will be Adam and Kui – you know, he seems not to have a bone in his body – he's the Serpent.' Crystal could see that Kui would make a wonderful serpent but, 'Has Doone anything to do with this?' she had asked.

'Yes. He's God.'

'God?'

168

'Yes, literally. He plays a tremendous roll of drums, God's voice when God gets angry. That's because you and Charles suddenly know you're naked.'

'But we don't dance naked.' Even Crystal had seen that in school choreography they could not go as far as that but, 'In the Wardrobe I found some marvellous flesh-coloured tights,' said Ruth. 'My mother's helping me to dye vests to match, so you do look naked, except that Charles will have to wear a jock-strap and you'll have a garland of flowers across you and flowers in your hair. You'll look so lovely!' Ruth's admiration had been unmistakable. 'Then, for after the Serpent, Charles has helped me make you a tiny apron of fig-leaves, and Charles has an outer fig-leaf jock-strap.'

'That ought to make them sit up!' and Crystal had given in.

Each ballet was allowed just three minutes. 'So we can only use bits of the music,' Doone explained to Roger and Ruth. The boy or girl choreographer had to come to the Judges' table and say: 'My name is Roger – Ruth – Amanda – Jonathan – Kui – Justin. I'm twelve – thirteen – fourteen. My ballet is called. . . .' The programme had to describe the ballet and how, ideally, it should be set and dressed. 'But actually they have to make do with what they can find in the school wardrobe,' said Mrs Challoner, and added, 'There are some tussles over that, I can tell you.' High indignant young voices: 'I need at least eight white tutus, and there are only six.' 'Hasn't anyone got a sky-blue cat-suit?' 'I want that blue veil for my Moon,' said Amanda of the *Planets*. 'Well, I need it for my *Scheherazade*.' Justin was firm.

'I got it first.'

'You didn't.'

Fortunately no one else wanted Ruth's pink tights or Kui's green ones on to which Mrs Sherrin had sewn a shimmer of sequins.

'You see, it isn't only choreography,' said Mrs Challoner. 'The children have to find the music, design the dresses. They have to train their dancers but first persuade them to give up the time – a great deal of extra time. Remember, ballet classes and school work mustn't be interrupted. It's really a test of persuasive powers,' she said, 'and, oddly enough, not only of popularity; the children will often agree to be in a ballet by

169

someone not very popular if they can see it's worthwhile.' No teacher was allowed to help and, 'I think it's asking a great deal of them,' said Mrs Challoner but ballet always asked a great deal.

To Doone it was a halcyon time, 'and the end of the holidays was all right,' he said; he had gone to stay with Will and Kate, tactfully out of Ma's way. Above all, the Baroness had come back and, soon after, had summoned Doone. 'You had a good Christmas? No?'

'No.' She had seen Doone's eyes brim and, 'Ach! What a pity! Tell me,' and Doone told about Madame Tamara's piano as quietly as he could. 'No one can make it play. Will said it would cost as much as a new piano – besides, the case has worms.'

'It was worm-eaten. Poor tin kettle.'

'Yes. Men came and took it away – to the tip, Hughie said. Ma wouldn't speak to me. Pa gave me five pounds, but what's the use?'

'Plenty of use,' said the Baroness, that cheerful lady. 'Certainly you must put money in the pig.'

'I've only got thirty-two pounds, thirty-seven pence. Will says Steinway grands cost thousands.'

'Never do arithmetic, Doone,' and the Baroness said, 'Men in small houses see great mountains and one day, if they keep their eyes fixed on them, they climb them. You'll see.'

The Baroness seemed to have a kindly wand that could touch sore places, heal them and spirit worries away. 'Money worry,' said Doone; even his other particular money worry – what Crystal had told him – had been insidious. 'I *don't* want to be noble,' he told the Baroness.

'But this Crystal is diabolical,' and, 'Listen to me, Doone,' said the Baroness. 'No boy or girl has ever had to leave Her Majesty's Ballet School for lack of money. I doubt if your papa has to spend a hundred pounds a year for either of you at school. You would cost far more than that if you lived at home.'

'Pa says we mustn't take charity.'

'Charity! You are earning for the Ballet School every minute of your day because, when you make your début, you will pay them back handsomely. Handsomely.'

170

That found an echo in Doone; even in his first year it had begun to dawn on him that, if he stayed at Queen's Chase, his dancing did not belong to him alone, but to Her Majesty's Ballet. It was not what Pa thought or Ma thought that mattered now, it was what Miss McKenzie thought or Mr Max, all the teachers and, more importantly, those top people who would come in force for the Week, and, 'Thank you, Baroness,' he had said with all his heart. 'Ach!' she dismissed it. 'Let us get busy and find this music,' and soon they had been deep in the choreography.

For Roger's *Nightmare, Gaston de la Nuit,* 'that wonderful suite,' said the Baroness. 'We could take parts of "Le Gibet" – which means the gibbet from which people were hung. It is eerie! Frightening! They will all have shivers. By Ravel, Doone. You must remember the composers' names. And for the little Ruth. . . .' When Doone had told the Baroness the story of Ruth's ballet, she had laughed, not with amusement but delight. 'But I must meet this splendid choreographer.'

Doone took Ruth to see her – as the Baroness had asked Ruth, Ma could not say 'No' – and Lötte von Heusen had treated Ruth with the same respect as the ballet chiefs presently would do.

'There's a Hindemith suite,' she had said. 'I think we could find something in that.'

'Hindemith.' Doone did remember that name. 'Mr Felix said he was full of sound and fury, signifying nothing.'

'Hush!' said the Baroness and, 'Ach! Don't you say that. A lot of older musicians refuse to understand Hindemith; perhaps Mr Felix did not play him enough. In this suite there is a pastorale, the second movement, *perfect* for the Garden of Eden; next it becomes more complex, frightening, for the Serpent and also there is a passage that is – what shall we say? – yes, beguiling. After all, this is ballet music.' She had helped Doone make a tape and, 'If I made a piano score for you, you should try to play it,' she said. 'The Ravel is impossibly difficult but this you could do and it might open your tiny mind, which is like a nutpea – no, a peanut, du Dummerchen, and also you might need it for accompanying. I don't expect you can always use the tape,' which was true, especially when Ruth made Crystal and Charles and Kui work a part over and

171

over again. She was often white around the nostrils, curt, even bad-tempered, and there were fierce altercations with Crystal. 'No, no, no! It's *not* like that. You should be just innocent and loving. You're flirting, Crystal.'

'I think Eve should flirt.'

'Not till after the Serpent. She doesn't know how to,' and, 'The opening is an idyll. You can't flirt to that. Crystal, you're spoiling it,' Ruth fretted.

'Very well, I'm vulgar.' 'Vulgar' was Crystal's new word. Then 'Put me out. I don't care.' As a matter of fact, she would not have given up the part of Eve for anything and was secretly glad when the omnipotent Melissa intervened. Melissa was head girl now and spoke with authority.

'It's Ruth's ballet, Crystal. You said you would be in it and you must do as she says.'

'Absolutely,' said another girl, Lucy.

'You'll never get on if you go on behaving like this,' put in Galina, and Crystal felt again the unity of the others about her, a bond that said '*We* don't behave like this'. Perhaps, as a little girl, Crystal had been right to use that 'we'.

It still astonished her that her classmates and even those who, like Melissa, were in their fifth year, accepted the fact that a few of them, perhaps three or four or five, excelled the others, outshone them – she herself, Ruth and the small half-Russian, half-Irish Galina – without, as far as she, Crystal, could see, any trace of being jealous. 'What good would it be if we were?' asked sensible Melissa. 'It doesn't matter how we try; we're not as good as you are. It's not our fault. That's how we were born.'

Miss Baxter often said something of the same kind. 'It really makes one believe the stars have influence. How does it happen that three or four of these – one could call them "plus dancers" – come in one year, sometimes almost a whole batch, another year none?'

'So just think how lucky you are,' Melissa told Crystal.

For the Adam and Eve ballet, Doone had to sit at the side of the classroom with the two big boys, Philip and Louis, who were responsible for running the tapes or records. 'The flute is the Serpent,' Doone told Philip. 'The drum is God's voice. I'm

172

God. I come in just after the trumpets,' and it was there that they stopped the tape and, at a nod from Philip, Doone beat out God's voice. He thought it should really have come from the ceiling and wished with all his heart he had one of the Royal Theatre's huge drums instead of a single small one from Dalcroze classes; he did his best to make it fearsome and, when the staff came to rehearsal, he was surprised, even offended, when they laughed as Eve and Adam, in their fig-leaves, stepped out from behind the hat-stands. Soon he understood it was what Ruth had meant – Ruth had a quiet sense of humour – and then he waited for the laughs. 'I *love* being God's voice,' he said.

This time, thought Crystal, this time the person in the Penny family they'll look at will be me. I'm in *Giselle* and the *Dance of the Cygnets*, I'm the Diamond Fairy and Eve. This time it must be me, thought Crystal but, 'Crystal, have you seen your brother as Mars?' said the girls. 'As the left-out boy in *Trouble?* In Colin's hunting ballet as the Fox? Crystal, have you *seen* him?'

Crystal went to Miss Thompson in the boys' wing. Instinct told her not to go to Miss Walsh.

'What are you doing over here?' asked Miss Thompson at once. 'You know you're not supposed. . . .'

'I had to come,' Crystal interrupted. 'Please may I speak to you, Miss Thompson? Miss Walsh wouldn't listen, but I thought I could talk to you. . . .'

'If Mr Ormond . . . Well, come outside,' and Crystal knew Miss Thompson was flattered.

'It's about my little brother, Doone. We're worried about him at home.' Crystal's voice was earnest and concerned. 'My mother knows that parents can't interfere over dancing, but. . . .'

'But what, Crystal?'

'Miss Thompson, it's this choreography. Doone's only twelve and he's in four ballets – four – and does a lot of accompanying, and of course there's all our usual work as well. He's so strung-up. Last weekend he hardly slept at all and he's not eating.'

'I haven't noticed that.'

'I mean – at home,' Crystal said it hastily. 'I should have thought one ballet was enough. *I'm* only doing one – and his part as Mars in the *Planets* ballet is terribly exhausting. What do you think?'

'I think. . . .' Miss Thompson was completely won over. 'He's a lucky boy to have a sister so concerned for him. I'll see what I can do.'

'Oh, thank you. Thank you.' But Crystal had reckoned without ballet tradition.

Miss Thompson took it upon herself to beard Mr Max. 'Understand,' Polly Walsh had told her when she was engaged, 'you never, never interfere on the ballet side unless it's a case of illness and then it's wisest to go through Sister', but, 'They've a fetish about this dancing. I'm thinking of the child,' Miss Thompson told herself, and Mr Max was surprised by an incongruous figure in a white overall. 'I should like to speak to you about Doone Penny.'

'What about Doone Penny?'

'Do you know, Mr Max, that for the choreography afternoon he is dancing in four different ballets?'

'Indeed I know. It's giving me quite a problem having to get them all on, off and changed, but I don't see any other problem.'

'I do.' Miss Thompson spoke emphatically. 'It's too much, with all the piano-playing as well. Doone's getting too tired.'

'If he's going to be a dancer, he'll have to get used to being tired.'

'Over-tired?' Miss Thompson was slightly belligerent.

'He'll recover. They always do. I must go, Miss. . . .' Mr Max had no idea of Miss Thompson's name but, seeing her chagrin, he said kindly, 'If you're worried about the boy, give him all the rest you can – early bed.'

Crystal, of course, did not know what Miss Thompson had tried to do, but Doone was still in all four ballets and, 'He's always in my way,' Crystal burst out to Ma that weekend.

'How can he?' Ma was mystified.

'He always, always goes one better than I can and he doesn't even *try*.' Ma could hear the envy and frustration.

'Dearie, you're building this up. . . .'

174

'It's built.' Crystal was terse, then cried, 'Ma, *why* couldn't he do music?'

'I'd rather not discuss Doone's music.' Ma was still bruised from the disaster of the piano.

'*Please*, Ma,' and it was then that Ma asked, 'Have any of the ballet people ever heard Doone play?'

Crystal's eyes brightened.

She laid her plans with a strategy that made Colonel Ingram, that skilful soldier, say when Charles told him the whole story, 'That little girl is wasted on dancing. She ought to go into politics.' There is just one person, thought Crystal, Doone might listen to, and, 'Is Madam coming for the choreography?' she asked Miss McKenzie.

'Well, she has a bad cold and shouldn't come out, but I expect she will,' said Miss McKenzie.

The day before the choreography afternoon was always given over to its dress rehearsal, to which Queen's Chase teachers, both ballet and academic, were invited as well as all the domestic staff. Mr Max and Miss McKenzie marshalled the boys and girls; Mrs Gillespie and the other housemistresses helped with quick changes; senior girls and boys did the make-up for the dancers. There was fun and jollity but a great deal of tension. Ruth was pale and taut but held herself in control. 'Crystal, you will listen to the music,' she begged. 'You will remember.'

'I might.' Crystal was tantalising to the last. As for Doone, he was having an orgy of an afternoon; when his dancing was finished he scurried across to Philip and Louis's corner to take his place at the drum as, '*It Happened in Eden*,' read out Mr Max.

Ruth came in, made her little speech; it had to be to Mrs Challoner, who was deputising for the Judges. Ruth put the programme on the table and moved to sit down by the 'orchestra' to make room for the dancers.

'Eden' was only the classroom; the trees, two hat-stands, but they looked quite humorous when a big cardboard apple was hung on one, on the other the fig-leaf apron and jock-strap. Ruth knew she had achieved a good balance between wit and poetry. For once she was confident and,

'When you and Charles walk through the Garden of Eden to that pastorale, it really is beautiful,' she told Crystal. Happy tears were in her eyes.

With a small click Philip started the tape and, instead of the glorious melody of the idyll, came silence – a silence only broken by the sound of a car outside; of a voice speaking in the garden, a rustle of paper, and, 'Someone has erased the tape.' Philip spoke as if he were strangling.

'You're playing the wrong side.' That was Louis. 'Reverse it,' and, 'You've mixed them up,' said Miss McKenzie.

'I couldn't have.'

'You must have.'

When that was useless, 'Go through them all,' ordered Miss McKenzie – she and Mr Max had come over. 'I'm sure they've been mixed up, that's all.'

'They couldn't have been.' Louis was a proud boy. 'As soon as a tape's finished, we take it out and back it goes into the stack. Look.' They looked and there was no mistake in the order. 'It's labelled "Garden of Eden, Hindemith",' said Louis. 'It's labelled still,' and Philip stood up and faced them all. 'Someone has deliberately erased it,' said Philip.

'Who would have done a thing like that?' was asked in the Staff Room.

'To begin with, someone who knew how,' said Mr Max.

'My dear Leo,' said Mrs Challoner, 'there isn't a child in the school who owns a transistor cassette who wouldn't know. Philip or Louis must have muddled the order of the tapes.'

'If they had, it would be there,' said Miss McKenzie, 'and it isn't.' That was irrefutable.

'Someone was jealous of Ruth,' said Mamzelly.

'That's Crystal,' Miss Hurley spoke. 'But she would hardly have destroyed a ballet in which she had the chief part.'

'Crystal herself's been growing unpopular. Some other boy or girl. . . .'

'They wouldn't have penalised Ruth.' Miss McKenzie was sure of that.

'Doone Penny's allowed in that corner. It was he who made the tape with Lötte von Heusen. Do you think he played it over and did this by accident?'

176

'If he had, being Doone, he would have called for help at once,' said Mrs Challoner. 'He cared a great deal about that little ballet.'

'Then who? Who?' but, 'There's no time to waste wondering about who or why.' Miss McKenzie was always practical. 'We'll hand that over to you, Clio,' she told Mrs Challoner. 'We have to think what can be done.'

'If anything can be done.'

'We have just twenty-four hours.'

'Do you think Lötte von Heusen, in her kindness – she is so kind – would make another tape for us?'

'The Baroness is on tour in Australia,' said Doone when he was asked.

'We could find the record.'

'Try the BBC.'

'But she only took bits,' Doone objected, 'then had to arrange them.'

'If we found the record, could you do that?'

Doone shook his head. 'She made them match . . . transposed bits. . . .'

He, the Garden of Eden dancers, Philip and Louis, Miss McKenzie, and Mr Max were gathered in the classroom. 'Doone has the piano score,' said Crystal.

'Ye-e-s.' Doone had to admit it.

'And you can play it?'

'Of course he can,' said Crystal. 'He's been playing it all the time – so what's all the fuss about? We can do it to the piano.'

'It wouldn't be the same,' said Ruth, but she looked less wan.

'We could make it the same,' argued Crystal. 'Listen, Ruth. Take the bit about the Serpent; José plays the flute. You could pick up the melody from Doone, couldn't you, José? Well, then?'

'Go and practise,' Miss McKenzie ordered Doone, José, Charles, Crystal, Kui and Ruth. 'Practise while we run through the other ballets. Then we'll see,' but Doone hung back.

'Couldn't Jonah?' Jonah had come to see if there were anything he could do to help. 'I mean, Mr Jonah . . . sir?'

'I'm a bit late on the scene,' said Jonah. 'I shouldn't do it as well as you. Come on, Doone.'

177

'Splendid,' said Miss McKenzie. 'Well done, Doone and José,' but, 'Will the piano be turned back to the room so I can watch the dancers?' asked Doone, which was not the real reason. That he had fathomed at once. So that no one will see me was the truth.

One more blow was coming to Doone. 'The piano has to come over the drum rolls at the end,' said Mr Max. 'Louis, you will have to take over the drums.'

'So I'm not to be the voice of God,' said Doone.

'It *is* Yuri Koszorz.'

Although Crystal and Melissa had watched him dance at the Royal Theatre, looked at his photograph in magazines and newspapers – Crystal had one pinned up over her bed – it was a shock to see him 'live' and so close. Crystal was in her dress, or no dress, as Eve, the pink silk tights and vest, a band of flowers – 'carefully placed,' Charles teased her – more flowers in her hair. She was waiting to go on. Her ear should have been tuned to the Hindemith pastorale but, as she looked at that figure, so brilliantly alive that it seemed to outshine everyone else, even Anthea Dean and Ennis Glyn, at the gold-brown head and hands that moved eloquently as he talked, other music woke in Crystal, music that should not have been there:

'Some enchanted evening
You may see a stranger. . . .'

Valerie had been in the chorus of the musical, 'until I got thrown out,' said Valerie, 'when they found how old I was.' In that brief glory she had taken Crystal to see it, and the song had touched deep chords.

'You may see a stranger
Across a crowded room. . . .'

He was laughing and talking, especially to Anthea Dean. Of all people in the world, Crystal would have liked to be Anthea Dean. 'It's not fair,' Mr Yeats had once said, 'that any girl should be so pretty and dance so well.'

Anthea was adored by the public and, more importantly, by other dancers. The boys at Queen's Chase could not take their

178

eyes off her, nor could most of the girls; to them it seemed impossible to believe she had once been one of themselves, a gawky little girl, newly come to Queen's Chase, her hair done up in plaits just like theirs, wearing the same blue, with rose-coloured belt, working in the same classrooms. 'I had knobbly knees and my teeth looked too big,' Anthea told them. Now they looked like pearls and she must have had the same witchery; she had gone from the Senior School straight into the Company, and at twenty-two was a Principal with a brilliance about her, a diamond sparkle that eclipsed even the elegant tried and trusty Ennis Glyn; but they, and Yuri Koszorz, thought Crystal, and a few, rare others were like precious stones that had been cut and polished, polished and repolished, as indeed they had.

Now Crystal looked past Anthea Dean to Yuri Koszorz.

'You should see him move,' whispered Melissa.

'I have.'

'Not in the same room with you. He gave us fifth-year girls a Workshop. Miss McKenzie said it was a great privilege, and it was. He has such power.' It was an odd word for the unimaginative Melissa to use. 'He danced with Amy.'

'Amy!' and a horrible possessiveness rose up in Crystal. Then, as he sat still for a moment, withdrawn, his face looked older, far older than the hair cut longer than most of the men's; older than his eyes, which were small, brown, merry, even mischievous, and yet, 'Why does he suddenly look so sad?' whispered Crystal.

'I expect he has suffered.'

'Is he Russian?'

'Polish, but he trained in Russia. Miss McKenzie told us he came to London with the Bolshoi and defected. We took him into the Company' – Melissa, too, used the proprietorial 'we' – 'until he found his way. Then he went to New York and did two world tours. With our Company he comes and goes, and now he's come back as guest artist till the spring.'

'But what's he doing *here*?'

'Come to look us over, I expect. He's a choreographer as well as a dancer and has just done a new ballet they say is sensational. He may be looking for future dancers,' and Melissa added, 'He was here yesterday for the solos.'

179

'I never noticed him.'

'Because you were too taken up with yourself,' said blunt Melissa, but, 'I danced the Diamond Fairy and never knew that Yuri Koszorz was there!' said Crystal.

'I did,' said Ruth and shuddered.

Miss McKenzie had given Ruth the timid half-flirting Serving Maid's dance from *The Gods Go a-Begging*. 'Thank God it was timid,' said Ruth, because when the music began she could not move. Jonah had had to start the piano again – this time there was no Doone to chant from the wings, but Miss McKenzie had given Ruth the sharpest slap she had ever had. 'Go on and *do* it.'

'And she danced it beautifully,' Miss McKenzie told Miss Hurley.

'Yes, but she won't always have a Jean McKenzie behind her'; and indeed Ruth had seen the Judges' heads close together as they consulted. Yuri Koszorz obviously put in a word for her, because they had turned to him, but, 'I never knew!' said Crystal. She knew now.

Ruth was presenting her programme. 'My name is Ruth Sherrin. I am fourteen. My ballet is called *It Happened in Eden*.'

'Please, please hum the pastorale's opening to Crystal before she goes on,' Ruth had begged Charles, 'or she'll never get the rhythm.' That was a wise precaution; 'Some enchanted evening' was loud in Crystal's ear until, 'Six, seven, eight,' she heard Charles counting. 'Slowly. Softly.' It was the Hindemith idyll; this was not evening but a serious work afternoon; discipline took over and Crystal danced, not Crystal Penny as Eve, but Eve as Ruth had imagined Eve. The Judges were pleased. 'Style with a good sense of performance' was the verdict. Crystal, though, was filled with remorse and regret. If only we had had the full orchestra on the tape, and, Why did I do it? Oh, why?

The sight of Yuri Koszorz seemed to have opened a bigger world, too big for spite. She winced at that word, which had only now occurred to her; spite and jealousy, they seemed petty now, and Why did I bother? thought Crystal.

* * *

180

'Excuse me, Mrs Challoner, but could I have Doone? He has to go to bed early.' Miss Thompson had been chasing him off to bed for the last week – 'As if I were a baby,' muttered Doone.

'Bed?' Mrs Challoner raised an eyebrow.

'Mr Max said he was to have plenty of rest. He has had a great deal of strain today.'

Who hasn't? Mrs Challoner wanted to say. It was the evening of the – to Doone and Ruth, at least – harrowing day, and Mrs Challoner had called all of those who were concerned to her study. She had let Philip, Louis, Charles and Ruth go, but kept Crystal and Doone.

Ruth, though, was happy. The Judges' comments had, on the whole, been good; all Queen's Chase knew they were there, not to praise but to appraise, sometimes pungently, and they could be humorous. Andrew Devereux, Director of Ballet at the Royal Theatre, read through Amanda's programme, and 'About the *Planets* ballet, Amanda: you say "the Moon falls to the ground". Did you mean that?'

'Yes,' Amanda said, puzzled. The young choreographers and their dancers were gathered, sitting on the floor, to hear the verdict, and, 'She falls to the ground.'

'What ground? Your ballet is in space.'

Even though a ballet could be fantasy, the fantasy had to be founded on logic.

Of *Trouble*: 'You didn't give your other boys enough to do. I think you concentrated on the girls and the left-out boy.' Of *Nightmare*, he told Roger: 'You were lucky in your girl' – she was Zara, who could act – 'but your boys were not properly drilled.'

Of *It Happened in Eden*: 'A stereotyped idea, Ruth, but freshly handled with originality, and that's not easy to do. Congratulations.' Congratulations from Andrew Devereux! and Anthea Dean had smiled and said, 'We loved your fig-leaves.'

'That's what I'm going to be when I grow up,' Ruth told Doone, 'a choreographer.'

'Well, I'm not going to do your music,' said Doone. 'Never again,' and now, 'Just a moment, Miss Thompson,' said Mrs Challoner – she did not ask Miss Thompson to sit down. 'We're trying to get to the bottom of the mystery of how and why Ruth's tape was erased or disappeared.'

'I believe I can help you there.' Miss Thompson shut the door. 'Being in charge of the younger boys. . . .'

'Under Miss Walsh,' said Mrs Challoner.

'I think I know them as well as anyone,' Miss Thompson went smoothly on, 'and I can tell you that from the day Doone Penny came here he has been trying to draw attention to himself.'

I should have thought that was Crystal – but Mrs Challoner did not say it; she had seen how Doone had given a gasp like a little fish exposed to air.

'Remember all that fuss about *The Dream*. . . . And you should hear him, as I have heard him, Mrs Challoner, talking about some Baroness he says he's friends with, and about Charles Ingram, making out he's as much at home with them as if he were Charles's brother – when we all know,' Miss Thompson said with a sniff, 'that Mr Penny runs a greengrocer's shop.'

Crystal jumped to her feet; Mrs Challoner put out a hand and caught her. 'Mr Penny is a greengrocer,' said Mrs Challoner. 'He is also one of the nicest gentlemen I know.' She emphasised the 'gentlemen' but there was no stopping the Tom Cat.

'Then Doone getting himself into all those ballets. Courting notice, overdoing it. Why, his sister had to come to me about it, didn't you, dear?'

'I'm not your dear,' said Crystal. It was getting dangerous.

'And of all the children,' said Miss Thompson, 'he was the only one whom Philip and Louis, good boys both of them and *trustworthy*' – Miss Thompson darted a look at Doone – 'the only one they allowed near the tapes and records, and it's my opinion' – Miss Thompson always had an opinion – 'that Doone wanted Miss Baxter, Mr Devereux, all those people and Madam, particularly Madam, to hear him play – and so he erased the tape.'

'Plausible, but it doesn't quite fit,' Mrs Challoner had begun when she was interrupted. Crystal was facing Miss Thompson. Doone, too dumbfounded to speak, had never seen her as angry, even in her confrontations with Pa. Her cheeks were scarlet, her eyes like blue fire, as she moved in front of Doone.

'That's the last thing,' blazed Crystal, 'the last thing my brother would have done. He of all boys! How dare you! How dare you even suggest it, you lying bitch!'

'Crystal!' Mrs Challoner's voice cut in. 'How dare you use language like that to one of the staff. Apologise to Miss Thompson at once.'

'I'll apologise for the words,' Crystal was still shaking, 'if she'll apologise to Doone.'

'Ap-apologise?' Miss Thompson's astonished whisper seemed to come from high up in the ceiling.

'Apologise first,' Mrs Challoner commanded Crystal. She was so crisp that Crystal had to say, 'I apologise for calling you names.' Then she walked to the window and stood with her back to them.

Why did I do that? she was asking herself. What's happened to me? There was Tom Cat playing my game and I went and spoiled it. Why? What's got into me? asked Crystal.

'Doone, come here', and, as if he had been caught in a bad dream, Doone got up and came to Mrs Challoner. 'When Miss Thompson pointed out that you were the only one, besides Philip and Louis, who had access to the tapes, that was true, wasn't it?' Doone nodded. 'But did you do what she said you did?'

'Of course not.'

'I didn't think you did', and, over Doone's head, Mrs Challoner told Miss Thompson, 'What you don't know is that Doone asked for the piano to be kept turned so no one could see him. He hoped Madam wouldn't be there. Baroness von Heusen is one of his dearest friends and I think the Ingrams look on him almost as Charles's brother. If he has to be "put to bed", though I'm sure he's perfectly able to do that for himself, please ask Miss Walsh to come and fetch him. You may go, Miss Thompson.' Go for ever if I had my way, thought Mrs Challoner.

When Miss Thompson had shut the door behind her with an angry crack, 'I think you have something to tell us, Crystal,' said Mrs Challoner.

'Does everyone have to know?' Crystal asked Mrs Challoner. 'Everyone?'

183

'I shall have to tell Miss McKenzie and Mr Max.'

'Philip? Louis?' Since when had Crystal worried about Philip and Louis?

'I shall give out tomorrow that the mystery of the tape has been solved and no blame attached to Philip, Louis or Doone.'

'But they'll all wonder.'

'Let them wonder. It's nearly the Easter holidays and when we come back they'll have other things to think of. The summer-term School Performances, examinations – and remember, Crystal, no one need be told the truth except as far as it concerns them, and this really only concerns you, Doone and me. For myself, I am going to forget about it. I'm sure Doone won't hold a grudge against you, particularly after the way you defended him against the Tom Cat.' Crystal looked at Mrs Challoner, startled. Did the staff know, then, all the secret names? Did they know everything? Crystal was beginning to think they did. Her plan had worked perfectly; she had danced Eve, Doone had had to play, then came these subtle ... boomerangs. Crystal found the right word.

She had dared to approach Madam. It took more than a cold to keep Madam away from what she considered duty, and she had appeared, well wrapped up, and watched each ballet intently.

'Madam, you heard my brother play the Hindemith for the Eden ballet?'

'Your brother?'

'Doone. Doone Penny. I'm Crystal.'

'Oh, it was he. I couldn't see. He played very well.'

'Yes. He's only twelve. Madam, don't you think he's outstanding?'

The vagueness disappeared. The eyes which, as Doone could have told Crystal, 'seemed to look deep into you' this time looked Crystal through and through and, ' "Outstanding" is a big word,' said Madam. 'I'm sure his music will help him with his dancing.'

As Crystal had retired, beaten, she had caught Yuri Koszorz's eye; he had smiled at her and said, 'Well done.' He meant it for her dancing of Eve, but Crystal had not been able to smile back; instead she looked at the floor and blushed like any ashamed schoolgirl. Would Yuri Koszorz have said, 'Well done' if he had known about the tape? Would there have been that comradeship, instant between serious dancers, even if one of them is a world-famous star, the other a schoolgirl aspirant? She would have forfeited that. There might even have been a look of disgust, and when, in the study, Mrs Challoner said, 'I think you have something to tell us,' she, proud Crystal, had an urgent desire to – Don't they call it 'come clean'? thought Crystal – and, yes, to cleanse herself. She had told about the tape – and everything, thought Crystal.

Mrs Challoner had not dwelt on any of the obvious things: how jealousy was not only poisonous but also silly. 'It's not Doone who is poisoned and made unhappy, it's you.'

'I know all *that*,' Crystal would have said impatiently but, when she had ended with, 'I'm sorry I was rude,' 'I'm not,' said Mrs Challoner. 'That was the best thing I've ever heard you do.'

'The *best*?'

'Yes. You mustn't, of course, speak to a member of the staff like that again, but you stood up for your brother and, don't you think it's time,' Mrs Challoner spoke with extreme gentleness, 'time you got rid of all this nonsense and let Doone be Doone and, far more importantly for you, Crystal be Crystal – as I know she could be?' asked Mrs Challoner.

'I promise,' said Crystal. It was a fervent promise, and as she went up to bed she felt a new lightness of mind and heart, as if she had shed a skin that was too tight for her or broken out of a hard shell and had taken a leap into the future, a leap that matched Yuri Koszorz's when, as the Rose, he leapt through the open window into the night, seeming never to come down again. Crystal, like Ma, had seen him dance *Le Spectre de la Rose* and, too, had marvelled. Suppose I could be that girl dreaming in the chair? The thought sent tremors through her. Why not? she thought. Yuri Koszorzes of the dancing world go on almost for ever, and I am coming on. It might happen, but it was enough for now that he had smiled at her, spoken to her, and, I'm glad I was Eve, she thought; but the tune she heard, as she undressed, washed, brushed her teeth, brushed her hair, wearing her little-girl quilted, rosebud-printed dressing-gown was not the pastorale. 'Some enchanted evening,' hummed Crystal.

Chapter Seven

'LET Crystal be Crystal.'

'She doesn't need any encouragement to be that,' Will would have said. Crystal had tried to keep her promise, but Queen's Chase and Porlock Road were different worlds and that holiday, 'Doone's going to Paris'. She said it almost in a shriek. 'Paris!'

'Yes, I've got his passport,' said Pa.

Miss Thompson had left. 'I can't cope with these children.'

'No, I don't think you can,' said Mr Ormond.

'I shall write to the Governors.'

'Do,' said Mr Ormond.

And now, 'If I have to have an assistant,' said Polly Walsh, 'this time please let me find my own.'

To Doone, Miss Thompson's going was a relief. Next term will be great, he had thought but, 'I'm leaving, too,' said Charles.

'*You!*' That was a bombshell and, 'Why?' Doone had wailed. 'Why?'

'I've had enough,' said Charles.

'I thought you loved it.'

'I did. I do ... but not with all of me.'

'Then what – what will you do?'

'I'm going into the Army. That's my other half. I'm my father's son as well as my mother's. Besides, she knows now I'll never make the top.'

'But you dance so beautifully.'

'Not beautifully enough. That'll be you,' said Charles, but Doone was not taking any chances.

After that choreography day, he had written to the Baroness – she would be back from Australia, he had thought. It was the first letter he had ever written and he had no idea how to address her. He had, though, once taken a letter to the postbox from Mrs Challóner to the Vicar and noticed it was addressed to 'The Reverend', so he addressed the envelope to The Reverend Baroness von Heusen.

'Dear Reverend Baroness', but it did not feel right, and he wrote as well:

> Dear Dear Baroness,
>   Please could you send me a surtifficate to say I am *not* good at the piano. It would be a grate help.
>
> Love,
DOONE
>   PS. I hope you are well.

and she had telephoned that he should come at once and see her.

The Baroness was a godsend. Doone could not have told Pa, Ma or Will about the tape, it would have been too cruel; nor could he betray Crystal to Miss Glyn or Stella but the Baroness was different, far outside the family and school. 'Ach!' she said when he had finished. 'What a little serpent!'

'No, that was Kui.' Doone still took everything literally. He sighed. 'Ma says I make nothing but trouble.'

'*You* make nothing but trouble?'

'Yes. Crystal did that because of me. Baroness,' Doone asked in anguish, 'do you think I ought to leave Queen's Chase?'

'Nicht um alles in der Welt!' As always, when she was angry the Baroness exploded into German.

'What does that mean?'

'Not for all the tea in China!' and, 'Tell me, Doone,' said the Baroness, 'when we go to our concerts, what happens to you?'

'I see pictures,' said Doone.

'Pictures?'

'Yes. Pictures but with dancing steps and how they fit.'

'Then, my little man, you are a dancer and not a musician', and, seeing Doone's troubled seriousness, she began to play-act. 'Dolt that I am!' She struck her forehead. 'I have been wasting my time.'

Doone was only more deeply perturbed and hurried to reassure her. 'You haven't been wasting your time. Really you haven't. Baroness, you have been very useful.'

'Useful?' For a moment that nettled her into real wrath. 'I, Lötte van Heusen, to be called useful!' Then she had to laugh. 'Useful!'

She laughed so much that tears came out of her eyes so that Doone thought she was crying and tried to console her. 'You are useful,' he said earnestly. 'Baroness, you are. At least to me.'

'Ach, Doone!' she said, wiping her eyes but still shaking. 'I think one day you will kill me.'

That worried Doone. 'Mr Felix died,' he told Ennis Glyn when he went, as he did every holiday, to see her and Stella.

'Baroness Lötte won't die,' said Miss Glyn. 'She'll live for ever.'

'Nothing is for ever,' Doone could have said; he had already learnt that.

'I suppose I won't see you again,' he had said to Charles, trying to keep the soreness and sadness out of his voice. 'I won't see you again.'

'Don't be an ass,' said Charles; already he was beginning to speak like his father. 'You're my mother's hope and joy now! Very convenient for me, so don't *you* go and join the Army. Matter of fact,' said Charles, 'my mother's writing to your mother to ask if you can come and spend these holidays with us in Paris.'

Ma foresaw trouble and tried to object. 'William, think of the expense.'

'There won't be much expense. It seems the Ingrams' chauffeur is coming to fetch them – Charles has been at his grandmother's for a week. They'll come back the same way. Charles is starting his new school. All Doone'll need is a little spending money. Suppose that will have to be francs', and Pa chuckled. 'Mrs Ingram says three weeks in Paris will improve your French, Doone. I didn't know you had any French.'

'Nor did I.' Doone looked so bewildered that Pa stopped and said, 'Surely you want to go.'

'Of course, but. . . .' Doone had caught the look on

Crystal's face. 'Couldn't Crystal come, too?'

'I don't go where I'm not invited,' said Crystal but when she was alone with Ma, though she tried to stop the words, they came. 'It's not fair. Doone's too young to appreciate it. I've always longed and longed to go to Paris.'

'Look, dearie.' Ma had been to the travel agency – to her a big adventure – and brought back brochures. 'You shall go to Paris. Pa and I have had an idea. Here's what we thought; it's a nice little package and good value. See, we leave London by coach, go overnight on the ferry, spend Saturday in Paris, staying the night at this hotel – two-star, it says. We'll have all Sunday and come back on the coach Sunday night. We can see the shops, have dinner in a French restaurant, and it includes a sightseeing tour of the city.'

'*And* if you work in the shop for a week,' said Pa, 'so Mrs Denning can have a short holiday, you can earn what she does and pay your own way. I'll pay for Ma. How's that for a plan?' asked Pa in triumph.

'Work in the *shop*!' Crystal spoke in so deathly a whisper that the triumph stopped abruptly. 'In the shop!' Her horrified eyes went from one to the other of them as if they were monsters. 'Go to Paris on a package tour with Ma! While Doone, *Doone* goes in a private car with a chauffeur and stays with the military attaché at a lovely house in Paris, meets the best French people,' and, 'You must be *mad*!' cried Crystal. 'Mad!' She went into her room and slammed the door. The travel brochures fell to the floor.

'We just can't think what to do with her.' Ma was near weeping.

'Little bitch,' said Will.

'Don't call your sister that,' but Ma dissolved again. 'We can't think what to do.'

'I think I can,' said Kate.

'We haven't taken enough notice of Kate,' Ma had to say afterwards in grudging admiration.

Will, these days, looked a happy man – Man, not boy, thought Ma – and now, back in the old perplexities that this impossible young sister made for them all, he turned at once to

Kate.

'You don't understand,' Crystal had flown at him. 'There's nothing for me to do here. Nothing.'

In the rooms above the shop there really did seem to be nothing except going out shopping with Ma or to the cinema. 'Would you like to go to Devon to see Uncle John and Aunt Mary?' Ma had said.

'They're dull as ditchwater.'

'I hear Ruth Sherrin's starting holiday play-school dancing,' said Pa. 'Why not go and help Ruth?'

'Help *Ruth*?'

'Hughie would take you to a disco – where Chuck and Thomas go,' offered Ma.

'Clumsy suburban boys. Any other bright ideas?' but now 'Have you ever thought of living?' asked Kate.

'Living?'

'Yes, being a dancer isn't all dancing, you know. One day you'll marry or find someone to live with and have a home or a flat of your own. What will you do then if you go on letting Ma do everything for you?'

That brought a painful memory. At Queen's Chase, when Crystal had been given her first *pointe* shoes, her guide, Moira, had told her to darn the tips like the other girls, 'to make them less slippery and the satin last longer'.

'I'll do them at home,' said Crystal.

'And get your mother to do them for you,' Melissa, Crystal's senior by a year, had taunted and, 'Dancers have to learn to be independent,' said Moira, 'manage for themselves. As you're going to spend hours and hours of the rest of your life darning shoes. . . .'

'And battering and hammering them,' put in Amy.

'Yes. If you don't break your shoes in properly, you'll have sore toes,' Moira explained.

'They bleed,' Galina had said, her eyes wide.

'You may as well start from the beginning.'

'Mummy's darling,' Melissa had mocked and now, 'You mean housework, Kate?' Crystal was doubtful.

'Well, housekeeping,' said Kate. 'I know it's difficult for you to like it here – poor Ma's work is so heavy – but come and stay with Will and me for the rest of the holidays and help me.

190

May she, Ma?'
'It would be a merciful release,' said Pa.
'I'm having cookery lessons,' Kate coaxed Crystal. 'You could come, too.'
'Cookery! Me?' but Crystal's voice was brighter.
'You'll want to cook sometimes, and I'm going to flower-arranging classes.'
Crystal looked at her sister-in-law with respectful amazement. 'For me,' said Kate, 'it's so I can help Will with the bouquets and wreaths and sprays, but for you it would be fun – and we're painting the bathroom.'

Housekeeping – polishing a sideboard until the wood glowed, vacuuming and dusting a room, making clean and fresh what was dirty – was curiously satisfying, as was putting a pile of good-smelling, neatly folded clothes and linen in the airing cupboard and laying a table invitingly. 'Of course, sometimes we have a tray in front of the television,' said Kate, 'but it doesn't compare. It depends how you look at it,' said Kate. 'When I was younger, I often thought, to hell with it, all that work and care; might as well eat when you like, buy junk food, don't make the beds or bother cleaning . . . but then it's just any old house, any pad. I want a home.'
'I think I would, too,' said Crystal.
'But you have to make it.' Crystal was beginning to find that out and found she was unexpectedly skilful. The independence taught her at Queen's Chase stood her in good stead; more unexpectedly, she found she liked housework. 'Ma won't believe this,' and, 'I tell you what,' said Kate, 'we'll ask Ma and Pa over for coffee and you shall make a cake.'
'A chocolate cake,' said Crystal.
The chocolate cake was never made and Kate, in her turn, had to learn what the rigours of being a dancer meant. Ma arrived early next morning with a letter from Queen's Chase.

Owing to a change of plan for the School's annual Performances next July, all fourth and fifth year pupils are to return to Queen's Chase five days earlier than the given date for commencement of the Summer Term, i.e., Monday instead of Saturday.

191

'They don't mind inconveniencing you,' said Ma.

'Listen to what it says!' Crystal had snatched the paper. ' "A new ballet has been designed especially for the Junior School by Yuri Koszorz." Yuri Koszorz!' I knew, I knew, thought Crystal, I should see him again.

Ma read on: ' "This is to the students' interest as Mr Koszorz will himself be available during these few days for coaching and preliminary casting," ' and 'Suppose he casts me!' whispered Crystal.

'I expect it's chiefly for the boys,' said Melissa, but soon they heard there were to be four girls. 'Which four?'

Usually a new school's performance ballet was for the Senior School boys and girls who were beginning to rank as young men and women capable of dancing a full *Swan Lake* or *Giselle*. 'But for us it's always boring old folk dances,' Crystal had said.

The folk dances, as a matter of fact, were extremely demanding and nothing could better have shown off – 'or shown up,' Miss McKenzie said wryly – the children's footwork and posture, but this of Yuri Koszorz's, still a secret, was for the fourteen and fifteen year olds. No one had written what equalled an adult ballet for them before, 'and with Yuri Koszorz to coach us!'

All of them felt the excitement of that – 'The privilege,' Miss McKenzie would have corrected them. The boys' thrill was chiefly for their dancing; though they were susceptible to Yuri Koszorz's charm, some to the extent of hero-worship, they were not as susceptible as the girls, 'Thank heaven,' said Miss Hurley, and, 'Be careful, Yuri,' Miss McKenzie told him, 'or I shall have my girls failing to dance because they are so in love with you.'

'It should make them dance better,' said Yuri. 'To fall in love is to wake up.'

'As long as you can quickly fall out again. I don't want them to get hurt.'

'I wouldn't hurt anyone – anyone,' said Yuri in a voice that could almost have wooed Miss McKenzie herself.

*   *   *

192

The coaching, of course, was an expedient, 'to look us over'. Melissa had speedily fallen out of love when she was not chosen. 'I can't choose *all* of you,' Yuri had told them, 'alas.'

The ballet was called *Cache-cache*, a game of hide and seek; but, though it was set to Bizet's *Jeux d'enfants*, it was designed to be danced, not by children, but by grown boys and girls having their first taste of love, some changeable, some already steadfast – there was a moving young *pas de deux* – but all different. It was serious under its fun and lightness and also highly skilled, making the most of the limited powers of the dancers, still so young.

'It is chic. It has style,' said Mamzelly. She had always said, of fourteen and fifteen year old girls, that it was a marvellous age at which to teach them. 'They are just breaking through, losing their – I do not know how you call it. . . .'

'Gawkiness,' said Miss McKenzie. 'For some it's puppy fat, which can be quite a problem.'

They all, too, now had their periods, 'of which you in England take little notice,' said Mamzelly. 'In Russia the girls are made to rest for two days. It all makes them so vulnerable,' said Mamzelly. 'But with this ballet they are blossoming,' and, 'Really, Crystal,' she said at the end of a class, 'I have never seen you dance like this, or work like this!' and Crystal, who was reluctantly pulling her tracksuit over her leotard – 'You're so hot you mustn't risk a chill' – gave Mamzelly a ravishing smile and said, 'I never loved it so much.'

'It's giving them just what they need,' said Mamzelly.

The trouble was that *Cache-cache* could use only five boys and four girls, 'and Yuri refuses to have alternating casts, just the usual standbys,' said Miss McKenzie.

'What I have chosen, I have chosen,' said Miss Hurley. 'Yuri really is a little God.'

The choice was surprising. All the boys were fifth-year, except fourth-year Louis, who had a gift for comedy and would dance the odd boy out who, in the end, would be rejected. Of the girls, only Amy was senior; the other three were fourth year girls: Galina – 'a foregone conclusion,' said the School – Ruth and Crystal. Crystal rushed to the telephone to tell Ma.

Miss McKenzie took the rehearsals now but Yuri often

193

came down. 'I hope I'm not interfering.'

'It's your right to interfere,' said Miss McKenzie. 'I'm only here to try to carry out what you want.'

'And see I get perfection.'

'I wish it could be perfection!' but Miss McKenzie smiled as she watched him take her place and, after that day's rehearsal, 'Mamzelly's right,' she said. 'Yuri, you're giving them a lot.'

When it came to dancing, the charming, almost playboy Yuri disappeared. 'You must *think*,' he told his chosen nine. 'A ballet is a design and must be worked out as that design, which matches . . . delicately – no, not delicately. What is that word that I want?'

'Subtly,' said Ruth.

'Yes, subtly, the design of the music, not obviously but always. *Always!* So you must listen. Crystal, *you* must listen.'

Every time Yuri spoke to her, self-possessed Crystal blushed.

'For *Cache-cache* you must imagine a summer evening in a park with its alleyways and byways; you will have to suggest them as we have no scenery – yes, you must learn the geography. You, boys and girls, have come together and you are conscious, most conscious, of one another. You must not forget that as you weave – yes, I mean that; it is like weaving – weave your way through the music – and, remember, each of you is only part of the design – you must not spoil the shapes, the lines you are making and, because all of you are equally important, no one must show off.' Crystal felt he was looking at her. 'Now get up and do it,' commanded Yuri.

He swore at them, and in argot. 'That's a kind of French I've never learnt,' said Louis, and, 'Philip! Philip!' – only, Yuri said 'Philippe' – 'you are not just a *porteur* carrying – how do you say? – a sack of potatoes. It is a girl, a *girl*, Philippe. You must be tender and protective.' For lifts, Mr Rotham, who took the *pas de deux* classes, was always telling the boys, 'It's the girl who's in the ascendant,' but Yuri contradicted that. 'No, not she, Philippe. It's you!' said Yuri. 'Watch over her. Be romantic.'

Philip reddened and said stiffly, 'I'm not romantic.'

'Not when a girl has a skin like this, warm, sweet, like peaches?' Yuri drew his finger down Crystal's cheek and then

194

drew Philip's finger in the same way. Crystal did not feel Philip's finger at all, but Yuri's sent an odd tingling through her. He showed Philip the lift himself and, for the first time Crystal felt what it was like to be lifted, spun, supported by a man, not an inexperienced boy; a man so virile, so sweet, thought Crystal, that she seemed to throb with response in every nerve. She did not sleep that night and, 'One day, perhaps,' she told Ma, 'I'll really dance with him, not just a few steps to show Philip, but a *pas de deux*. Oh, Ma!'

'Crystal,' Ma felt bound to say. 'He's already a famous dancer and you're just a little girl.'

'He calls me "chérie",' said Crystal. 'That's French for darling.'

'Darling!' said Ma.

'Les pauvres petites,' said Mamzelly, who herself was a little afflicted.

'The agony's part of the ecstasy,' Miss Hurley reminded her.

'But Yuri forgets they have feelings,' said Miss McKenzie. 'And such feelings!'

'What is the harm,' asked Yuri, 'if I do it to each one?'

The trouble was that he did it one by one. Ruth came upon Crystal gazing at a photograph: 'To my little Crystal from her loving Yuri' – he was genuinely fond of his 'little four', as he called them. Crystal thought she was alone in the library until she heard Ruth's exclamation. 'He gave you one, too!'

'You mean . . .?'

' "To my little Ruth . . .," ' said Ruth. ' "And Galina and Amy." '

Crystal tore her photograph in half.

Then, once again, Doone went past her. Home for the weekend, he saw Ma and Crystal poring over a newspaper and looked over their shoulders. 'That's Yuri,' he said. 'I like him. He's nice.'

'Like him? You don't know him. He never goes near you young ones.'

'He was in Paris,' said Doone. 'He came to one of Mrs Ingram's "salons". A "salon" is a kind of party,' he explained to Ma. 'Yuri asked me to dance for him.'

'And you did?' Pa was pleased.

195

'Yes,' and Doone said with some pride, 'I thought I'd try the big boys' Pierrot dance and I did. Charles had been teaching me and Mrs Ingram could play the music. Charles said I was daft.'

'What did Yuri say?' Crystal was on tenterhooks.

'He said "Bravo!" – they all said "Bravo!" – but afterwards he took me away and said, "Shocking!" and showed me how he would dance it – quite different from Mr Max – but the Baroness—'

'She was there, too?'

'Yes. She gave me a big box of crystallised fruit. The trouble with crystallised fruit,' said Doone, 'is that you can't eat more than a little bit of it, nor could Charles, so I gave it to their chauffeur man, Carlos, because he'd promised to take me up the Eiffel Tower, but he was too busy making love to Mrs Ingram's maid.'

'Doone!'

'He was. Right in the kitchen, too! So Yuri took me instead.'

'Yuri – Koszorz – took – you – up – the Eiffel – Tower!'

'Yes. He must have some fun sometimes,' said Doone. 'We had a gorgeous time. We went on the Métro – Mrs Ingram never goes on the Métro – and when we came down from the Tower we had hot dogs and Coke.'

'I think you're the most hateful boy I've ever met,' choked Crystal. Doone was not listening. 'Let's ask Yuri to tea, Ma, and give him hot dogs.'

'Mrs Challoner,' said Crystal, 'do you think, one Sunday, I could ask Mr Koszorz to tea?'

Mrs Challoner was silent for a moment, then asked, 'How many young dancers do you think Mr Koszorz trains and encounters in a year?'

'Hundreds,' Crystal had to say.

'Yes. Suppose they all asked him to tea?'

'They wouldn't think of it.'

'No, they wouldn't. They understand,' Mrs Challoner put an uncomfortable emphasis on the 'they'. 'Understand that someone like Yuri Koszorz, who has to spend so much of his time in the limelight, wants to keep his private life to himself. *Private*, Crystal.'

196

'Private' is always something of a snub, but Crystal still argued. 'He made friends with Doone in Paris. He took him up the Eiffel Tower.'

'*He* took him. That's the difference. I'm sure Doone didn't ask. I think you'll have to wait, Crystal, till he makes friends with you, too.'

'What if I have to wait for ever?' asked Crystal desperately.

'Then you'll have to wait for ever, and I'm sure by now Yuri has forgotten all about Doone.'

It was ironic that, not five minutes later, Crystal herself made Yuri Koszorz remember him.

She had come out of the study and, as she made her way down the long basement corridor to the rehearsal classroom, met Doone. Crystal was carrying her block shoes and, suddenly overcome with chagrin she gave him such a bang on the head with the shoes that he reeled and his eyes watered. She was giving him another bang when a hand caught her arm, a strong familiar hand; a voice said, 'Not nice to hit someone so much smaller than yourself,' and Yuri Koszorz was looking down at her with those small brown eyes, not bright with teasing or merriment now, but indignant. 'Not nice at all!' said Yuri.

Doone had recovered himself. 'It's all right, Yuri. It's only Crystal. She often thumps me.'

'Isn't it Doone?' asked Yuri. 'I remember now they told me you were here – Doone . . . Pierrot . . . hot dogs.' Gently he touched the place on Doone's forehead where a red mark was beginning to show. 'One day,' said Yuri, 'we'll eat hot dogs till we burst!'

'Yes!' Doone was delighted. 'But don't be cross with Crystal. It didn't hurt, really it didn't – and she can't help it.'

'Ah!' Yuri transferred his gaze to Crystal. 'You lose your temper, too. Like Yuri Koszorz.'

'You? I don't believe it,' Crystal managed to whisper. 'You're so kind.'

'Not always. Remember the poor Philippe. One day I expect I shall – how do you say it? – blast you all out of the ballet. Out! Out!' he mimicked. Then, seriously, 'But one has to be calm and not – what did Doone say? – thump people. Don't cry, chérie.' He put his arm round Crystal and gently kissed her on both cheeks, and 'Come, we shall be late. Hi, Doone,' and in quick strides he was gone.

The School's Annual Performance ran for a week at the little Princess Theatre. Ma and Pa had booked seats and brought Will, Kate and even Hughie. 'I s'pose I'd better see what it's all about.'

'If only it had been the Royal Theatre,' said Ma. 'This is such a shabby little place.'

'It's a dear theatre,' said Doone. He was one of the 'red' boys in the Scottish dances, partnered by his friend Amanda; his opposite number in the blue was Kui. 'And very handsome they looked in those kilts and jackets,' said Pa, 'and very well they danced. I liked the little Irish girls, too, in their green skirts and white blouses and the green ribbons tying their pony tails. The way they picked their feet up!' marvelled Pa. 'And to think I was one of the Irish girls two years running,' said Crystal. Now it was *Cache-cache*.

She was the girl in rose colour, a deep rose, with her partner, Philip, in faintest pink. 'Beautiful,' breathed Ma. Amy's dress was azure, her partner in pale blue; Galina was in ochre, the partner in pale yellow; Ruth amethyst, her partner in mauve. Louis, the left-over boy, was in cream with sage-green stripes. Louis was truly comical and, 'I didn't know a ballet could be funny!' said Hughie.

'And fun,' the critics said. To Pa's surprise, the School's Annual Performance was deemed sufficiently important to be reviewed in *The Times* – Pa had taken all the papers. One critic had picked out Crystal; she was given only two lines, but 'Crystal Penny danced with panache and, more importantly, a strong clear line. She has extraordinary looks and was clearly a magnet for the boys.'

'Pity Yuri Koszorz wasn't in it himself,' Ma said afterwards to Crystal.

'Ma, it was for children – that's what we are officially. Of course he doesn't dance in ballets like that.' Crystal tried to speak evenly but it was difficult. On the last night all four girls had had a posy of flowers from Yuri and all four were identical. 'Perhaps he is learning wisdom,' said Miss McKenzie. 'All exactly the same!' The girls were disappointed; it was

Crystal alone who had thought of detaching a little apricot rose and giving it to Yuri.

He had kissed it and given it back to her as in Ma's dream, and that was not all. Ma and Pa were not allowed backstage to see Doone or Crystal – as soon as Queen's Chase pupils had danced, they were always driven straight back to school by coach or taxi – but Ma had taken the family round to the stage door, 'just to show them I know about stage doors,' she said. 'And who was coming out just *then*,' she told Crystal, 'but Yuri Koszorz himself.'

'Ma, you didn't speak to him!'

'I did. Pa didn't want me to, but I did. I wasn't going to miss an opportunity like that. I went up to him and said, "I'm sure you will excuse me, but *Cache-cache* was delightful. I had to tell you that and to thank you. You see, I'm Crystal Penny's mother." '

'And he squashed you?'

'Not at all.' Ma was triumphant. 'He said, "Ah! The pretty little Crystal!" That *was* a compliment! And, Crystal, he kissed my hand.' Never in her life had Ma met a stranger who kissed hands. 'He kissed my hand. Oh, I so hope it didn't smell of onions,' said Ma.

'If it had been Crystal, I can guess she wouldn't have washed her hand for a week,' teased Pa.

Crystal did not tell him she had been kissed, too, not on a hand, on both cheeks – twice! thought Crystal; once when she had hit Doone and again after the ballet when he had said goodnight. But that was the same for all of us, she had to admit; the time in the passage was hers alone.

Crystal did wash her face but she slept with the apricot rose under her pillow.

'We're going to Devon!' To Doone, the summer holidays could have brought no greater joy; he loved the farm. 'They'll have finished haymaking, but I can go to market with Uncle John.' Uncle John was one of Doone's heroes. As for Aunt Mary, she had always petted Doone – she and Uncle John had no children. 'And there's the pigs.' Doone particularly loved piglets, 'and going on the moors, and I'm sure we'll go to the sea.' It was, too, in a way, Doone's country; his very name

199

belonged there, and to crown the bliss, 'Pa is coming with us,' he said. Pa had sent them without him last year.

This year he had consented to leave the shops to Will and Kate – Kate had proved her usual strength and, 'It'll be for a whole fortnight,' crowed Doone. 'The first of August until the fifteenth.' He might even be left behind at the farm and, 'There's hardly a week to wait.' He was crossing off the days on the calendar until one evening, as they were finishing tea, the telephone rang. Hughie beat Crystal to answer it. 'Coo! It's Yuri Koszorz.' Even Hughie knew that name.

'Yuri!' Crystal could not believe it. 'Then it's for me,' she said, dazzled, but Hughie fended her off. 'He wants to speak to Ma or Pa.'

'*Ma* or *Pa*?'

'Yes, Miss.'

'It must be about me.' She waited agog.

It was Ma who went trembling to the telephone. 'Good evening, Mrs Penny. You may not remember me. . . .'

'I do. I do.' How could she forget that moment outside the stage door. 'Of course I do.'

'I am telephoning' – it sounded formal, foreign – 'to ask you a favour. . . .'

'Me? A favour?' Crystal was champing with impatience.

'Yes, I think Ennis, Miss Ennis Glyn, will explain to you better than I can. I'm sure you remember her.'

'Of course,' but before Ma could go on, Miss Glyn was on the line. 'Good evening, Miss Glyn.'

'Miss Glyn!' Pa got up. Crystal tried to overhear but Ennis Glyn spoke too rapidly, softly, and at great length. Then Ma said, 'And the Ballet School wants this? I thought there were to be no outside appearances. . . . I see. We'll get a letter from the Director? Yes, it's a wonderful chance but. . . .' Miss Glyn had cut off, and Ma put the telephone down, half-fearfully.

'What is it? Ma, what is it?'

'A television company, ITV, is doing a documentary on Yuri Koszorz, how he was a little boy in Poland and trained and worked in Russia until he came here. They want a boy for when he was a boy himself, training in Leningrad, a boy who could dance the first part of the ballet he, Mr Koszorz, did in New York, something about a swan.'

200

'*Leda and the Swan*,' said Crystal. 'He told us about it. It's the story of the great Greek god Zeus falling in love with a girl and coming down disguised as a swan to mate with her.'

'Doesn't sound very nice to me.'

'Ma, it's only a story. Zeus was always doing things like that.'

'Disgusting', but 'Can't you imagine how beautiful Yuri Koszorz would be as the Swan?' and, as the full meaning of the telephone call dawned on Crystal, 'But why Doone? What dance could there be in it for him?'

'A dance for something called a cygnet. It seems Mr Koszorz saw Doone dance in Paris and was impressed enough to come and watch him in class.'

'He didn't,' said Doone.

'*You* wouldn't know,' said Crystal.

'They're engaging Mr Max to coach him.'

'Mr Max! Isn't he the Senior Ballet Master at Queen's Chase?' and, 'They're taking this very seriously,' said Pa.

It was difficult to know who was the more unhappy over it, Crystal or Doone.

'When is it to be?' Pa had asked.

'They want Doone tomorrow.'

'Tomorrow! Maudie, you're joking.'

'I'm not, William. Mr Koszorz wants to finish the television before he starts a Summer School it seems he's giving in Switzerland – the dates are fixed for that – so they have to begin coaching now; filming will be from the first of August till about the fifteenth.'

'That's when I go to Devon,' cried Doone.

'That's when you don't go to Devon,' Hughie put in.

'Not go? Not see Uncle John and Aunt Mary? Not the beach or the moors or the market? Pa? Ma?' Doone besought one, then another.

'I know it's hard, son, but you know you have to do as they say. Will and Kate will look after you.'

'You liked being on telly.' Even Hughie was moved to try to comfort him. 'You liked it.'

'I don't like it now. Please, Pa. Ma.'

'Don't bleat.' Crystal turned on Doone. 'When you have a chance I'd give my eyes for.'

'I'd rather go to Devon.'

'Then you're a stupid ignorant boy.'

'Hush, Crystal,' Pa was peremptory.

'All right, I'll hush. What's the good anyhow? I expect I'll have to hush for ever.'

'What are you looking at, Ma?' asked Crystal.

In the momentous week before they went to Devon, a hectic week of hard work for Doone, an empty one for Crystal, what had worried Pa and Ma most was Crystal's numbness. It was as if she did not want to speak or move. She would not even go to Kate as in the Easter holidays. 'Don't you feel well, dearie?'

'Perfectly well.'

'Then . . .?'

'Can't you understand?' Crystal had broken out at last. 'I thought that call was for me – or about me – and it was Doone. It's always Doone, and I realised,' the misery overflowed, 'I shall never see Yuri again.'

'I'm sure you will.'

'When he's on stage and I'm up in the amphitheatre.'

Ma had to acknowledge that Crystal could produce tears when she needed them, but these tears were real and went to Ma's heart, and when that was wrung she acted.

'Now what are you looking at, Ma?'

'The brochure for Yuri Koszorz's Summer School.' Ma tried to speak calmly. 'Do you know anything about it?'

'Of course. We all know.' Crystal's Queen's Chase contemporaries had laughed at it. 'Senior students and dancers! What dancers?' Melissa had asked.

'From all over the place. Anyone with two legs.'

' "Two sessions daily," ' Amy read out. ' "Practice under the supervision of Mlle Gilberte Giroux." '

'So Mamzelly's fallen for him!'

' "History of the ballet. Evening lectures. Demonstrations, *pas de deux* and solo by Yuri Koszorz and invited artists. Accommodation and transport can be arranged. Tuition £150 per week. . . ." ' and, 'A hundred and fifty pounds a *week*!' cried Amy.

'For Yuri they'll pay anything,' said Galina and, 'He must be making a fortune!' said Melissa.

202

'He isn't. He's giving his services free. It says so,' said Crystal. 'It's for Polish charities.'

'If people are crazy enough to pay that money . . .,' Melissa shrugged.

'And think, we have had it all free!' said Amy. It did not seem funny to Crystal. To be with Yuri Koszorz away from the School, two whole weeks of him! To see him every day, not just when he chanced to appear! 'Individual attention.' That meant perhaps he would dance with each girl or woman – it said '*pas de deux*'. 'I wouldn't care if the whole world thought I was crazy.' She had wanted to fling that at Melissa and Amy, but was glad now that she had held her peace, because, 'When we come back from Devon,' asked Ma, 'would you like to go to this Summer School?' She said it as if she were asking if Crystal would like to go to the cinema in the next street.

'Go to Yuri's Summer School?' Crystal looked at Ma, as if Ma had lost her mind. 'It's in Switzerland.'

'I know. In Montreux, but I didn't ask you where it was. I asked if you would like to go to it.'

Long ago, when Ma had arranged for Crystal to go to Ennis Glyn, she had taken Crystal's breath away. Now, again, Crystal was speechless until, 'Answer me,' said Ma. 'Would you like to?'

'More than anything in the whole wide world, but you know I can't.'

'Can't? When we come back from Devon,' said Ma, 'Will and Kate will be taking you to Switzerland. It'll be a new kind of holiday for them; Kate's putting her holiday money towards it, but their fares will be paid, and yours of course and your board – that's at what they call a "pension" – and Mr Koszorz's fees, of course.'

'Ma!' but Ma swept on: 'Miss Glyn thought you weren't ready. . . .'

She would, Crystal wanted to say, but Ma was saying in triumph, 'So I went straight to Mr Koszorz. He said he'd be delighted to have you.'

'He probably doesn't remember who I am.'

'He does. He said, "Ah! One of my four little girls. I wish I could have them all." '

'Oh!' That was something of a cold shower, but Amy,

203

Galina would not be there, nor Ruth, and, 'Ma! Even with Kate's money it'll cost . . . hundreds of pounds.'

'Yes,' said Ma complacently.

'But Pa. . . .'

'It's nothing to do with Pa. I've arranged it with Will.'

'*For* Will' would have been nearer the truth. 'Mother,' Will had said – when Will was exceptionally grave, he called Ma 'Mother', just as Pa called her 'Maud', not 'Maudie' – 'Mother,' Will had said, 'you can't lay this on Pa just now.'

'I have no intention of laying anything on your father.'

'Then how?' Crystal was to say the same thing.

'I have a little nest-egg,' said Ma, 'that none of you know about.'

It had had to come out. Just as they had been leaving for Devon, 'Maudie,' said Pa, 'give me your emeralds and I'll put them in the safe.'

'They're all right in my drawer.'

'Better be safe than sorry.' It was seldom Pa made a pun. 'We're late already. Bring them.' Then, 'What's the matter, Maud?'

'I can't bring them, William. They're sold.'

'And what did they give you?' Pa had not been as put out since the day he had learnt about Doone's dancing. 'What? Twopence halfpenny?'

'I'm not a complete fool, William. I went to the West End, Bond Street, and to several jewellers and I took the insurance certificate.'

'You'd only get about a third of that.'

'So I learnt, but jewellers have overheads to think of and their percentage to make. They explained all that.'

'I bet they did and cut you down, four or five hundred instead of five thousand pounds.'

'I got thirteen hundred, which is what I need,' said Ma.

It had not been without pain; when, for the last time, Ma had shut the velvet case and lost sight of the diamond-set green glow of the emeralds, she had had to go hastily out and find the nearest coffee-shop – 'They don't seem to have tea-places nowadays' – and have a private weep. She had not only lost the emeralds; she felt she had lost Aunt Adelaide and as if she, herself, were sinking out of sight with no claim to anything. It had been a modest claim, even what Pa had always called it, a far-fetched one, but still a claim. Now. . . . but, 'You *sold* your emeralds for me, so I could go to Yuri's school!' said Crystal.

'Well, you would have had them when I'm dead, so I thought why not now?' Ma tried to be casual, but Crystal was as near dissolving into real tears as she had ever been and, 'Nobody, *nobody's* ever had a mother like you,' she said, 'and after all the things I've been saying to you. . . .'

'We needn't think of them now,' said Ma.

'I need', and Crystal promised, 'I'll never let you down, Ma . . . never.' ¯

Chapter Eight

'THEN it's true!' said Crystal.

It was September again, the beginning of the autumn term and another new school year. Melissa had left, Amy gone to the Senior School. Crystal, fifteen in August, was in her fifth and last year; she had been moved up to an attic bedroom and had the privilege of the seniors' private common room. Doone had begun his third year, though sometimes he worked with fourth year boys. Neither he nor Mr Max said much about the television, though there were rumours until a new exciting one began to filter through Queen's Chase and blotted them out. Soon the new rumour was fact.

Yuri Koszorz had been so delighted with the young performers of *Cache-cache* that he was reviving *Casse-noisette* – *The Nutcracker* – for the Company's Christmas season, 'at the Royal Theatre!' and not in one of the modern versions, 'which have made it all different and spoilt it,' said Ruth but in its original and traditional Petipa version, where the children's parts were danced by children – 'Us!'

'Not exactly children,' said Galina.

'We do look very young on stage,' said Ruth and tried to steel herself. She would not let anyone know how she dreaded being a performer on any stage.

The children of Queen's Chase, besides the Annual School's Performances at the Princess Theatre, often took small parts in the Company's ballets, as pages, the peasant children in *Petrushka*, the youngest dancers in *Konservatoriet*. Now and again, as with the children in the ballet *Isadora*, the chosen two were named; usually, though, prominence was discouraged, but to Yuri Koszorz even Her Majesty's Ballet could not say 'No'.

The rumour soon became fact. Miss McKenzie made her

predictable speech: for those who would be chosen to take part, this was a great privilege – 'to work under Yuri Koszorz; to dance with the Company; with principals like Anthea Dean, Ennis Glyn and Peter Morland; to watch the *corps de ballet*. Those of you who are not chosen mustn't be disheartened. Your turn will come.' For once, Crystal was not among the ribald young who made a show of mocking the earnestness. 'It *is* a privilege,' she said. This was after Yuri Koszorz had come down to talk to them about his *Nutcracker*.

'It is a little girl's dream,' he had said, sitting sideways on a table while they sat round him on the floor. 'You may say it is banal, baby nonsense, but is it? Is it simple to weave magic? Magic, not only for the children in the audience, but also for grown people who perhaps have half-forgotten, poor things, what magic is.' There seemed already a ripple of magic in the room.

'We begin with a scene in old, old St Petersburg – Leningrad now – where I trained and was the smallest boy in the *Nutcracker*'s party scene, as you, perhaps, James or Claude, will be. I remember I had to wear a blue satin suit with a huge white bow that got into my mouth as I danced. We won't do that to you, James or Claude. The first scene is the Salon of the little girl Clara's parents. It is Christmas Eve; footmen are lighting candles on an enormous Christmas-tree – this Christmas tree is an important part of the magic. There is a table piled with presents. The old nurse trots about – and do you know who the old nurse will be? Your Mr Max,' and, as the younger children burst into giggles, 'Mr Max was a great character dancer and still is,' said Yuri Koszorz.

'The guests begin to arrive, boys and girls with their mothers and fathers. The children dance, and here,' said Yuri, 'I am putting in a short dance for Clara and her friend Sophie, just for the two of you.' Which two? Which? Heads turned from girl to girl. Yuri appeared not to notice.

He told of the Magician who gives the Nutcracker – which is in the shape of a soldier – to Clara, and of the battle that night between the Rats and the Toy Soldiers. 'You eight girls who will be chosen to dance the Rats may at first feel disappointed. Who wants to dance a rat? But it is wonderful dancing, wriggling, squirming, pouncing, clawing.' Yuri demonstrated as he spoke and so funnily that they were helpless with laughter. Then he said seriously, 'There is, in all of us, a feeling of wanting to be bad and cruel, and you can be as mischievous and cruel as you like.

'I remember once when I was a Toy Soldier and a Rat girl was wrenching my gun away from me. She had to shout – the orchestra was making a big din – "Yuri, give me that gun. *Give* it to me, or we shall be late." I had forgotten it was a ballet. There is a cannon, too, that fires sweets. The Rats have to gobble them up. A good Rat – or shall I say a bad Rat? – can have a very lovely time.'

He told them of the snow scene. 'The *corps de ballet* are snowflakes when Clara is whisked away in a golden sleigh, the Nutcracker having turned into a handsome prince. You can see how handsome,' said Yuri. 'He is me,' and He's showing off, thought Doone. This was not the comradely Yuri he knew, but a tremor had run through the girls, even though each was determined not to show what she was feeling – except Crystal, who sat rapt, her arms round her knees, her eyes like blue stars fixed on Yuri.

'I am telling you so much of this first Act because it is the one some of you will dance in – some of you,' said Yuri. 'After it, I expect you will be sent back to school by coach. I used to hate that. The only one of you who stays right through the ballet is the girl who will dance Clara.'

Which girl? Which? There could be no answering that – yet.

'It really is a sentimental fairy-tale,' said Galina.

'Well, you were hooked like the rest of us,' said Lucy.

'And when you come to dance it, dance Clara. . . .' Crystal tried to keep the longing out of her voice. Would Yuri remember her?

Two years ago she would have boasted about his Summer School; now she did not say a word – 'and you're not to, either,' she told Doone.

The Staff knew, of course. Permission had to be given. 'It will be crowded,' Miss Baxter had warned Ma, 'and Yuri Koszorz himself doesn't take many classes. It's also absurdly expensive and Crystal may come back rather dashed.'

Crystal had been anything but dashed. She had come home

208

laden with presents for everyone, and overflowing with happiness. 'Ma, I think you've made me. Miss Glyn said "individual attention" meant from Mamzelly and the other teachers; of course that was true for most of the time, but Yuri came every day and he picked me out' and, 'If this has made Yuri Koszorz take an interest in Crystal, that was money well spent,' Ma told Pa.

As a matter of fact, Yuri and Mamzelly had found Crystal useful. Of the near sixty dancers, most were 'not up to it,' said Mamzelly. 'They came for the wrong reasons, which was to be expected. We had to simplify,' and Crystal, impeccably trained in the classical tradition, could be relied on to demonstrate. 'He danced with me four times, though there were girls far older.'

'A pity,' said Miss McKenzie. 'It has encouraged Crystal until Yuri's becoming a passion.'

'All the same, her work has improved out of all knowledge,' said Miss Hurley. 'Some of the others could do with a touch of passion, too.'

'They probably have succumbed,' said Mrs Challoner, 'but would rather die than show it.'

'Crystal shows every time Yuri appears or is even mentioned,' said Miss McKenzie. 'Her face and eyes!'

That October there was a private showing of the television documentary *Yuri Koszorz, Dancer*, and the television Company invited Pa and Ma. 'Well, I *am* surprised,' said Ma. Since Crystal and Doone had gone to Queen's Chase, she had grown accustomed to being 'left out of things', as she would have put it. She and Pa were more surprised still when half the ballet world seemed to be there.

Doone, of course, had seen the film and had been anxious. 'I had to make mistakes,' said Doone, 'had to on purpose, because Yuri did when he was thirteen, but I hope people will understand.'

They did. After it was over, Mr Yeats and Elizabeth Baxter came across to Ma and Pa.

'What did you think?' Pa asked anxiously.

'Simply that it was one of the most beautiful and moving things I have ever seen on television,' said Michael Yeats.

209

'I meant Doone's part.'

'So did I.'

'I was amazed,' said Miss Baxter.

'That scene,' said Mr Yeats, 'when he was trying to do the Cygnet dance alone in the empty classroom, the snow falling outside the window. You could feel the cold and the desperation.'

'It was Yuri's time of despair,' said Miss Baxter.

'Did Mr Koszorz have a time of despair?' To Ma it did not seem possible.

'Of course. I think all dancers do, but for him it was even more desolate, and Doone caught that wonderfully.' They both sounded so happy that they might have been his parents – 'as I suppose in a way they are,' Pa said afterwards.

'You have a really gifted son, Mr Penny,' and Mr Yeats added the usual rider, 'Of course, he has a long way to go, but we shall take good care of him.'

'Indeed we shall,' said Miss Baxter.

'You see, Maudie,' said Pa on the way home. 'There are some things you can't buy. . . .' 'Not even with emeralds' hung on the air, though Pa did not say it. Ma was nettled.

'I wouldn't be too sure. Doone did very well but did you know, William, Crystal might be chosen for a big part in the ballet Yuri Koszorz is producing for Her Majesty's Ballet at Christmas? It's called *The Nutcracker* and it's for the Company this time, not the School, and at the Royal Theatre. It's not the ballerina part, of course – that's the Sugar Plum Fairy.'

'Nutcracker. Sugar Plum. Sounds crazy to me.'

'It isn't. It's a famous classic. The young part is the heroine, Clara. Crystal doesn't say much, but I know that Yuri Koszorz has taken a great deal of notice of her since the summer school, and he wouldn't have done that without the emeralds.'

The part of Clara was narrowed down to three: Galina, Ruth and Crystal.

'It will be Galina.' Most of the School thought that; as Galina was half-Russian, she must, they thought, be closest to Yuri. 'I'm not really,' said Galina. 'I know he doesn't think

210

much of me.

Crystal did not trust herself to say anything, nor did Ruth, but, 'I've just remembered,' said Doone, 'Clara's dance, when she's given the Nutcracker, is the one you both danced at that Competition.'

'Be quiet!' Crystal and Ruth said it together.

Doone's star seemed still to be in the ascendant. To his surprise and delight, he was to be the Captain of the Toy Soldiers. 'It will be amusing to have a smaller boy in command,' said Yuri – the rest of the Soldiers were fifth-year boys – and, 'I have to fight the King of the Rats,' said Doone. 'That's Peter Morland and he's *big*' – that same Peter who had been so commanding an Oberon. 'He's coming down specially to rehearse with me.' Best of all to Doone was that 'the Conductor has to conduct me when I play my drum so as I can fit in with the music. I have to come right down to the footlights. Of course, the real drum will be in the orchestra and the drummer has to fit in with me. Miss McKenzie says the Conductor will talk to me at rehearsal – the *Conductor*! but I conduct the battle.'

'Yes, dear,' said Ma, to whom this had been breathlessly told. 'Crystal, does Mr Koszorz rehearse Clara's *pas de deux* with you?'

'Of course not. One of the *corps de ballet* from the Company comes down and stands in for him.'

'Doesn't he ever?'

'I wish to goodness,' Crystal told Doone, 'I hadn't said anything to Ma.'

Half-term came and Yuri Koszorz still had not made up his mind. 'Typical,' said Miss McKenzie. 'With *Cache-cache* he wouldn't wait and let them show their paces; now. . . .'

'Galina, Ruth, Crystal. All are good, so what does it matter?' asked Yuri.

'It matters intensely to the girls and we have to choose a second cast.'

'You can do that.' Yuri took little interest in second casts. 'Only for replacement; I keep to the first.'

'Then you had better choose who is to be in it.'

'Presently. Presently,' Yuri said with his charming smile. It

did not charm Miss McKenzie now. 'I'd like to shake him.'
'Galina's the best dancer but she has so little personality,'
said Miss Hurley. 'Almost too unpretentious.'
'No one could say that of Crystal.' Crystal was Mr Max's
choice.
'I always think Ruth has a quiet appeal,' said Miss
McKenzie.
'No guts,' said Miss Hurley. 'When it comes to the moment
she might very well panic.'

Doone was sent for by Miss McKenzie. With her was Mr Max.
'There's been a change of plan.'
For this short Christmas season, Yuri Koszorz was to dance
every night alternating *The Nutcracker* with *Petrushka*, one of
his best roles and, 'As *Petrushka* is a little short,' said Miss
McKenzie, 'Mr Koszorz has decided to give *Leda and the
Swan* its première in London.'
'The one from the documentary?' Doone's lips hardly
moved. He could guess what was coming next.
'Yes. Of course, dancing it on stage will be very different
from dancing it in the television studio, and it will be full
length, but don't worry. Mr Koszorz himself will coach you.'
'You mean I'm to dance the Cygnet at the Royal Theatre?
But I can't,' said Doone. 'I'm Captain of the Soldiers.'
'You'll have to hand that over to Kui, I'm afraid,' and, to
Doone's dismay, Miss McKenzie emphasised the stock words:
'This is a great, great privilege, Doone.'
'I don't like great privileges,' said Doone.
He liked them less as the weeks went on. He had to endure
the other boys' teasing: 'Flutter, flutter, flap, flap.' 'You'll wear
a white tutu and a little crown of feathers.' There was general
discontent. 'Kui's not half as good as Doone,' complained
Peter Morland.
Still, Doone would not have given up the Cygnet; as a
dancer every fibre of him felt the power and beauty of the
ballet. Yuri had given him chances and made them possible,
and opened a new vista that he, Doone, had not dreamed of and,
'Why can't I do both,' he asked Miss McKenzie, 'the Cygnet
and the Captain? Yuri's dancing every night. Why can't I?'
'There are licensing laws, Doone. A child may only dance

212

five times a week and, counting the matinées, we're giving eight performances each week – four *Nutcracker*, four *Petrushka* and *Leda and the Swan*. I'm sorry, Doone, but you'll have to accept it, willy nilly.'

'Willy nilly.' He did not like the sound of that and, 'I'll never, never beat that drum,' mourned Doone.

'Do you know, son,' said Pa, that weekend, 'I calculate that you've earned more than four hundred pounds with your televisions.'

'Can I have them, please?' Doone held out his hand.

'Have them?'

'To put in my money pig.'

'Don't be absurd. Money like that's not for boys to spend. The money for the Cygnet goes to the ballet people. With the Debussy, the television company paid it to me and I put it in the Post Office for you so it will grow. Think, when you're eighteen you can use it for a holiday or put it towards a car.'

'That's not what I want to do with it at *all*. I earned it,' said Doone, 'then why can't I have it?'

'But he wouldn't let me,' Doone told the Baroness, to whom he had fled.

'He couldn't let you. It is the law. Now, sit down,' said the Baroness, 'and tell me again, quietly and exactly, all about Mr Felix and his piano. All.'

As Doone told, Mr Felix seemed to be there, tall, thin, dignified in his threadbare clothes. 'He didn't say goodbye to me.' The old grief gushed out. 'Pa said I was being silly and I suppose I am. Even four hundred pounds isn't nearly enough for my grand piano, and I've only got thirty-two pounds, thirty-seven pence in my pig, even though I've gone without sweets and comics. I'll never, never have my piano. Why, I don't suppose I could even find it.'

'A Steinway grand piano doesn't just disappear. They have numbers. We'll ask at Steinway's tomorrow' – which was how a rumour ran through musical London that Lötte von Heusen, to Blüthner's dismay, was changing from a Blüthner to a Steinway.

As far as it could be traced, there had been no such sale and, 'It is lost,' said Doone in despair.

'Mrs Sherrin, can you shed any light on where this piano could be?'

'Where it has always been – in Mr Felix's flat.' Mrs Sherrin was astonished. 'I thought the Pennys knew. Mr Felix died intestate and two cousins are wrangling over his poor old bones.'

'Not all that poor to possess a Steinway.'

'He went without almost everything else. Until things are settled, if they ever are, nothing must be moved, but the lawyers asked me to keep the key so that I could go in and see everything is all right, particularly the piano, and have it tuned. He loved it so much. Would you like to see it?' asked Mrs Sherrin.

The Baroness looked round the big room, tidy, clean, dead. 'Like a tomb,' she whispered. The piano was shrouded in a green baize cover which Mrs Sherrin drew off and, at once, the polished wood gleamed. The Baroness lifted the keyboard lid and ran her plump experienced hands over the keys, thinking of the small fingers that had laboured on them. She played Doone's familiar nocturne and the silent room woke to life; except for the tuner's visits there had been no sound in it all these years. The pity of it, thought Mrs Sherrin, the pity. As Crystal had, the Baroness closed the lid, and, as she stood up, 'Ach!' she said. 'This must be Doone's.' On the rack, now put down, was a music-book of Czerny Exercises. 'Yes. See.' Inside was written his name: 'Doone Penny'.

'I wanted to give it to him,' said Mrs Sherrin, 'but of course I couldn't.' She added, 'Perhaps it was better not.'

The Baroness turned the worn pages, marked through and through with fingering carefully pencilled in, then stopped. 'What is this?' She had gone back to the first page and, fastened into it, was a letter. 'To whom this may concern,' and, 'For Doone.'

'There's a big letter for you,' Pa told Doone as soon as he and Crystal came home next Saturday.

'Probably some form or other from the television people that he has to fill in,' said Ma.

214

'It's addressed "Master". "Master Doone Penny",' Hughie teased but, 'Stop it,' ordered Ma. 'That's the way boys are addressed in the best circles.'

'So Doone's in the best circles. Wow!'

It was not a form. 'My Czerny Exercises! Why?' Light broke. 'It's from Mr Felix!'

'It is in a way,' said Pa. With the Czerny was a letter typed on thick paper with a heading in black, 'Spooner & Fitzgerald, Solicitors'. It began, 'Dear Master Doone' and, 'I don't understand,' said Doone. 'It's something to do with Mr Felix, but how can it be?' He gave the letter to Pa. As Pa read it, his eyebrows went up and up, his whole face changed and, 'God Almighty!' said Pa.

'What is it, William?'

'A letter has been discovered – no, not a letter, a Will. It seems Mr Felix had written it just before he died and put it inside that piano-book for Doone or somebody to find.'

'An odd way to do it,' said Ma.

'Mr Felix was odd; besides, he wasn't to know Doone wouldn't be allowed to go in. It's properly witnessed.'

'But what does it say?'

'Mr Felix,' said Pa solemnly, 'has left his Steinway grand piano and all his music to Doone.'

For the first time when so many Pennys were gathered in the same room there was utter silence. At last Ma said, 'You mean Mr Felix has left his piano – a grand piano, not like mine – to Doone?'

'For my very own?' asked Doone.

'For your very own, son'; and Pa seemed to hear, like an echo, Doone saying on his eighth – or was it his ninth? – birthday, 'I wouldn't mind a grand piano.'

'It must be worth at least three or four thousand pounds,' said Pa.

'William!'

'Jesus!' said Hughie.

'It can't be,' said Crystal.

But Doone had picked up the Czerny Exercises book and was cradling it, as he said, as if at long last a hurt had been healed, 'Then Mr Felix did say goodbye.'

Mrs Challoner told Miss McKenzie, 'Jean, that child, Ruth Sherrin, is unhappy.'

'Ruth? She couldn't be. She's had perhaps one of the best years a girl in this school has ever had; a real success with that effort in choreography, and then to be one of the four in *Cache-cache*.'

'The one of the four who "gave" least,' said Miss Hurley.

'Maybe, but now she's in the running for Clara. She may be disappointed, of course. All the same, unhappy?'

'Read this,' said Mrs Challoner.

It was an essay written in class; the subject had been free and Ruth had called hers 'The Closed Door'.

She was sure that there was something behind the closed door; but could it be worse than the storm she was in?

She listened at the keyhole. No, there seemed to be nothing – nothing moving at least. Anyway, what was in there could not be worse than this terrifying storm.

A streak of lightning made her jump; she twisted the stiff handle violently; the door creaked open and, miserably, she went in and shut it behind her.

There was nothing, except the same storm blowing at her, blowing round her, and another door. She sighed, wrung her hands, then shook back her long brown hair. Behind this door, she thought, there had to be shelter from the storm, a haven reached at last.

She shivered and once again opened a door.

'Aaah!' she screamed as she was greeted by the same storm and yet another door. Filled with fury she tore it open and went through with her eyes closed, hoping – yes, hoping.

When at last she opened her eyes, she began to cry. She was still in the storm with, yes, still another door. She raised her head and stared; where the ceiling should have been, it was a frothing sky where the clouds seemed to roar with laughter at her.

'I'll show you,' and she pushed through another door, then another. Yet, still, she was wet, cold and blown breathless.

She collapsed, exhausted, and the storm was still all

round her, deafening her, blotting out hope – yes, she had given up hope, her strength had gone – but wait, what was this? Through the door in front of her she heard people laughing, talking . . . a voice ordering . . . heard music. She sat up and put her eye to the keyhole. She saw movement. Yes, there were people, all smiling in a warm lit place. There was no storm there, only moving . . . music, laughter, clapping.

Fiercely she twisted the door-handle again. The door wouldn't open. She tried until sweat ran down her neck, but the storm had beaten her.

She cried and cried because she knew she was meant to stay in the storm for ever. She would never know what it was like behind that closed door, never, never. She was shut out.

'Shut out? By whom?' asked Miss McKenzie, and Miss Hurley said, 'By Ruth.'

'Mrs Gillespie. Mrs Gillespie.'

The Housemistress had just had a bath, made herself a hot drink, and was sitting by the fire in her bed sitting-room watching late-night television. She was, as usual, tired, her feet ached; she was beginning to relax in the pleasant glow, when there came those taps at her door. 'Mrs Gillespie.'

Galina, Anne and Lucy, in their nightclothes, stood in a worried group.

'What is it, girls?'

'Ruth's crying and crying. She won't say why and we can't stop her.'

'It's this wretched *Nutcracker*.' Mrs Gillespie often had cause to abhor ballet and its consequences but, in spite of her weariness, 'Go back to bed, girls,' she said. 'I'll see to her.'

She brought Ruth into her own room and chafed her cold hands and feet by the fire until the crying stilled. Then, 'It's *The Nutcracker*, isn't it? And this indecision as to who will have the part of Clara?'

'Yes,' said Ruth and shivered.

'Don't anticipate the worst, Ruth. It may still be you.'

That only brought a worse outbreak of tears. Mrs Gillespie

had meant to give hope; now she was at a loss. The only thing to do, she felt, was to apply immediate common sense – Yuri Koszorz called it 'Come on sense' – and, 'No matter what you think or feel, you can't do anything about it tonight,' said Mrs Gillespie. 'Ruth, the only way, when you are so taut and anxious, is to take things day by day, even hour by hour. You have to be fit for classes and rehearsal tomorrow, and you won't be that if you cry yourself sick. I'll make you a hot drink and, when you're nice and warm, inside and out,' Mrs Gillespie said it with a tender smile, she liked Ruth, 'you'll go to bed and *sleep*. There isn't anything else you can do tonight.'

'I believe Crystal knows something we don't,' said Miss McKenzie.

For the last three days Crystal seemed to be lit with happiness. It bubbled out of her; she worked with an enthusiasm Miss Hurley and Mamzelly had not seen before and seemed suddenly impelled to hug Galina, Anne or Lucy; she was even sweet to Ruth – 'Even Ruth!' said Mamzelly. 'Could Yuri have said something to her?'

'Surely not before he had told us. We have *some* rights.' Miss McKenzie was warm. '*We* have to approve.'

'The Yuris of this world jump fences,' said Miss Hurley and, 'He's said something, I'm sure.'

Three days ago, Crystal had been late for rehearsal; she had had to see Sister about a septic finger and, running down the stairs into the lower hall on her way to the Pavlova classroom, she had seen Yuri Koszorz studying the noticeboard, obviously wondering where the rehearsal was being held. 'It's in Pavlova,' said Crystal, as always a little breathless when she spoke to Yuri.

'Ah! Come, we'll go together. We're getting on; only two more rehearsals here,' said Yuri, 'then we shall go to the rehearsal rooms at the Royal Theatre. Come,' but Crystal had stopped. Could she dare? As she looked up at the face that so bewitched her, the yearning had become so strong that she had found herself saying, 'Mr Koszorz. . . .'

'Yuri.'

'Yuri.' Her heart seemed to be beating in her throat. 'Please tell me . . . *please*. Am I . . .? Are you . . .?' It came with a rush.

218

'Are you going to choose me as Clara?'

For a moment his eyes had flickered, then an amused little smile came at the corners of his mouth; Crystal did not know it, but it was the smile with which some people can watch a little insect wriggling on a pin, then, 'Why not?' asked Yuri. 'You will be so very pretty.'

'As pretty as Anthea Dean?' Crystal did not know why she was naïve enough to ask that but Yuri had evaded it. 'If Anthea is the flower, you are the bud,' he said gracefully, too gracefully, and, He's putting me off, thought Crystal. With a new determination she asked: 'But am I?'

'Pretty?' Yuri came closer. Crystal had never looked prettier; her hair was drawn up into the customary knot on the top of her head but small gold rings had escaped on to her forehead and her neck was invitingly bare; her eyes, deeper blue with longing, were beseeching. 'Am I to be Clara?' Yuri did not hear the last words. 'Am I pretty?' was still in his head, and, 'My little bud,' said Yuri, 'I believe you are. Indeed you are!'

Few people at Queen's Chase would have credited that Yuri Koszorz could be swept out of himself by a schoolgirl, certainly not any of the ballet faculty, but the next moment Yuri had Crystal in his arms and was kissing her. 'Really kissing me!'

It was only for a moment. Footsteps had sounded in the hall above and Yuri remembered where he was – in a school, a ballet school. Abruptly he let her go. 'Rehearsal! Rehearsal!' he cried and was gone.

He left Crystal so dizzy that she sank down on the bottom step of the stairs. She had been crushed in Yuri Koszorz's arms; his body had pressed against hers; his mouth had been on hers with such force that her lips felt bruised – she put up a hand to touch them, a hand that was shaking. She had felt his tongue, which had made her recoil until, thrusting, it had found her own. Then . . . and, 'Yuri!' In a trance Crystal leant her head against the newel post. 'Yuri. . . .'

'Crystal, shouldn't you be at rehearsal?' Mrs Challoner, coming downstairs, was looking at her closely. Suppose she had been a minute earlier! thought Crystal. 'Don't you feel well?'

219

'Well? Very well!' And Crystal leapt up, gave Mrs Challoner a radiant smile and, like Yuri, said, 'Rehearsal.'

'You needn't have run,' said Miss McKenzie when she saw Crystal's flushed face and panting chest. At this rehearsal Galina was dancing Clara, yet, as Crystal took her place among the Rats, there was an air about her, as if she were sleepwalking, and was yet exhilarated. She did not look adoringly at Yuri as she usually did, but down at the floor or straight in front of her. Every now and then, a blush came that spread down her neck to her arms, and her eyes, when she did look up, were shining. H'm! thought Miss McKenzie.

Next Saturday, Miss McKenzie came into the lower hall and pinned a notice on the board.

The first cast had been rehearsing all morning for the final full rehearsal at Queen's Chase. Yuri Koszorz had come down and danced the *pas de deux* with all three girls, praised all three and gone away. Now it was after lunch; the boarders who were going home for the weekend had packed their overnight things; parents' cars were beginning to arrive and the school bus stood ready to take those who were going by train to the station, but the moment Miss McKenzie pinned that sheet of paper on the board the whole school gathered round.

Franz, Clara's brother	Louis Mayer
'Well, we knew that.'	
Captain of the Guard	Kui Wang
'We knew that, too.'	
Rats	Ann Darcy
	Lucy Entwhistle
	Crystal Penny
There was a ripple.	
	and five other names
Soldiers	
Child guests at the party	
Sophie, Clara's friend	Galina Posniakoff

An even deeper ripple.

Clara   Ruth Sherrin

'Clara – Ruth Sherrin'! That was the line that riveted everyone, including Crystal.

She had come running, confident, happy. Silently the others made way for her. Crystal read and stood dazed while, slowly, two patches of scarlet came on her cheeks. 'She looked as if she had been slapped in the face,' Miss McKenzie said afterwards.

She put her hand on Crystal's shoulder. 'Another time it may be you, and look. . . .' Below the notice was a line: 'Understudy for Clara – Crystal Penny.' 'That means Galina's out of it, but you may yet dance the part.'

Crystal nodded. For a moment it seemed she could not speak, then 'Where's Ruth?' she asked.

'Her mother came for her as soon as we knew. Ruth was a little overcome.'

'Overcome? To be dancing Clara!' Crystal obviously did not understand that, and, 'Try to be glad for her,' said Miss McKenzie. 'She and her mother have had a hard time,' but Crystal only said, 'Could I make a call, Miss McKenzie?'

'I expect the poor child wanted to tell her mother before she got home,' said Mrs Challoner, 'and one can't blame her.'

'Indeed no. Mrs Penny will feel it even more than she does,' said Mamzelly, 'and it *is* difficult. Her precious darling Crystal's first appearance in a full ballet at the Royal Theatre and she has to be a Rat!'

'It can't be easy to accept,' said Mrs Challoner, troubled, then asked, 'Jean? How did Crystal take it?'

'Well.' Then 'Too well,' said Miss McKenzie, and, 'I don't think that call was to her mother.'

Miss McKenzie's guess had been right. Crystal's call was not to Ma. After she had made it, she wrote a note, carefully copying Ma's handwriting – not that Ma wrote often; Will usually did it for her – and when the bus had decanted the Queen's Chase travellers at the station and Mrs Gillespie had seen them on the train Crystal gave the note to Doone. 'When you come back on Sunday night, give this note to Mrs Challoner or Mrs Gillespie,' and, before Doone could speak,

221

'Don't say anything,' Crystal commanded. 'I'm not coming home. Tell Ma I'm sorry, but Amy has invited me for the weekend.' Crystal had calculated that Ma would not know that Amy had gone to the Senior School. 'Tell Ma I'll ring her. You'll need the note because I shan't be back till Monday morning; Amy's taking me to see the Senior School.'

She knew Doone did not believe her. 'They'll know it's not Ma's writing.'

'Daphne might, but she's not here on Sundays,' and, as Doone was still reluctant, 'You once said you'd stick by me, no matter what I did. Remember?'

'Ye-es.' He could not fathom the whole of Crystal's distress, but enough to distress him, too. He had seen the amount of make-up Crystal was wearing when she had boarded the school bus and, on the train, seen her change her stud earrings to the forbidden drop ones, and bring out all her bangles, and guessed where she was going. He did not like it, but Crystal was pleading. *Pleading!*

'Stick by me now. Do exactly what I say. Tell Ma what I've said, and on Sunday evening, when you come back, give the note to Mrs Challoner or Mrs Gillespie. Above everything else, don't tell Ma or anyone that I'm a Rat. Promise.'

'I promise,' said Doone.

'Something's happened, hasn't it?

'Nothing.'

'Oh, well, I'm a liar, too,' said Valerie.

It was easy and comforting being with Valerie; there was no need to pretend or behave, though at first Valerie had been prickly.

'To what do I owe the honour of this visit?'

'Oh, Valerie, don't. I wanted to see you, that's all.'

'You didn't want to see me all summer.'

'You don't know what a summer it's been. Work! Work! Work! In July there were the School's Performances at the Princess Theatre, and there was a ballet, too, that I was in. . . .' It was too painful to talk about that, 'and, as if it wasn't enough, I had to take my mock O-levels.'

'You don't mean you have to do examinations as well as all that sweat!'

'A dancer has to be educated!' Crystal jibed, as she always did with Valerie. 'I'm taking five.'

'Did you pass the mocks?'

'Managed to.'

'Well, all I can say is I'm glad I got out when I did.'

'Let's forget about it,' said Crystal; she had not said a word about *The Nutcracker*. 'Let's have some fun.' Anything to distract Valerie's attention. 'Couldn't we go to a disco?'

Saturday had been lived through, and with credit. 'I've seen you wild before,' Valerie said in admiration, 'but never like that.'

'Because I'm not like that.' Crystal knew it this Sunday morning; she had a throbbing headache, and a sour taste in her mouth. Valerie had taken a flask of her father's whisky to the disco – given Crystal another. 'But be careful. Hide it in your bag', and now, 'I'm sure I smell,' said Crystal. 'I was disgusting, and so were you.'

'That's what I get for taking you out and trying to help you. Thanks very much.'

'I'm sorry. . . .'

Crystal could not eat any lunch. They had it with Valerie's father. 'It's the one thing he insists on when I'm at home,' said Valerie. 'He thinks he can keep tabs on me. Dear Daddy! Mother couldn't care less.'

'Where is your mother?'

'Away as usual at weekends,' and Crystal had a fleeting thought of Ma, who would never have been away if her husband and children were at home; she had a sudden yearning for that steady presence.

'Don't you feel well, my dear?' asked Mr Kydd Mortimer.

'Just a headache', and 'I must say, having you to stay is like a wet week,' said Valerie. Then she relented. 'You do look awful.'

'Outsize hangover,' Crystal tried to shrug it off, but a hangover from what? Not just the disco; from that moment of shock when she had seen the cast-list on the noticeboard, shock and disbelief. 'Yuri *said* . . .', and like an echo she heard his, 'You will be so very pretty.' 'Yuri said. . . .' Mercifully she had not spoken aloud, but each time she thought of it she smarted again and, 'I feel sick,' she said. 'I don't mean I'd *be* sick,' she tried to explain, 'sick all through me.'

Valerie, thick-skinned as she was, divined there was a deeper trouble; something beyond her sensing; under her boldness and sauciness, Valerie could be kind and, 'Chris, I think that you've had enough of that place,' she said. 'All that teaching and preaching. On Monday I'll take you to Apply Dapply – that's the agency. You have the looks and could dance any of us off the floor. It's simple.'

'Not that simple.'

'It is. Just don't go back.'

'Val, I'm not sixteen yet. I'd have to have a licence, all kinds of fuss.'

'Hell! I'd forgotten what a child you are.'

'I wish I was a child,' and Crystal burst out, 'Fifteen's a terrible age to be. You're too young and too old.'

'We could probably rig it,' but, 'It isn't only that,' said Crystal. 'What they get for you at Apply Dapply isn't dancing.' She was remembering *Christmas Crackers*. 'It's not dancing.'

'That's a bit of an insult.'

'I'm sorry. . . .'

'All you seem able to say is, "I'm sorry",' and, 'For God's sake,' said Valerie, 'don't let's go on and on. If you don't want to go to Apply Dapply, you don't. That's no skin off my nose, but we can't stay shut in this morgue all day. Let's go up on the Heath. Being Sunday, there'll be heaps of people and it's a lovely day.'

It was. The sunshine was so bright it hurt Crystal's eyes; she could hardly see as they went up the hill. Then, 'Talking of dancing,' said Valerie, 'I've something to show you.'

She turned off the Avenue into a lane of small terraced houses and, for Crystal, the dazzle cleared. The little houses, all painted white, each with a balcony, hung with creepers – 'Roses, wisteria, honeysuckle,' said Valerie – each with a little hedged front garden, seemed immediately and deeply etched on Crystal's mind as, 'Isn't it a dream?' asked Valerie, 'and so quiet. It's a cul-de-sac, so there's hardly any traffic. It's as exclusive as anywhere in London, and who do you think lives in number 4? Someone I'm sure you know of and have probably seen – Yuri Koszorz.'

224

'Yuri?' For an unguarded moment, only the first name slipped out. Then Crystal covered up. 'Yuri Koszorz lives here? How do you know?'

'I saw him shopping in the High Street, followed him home and asked for his autograph.'

'Valerie!'

'Well, why not? If I want something, I go after it,' said Valerie, and, 'I must say he's ecstatic.'

Ecstatic! For a moment Crystal was back on the staircase at Queen's Chase; Valerie's bold eyes saw her flush and, 'You know him?' said Valerie at once.

'Hardly,' Crystal fenced her off. 'I was in a ballet he choreographed.'

'Hardly? Then why are you looking like that?'

'Because, somehow, you never think of a famous person living, actually living, anywhere.' It was a lame excuse but, for once, Valerie refrained from probing. Crystal could not tear herself away; she stood in the sunshine gazing until, 'It's not a shrine,' said Valerie. 'Come on.'

'Nothing's happening this evening, is there?' asked Crystal.

Valerie's eyes opened wide. 'Of course there is. We've been asked to Justin's; not everybody's asked to Justin's, I can tell you, but you went down well with the crowd last night. We're to take some eats and every boy will bring a bottle.'

And get drunk again. Crystal did not say it. All day she and Valerie had been on the verge of a quarrel. Instead, 'Won't your father . . .?' she asked.

'Daddy's given me up long ago,' Valerie laughed. 'He goes to his Club and stays late playing bridge. He won't know what time we get in.'

How different from Pa! Again Crystal had to fight down that unaccustomed homesickness.

Silently she watched Valerie pack a basket and, 'You could butter some rolls instead of standing there like a gravestone.' Silently Crystal buttered until, 'That's that,' said Valerie. Then, sharply, 'Go and change.'

'I can't change,' said Crystal. 'I didn't bring anything. You see, I thought I would be going home.'

'Pity you didn't. Well, put on some make-up – you're pale as

225

a ghost – and those snazzy earrings.'

Crystal obeyed but in the hall she suddenly hardened. 'Val, I'm not coming.'

Valerie put down the basket she had just picked up. 'Not?'

'No, I'm. . . .'

' "I'm sorry," ' Valerie jibed. 'Say, "I'm sorry." '

'I am. It's . . . just – I can't.'

'I've had enough,' blazed Valerie and she slapped Crystal hard on both cheeks, so hard that tears sprang. 'Take that! Little prig! I'll teach you not to patronise me.'

'Val, it's nothing to do with you.'

'Oh?' The black eyes probed, then Valerie said, 'I see. You're going down to that shrine to worship Yuri Koszorz.'

'Don't be horrible.' To Crystal's chagrin the tears had overflowed. 'You don't know him,' cried Crystal. 'He's mean and cruel.'

'Cruel? How heavenly!' Valerie came nearer. 'Tell.'

The avidness made Crystal shrink. 'There's nothing to tell.'

'Liar.' Valerie's patience snapped again. 'All right, don't tell and don't come. Don't do anything. I'm tired of Weeping Marys. There's food in the refrigerator if you want some. Amuse yourself, Misery. Goodnight.'

There were never any hours as desolate as those Crystal spent in the Kydd Mortimers' big empty house. The lights were on but it seemed dark, with eerie shadows. She turned on the television but could not take anything in. Her headache had given way to a strange lightheadedness and, I suppose I must have something to eat, she told herself. She did not want to explore the refrigerator but found a tin of soup and opened it. Valerie had taken all the bread, but Crystal knew there were water biscuits in a silver jar in the dining-room; she carried her tray there and ate, sitting at the long polished table. 'The dining-room's never been changed since my grandfather's day,' Valerie had told her; it had dark panelled walls, a sideboard heavy with silver, brown velvet curtains and, over the empty fireplace, a huge stuffed buffalo-head with wide horns; its glass eyes seemed to stare down at Crystal's forlorn figure. She could not bear it and went back to the television. Valerie has this night after night, she thought, if she doesn't go out, and she can't go out all the time.

'Wait till I'm eighteen,' she seemed to hear Valerie say. 'One day you'll find you'll have to break with Valerie,' Kate had warned her.

'Just because she's rich and we're poor,' Crystal had flared.

'It's Valerie who's poor,' Kate had answered and Crystal saw now that was true and, 'Even though she hit me, I'll never break with Valerie,' she vowed. In her own desperation she poured herself a glass of Mr Kydd Mortimer's whisky. It tasted abominable but soon she felt it warming her and she sat turning the glass round and round in her fingers as, 'I must,' she told herself, 'I must decide what to do. I must.'

'Tomorrow morning I have to go to my despicable Agency,' Valerie had told her, 'and you can take yourself back to your top school.' So I can't stay here, thought Crystal. I could go home but, 'Ma, I'm a Rat.' Ma would accept it – she'd have to, thought Crystal, but she sold her emeralds for me. That had become a lacerating thought. Sold them for nothing, thought Crystal. Go back to Queen's Chase? Crystal did not know the word 'humiliation' but sensed it and knew that everywhere she went she must inevitably meet it.

There was a grandfather clock in the Kydd Mortimers' hall that chimed the quarters as well as the hours; the chime echoed through the house, and every time it struck she jumped. Now it struck half-past ten and, There's nowhere for me to go, thought Crystal. Nowhere. So. . . . She tossed off the rest of the whisky as if it were a toast and went slowly upstairs.

Drink was not the only thing she and Valerie had taken to the disco. 'Let's see if we have any luck,' Valerie had said and had led the way into her mother's surgery with its desk covered with papers, its covered tray of instruments, weighing-scales, a couch bed with a neatly folded blanket all held in a smell of disinfectant. Crystal followed her with awe. 'Val, should we come in here?'

'Sh!' Valerie had said. 'Daddy's in. Be quiet.' She went to a cupboard hanging on the wall. 'Drugs cupboard,' Valerie had whispered. 'She keeps it locked but she doesn't know that I had the key copied. Clever me! You see, when a patient dies, the drugs are all brought back and . . . goodie!' said Valerie. 'We are in luck!'

227

She had brought out a bottle of small pink-orange pills.
'What are they?'
'Never you mind.' Valerie was counting them out.
'Won't your mother miss them?'
'She's too busy – or, if she does, she won't suspect me. "What! My little Valerie!" She still thinks I'm about six,' and, 'Just what we need,' whispered Valerie in glee.
'To take?' Crystal was mystified.
'Of course not.'
'Then for what?'
'Spending money. Daddy thinks if he keeps me short it'll stop me going out, poor innocent! I told you, if I want something, I go and get it – so these are to sell. The Crowd'll give us a pound each for them and we shall be very, very popular.' The way Valerie said that had sounded sinister to Crystal and she drew back, but Valerie had taken two envelopes from the desk and was counting the pills into them. 'Eight for me, eight for you, but mind,' said Valerie, the doctor's daughter, 'don't sell more than two to any one person, no matter how they try to make you. One pill can make you feel good and high but they can be lethal.'
'Lethal? You mean they could kill you?'
'Certainly they could, especially if you've had much to drink. Mother only gives them to patients who are dying anyhow and are in great pain. So be careful.'
Crystal had not sold any. Somehow she couldn't. Now she shook them out of the envelope, eight prettily coloured, harmless-looking little pills, and, it would be all over, Crystal told herself. I wouldn't have to go anywhere. I wouldn't feel anything any more. Doone could be famous without my minding – she saw Doone's trusting hazel eyes looking at her and hastily shut them out. Ruth can dance Clara and I wouldn't care. Yuri . . .? Yuri would be sorry but how would he know? thought Crystal. It would be hushed up. She could imagine the scandalised grave faces at Queen's Chase. Ma and Pa? Better not think of Ma and Pa. But at least Ma wouldn't have to know I was a Rat. Crystal could almost hear Ma weeping, 'Just when she was getting a star part.' Clara was not a star part, but still. . . . Crystal came back to Yuri. No, he wouldn't know unless – a daring thought occurred to her, so

daring that she caught her breath – unless I did it in his garden. In a romantic picture she saw herself lying, her golden hair spread round her, on his doorstep – like Juliet with Romeo, thought Crystal. Perhaps not on the doorstep – gleams of sense intruded themselves – someone might see her from the road. Lying on the grass, then, a distraught Yuri bending over her. At least he'd know how much I love him. Then she heard, or seemed to hear, Valerie's down-to-earth calculating voice, 'What good would that be to you if you were dead?' and Valerie's perpetual saying, 'If I want something, I go and get it.'

The small white house was close, so close, and, Suppose I went there, thought Crystal and caught her breath again. She studied her reflection in the looking-glass. Yes, it was a lovely face: her skin, her eyes – what luck that they really were what Ma called them, 'violet blue'. Their lashes, too, might so easily have been gold, not half as effective as their darkness. I should have had to dye them, thought Crystal. In any case, she would not have gone without her gift of golden curls. Yuri gave his photograph to all four of us, she thought. Those miserable little bouquets were all equal but – and she was certain of this – none of the others had been kissed as she had. 'Little bud!' In those moments, Crystal had not been fifteen, nor he a great dancer; they were man and woman, woman not girl. She had been held against him. 'I'll never let anyone else hold me ever.'

She put her hand up to feel her mouth, remembering that glorious fierceness and, I'm damned if I'm going to die, thought Crystal. Was it the whisky or Valerie's maxim that had given her a new boldness? 'But I'm going to make him hold me again,' said Crystal to the looking-glass. 'I can, I know I can, and more. . . . I'll offer myself to him.' Now it was not Romeo and Juliet but the Sacrificial Maiden; she remembered how, in *Rite of Spring*, she had seen the *corps de ballet* girls' dresses stained with blood, virgin blood, and I almost hope it hurts, thought Crystal.

She left a note for Valerie. 'Goodbye. Love and thank you', put on her coat and picked up her overnight bag. It held her nightgown, but would she wear a nightgown? People are usually naked. . . . Don't! Don't! The vision was overmastering and, suppose, suppose I had Yuri's baby? That thought

229

made Crystal dizzy; it's perfectly possible, she argued, but the baby seemed to have eyes like Doone's and, I think Pa would kill Yuri. As for Queen's Chase! Crystal was getting more and more dramatic. She had to put the pills back in their envelope, which brought a chill. If he sends me away, I'll take them, but he won't. I know he won't, and she flushed them down the lavatory.

She stood just inside the gate, that magical gate. Half the houses in the lane were in darkness but, in Yuri's, a line of light showed through drawn curtains. Timidly she stepped across the square of lawn; fallen leaves rustled, there was the sound of traffic from the Avenue, but the house was quiet, so quiet that he must be alone, thought Crystal. What luck! Her heart seemed again to be beating in her throat but I'm ready, thought Crystal, ready, and a thrill ran through her from head to foot as she raised her hand to the lion's-head brass knocker.

The front door opened, a shaft of light blinded her, so that she jumped back. 'Darling,' a clear voice called back into the house, 'I'm just taking Whiskers out,' and a young woman stepped into the light. Not many years older than Crystal, she was cuddling a kitten, and wearing night clothes; Crystal took in all the implication of their lacy softness. The feet were in silver mules, the beautiful hair tumbled on the shoulders, the brilliance shone as, with unmistakable grace, the girl bent to put the kitten down on the path. She was Anthea Dean.

The garden seemed to run away from Crystal and then ran back again as if Anthea, too, had hit her, but with a devastating blow. They stared at one another and, She doesn't know me, thought Crystal. Of course not. I'm not important enough. She did not realise that she had jumped back into the shadows so that all Anthea saw was a silhouette, a glimpse of a young, young face, a hand gripping a travelling-bag and, 'Go away, you little silly,' hissed Anthea.

As if more were needed, Yuri came to the door, Yuri wearing dark slacks, a black high-necked jersey, a bracelet – Crystal saw every detail as she had with Anthea. There was a gleam of gold from the bracelet as he put his arm round Anthea, holding her close as he peered into the darkness. 'Who is it?'

230

'Another of the poor little things who have a crush on you.'
'Pests!' said Yuri lightly, and then, 'Shoo!'

Perhaps he was speaking to the kitten – it was a gentle 'Shoo' – but to Crystal nothing could have been more ignominious. 'Shoo!' With burning cheeks she turned and ran into the Avenue and down the hill; she had a stupid thought that Yuri was running after her and she ran pell-mell until she reached the bottom where, for a second, she stood panting as, across the road, she saw an Underground station. She knew it well; it was the station she and Doone had used three times a week in the far-off days of Ennis Glyn. The road was a whirlwind stream of traffic, but Crystal could not wait for the lights to change. She dived straight in.

Brakes shrieked, drivers shouted at her, one car almost sent her down, the lights blinded her still more but, 'God looks after drunks and fools,' Pa would have said and, turning, twisting, dodging, Crystal reached the pavement on the other side.

She did not wait to take a ticket. There was a railing beside the collector's booth, his back was turned to her, and she vaulted the railing. On the downward-moving staircase she saw the familiar Northern Line sign; a train was standing at one platform and, without reading the notices, she ran to it. The doors were closing, but she forced her way through. They closed and the train left.

Chapter Nine

DOONE put the receiver down.

That same Sunday evening when Will had driven him back to school, the first person Doone had seen was Amy. She and her father were dropping Amy's small sister at Queen's Chase before going on to Amy's hostel. So Crystal had not spent the weekend with Amy. Well, I knew that, thought Doone.

'I do think she might have come home,' Ma had lamented. 'She knows I'm on tenterhooks. Has Yuri' – Ma, too, called him Yuri now – 'has he been down?'

'Yes, he danced Clara's part with all three of them.'

'And told them nothing.'

'No.' That was the truth. It was not Yuri who had told them.

It should have been the happiest of weekends. The Steinway had arrived. 'I thought we should have to take the banisters down,' Pa told Doone. 'The men just managed to turn it on the landing. It was on its side, the legs taken off,' and there it was, at home. 'Over Ma's dead body,' said Pa, putting his arm round her and squeezing her shoulders.

'Dead body?'

'That's what she said.' Then, seeing Doone's alarmed face, 'It's all right, son. She didn't mean it.'

'But she said it. Why?'

'I've had difficulties,' said Ma. A heartbreak was more truthful. 'We can't have that piano, William,' she had told Pa. 'We can't.'

'We must. I see it as a sacred trust.'

'Sacred or not, we can't have it, unless we move house. We've nowhere to put it.'

Pa had not thought of that; put in the sitting-room, it would take up half the room, 'and imagine what would be done to it'.

232

'And Doone couldn't play it,' said Will, 'which is the whole idea.'

Ma had asked Will to come. 'Someone must talk sense to Pa', but it was Ma who had had to hear devastating sense.

'I know you always think I'm against Doone,' she had said. 'I'm not. I would do anything, anything to wipe out how stupid I was over Madame Tamara's piano. That's why I was so glad, extra glad, about this one, but I'd no idea it was so huge. There simply isn't room.'

'There is,' said Will.

'If you're still thinking of the sitting-room. . . .'

'I'm not thinking of the sitting-room.'

'Then where? Unless you turn Pa and me out of our bedroom.'

'Of course not.'

'Then where? There isn't another room big enough.'

'There is.'

'Which?'

'Crystal's.'

'*Crystal's!*'

'Yes. It would go in there.'

Pa came to Ma's rescue. 'She's our only girl, Will. She has to have her own room.'

'She can. Doone has my old one now. Let them change. You'll only have to paint and paper his, cut Crystal's carpet down. Yes, we'll make her bedroom into a workroom for Doone.'

'You wouldn't even have to paint it,' said Kate, 'just stain the floor.'

'He can have my rugs,' said Will. 'It'll hold the piano. . . .'

Ma shut her eyes in dread but she still saw the room she had cherished so carefully: its blue carpet, muslin curtains, bedcover and dressing-table skirts she freshened every week; everything in it, from the big wardrobe to the least little china animal of Crystal's collection was kept immaculate and, 'Over my dead body,' cried Ma and, 'You're all trying to take her away from me. All of you.'

'Not us, Ma. It.' Kate was full of pity.

'It?'

'The dancing you started, Ma,' said Will.

Crystal herself clinched that. 'I don't mind. Even now, I'm only here for weekends and the holidays. When I go to the Senior School next year' – she had not a doubt she was going there – 'I'll live in a hostel. When I'm in the Company, I'll have a flat of my own and will scarcely be coming home at all.'

As far as Doone could see there was nothing but truth in that. Then why had Ma been so upset when he had played to them all after Sunday dinner? Jim and Tim were there, proper soldiers now, and they had listened to him with surprising respect, as had Hughie, but Doone had seen Kate get up, go to Ma and sit by her, patting her hand and he saw that Ma was crying.

Was it, he suddenly thought, because of the difference between the Steinway and the tin kettle? She had meant to be kind and he had loved her for it and had had to hurt her. How can I show her I love her? wondered Doone. How? Then he had an idea. When he had finished and everyone had gone back to the sitting-room, he went to his chest of drawers, picked up his china pig, opened it with its little key and, taking it to Ma, showered coins and notes into her lap. 'There's thirty-seven pounds, thirty-seven pence. I don't need it any more. It's not very much, but perhaps you could buy yourself an emerald.'

Now he had faithfully delivered Crystal's note. 'Mrs Challoner's not here this evening,' said Mrs Gillespie. 'It's her nephew's twenty-first birthday,' and, when she had read the note: 'What a pity Crystal has this cold. Never mind. Your mother thinks she can be here first thing tomorrow morning. I suppose you've heard the news?'

'What news?'

She told him and Doone gasped; then he had run to the telephone, feeling in his pocket for his purse.

He knew where Valerie's house was, he had taken messages there for Crystal, but the telephone number? There was a queue of boys and girls at the kiosk and he had dared to go into Mrs Challoner's office; Daphne did not come on Sundays and it was mercifully empty. He was able to look up the number in peace. There were two Kydd Mortimers: A. J. Kydd Mortimer and Dr Isabel Kydd Mortimer. Which? He decided on A. J. and dialled the number. Valerie had answered.

'Valerie? It's Doone.'

'What do you want?' The voice was hostile.

'I must speak to Crystal.'

'You can't. We're just going out and she's changing.'

'Get her. *Please*.'

'Listen,' said Valerie. 'We're going to a party and she doesn't want to be bothered with you or anyone else.'

'Valerie!' Doone had been frantic. 'It's – it's life or death!' Somewhere he had heard that phrase but, 'Life or death!' Valerie had laughed. 'Your School's not *that* important. Anyway, Crystal's not coming back to it.'

'She would if . . . Valerie!' but she had put the receiver down.

Doone had tried again, twice. There was no answer. 'A call for Mother, I expect,' Valerie had told Crystal and, 'As she's not here' she had let it ring. When Doone came out of Mrs Challoner's office it was late. If Mrs Gillespie caught him in this part of the house, he knew there would be trouble, but he had made a plan, almost as desperate as Crystal's. 'All right,' Doone had said to an imaginary Valerie. 'All right. You won't let me speak to Crystal, but as soon as I can get out in the morning I'll come and fetch her.'

In the train someone had left a newspaper on the next seat. Crystal picked it up and opened it so that people would not look at her; they had stared enough as she had pushed open the doors – she knew she was scarlet with running and the shame that was still scalding her. 'Another of the poor little things who have a crush on you.' 'Crush' for love, true love if ever there were love, and, always, that cruel word 'little'. Then 'Shoo!' as if she, Crystal, had been that kitten. I'll never look at a kitten again. I wish I had kept those pills.

How easy to get off the train, go into the station lavatory and die – but would I die? asked Crystal. Some busybody would find me and take me to hospital. They do horrible things to you – and anger set in. I don't wish I'd kept them. How stupid to die when I don't love Yuri. I hate him. He *is* mean and cruel. I hate him! All the same, she gave a hard little sob. She was raw, as if from a beating, yet, if she were not going to die,

235

she would have to live, and how? Where? She was too tired to think but, What to do?

'What to do? What to do?' The noise of the train seemed to say that over and over again in her head, but where did any of the Pennys go in a dilemma except to Will, and I'll go to Will and Kate, decided Crystal. Even if they've gone to bed, they won't mind. Will can explain to Ma and Kate'll help me think what to do. It was only then that Crystal realised the train was not going north but south. How odd, she was often to think, that getting into the wrong train can alter your whole life; the train was taking her steadily in the direction of Buckingham Park and the Ballet School.

She could easily have changed; at every stop she had only to walk across the platform and there would be a northbound train, but she did not move. Just as she had veered away from Yuri – I hate him – she was pulled back again. For all the pain, he's made me know where I belong, thought Crystal. He and they – she meant the Ballet School: Miss McKenzie, Miss Hurley, Mamzelly, Mrs Challoner, particularly Mrs Challoner; the girls and boys, Amy, Galina, Lucy, Philip, Louis and Ruth. If she flinched away from the thought of Ruth now, it was because of how much Ma would mind that it was Ruth who would dance Clara. 'That's what you've got for your emeralds,' whispered Crystal aloud. 'Poor Ma.' For herself she was thankful that she was to be a Rat. She would, of course, have to see Yuri. But he won't see me, among so many, and soon I'll have a mask. I won't be there when he meets the Sugar Plum Fairy – Anthea. To think of Anthea still brought a stab, but for the rest? What has happened to me? Crystal asked herself. Mysteriously she was, as she had thought she would have been if she had died, no longer caring about Ruth: knowing without envy that Doone was more talented than herself; humbly willing to be one among seven other dancers, and Perhaps part of me did die today, she thought, not from pills but from what happened to me. Perhaps, too, a new part of her had been born, a new resolve, and I'm going back, no matter what, thought Crystal.

The train went on but, 'What to do? What to do?' had changed to, 'No matter what. No matter what,' and it began to dawn on Crystal that, as far as Queen's Chase was concerned, nothing was the matter. Unless Doone had talked, and Crystal was sure he would not, the Ballet School did not know anything except that Crystal Penny was kept away by a bad cold, but would be back on Monday morning. What luck that I wrote that note. If I could get into Buckingham Park, find some way of spending the night, troubling nobody, telling nobody, thought Crystal, I could slip back in the morning, perhaps when everyone's at breakfast, and no one, except Doone and me, would have the least idea.

A clock struck midnight as Crystal walked through the sleeping town. It had been a long journey and, at times, a frightening one; she had had to change trains and all the stories she had heard of gangs lurking in the corridors, strangers trying to speak to her, had started up in her mind but, luckily, the station had been busy with weary people going home from late work and she had passed unnoticed. At Buckingham Park turnstile, though, there was a ticket collector.

'I haven't a ticket, so I'll have to pay.'

'Where did you get on?'

Crystal, too tired to concoct, had answered truthfully, 'Swiss Cottage.'

'Swiss Cottage! That's a mighty long way!' The collector was a West Indian, a comfortable big black woman with a gentle voice. 'A very long way,' and, 'Where you going, child? The last bus done gone.'

'I'm going home,' which was completely true and should have sounded reassuring but, as Crystal walked quickly away, she had known that the woman was looking after her.

Most of the houses she passed were in darkness but now and again a car came by. Suppose one stopped and a big oily man – Crystal saw him as big and oily – opened the door and said, 'Where are you going, little girl?' I'd have to run into the first house with lights on and ring the bell, thought Crystal. But I'd have to explain and I can't, so every time she heard a car she opened a gate and hid below it or slid behind a hedge. When I'm in the Park I shall be safe. I'll only have to hide in the bracken and wait. The gates will be shut, of course. I'll have to find a wicket gate. 'Wicket gate. Wicket gate.' The words sang in her head as they had in the train – I must be very tired – and,

237

as she trudged what seemed the endless road, she remembered a wicket gate that was open day and night. She and the other girls had often used it when they went shopping.

To get to it, though, she had to turn off the road, go down an unlit lane into a wood where the trees cast deep shadows and there were benches. Suppose I found a tramp sleeping on one of them? Crystal tried to walk on the grass, making no sound, but there was gravel that crunched loudly, puddles that shone in the starlight.

She had, too, forgotten that the way led past a cemetery; she could make out the dim shapes of its crosses. A light mist lay between them and, perhaps there really are Wilis, thought Crystal, those ethereal shapes of girls from the ballet *Giselle* — girls who had died for love and rose from their graves if they heard a call. Well, no one will call for me, thought Crystal, but it was so eerie that she felt sweat start on her neck and she walked on tip-toe until she reached the wicket gate and stepped into the Park.

A cool air was blowing but luckily the November night was not cold. There was, too, what seemed to her an immense silence. Even in the almost deserted streets there had been human sounds: the sound of television, a telephone ringing, the swish of cars, footsteps, voices. Here was quiet but, when leaving the footpath Crystal stepped on to the grass, she could hear sounds. In the stillness they frightened her, though now and then she knew what they were; to her, a town child, they were something foreign, not natural, animal and bird sounds, sudden rustles in the grass, stirrings, and deer grazing with a quiet steady munching. She did not startle them they were too accustomed to humans and soon she could see them but only as shapes, until a stag lifted its head and she saw its antlers against the sky.

It gave her a strange thrill as if its majestic shape was the symbol of all proud males like ... like Yuri. Stop thinking about him, she told herself.

Now she could see, too, the rise and fall of the land: the dark thickets of woods and trees blurred against the horizon and, over it all, the vault of the sky with its stars and, I never knew, thought Crystal, I never knew the sky was so huge. A strange peace fell on her, perhaps because she was so tired. Then an owl hooted and her blood ran cold from her head to her feet. It had sounded like a human mocking and she remembered that tramps slept out in the Park as well as in the lane, and loonies, too, thought Crystal. As if on that thought, she saw headlights and a car coming, the beam of a torch sweeping and scanning trees, bracken, deer, each springing into prominent light. She just had time to crouch down. Perhaps they're looking for me, she thought; perhaps that ticket collector. . . . Then she remembered that Mrs Challoner had said that the police, in their Land-Rover, toured the Park twice nightly, particularly round Queen's Chase, and I can't be far off, thought Crystal. I have only to wait.

She knew now that the owl was only an owl because its hooting was steady; the deer had gone on grazing without lifting their heads when the police passed. As Crystal walked, something crossed in front of her, so close it almost brushed her legs, but took no notice of her. Quiet, almost soundless, she was one with the creatures, with all creation.

She knew she had only to walk on, find Queen's Chase and, though there would be scolding, punishment, disgrace, she would find warmth, food and bed – above all, bed. She was cold now and hungry but, 'I won't give in,' she said aloud. 'I'll wait.' Her own voice startled her, then again peace fell. She stepped into the bracken and, like a doe caring for her faun, trod it round and round until she had made a nest. The ground was wet but she put her newspaper down and curled herself round, her feet drawn under her coat. It might have been the last effect of the whisky or the tiredness, or perhaps the peace, but in a moment Crystal was fast asleep.

Once a doe almost stepped on her but she was not startled, the feet were so light. Crystal put out a hand and felt a hairy coat, cold and damp on the outside, but when she parted the hair the skin was warm. 'I wish you would come and sleep with me,' said Crystal, and slept again.

Doone knew it was no use being up too early; for one thing, he could not get out of the house; for another, had Miss Walsh found his bed empty, there would have been an alarm. No, breakfast's the time, he told himself, and planned to come downstairs with the other boys and, when they crossed to the main house, he would not go into breakfast with them but, Just go, thought Doone. How he wished he could have borrowed Mr Ormond's son's bicycle, but he did not dare; besides, it might have attracted attention. No, he would have to walk to the gates of the Park and hope to catch a bus on the road and, if that failed, walk to the station. He knew, from his Underground journeys home, what a long one lay before him. Buckingham Park to Swiss Cottage and, after that, he would have to walk up the long Avenue to Valerie's house. He could only pray that Crystal would still be there. Even then, It'll take us ages to get back, thought Doone. It was the best he could do and he left a note for Mr Ormond.

'Please, Sir, I haven't run away but I have erjent bisness. Back at lunch time I hope. Love, Doone.

He pinned the note to his pillow – by the time the boys came back to make their beds he would have gone.

Keeping close to the walls, Doone crept round the house, bending double under the windows. No cars were in the courtyard except Mr Ormond's, Mrs Gillespie's and the school bus that would presently fetch the cleaning women. It was too soon for the teachers, ballet and school, to arrive. When he was past the wall of the King's Pavilion, closest to the entrance posts, Doone stood looking left and right. No one – and, as fast as his legs could carry him, he ran down the long open drive towards the Park.

Crystal had woken later than she had thought possible; she had been sure she would stay awake all night – I suppose I was too tired. As she tried to stand, she was so stiff and cold she had to pull herself up by the bracken; it came hip-high, almost hiding her as, shaken with shivers, she stood and looked far over the Park.

Crystal had never seen the dawn before. The clouds were still pink in the sky and, as the run rose, it sent long beams slanting across grass, bracken, trees. It was one of those rare late-autumn mornings that sometimes happen in November, when the sky becomes a pale clear blue and, as the sun rose higher, the whole Park seemed held in thin sunshine and dew that sparkled on every frond and leaf, on blades of grass and on the deer's coats, turning their russet darker as they grazed. She was standing in the middle of a herd; again they took no notice of this quiet human. She herself was soaked, jeans, anorak and hair; she could feel her sodden curls clinging to her wet face and, I've never been washed in dew before, she thought. She seemed cleansed inside and out.

It was still too early to appear at Queen's Chase and she saw now she was quite a long way from the house. Walking would warm her. I'll start now, thought Crystal, and wait just outside. No one must see me; being washed in dew was poetical but Crystal knew how she must look; she had had to relieve herself amongst the bracken and even her bottom was wet but, if anyone sees me, the whole thing would come out, she knew that. If I can slip in while they're all at breakfast, with luck. . . . Breakfast's the time. If she had known, that was the exact moment when Doone was calculating the same thing.

At the crossroad where the private drive led to Queen's Chase, Crystal looked at her watch, but it was still too early; she had half an hour at least to wait, lurking in the nearest thicket of trees.

Now there were riders in the Park and she watched the horses. The wardens came by in their Land-rover, wardens now, not police. In the trees around her, birds were busy. There was plenty to watch, but that half-hour was the worst time for Crystal; it seemed longer than the night, longer than that clanking journey in the train but, wait, she told herself sternly. You must wait. If anyone sees you now, the whole thing will be spoiled. You must wait.

At last the Queen's Chase bus drove out, which meant breakfast would have begun. Crystal came out of the thicket on to the drive, walked along the grass verge and stopped abruptly. A boy was running towards her, a Queen's Chase boy – she had caught a glimpse of a green blazer under his duffel-coat; the hood hid his face.

Panic seized her and she dived back into the thicket. The School has been alerted. Doone must have told or Valerie's father has telephoned – Crystal could imagine his doing that when he came back from that late game at his Club; perhaps he had looked in on their rooms, because he does care about

Valerie, Crystal was sure of that now. He would have seen her empty bed. Perhaps he had rung Ma and Pa, who had rung Queen's Chase. The police had been searching for her. Perhaps the nice ticket-collector had reported. In her fevered imagination she thought the boys might have been posted as sentries. Perhaps. . . . The panic was too much and Crystal, too, ran. She was only just in front of the boy but her legs were longer.

'Crystal! Wait! Wait!' The voice floated out on the air. Doone was running too fast to have much voice. 'Crys-tal. I've something to tell you. Wait.'

Crystal would not wait. She was running blindly for the nearest Park gate, so blindly that she almost came under a horse as the rider crossed the road. He swerved and cursed, just missed her, swung round only to meet Doone running as hard. 'God damn all children! What the devil's got into you . . .?' Doone did not even hear. There was a thud; Crystal had run full tilt into a car; fortunately it had stopped at the sight of them, but she, hit hard, reeled back, then was precipitated forward as Doone dashed into her. They both lay breathless on the bonnet as, 'Do you want to get yourselves killed!' cried a furious voice. A lady flung open the car door, sprang out, and, 'What in heaven or earth?' Then, 'Crystal! Doone!' The car was a familiar dark-blue Renault, the lady was Mrs Challoner, an exceedingly angry Mrs Challoner.

'What do you think you're doing? And at this time of the morning?' and, 'Crystal, look at you. *Look* at you!'

For once Mrs Challoner was ignored. 'Why did you run?' Doone was demanding of Crystal when he could speak. 'You needn't have. You needn't. Crystal, Ruth's ill and she's not dancing. Crystal, you're Clara.'

'Clara?' Crystal spoke as if she had never heard of Clara.

'*Clara* in *The Nutcracker*', but Crystal still seemed to be numb.

'It's true,' said Mrs Challoner. 'Miss Baxter rang me last night. Ruth's made herself ill with nerves, poor child, and is leaving. You are to dance Clara.'

'No!' cried Crystal. 'No!'

That took even Mrs Challoner aback, while Doone nearly fell off the road with surprise.

'Never! Never! Never!' Crystal seemed almost in hysterics.

242

'I can't,' but Mrs Challoner had recovered her calm and, 'Be quiet, Crystal,' she said. 'Get in the car, both of you.'

'*Please!* I can't dance Clara. I can't.'

Mrs Challoner did not answer but looked straight ahead as she drove until she drew up in front of the house. Then, 'Doone, go in to breakfast,' she ordered. 'Crystal, I'll have yours sent upstairs, but first you will get into a hot bath and dry your hair. You can skip Assembly.'

They had forgotten: Monday was Assembly morning, which was why Mrs Challoner was early. Now she was cold and formal. 'Later, perhaps you will be able to explain this extraordinary behaviour,' and, 'Crystal, concerning the role in *The Nutcracker*: I assume that, unlike Ruth, you want to stay at Queen's Chase?'

'Of course.' What else, after all I've been through? Crystal's expression seemed to say that for her.

'Then you should remember,' said Mrs Challoner, 'Queen's Chase children dance exactly what they are told.'

Epilogue

THE whole family, Pa, Ma, Will, Kate, the Twins and Hughie came to *The Nutcracker*'s opening night, eight seats in the stalls circle. It was almost Ma's dream. True, Crystal was not in a cloud of white tulle with flowers in her hair; the Prince was not for her but for the Sugar Plum Fairy — 'Anthea Dean,' read Ma from the programme. Anthea had a pale pink tutu sparkling with diamanté, silver wings and a silver wand, while, for most of the ballet, Crystal, as Clara, had to wear a nightdress, bare feet which meant no *'pointes'*, as Ma had learnt to call them. For the party scene, though, there was a white satin dress, low on the shoulders, with a high waist, deep-blue sash, white pantalettes edged with lace and blue *pointe* shoes. 'Crystal could not have looked prettier,' said Ma.

Even before the curtain rose, from the opening bars of the overture, she had been as deep as any child in the fairy-tale. For her its zenith was Clara's short *pas de deux* with the Prince after he had been transformed from the Nutcracker and before he whirled her away in a golden sleigh, as the Christmas-tree rose to reveal the fir forest and snow lake. 'And the end!' said Ma. 'When the whole company was on the stage!' When the curtain came up and Yuri, with Anthea, stepped forward to take his bow, he had held out his other hand to Crystal.

Not Ma, nor anyone else, except perhaps Mrs Challoner, knew what it cost Crystal to take that hand, come forward between Yuri and Anthea, curtsy and smile.

Rehearsals had hardened her slightly, though the first had been, for her, like that little mermaid in the Hans Andersen story, thought Crystal, who, when she walked, felt as if she trod on knives — Only I had to dance on them — but the dancing saved her, as it always did and, too, she had overheard a

244

conversation when she had gone to the study, hoping to see Mrs Challoner.

'Poor little Anthea.'

Why 'poor'? thought Crystal and, for Anthea, 'little'?

'She ought to have known better.' Did Mamzelly speak with feeling? 'Yuri's reputation. . . .'

'Anything pretty on two *pointes*!' That, of course, was Miss Hurley.

'Well, thank goodness all of ours have escaped,' said Miss McKenzie.

Mrs Challoner was silent.

Ruth had left Queen's Chase, and Crystal had protested, 'But what will you do? You have been accepted at the Senior School.'

'I'll go there when I'm eighteen and take the Teachers' Course. I know now I like making people dance, not dancing myself,' and Ruth said, 'One day, if I'm lucky, I'll be a choreographer, and you, Crystal, will pass straight into the Company.'

'What a hope!'

'You will. Almost at once you'll be a Soloist and then a Principal – a famous Principal.'

'That'll be Doone.' Crystal was able to say it without emotion, as a matter of fact. 'That'll be Doone.'

'It'll be you.'

Certainly *The Nutcracker* seemed a good augury. 'The applause,' said Ma, half-weeping with pride. 'The applause!'

Finally, a big Negro footman in all his panoply of wig, gold-braided coat, white breeches and stockings brought on bouquets for Anthea; the audience cheered as she curtsied. Then he came back with a big bouquet for Crystal – it was from Her Majesty's Ballet – and another, a posy from the family. Will had chosen that. 'It's too small!' Ma was disappointed but when Crystal, in her turn, curtsied, 'She's every bit as graceful as Anthea Dean,' said Ma. The cheers were so persistent that when the big curtain came down Crystal was the first, when the heavy velvet parted, to have a curtain call of her own. Ma's cup was full.

Almost full. 'This was the opening of the season,' she said to

Miss McKenzie – the family, for once, had been allowed backstage to see Crystal. 'The opening – why wasn't it the Gala?'

'*The Nutcracker* is almost a perennial,' said Miss McKenzie. 'It's done every Christmas, if not by us, then by some other company. For a Gala you need something special or new.'

The World Première of Yuri Koszorz's
LEDA AND THE SWAN
In the gracious presence of
HER MAJESTY QUEEN ELIZABETH

' "The presence of the Queen." We can't not go,' said Ma. 'What do you mean, not go?' Pa looked searchingly at Ma. 'You're not still jealous for Crystal?'

'A little.' Ma had to confess it, yet, strangely, it was only a little. On her finger was a ring, a new gold ring set with a single stone. 'I couldn't run to more than one, Maudie, but it *is* an emerald.'

'Doone thinks he gave it to me,' said Ma. She looked at it often, but now she simply felt she had had her fill of glory, and all she really wanted was to be still and savour it. Still – the Queen!

Pa felt as if they had been given a Royal Command and, in the first long dress she had ever had, Ma took her seat beside Pa in his hired dinner-jacket.

They were not alone for long. To their gratification, they recognised, 'and were recognised by,' said Ma, many in the audience: Mr Yeats, Miss Baxter, Mrs Challoner. 'You were quite right, William,' whispered Ma. 'It is full evening dress.' Stella came to speak to them. 'Ennis would have come,' she said, 'but she's dancing the Goddess Hera.' The Baroness was there, with a party in a box, and waved to them. They saw Mrs Sherrin and with her another person, frail and in black, but full of happiness, Madame Tamara.

'Everyone's here,' Doone told Mr Max. The Baroness, though she was there in her box, had sent him a greetings telegram. Charles another, from his school. A note had been left at the stage door by Colonel and Mrs Ingram. 'We'll come round and see you afterwards.' Mrs Sherrin and Madame

Tamara had sent the same.

The Conductor was tall, silver-haired like Mr Felix. Even Beppo was there in a way; the second ballet in the programme was *Petrushka* when Yuri would dance the puppet Beppo-Clown. Queen's Chase entire school was at the Gala. 'The amphitheatre seats haven't sold, that's why,' said Mrs Challoner.

'No wonder,' said Ma. 'Even up there at the back, a seat costs six pounds.'

'We'll sit where we sat before, even if each seat costs a hundred pounds,' said Pa. 'We're not going in the back of the amphitheatre.'

'It's up there, though,' Mrs Challoner told them, 'that you find true balletomanes and they don't like these dressed-up occasions. They'll be back for the next performance.' Meanwhile the seats were filled by Queen's Chase boys and girls, though six of them, chosen to be in the crowd for the peasant scenes of *Petrushka*, went straight backstage to get ready.

They had all arrived in three coaches; the police held up the traffic while the girls in their green cloaks, boys in green blazers crossed the road, and people in the crowd murmured. Doone was glad they were there; though the boys had teased him, he knew that, from the amphitheatre at least, he would get a tremendous hand.

Expectantly the moments went on. Then the audience rose to its feet while the orchestra played, 'God Save the Queen'. Through his crack, Doone could see, beside the be-diamonded regal figure in the Royal Box banked with carnations, that there was another lady, white-haired, erect though she had to use a cane – Madame. Doone knew that part of the clapping was for her.

With a quiet rustle the audience sat down. The lights in the auditorium dimmed as the footlights came up on the stage. The overture began and the music swelled over the auditorium.

It changed. Anthea's gone on, thought Doone. The melody of her music was brought out on the harp as she danced, looking for shells, along the lake shore. The clouds came down and Doone felt the magnetic stirring run through the audience

247

as Yuri – Zeus – and his Goddess wives began their mime. The stirring changed to laughter. Then the mime was over – the ballet seemed to be going with extraordinary swiftness. This was the poultry-yard, the egg had been pushed on with Claude; Doone could hear the oohs and ahs. The hens gathered round the Cock, they danced. Doone felt Mr Max's hand on his shoulder. 'Steady.' The Conductor held his baton still. 'Now,' said Mr Max. 'Now.'

Claude did not steal all the applause. Even on an occasion like a Gala, when many of the audience had come as a gesture to the charity, rather than for the ballet, the British public knew a rising dancer when they saw one and Doone, coming out before the curtain, was almost stunned by the clapping. Yuri had sent him out alone and he could only bow and bow again, to the Queen and to his Lady, to the ladies and gentlemen and up, far up, to his friends and fellows who were clapping until their hands tingled, bouncing up and down in their seats and shouting.

He came out again between Yuri and Anthea and they loosed his hands and pushed him forward again alone, and Ma's footman, as she had begun to call the black one, came on and gave Doone a big box of chocolates, 'the hugest one I've ever seen,' he said afterwards. It was from Yuri, and after the last call, as they went back behind the curtains, Yuri put his arm round Doone's shoulders.

'I'm afraid you'll have to wait,' said Miss McKenzie.

She was marshalling the children for *Petrushka* when Ma and Pa came round. With them was Crystal, tonight just one among a hundred other schoolgirls. She had been allowed to come down from the amphitheatre and join them in the interval. Her uniform made her distinctive and several people had looked at her and whispered. Ma imagined them saying, 'That's the girl who danced so beautifully as Clara.' Secretly Ma had made plans to go and see every performance of *The Nutcracker*.

Though he was indulgently proud of Crystal, Pa had thought *The Nutcracker* a piece of pretty nonsense, but *Leda and the Swan*!

Ma had been shocked by the ending. 'They oughtn't to show things like that on the stage.'

'The ballet needed it,' said Pa. He had been so deeply moved that he could not keep huskiness out of his voice as he said to Miss McKenzie, 'That's a wonderful ballet. I didn't know ballet could be so strong. Marvellous.'

'It is,' said Miss McKenzie, and, 'They shouldn't be long. They are being presented to the Queen.'

'The Queen!'

'Yes, she asked to meet the Principals.'

'Doone isn't a Principal,' said Crystal.

'Of course not, but tonight. . . .' Mr Max was as proud as Pa.

'Doone – *Doone* is meeting the Queen.'

They were joined by Colonel and Mrs Ingram, Madame Tamara and an elated Baroness. Doone came back and was surrounded. 'And to think,' Ma told them, 'it all began when I suggested a *Harlequinade* to Madame Tamara, and Doone was her little Clown.'

'It didn't,' said Doone. 'It began with Beppo and then I was allowed to carry Crystal's shoes.'

Tundergarth,
January 1980–May 1983

249

Author's Note

As this is a novel not a portrait I have allowed myself a certain licence: for instance, in the description of the Exhibition of Ballet Costumes, the entrance display is taken from the version shown in Edinburgh, not from that of the Victoria and Albert Museum in London.

Now and again, an author, without any intent of plagiarising, lights on an episode or saying that has been used almost identically in another author's book. This has happened to me with the late Kitty Barnes's *She Shall Have Music*. I can only apologise and make acknowledgement to her and Dent's her publisher.

Rumer Godden

Go

777

© THE BAKER & TAYLOR CO.